Sentimental Journey
THE BLOOD CASTE

By D.M. Cipres
Special editor |K. Fulton|
Cover designed and illustrated by |Mekenna Cipres|

ISBN: 9781731314055

To Sage ... Welcome to the World!

FOREWORD

A part of me always resisted bedtime, even to this day. Sometimes, I felt sad that the things I had anticipated were now over. Sometimes, I would be ruminating on the uncertainty that each new day could bring. I felt a separation and loneliness, as bedtime was the longest amount of time that I was ever truly alone. Feeling that aloneness made saying, "Goodnight, Mama" feel more like saying, "Goodbye."

Oddly, bedtime was also a cherished time. Being tucked in by mom was foundational to my life in so many ways. She showed me that I was important, as she listened to both the big and small of my day. She taught me what it meant to be selfless, as she placed her four children before her own tiredness while patiently and consistently tucking us in. She taught me how to see each day through eyes of thankfulness, as we held hands and prayed together. She gave me the gift of her imagination, as she artfully crafted stories I would get lost in. They were the last words I wanted to hear at the end of every day. I always wondered if the depth and intricacy of her stories served as a tool forged by her desperate efforts to soothe my soul and conquer my stubborn sleeplessness.

However, my mom's stories, creations, words, ideas, and imagination are too beautifully woven together to be rooted in desperation, they were, and still are, an act of love. When she finished the third book of the Sentimental Journey Series, The Blood Caste, I was able to see the same foundation that she laid out for me in childhood: the importance of people, selflessness, eyes of thankfulness, and imagination. This journey is walked by seeing the value in other people, on a mission that requires great sacrifice, survived by seeing beauty and victory in hopelessness, and fulfilled through great imagination.

While my mom originally created stories to help silence my fears, I have a feeling that they might help you as well. And just as her voice and imagination were the last sounds I wanted to hear before closing my eyes, I have no doubt that you will feel the same way about reading the adventures that she's woven together especially for you.   *Mekenna Cipres*

||||||||||||||||||||||||||||||||||||||||||||||||||||||||||||||||

Growing up, I looked forward to having days where it was just me and my mom. I will always love and cherish the special things that she did for me, and the times we had together.

These are the memories that shaped me into the person that I am today, the unseen sacrifices that as a child, flowed like honey, but were even more highly valued as maturity set in. The inspiration of a limitless imagination that turned a young boy's homemade tent that consumed the entirety of his room with leftover Christmas boxes, into a real-life castle that he colonized for days. Even after all the money was spent on gifts and recognizing that my favorite part of it all was the boxes, she still engaged in my Narnia.

Lost in my world of fantasy, while somehow remaining in the real life of the ever-present, was an everyday job. Through it all, and no matter what, there was always a new adventure filled with pirates and Darth Vader joining in on the adventure.

As I got older, I realized that this ability to go into a world of fantasy was not an act, but a gift that my mom used to journey alongside me; her creativity, innovation, and imagination were gifts that she had possessed her entire life, and now shared with me.

As life is forever changing, so our roles changed as well. Today, she is not just my mom or my adventure-seeking comrade, but my best friend whom I can rely on. Someone who I know would do anything for me, and over the years has gone above and beyond what anyone's done for me in my life. Although she doesn't have her little boy who will build tents and get lost in Star Wars fantasy any longer, she has taken her abilities elsewhere, recreating a world and story where anyone would long to be lost.
                    Austin Cipres

|Table of Contents|

"Those from the Tribe of David, while mere mortals, remain united by a tie of blood. This divine authority to take vengeance, enacting the final Evening of Score or Justice, is now given to you."

|Ivan Taggart|

Chapter 1

Restitution

"Her appearance curdled my blood. If I were merely judgin' by her condition, and if not for the warmth of her shallow breath on my skin, I would have thought 'er dead."
~Carig Hammel~

A sudden collision of frenzied emotions consumed me at the chargin' rate of a locomotive that had recklessly careened from the tracks. It wasn't just fear for Beni's well-bein', but a disorderly fury that I had never known before. There was no denyin' that only Beni could still my world and weaken my knees with one glance, but as I kneeled at her side and embraced her limp body, I felt nothin' at all, and feared she was dead. Judgin' by her ashy coloring and the feel of blood gushin' from her wound, she was barely holdin' onto life and needed better help than what I was capable of givin'. My mind and spirit burned with a staggerin' sense of urgency to get up and care for the one I loved most in the world but was quickly trumped by an abrupt and peculiar feelin' of paralysis, similar to the one I had a few days prior. It overcame me in such a way that no matter how hard I tried, I couldn't move.

The familiar stupor smothered me faster than before and took me into a far deeper hollow. *What was this? What in the hell was happenin' to me?* At the bloody mercy of whatever this was, I felt as though my body was movin' from this place into another, while at the same time, light and air was swiftly snatched from me. I had never experienced such darkness or lack of oxygen; I couldn't see, nor could I breathe! But like the sun rushin' to be noticed on a summer mornin', a light appeared. It wasn't the flame of a fiery star that brought light to my dusk, but merely my own outstretched hands altogether set aglow. I knew that they were mine and mine alone, as they were branded by the port wine stains that had marked my palms since birth.

In the dense shadiness beyond the now burnished light, I sensed a war ragin' all around me. I could even hear the sounds of metal piercing into flesh and screams of mercy from dyin' men. My vision of tribulation next revealed these same hands, *my hands,* drippin' with blood that reeked of the stench of one whose soul was beastly - the one responsible for this barbarity done to my wife. In that heartbeat of time, I was squarely yoked with a burden of justice and a callin' of vengeance. I didn't know how or when, but I knew that someday I would come face to face with this evil, and I wouldn't stop until it perished by *my* hand and plummeted into the pit of hell itself.

When the madness stopped, I found myself still sittin' on the floor with Beni in my arms, but now I felt her hand on my face and caught a glimmer of focus in her gaze. Her normally blue eyes were veiled in gray, and then she unexpectedly whispered simple but profound words that shook my world.

"So angry ... don't be angry. Love wins, it always wins ..."

With that, she fell back into a faraway slumber, almost death-like. To be sure, I was a bit stunned by the weirdness of it all. It was both a blessin' and a curse all at the same time. A divine godsend for me, to see her alive in my arms and hear the sound of her voice, but for her, a curse to wake to my tortured trance. Was it my fiery hot anger and bitterness that woke 'er from death itself? I didn't know what was makin' me feel so strange or think such things, but none of it mattered if Beni didn't survive. *I* no longer mattered without her.

As fast as I could, I jumped up and carried 'er to the surgery, and gently laid her down. Until that very moment, no words would come from my mouth.

"Beni, Beni. I'm here, lass. Everything's okay - you're home now!"

Her appearance curdled my blood. If I were merely judgin' by her condition, and *if not* for the warmth of her shallow breath on my skin, I would have thought 'er dead. Even though I knew Annaliese to be a complete loon, her prophetic words rang through my mind, playin' out exactly as she had foretold. After bein' shot in the back, Beni vanished with but a few onlookers, Annaliese bein' one of 'em. For this child witness of the impossible, the mystery was never solved but, in fact, ended there. Or perhaps the sudden disappearance of Beni was the dawnin' of Annaliese's insanity.

But for Beni, this marked a different story to be sure. Even if ye stacked one upon the other of every bad thing that had come into her path, it wouldn't compare in the least to this hell of a mess that she was facin' right now. Truth be told, I could hardly count this as a struggle at all, but more of a fight to live, or to go one bloody step further, a battle of good versus evil. It was clear by her still-fresh wounds and bloodstained dress that it had been but a few minutes since leavin' that clatty post, and comin' along for the ride was an evil bent on killin' off what was left of 'er. It wasn't even the blood really that sent chitters down my spine, but the defilement of scarlet veins seepin' onto the purity of white lace that made me wanna boke my guts out.

Was it only me that heard a gauntlet drop the moment I set eyes on my one love who appeared more forsaken than adored? Although alarmed by this hell-bent enemy, I knew that the power within me was greater than the one roarin' about like a wild beast. As far as I was concerned, war had been declared and I was pissed and ready to fight. Until this very moment, I only half-believed in the violent tale told by Richter's unhinged daughter, hopin' that it was but a tainted dream that would never come to pass. Nonetheless, as terrible as this was, I was most thankful to God that Beni made it back alive, and I knew one thing for damn sure, she would never again be at the mercy of that bloody frame. Her days as the Carrier of the Tempus Vector ended here and now.

With sorrow, I beheld the state of the lass I had promised to love, honor, and protect until my last breath, and knew that I had failed.

Did my notions of riddin' it forever actually fan it into flame? Curse this plague that had moved in like a storm! How many times did I see Adina holdin' that frame and my Gran sittin' there waiting for her as if she'd just run to the market for fresh oysters and potatoes? I never heard either of them complain of sufferin'; they were faithful and mild-tempered about it all. Maybe times have changed, and the world we've found ourselves in is darker than the one they encountered. That must be it, because everythin' felt pitch-black! Until now, I believed in the callin' of the Tempus Vector and that it was only meant for good. I believed it with all my heart. But thus far, it's only brought about evil.

Even while unconscious, she still clung desperately to each side of the frame. Her white knuckles were evidence of a frightful and narrow escape. Like her, the frame was even more marred than when they left on the journey. One by one, I unclasped her fingers and when I did, a wedge of mud fell from her right hand, encased within it was her weddin' ring. I was both moved and troubled by her conviction in the middle of the confusion. The fortitude to grab up the symbol of our union when she should have been thinkin' about so many other things, confirmed her devotion to me. Even so, I was bombarded by wild emotions hittin' me all at once, an affliction that left my soul in turmoil. On the one hand I was so blessed, so thankful that she was back. But on the other hand, images of her and of Alrik played like an old movie in my mind, and the thought of them together infuriated me. I kept remindin' myself that she could have stayed there, but she fought to come back and almost died in the midst of it.

All of which brought to mind that the doc should have been here by now! What could be takin' so long? Either I was completely outta sync with the hour, or he was takin' his sweet time.

Disregardin' the order not to do anythin' till he got there, I pulled a cluster of gauze from the box of supplies and pressed it on her wound. I didn't know much about doctorin', but she wasn't gonna survive much longer if I didn't at least slow down the bleedin'. All that was left to do was to tell 'er to hang on just a little longer and hope to God she was hearin' me.

"Come on, Doc, where are ye?"

To my great relief, I heard him callin' out my name from the stairway. Finally, he was here.

"Son! Carig, where are ya?"

"Yeah, up here! Hurry! She's not doin' good!"

Doctor Dean rushed into the room, and skillfully began tending to Beni. He wasted no time gettin' to work.

"Help me get this dress off of her right now! I gotta see what we're dealing with here."

He took out a pair of scissors and began cuttin' the gown from her body.

"When I lift her head up, you take the necklace off ... GENTLY! We don't know exactly how hurt she is."

I turned her over slightly to unclasp the choker of pearls. As the strands fell from her neck, the doctor gasped.

"What? Oh, my sweet Jesus! What in the hell is this? She's been strangled ... again?"

"Strangled? What do ye mean *again*?"

"This isn't the time to explain - she's barely breathing!"

After seein' the swollen bruises on her neck, I was sickened to my stomach. The doctor swiftly and efficiently cut off the rest of the dress, ran over to his table of supplies and pulled out a needle, insertin' it in her arm. Within minutes he had her connected to fluids and was injectin' small vials of medication into the tubes. He moved about so competently, knowin' exactly what he was doin', tryin' to remove anythin' and everythin' that stood in the way of helpin' 'er. He was obviously frightened for her life, and in frustration, threw the ruby ring onto the table where it landed alongside the pearls. Not once did he deviate from his task but was completely focused on Beni.

I, on the other hand, was once again strugglin' with a blazin' anger at the sight of it all, tryin' to recall Beni's voice tellin' me that love always wins. All of it together though, was like a wave crashin' down on me. Beni's injuries, the ring, the pearls, the weddin' dress. It was ludicrous, and love played no part in this game! For the life of me, I couldn't even make sense of any of it. I knew better, but like a fool, I lashed out at the poor doctor.

"Don't ye see now why I can't ever let her go again!"

He could tell that I was as pissed as a fire ant, and he was right. I was seein' red for sure, and I was fit to be tied. With that, I began cursin' up a storm. I felt like I was standin' on the outside of myself, watching the rantin' and ravings of a lunatic. I had no doubt that I was bein' an idiot, but I lacked control of my tongue. There was the doc, tryin' to save Beni, and my madness wasn't helpin', but was only causin' him to have to stop and deal with me. I soon found out that my Scottish temper didn't hold a candle to his wisdom and experience. He had no problem dealin' with the likes of me and stopped me in my tracks.

"Mr. Hammel, THAT is enough! Your grandfather would be ashamed of you! If you want to save your wife, STOP. RIGHT. NOW! Believe you me, we *will* talk about your destructive frame of mind, but this is neither the time nor the place! Stay focused, son!

Decide right now what you're made of! Steel or straw?"

With no time to spare for such nonsense, he dropped everything he was doing and barreled towards me with laser-focused eyes that glared straight through to my collar button.

"Now listen here. I understand that you're dangling over the fire right now and feeling the burning flames, but this my friend is a fork in the road of your life, so I ask you one more time, what are you made of? I know this is hard - life is hard! I also believe that you are stronger than you realize. Now, if you're finally done with this little temper tantrum, I'd say it's time to get to work!"

The moment he mentioned my Gran, I was set right. His advice to me was correct. I was bein' as stubborn as a mule and needed to be put in my place. His words of truth were like cool waters that washed over me.

Once Dean was done dealin' with the likes of me, he again set his sights on takin' care of Beni. He had many gifts to be certain, one bein' the ability to stay a step ahead of me or any other daft moron that might stand in his way. I was glad for his insight. He knew, for instance, that what he was about to do would be better done if I wasn't there. So, his gaze not varyin' from his task, he held out small plastic bags and instructed me to hurry outside and fill them with fresh snow.

I did as he said and ran downstairs, thankful that he cared enough to set me straight, and thankful for how he was tendin' to Beni. I was so troubled at how I'd acted. I was no saint to be sure, but in all my life, I had always been able to rise above difficult circumstances, until now anyway. I found that the battle for peace continued rearin' its ugly head though, fightin' for my attention. How could Alrik, that son of a bitch, allow this to happen? I couldn't even fathom what he put her through.

The doctor's voice yellin' for me, jolted me out of my venomous thoughts of Richter and back to the reality of the moment.

"Ice! I need it now. Her throat's closing up!"

With ice packs in hand, I ran up the stairs, arrivin' just in time to see him insertin' a tube into Beni's throat. The sight of such a disturbin' thing made me stop, frozen in my tracks.

"Are you gonna stand there and watch, or are you gonna help?"

He was bellowin' out information with every move as if he

were instructin' a crew of interns. To me, they were short phrases of muffled words ... "throat closin'" ... "intubate" ... "windpipe closin'."

"Carig, Carig! Are you with me, son? Take this collar and insert the ice bags!"

His hands were the finest instruments I'd ever seen. Obviously created to heal, their smooth but rapid movements reminded me of a symphony. With calloused mitts that were more suited to guide a chisel and hammer, I felt like an ill-equipped flunky working beside this pillar of excellence. Nonetheless, I was his only choice as an assistant. Maybe it was the stress of it all, but in the blink of an eye, he had finished and was makin' the final adjustments on the collar around her neck. The tedious task was done; he had saved Beni's life.

As the gravity of the moment subsided, my gaze shifted downward. Durin' this entire god-awful ordeal, my thoughts had been so caught up in Beni that I was unaware of my shambled state. Not only was I covered in Beni's blood, with tinges of scarlet stains runnin' up and down my arms but I was also standin' in a pool of it. It stirred into flame my earlier hallucination of my red palms, drippin' with blood. Desperately lost in my own thoughts, I heard the far-off echo of the doc's voice callin' my name.

"Carig, you alright?"

"Yeah, fine. What now, Doc?"

"For now, we lay low until the swelling's gone down, before I risk removing that bullet. She's so dehydrated and I'm concerned about her breathing. Let's just focus on one thing at a time."

For the next four hours we watched and prayed. After cleanin' all the blood from her body, I sat there holdin' her hand, so thankful that she was back. In the early hours of the mornin' she started runnin' a high fever, and the doc said we couldn't wait any longer - the bullet had to come out.

"Alright son, I'm gonna need your help. First things first though. Go change into these, then take this cleanser, scrub your hands, and dry with this towel. Don't touch anything, and when you're done, come right back here, then put on these gloves."

He carefully instructed *me* exactly what to do, taking every precaution to be sterile but he did the same before beginning the dreaded and delicate process of removing the bullet from Beni's shoulder. Changin' from the tattered overalls into pale blue scrubs, the uniform of his craft, was like watchin' a warrior prepare for battle. With each piece he cinched into place, I witnessed a boldness I hadn't yet seen; a salty seaman turned skilled surgeon. His demeanor seemed unshakable, and his instructions precise and militant, like a well-oiled machine that functioned best under pressure. It was obvious that this was not the first time that he had performed surgery under less-than-ideal circumstances.

His transformed appearance spurred a memory of an experience from not very long ago. One that was still fresh in my mind. His surgical mask fully covered everythin' except the windows into his soul. Like a closed book that was suddenly opened, I knew who he was. He was the doctor at the hospital after the Devil's Knuckles episode, who told me to go into the chapel and pray! He was the mysterious physician who revealed himself to *only* me, and then disappeared leavin' everyone thinkin' I'd lost my mind.

"It's you! Dr. Dean, you were at the hospital! Who are ya really?"

His look was one of kindness. Just like at the hospital, givin' me hope when things seemed so dark. Even though I couldn't see most of his face, I could tell by his smilin' eyes that he was grinnin' beneath the mask at my discovery, but everythin' about him left me feelin' confused.

"Truth be known, Doc, I've been livin' here since I was a lad, and I don't recall ever seein' ye with my Gran or Adina ... never up workin' on the tower even. Am I missin' somethin'?"

"I've spent many an hour here, son, but until recently, it wasn't time for us to meet. It's like the Good Book says, 'To everything there is a season, and a time to every purpose under heaven.' Do you really want to talk about this right now? Or do you want to save Beni's life?"

"Yeah, I'm here with ye, Doc. Let's do this!"

He instructed me to lift her up and prop her against my body, exposin' the gunshot wound on her back. On the other side of the table, he clipped on a lamp that lit up the entire area. I trusted him and felt confident that he knew exactly what he was doin'.

"Now listen carefully, son. It is imperative that you hold her *very* still, you understand?"

"Yes sir, I understand!"

While he prepared the area for surgery, I tried to turn my eyes away, but I couldn't help staring at the hole that marked her perfect skin, all the while feelin' her fever burnin' right through me. The damage that had been done to my beautiful Beni was unbelievable. She'd been with that man for less than a week and he had all but destroyed her. It was a good thing that the bastard was already dead, or I would have killed him myself. If he cared for her at all, how could he have allowed such a thing?

As I held her, I kept whispering in her ear, stories from our childhood, hopes of what our lives would someday bring, and reminders of how much I adored her.

"Everything's okay, lass. You're home now. I'm not ever gonna let anyone hurt ye again. I promise!"

For the next several hours I held her still as the doctor removed the lead slug.

Watchin' Dr. Dean's skills as he worked on Beni was impressive to say the least. I'm not exactly sure if his continuous talkin' was meant as a distraction to keep me from focusing on the grim reality right before my very eyes, or if it was just his normal way of doin' things. Although he was an older gentleman, I was amazed at his steady hands that seemed to be fueled by his endless chatter. His stories ranged all the way back through his grippin' family lineage, up to his own captivatin' life experiences. They were a much-needed distraction to be sure. Come to find out, he was the son of a Tuskegee Airman who flew in the Red Tails. Both his mother and father sacrificed everythin' to send him to the university so that he could go into the Navy as an officer and medical student. After many years of schoolin' and field training, he became a highly skilled combat doctor who served durin' three wars, endurin' the harshest of conditions.

Even though this situation, for me, was traumatic, and I was feelin' a bit defeated, Dr. Dean stayed calm and showed no signs of panic. Twice now, perhaps even more for that matter, this man who seemed to have a deeper understanding about me and Beni than we even knew about ourselves, had saved 'er from the clutches of death. He was somehow there, within the after-shadows of The Devil's Knuckles, and then here and now … knowin' exactly what to do, almost as if he expected it. Whatever it was that brought about the miracle of his presence, I was forever grateful! By the time he'd finished and began patchin' her up, Dean no longer seemed a stranger to me, but instead, a friend who had in reality rescued the both of us.

"The good news, son, is that the bullet didn't hit any major arteries or organs. No damage that won't heal, but she's lost a lot of blood. I'm gonna start a transfusion, and then she'll be on her way to recovery."

"Wait, do you know what her blood type is?"

"Of course, Adina made sure I did. A Positive, just like her aunt."

"Adina knew she'd need blood?"

"I can't say that I was aware of everything she had knowledge of, but it's a good thing she told me. The greater concern here is Beni's throat. The next twelve hours are crucial. I'm gonna keep her sedated. She needs the rest.

"Carig, I want to prepare you - I don't know if you realize this or not, but when Adina returned from her journeys, she would sleep for days, hurt or not. It was never easy on the body, ya know. Now, considering how long Beni was gone and all of her wounds, this will require time. When she wakes up she may not be herself for a while. By the time your grandfather died and left you in charge, Adina had done this for so many years that you probably didn't really notice a huge difference in her personality when she returned and while she was recovering. But it wasn't always like that. When she was just beginning as the Carrier, Killen told me that she had some awfully rough days. It's not an easy thing being thrown into, and consumed by, the lives of those in a different world, a different time. But I promise you, she'll get through it and so will you.

"What she needs now is lots of rest and time to heal. Even when she wakes up, she's gonna need time to work through the ordeal that she's endured the last week. Everybody handles traumatic situations differently. Just be patient with her. Why don't I take the first watch and sit with her; you're exhausted!"

"Na, that's okay. I've been waiting a week for her to come back, I'm not leavin' her now."

"Well, I'll tell you what. I'll get a little shut-eye, and then it'll be your turn. You won't be any good to her if you don't get some rest yourself."

"Will do, but really I'm fine. Really."

Before he walked out the door, he turned around and looked at me as though he pitied my situation.

"Carig, you did good! Call me if anything changes. I'll be down on the sofa.

Once he left the room, I scooted the chair close to Beni. I tried not to allow myself to get upset again; I knew that's not what she wanted. What was wrong with me? Instead of bein' angry, I should be thankful. I had everythin' to be thankful for, but whatever was stirrin' in my soul, was bewilderin'. I didn't feel like myself anymore. This callin' was far too much to ask of anyone. I just wanted a normal life with Beni. I had spent far too many hours of late by her bedside. First after her near-death experience at the Knuckles, and now this. I was sick of it. What kind of man would I be if I just sat back and let this bloody madness continue?

When finally I had somewhat relaxed and almost fallen asleep, I was startled by intense pounding on the balcony windows. It was a ragin' torrent of snow hittin' the door, soundin' as if it would burst through at any moment. In all my life I had never seen or heard a storm such as this. It was almost like a fury had been let loose and was beatin' with desperate fists tryin' to break out of hell and into the room. Somehow, I imagined the storm as the temper of Alrik Richter tryin' to claim what he believed was his. For a split second I could even see his face starin' at me through the pane. After blinking my eyes shut, and wiping away traces of illusion, I peered out the window once again, and he was gone.

Total exhaustion hit me all at once with a force like the storm, and it was all I could do not to close my burnin' eyes and let my head slump onto the side of the gurney. I knew I'd be alright if only I could rest my eyes for just a few minutes and try to let the grief and worry go, replacing them with thoughts of one day *soon* sleeping in a real bed *with my wife* ... I longed for it! Thinking of once more feeling her body next to mine made my heart beat like thunder in my chest and warmth rise up from my soul.

My passion was pierced through, when out of the corner of my eye I caught sight of the ruby ring and choker of pearls sittin' on the table in all of their showy pomp; a hauntin' reminder of another man who hungered for Beni. The scarlet stone was a sight to be sure, almost as large as a periwinkle shell. It took every bit of restraint not to throw *it* and the blasted pearls out the door. But then I saw Beni's wedding ring sittin' there as well, still covered in mud. Those brassy jewels may have been grand, but to me they were nothin' but symbols of a bad memory. Her weddin' ring, although dusky, was radiant with devotion, a sweet reminder that she was mine. I'd just as soon be damned than to let that ring stay another moment off her finger.

As I stood at the sink, watchin' the clear cool water sweep away the particles of silt from the tarnished stone, I wished that the pain of this journey could just as easily be washed away. I lifted her delicate hand and kissed it as if it were her lips. Feelin' exhausted and broken, I, for a second time, placed the ring on her finger and committed my life and my heart to her.

"You listen here, lass, there's somethin' ye need to know. No matter what, I'd marry ye a thousand times over. I've been empty … incomplete all these years until the moment you returned to Bar Rousse. Did I ever tell ye about that day you came back, right after Adina passed? When you walked up behind me, I could feel you, even before I saw your face. I'd dreamed of you endlessly, but would always wake and find that, once again, you weren't real. Only that day it wasn't a dream. My daft norm of seein' you in only the distant corners of my mind had come to an end. That mornin' that I found Adina, or the shell that her soul had left behind, I prayed that it was only a nightmare and I'd soon wake. But later, as I stood on the tower watching them drive away with her body, the Lord reminded me that when a door closes, He always opens a window. And then, you came. You were that breath of fresh air that blew in after the door of grief slammed in my face. Beni, all throughout my life I was half-done whenever you would leave! I now realize the emptiness that comes from your absence, and maybe I'm selfish, but I just don't ever wanna feel that again. Yet no matter what, I'll always be here for ye. So, listen here, you stubborn lass ..."

I could scarcely say another word, feelin' such a rush of emotions simply because she was near. I was afraid. Not 'cause of anything except how much I needed her, how much I ached for her. I was afraid of losin' 'er. Maybe not right now, but the future was like a thick fog.

"You're my everythin', lass!"

Beni was my everythin', wife and best friend. Do I dare say

out loud how my life nearly broke in two when I saw the pictures of her and Richter together? And that I surely would not survive somethin' like that again? What little knowledge I had about her journey overwhelmed me, and I had to decide whether or not I even wanted to hear her story of her week with this man at all. I'd rather pretend that none of it ever happened. What if she loved him too? What if …? My mind went off the rails with the "what-ifs."

Swayin' from reality into dreams, caused by too many wakeful hours, left me asleep at the switch, which was not like me at all. Before I realized it, I had fallen into a deathlike sleep and early mornin' had come. I was altogether startled as I was awakened by the touch of the doctor's hand on my shoulder.

"Carig, wake up, son! Bar Rousse has been hit by severe thundersnow, and it looks like the power lines are down. Probably got hit by lightning, or maybe the wind - not sure."

It was hard to tell if it was mornin' or night. The darkness of the room glowed like the sun one moment, and then the darkness of hades rolled in the next. Aside from the blindin' flashes and the neverendin' clamor, I realized that we were in the eye of a merciless and deadly storm. Explosions of lightnin' bounced off the walls. If Gran were here, he would surely say that Zeus himself was heavin' javelins of fire from one end of the sky to the other. The elements were fightin' for dominion, but the heavy winds overpowered them all, commandin' the downfall to divert to a lateral torrent. I prayed that the rage of snow peltin' against the windows wouldn't break through the French panes.

"Are you up, boy? We don't have electricity, and Beni's monitors are all off. It's not what I wanted, but I'm gonna need to remove her breathing tube and I need you to hold the flashlight while I do it."

As I watched him remove the long piece of tubing from Beni's throat, I was reminded that neither my gifts nor my callin' were even slightly related to anythin' to do with medicine. It wasn't the sight of blood that bothered me, I was more of a hunter than a healer. You could put me in charge of slayin' the Thanksgiving turkey or catchin' anything from the sea, but watchin' the center of my existence hangin' on for dear life was just too painful. I was sure thankful that she was asleep through it all. If she woke up with that thing bein' pulled from her throat and the storm blaring the way it was, it probably would have scared her to death.

Straightaway, he placed an oxygen mask on her face and then stood above her, intently monitorin' her breathin'. Like a father to his daughter, he began stroking her hair gently, tellin' her that everything was grand, and then whisperin' things that I couldn't quite make out. The gentle sound of his whispers miraculously comforted me as well. Just the part I could hear laid the groundwork of an unshakable faith, unmovable really.

"Listen here, child, the One who made you, the One who has dominion over all things is in the center of the storm. His ways are higher than our ways, and He's always good. He's not only in the storm but here also with us in this room, keepin' us safe. You rest now."

He stayed there for a half hour or so, sayin' nothin' at all. With eyes squeezed shut, he pressed his forehead against hers. I could see his lips slightly movin' while humming words in a silenced tone. Although hushed, I could tell that he was praying for her with intense fervency. When finally he lifted his head from the mercy seat of appeals, he exhaled intensely and once again became present in the third story room, lookin' over at me through eyes that had just visited the throne of God.

"Know one thing, son! You are but a man, flesh and blood. Your strength to move forward must come from God. He is present yesterday, today, and tomorrow … choose to lean on Him. Even if you are at the end of your rope, don't ya wanna be assured that the One holding the other end doesn't grow weary? You see, Carig, there's one thing that I've noticed in my many years of healing and watching mankind in its most desperate hour, clinging to life. Unless they're half-cocked, they always seek God in their last moments because they know that death is simply a door. If you want peace on this journey of life, stay close to the God who holds yours and Beni's lives in His hand. He makes no mistakes. *This* … right here and now, was no mistake. The Tempus Vector was created with that same wisdom. God is perfect, but man is flawed. Beni's journey is set and of the utmost importance. She can't do it without you, son. Stay strong!

"Now, one more thing - in addition to electricity, we don't have heat. While I keep a close eye on Beni, put some more wood in the stove. You may wanna go down to the woodshed and stock up, just in case. We'll stay in this room where it's warm until the storm passes."

I was amazed at the doc's strength and wisdom and did as he said. It was all I could do to trudge through the dense snow, not to mention practically bein' blinded by the blizzard that was attackin' from all sides. I had to keep my wits about me so that I wouldn't wander off in the wrong direction. It was crazy to think that this place that I knew like the back of my hand had so rapidly become a maze of confusin' routes, encased within snowy mounds that were swallowin' me up. As I looked back toward the house, all I could see was darkness, and all I could feel was the sting of the winds cuttin' through to my flesh.

From out of nowhere, somethin' out of the ordinary urged me to glance upward, almost like my name was bein' called from the heavens; surely my eyes were playin' tricks on me. The clouds above were stirrin' with pink and gray, and then with a crash of thunder that nearly knocked me to my knees, the billows twisted into blood red veins, movin' in all directions. If the stars had begun to fall from the skies, I would've known that the end of all things had come. But as briskly as it came, it turned once again to bitter darkness. In all my days, in all the skies at which I've marveled, I'd never seen one so unnatural.

Within the few minutes I'd been gazing up, I found myself waist-deep in powder, barely able to make it to the door of the shed. Even inside, it was bitter cold, so I grabbed a canvas tote and loaded it with as much wood as I could carry. If the snow continued, it'd soon become impossible to make it out here again. The air outside was almost too cold to breathe, and my lungs burned like fire. It took every bit of strength I had within me to make it back to the house.

Aside from not really eatin' or sleepin' for days now, the howling wind that had always filled my sails had now become a relentless enemy, set on destroyin' me. Half frozen, I finally made it back upstairs and set the pile of wood next to the stove. I watched as Dr. Dean was skillfully pullin' tubes filled with fluids out of the electric monitors, and creatin' a makeshift system that would function without power. He didn't seem a bit rattled as he held a small flashlight between his teeth, which was his only source of light. Bein' the kind of person who brought about a confidence, the doc made me, for one, feel that all would be well, no matter what;

he was well-skilled at makin' the best out of a bad situation. He obviously had done it many times before, and I felt so blessed to have someone here with the experience of an old-school military doctor. His training had taught him not only how to function and save lives in the midst of a war but he also knew how to improvise without electricity and technology. I had no doubt that he was the best of both worlds.

I began fillin' the belly of the stove until it could hold no more. Before I knew it, the cast iron glowed red with heat. After lightin' every candle I could get my hands on, the darkness was soon replaced by a warm and comfortin' glow. Finally bringin' the last candle and settin' it on the table, I collapsed into Gran's chair.

By that time the doc was no longer workin' on Beni, but instead, was sittin' by her side and once again whisperin' in her ear. Even though she was completely sedated, he continued with his most private and no-nonsense conversation. His normal jovial expression and constant smile, now yielded to a seriousness, almost as though he was nursin' to life her will to survive.

"How is she?"

"Well, son, I think she's gonna be okay."

He picked up the thick choker of pearls and held it up.

"Believe it or not, this strand of pearls saved her life. Whoever it was that did this to her had a difficult time getting a solid grip on these polished babies. Miraculously, they acted as a shield that protected her delicate throat."

"Ye said somethin' earlier about her bein' strangled '*again,*' like it had happened more than once. What did ye mean?"

"Come over here, I wanna show you something!"

He shined the flashlight back and forth across her neck.

"What is it? What do you see?"

"Well, look here. You can see the imprints of the pearls that left dots of bruises from being pressed into her neck. But then look over here!"

He pointed to other larger random bruises that didn't match the others.

"These other bruises in this area were not made by pearls. These are contusions made by someone's fingers around her neck. If I were conducting an investigation, my determination would be that she had been strangled once before, at an earlier time, most

23

probably by the same person."

"Bloody hell! Who would do something like that? What makes you think that it was the same person?"

"Well, in my experience, the act of strangulation is not a common one. It's an act of passion ... a strong desire to attain power. You see, when someone strangles another person, they find great pleasure watching life leave their victim. It makes them feel godlike. Whoever did this the first time was left unsatisfied at her survival. Although he found a sick satisfaction in the experience, he most probably felt unceasing pain at being forced to stop before the job was done. People like this don't stop until they can finally and completely accomplish their horrible act of violence. Somehow before Beni left, *right before she left*, she unfortunately had a second encounter with this psychopath where he tried to finish what he had begun."

Dr. Dean could tell that his explanation decidedly affected me, so he stopped and changed the subject.

"But the good news is that she is going to be alright, and hopefully will wake up tomorrow, or should I say today."

The tempestuous night had come and gone. With 4:00 a.m. came howling winds and snow flurries, but the worst of the storm had passed.

Chapter 2

The Gift of the Healer

"At first, I didn't recognize him, but the longer I studied his face,
the more familiar it became."
~Benidette Hammel~

I woke from my coma-like sleep curiously thinking about something Adina said on more than one occasion. "There is one absolute certainty in life." Pausing with a slight chuckle, she would reveal her profound and mysterious words of wisdom that inevitably turned into an all-night life conversation. "Statistically, my dear Beni, one out of every one person will die, that's a certain. But what matters most is what you do with that span of time between your first and last breath. God gives us but one lifetime to make a difference, either for good or for evil. Always choose what's right and good. Live in such a way that if your journeys were played back for the world to see, you wouldn't be ashamed."

As I laid there in the quiet unknown, her words continued spinning through my mind, and not quite sure if I was dead or alive, I half expected my life reel to begin playing at any moment. Even though my eyes seemed to be glued shut, I perceived a blinding brightness in the room outside of myself. If I was dead, I was thankful to be surrounded by light and a seemingly peaceful atmosphere. Even if I could, I wasn't entirely ready to open myself up to my surroundings, and was determined that before taking even a peek, I would contemplate the recent events of my life.

I was fully aware that I had just been party to my first journey with the Tempus Vector. But exactly how long I'd been gone, or for that matter, if I had even returned home, I wasn't sure. At this point, I seemed to possess only a handful of details about the whole ordeal. A haziness covered my recollections, and the Friedlich events were but a dream. No! Not a dream at all, they were as real as me. With each passing moment, my mind began to wake, and memories appeared like stars in a black sky. One by one my thoughts became vivid. Unfortunately, my memories surfaced along with a new and unwelcomed ache from my seemingly broken body.

Strangely, and above all else, my heart hurt. Actually, it was throbbing all the way down to my stomach, no doubt instigated by thoughts of Alrik. Alrik Richter. He was a very real part of my journey, but why I was grieving over him, I wasn't sure. Perhaps it was because I had left him behind and in the process of doing so, broke his heart. I distinctly remember observing his grief-stricken face just seconds before I clutched hold of the frame and disappeared. His expression, that spoke a thousand somber words, was one that I would never forget as long as I lived. The ache that now clenched my heart welled up into tears that burned as they trickled down over my scuffed-up face.

As if the pain I had caused Alrik wasn't bad enough, I suddenly felt an impetuous onslaught of fear that seized my soul, caused entirely by mental images of the demon-man of Halag Sauer. Even now, I could smell the foulness of his breath as I gasped for air and cringed as every muscle in my body tensed up. It became too much to bear. I felt as though I was being tortured by these incessant thoughts, but to add to my already agonizing state, I was also distressingly confronted with eyes of innocence that revealed a haunting display of disappointment.

I exhaled a breath of despair over thoughts of that sweet little girl who longed only for a mother's tender care. Annaliese, *I'm so sorry for leaving you!* In that blink of an eye, that heartbeat of time when we peered deeply into one another's eyes, I saw myself as a little girl, alone. All of her hopes were crushed as I was taken away. Unlike me, she probably didn't have an Adina who would come along and rescue her. I had ruined two lives who were depending on me for happiness, and gravely disappointed another because I survived his brutal attacks.

These endless thoughts were too much for me. The more I pondered, the more I felt as if I had done nothing right, and I was ashamed. No matter what, no matter where I would find myself, it was time to open my eyes and get up from this place.

The beaming rays that filled the room, to me were daggering shafts of painful light. It had been such a long and difficult journey, one that left me feeling hopeless at the prospect of ever returning home again.

At first, I couldn't tell where I was, as I was blinded by a brilliance that forced me to squeeze my eyes shut over and again. I was afraid to open them. Afraid that if I did, the third story room would be gone, and I would find myself back at the Richter Estate. I couldn't stomach the possibility!

Promptly detouring from that train of thought, I realized that every inch of my body, not just my throat, ached, and with every move I cringed in pain; even swallowing seemed impossible. I hurt everywhere! Anxiety gripped me like a vice, twisting at every part of my being, at not knowing where I was or what would be waiting for me when I opened my eyes. My only relief came from the intense warmth of the sun that was beating down on me, making the surrounding atmosphere feel safe and friendly. Even still, I was petrified at the idea of opening my eyes and discovering that I was still stranded in 1940 Germany. I didn't think that I could stand it. If I was still at the Richter Estate, I was probably there for good. Never again would I return home.

I couldn't just lie in this guessing state forever. I had to be brave and face whatever was waiting for me. Slowly, I peered through half-opened eyes, slightly squinting, but this time something or someone was shielding my face from the bright light. It was a someone. I could feel their presence and hear their breathing. Please Lord, don't let it be Halag. Please let me be home!

Blinking incessantly, I began straining to make out the face that was standing over me. As my focus came into view, I was practically blinded. Not by the light, but by the intense white smile of the man leaning over me. At first, I didn't recognize him, but the longer I studied his face, the more familiar it became, and then when he spoke I remembered who he was … it had been many years, but I recognized Ray Dean, the man who came over often to make repairs on Adina's lighthouse.

As I laid there looking up at his pleasant face, I was utterly confused, and for the life of me, I had no idea why the lighthouse repairman was here by my side. Perhaps I was dreaming, but the light that was glowing behind him almost made his appearance angelic. Maybe I was in heaven, and so was he. But then the excruciating flare of pain in my back and throat instantly reminded me that I was very much alive. Knowing that there's no suffering in heaven, I was painfully aware that I was obviously still here on planet earth … with Ray Dean as company.

"Well, good morning, sunshine. Welcome back!"

I opened my mouth, and tried to speak, but nothing came out.

Feeling sour and acidic air burning my throat, the realization hit me that an oxygen mask was on my face, causing me to panic and impulsively attempt to rip it off.

"Hold on, little girl. I'll help you with that. You're alright."

He could tell that I was trying to speak, and gently removed the mask from my face.

"Slow down, Beni. There's no need for talk right now, you're alright. Let's prop you up and try a few ice chips."

I nodded my head *yes*. My throat felt dry and burned like it had been laid out to dry in the Sahara.

"Okay, Beni girl, here ya go!"

He set one tiny but marvelous chip on my lips. I could feel every inch of the icy hot liquid seeping down my throat.

"Beni, I'm going to ask you a few questions, and all I want you to do is nod yes or no, okay?"

I nodded in agreement.

"Do you know where you are?"

As I glanced out the balcony door and across the room, I knew exactly where I was. I was home.

Yes, I nodded.

"Do you remember what happened to you?"

I looked straight at him without seeing him, as my mind began to recount even more of the events of my first journey with the Tempus Vector. It all seemed like a bizarre nightmare, but it wasn't a dark dream at all, it was my reality. Staring up into the eyes of this man who was asking such a haunting question filled me with grief as it awakened the ghosts of my journey. My eyes suddenly filled with tears. My agony not only stemmed from the horror inflicted by Halag and how I invaded the lives of Alrik and Annaliese but from the sadness and intense sorrow that consumed me over leaving Carson and Malachi, knowing that I would never see them again.

Even more bothersome was the fact that I was back, but Carig wasn't here. All of it together was too much to bear.

"You alright, kiddo?"

With that one question, I completely broke down and began to sob. His words were soft and kind and seemed to make everything in my torn-up being feel better, yet I couldn't stop crying.

"That's okay, just let it all out. All the emotions you're

feeling are completely normal. I saw it a hundred times over with Adina. Speaking of Adina, you're probably wondering why in the world the lighthouse repairman is here. Well, all those times that you thought I was here fixing the lighthouse, I was really here helping Adina, just like I'm helping you now. In all honesty, I do fix lighthouses, although I'm really a doctor, but mainly a friend. And as long as I'm alive, you can count on me to be here to help you and Carig. *You*, little girl, came back to us pretty beat up. Do you remember?"

I now remembered what had happened to me, or most of it anyway. In all of it, I felt like an absolute failure. I had failed. I took a deep breath and closed my eyes, unable to stop the tears from flowing down my cheeks.

"Beni, listen. I can only imagine what you've been through, but Carig has been through it right along with you. He finally fell asleep. He's been up for days, has barely eaten, and has been worried sick about you. I think you could use each other right now."

With his eyes, he motioned to the other side of the room where Carig was asleep in his grandfather's chair. *So, he was here!* Poor thing! Shame on me for not thinking the best of him. If anyone deserved that, he did. Dean was right, I needed him desperately and couldn't wait to see him.

I winced with every movement I made. My shoulder and arm were throbbing with pain. I knew why my throat was injured; I remembered Halag attacking me, but I couldn't quite remember what happened to my shoulder and why my arm was in a sling.

"Beni, you were shot in the back, right below your shoulder blade. You don't remember that?"

No, I didn't remember that at all. I had no idea who shot me. I sat up on the side of the bed, and just stared at Carig. Putting my feet on the floor, standing up and finding my balance was not as easy as I thought it would be.

"I don't know if this is a good idea, Beni. You need to rest!"

Although words wouldn't come, I gave him a glare that said, *"Just help me! I need to see my husband!"*

"Alright! Boy, if looks could kill! My word, *you are* stubborn, just like your aunt."

As he began unhooking my IV lines, he became very chatty about his time with Adina, and then he looked me straight in the eyes.

"Yes, it's not just your stubbornness. I see Adina in your eyes, yes, I do. You have a lot of that *firecracker gene* in there! Alright, little girl, nice and easy. Just lean on me."

Dr. Dean helped me walk over to the chair where Carig was sleeping. I had read about it many times in great novels and tales of romance, but until now I never knew what it meant to die in someone's arms. Yet the moment I sat down on Carig's lap, nestling close to him, the world seemed right and good. Like magic, my body melted into his and I was comforted by his ever familiar warmth and quietness. These extraordinary qualities were not merely superficial, but they radiated from deep within him - straight from his caring heart.

It was difficult to tell where *my* body ended and his began. I so badly wanted him to wake up, but he was clearly exhausted and in such a deep sleep that he didn't even flinch at my presence. Although he was pale and haggard from the worry and anguish that I had caused him, he was still so amazingly handsome. Like always, it was my great pleasure to watch him as he slept. If I could have spoken at that very moment, I would have told him how incredibly sorry I was for all of the worry that I had caused. Leaving a never-ending trail of difficulties seemed to be my lot in life, not only in the here and now but in decades of long ago.

As I sat there admiring Carig, I felt my mind being attacked from all directions; like a movie projector playing reel after reel of everything I'd ever done wrong. Feeling that I had disappointed everyone who mattered in my life, I was overcome by sadness. I'd been awake less than an hour and already I was unable to escape the harrowing reality of my failures.

Bar Rousse and the people here were my true home, but I had been too self-absorbed to see it. I ignored them until they were gone, and *now* it was too late. For that, I would never forgive myself. Why Carig even gave me the time of day, I had no idea. For years I was horrible to him. I couldn't begin to imagine what he thought about how I abandoned Adina, and my absence at the passing of his grandmother and grandfather. The times he needed me the most, I wasn't there.

But that wasn't me anymore. I had become a new person. The selfish individual that I had once been, self-consumed and driven by success, was no longer who I was, and was no longer welcome.

I tried to let the past go, to focus on Carig, but it wouldn't be that easy. Along with my tormenting grief and the fact that every bone in my body ached, I was suddenly bombarded by grim recollections of disloyalty. Did I cross the line? One by one, feelings of guilt began to stack up in my mind. Flashes of the man who tried to steal my heart with his obsessive romance, not to mention the things I allowed to happen between the two of us, came toppling down upon me. I did it all in the name of survival, but was this self-reproach a sign that I had gone too far? Would I understand if the tables were turned and it was Carig instead of me who had behaved in such a way?

Without too much thought, I answered my own queries. No matter what, I trusted him, and I would expect him to do whatever was necessary to survive and come back to me. My love for him was steadfast, and nothing would ever change that as far as I was concerned. He was my one and only and my best friend. I truly hoped that he felt the same way and would trust the decisions that I had made without questioning my faithfulness and devotion. I would never purposely do anything that would hurt him. As a matter of fact, I would rather die than see him sad or disappointed.

Countless scenarios crossed my mind of how this may or may not work out, but I couldn't seem to come to a resting place of "everything was going to be alright" and rid my heart of this agonizing feeling. I reminded myself that we both knew going in how taxing it would very likely be on our relationship and our marriage. We were even warned ahead of time that it would be better to stay single. I remembered arguing the point with Carig, but he wouldn't hear it. I wondered if he regretted marrying me now. Part of the problem was that we didn't even have twenty-four hours of married life together before I left. We hadn't yet built any kind of foundation where we could weather a trial of this magnitude without it tearing us apart. His eyes had now been opened to this unconventional life where he would always be left waiting and wondering. I knew it had been hard on him, and although I didn't want to add any more stress, I had to tell him everything, no matter the outcome. If I didn't, my silence would most certainly lead to a tormenting bondage. Every secret that I'd hide would be like a link in a chain forged by deceit, finally becoming a permanent weight around my neck and a symbol of my oppression.

I couldn't live like that. I *refused* to live like that! The more I reflected on everything, the more clouded and confused my thoughts became. I should have been ecstatic because I was finally home. After all, there were so many times that I thought I would never make it back, that I would never see Carig again. Amidst everything else, I couldn't think of one thing I did right on this perilous journey. I should have never gone. I should never have been chosen as the Carrier of the Tempus Vector.

My soul, so unsettled within me, and my continued flashbacks, only made everything worse. It was overwhelming, and I couldn't quite put my finger on exactly what was eating me up inside. It wasn't just the fact that I had only one task to complete, at which I had totally failed, but there was something else. If I were to be completely honest, I had come to care for Alrik very much. Too much really. Even with all of these complex emotions stirring my heart, I knew one thing, my fondness for him bordered on love, but only that of a devoted friend. The deepest and most powerful love I had ever experienced was reserved for Carig alone. Alrik was just so desperate for companionship and someone who would unconditionally and wildly yearn for him. Even though I wasn't that person, I was grieving over Annaliese and him. With all of my heart, I hoped that he had found the one that he was looking for, and that the rest of his days were happy ones. I wondered if Adina brooded over her journey acquaintances, or was that just me?

I began running my fingers through Carig's hair, twisting his auburn locks in spirals, then lightly skimming the base of his neck. I was mesmerized by his beautiful face. Not wanting to interfere, Dr. Dean stood at the window admiring the sunlight glistening atop the thick blanket of snow while watching me out of the corner of his eye. He could tell that I was ineffectively battling my own thoughts and knew that healing would never come without rest. Trying to save me from myself, he walked over and insisted that I lay back down.

"You want me to wake him up for you, Beni? The poor boy is exhausted though. He hasn't left your side once, and it nearly did him in being witness to the state you were in when you returned."

I shook my head *no*. As much as I wanted Carig to hold me,

I knew that he needed to sleep. Without waking him, I slipped off his lap, and Dr. Dean helped me back to my bed.

"Is there anything I can get you, Beni girl?"

I pointed to the light brown journal with the initials "AY" that was sitting over by Carig's chair.

"Alright, let's just make you comfortable first."

As he was tucking the blankets around me, his smile disappeared, and his face became solemn.

"Beni, I can't even begin to understand what happened to you on this journey, but there are some things that I do know. Your experiences will most certainly be different from Adina's. You can read through and study her journal, and it's good that you do, but you're not gonna find all the answers in there. One thing Adina told me shortly before she died, is that she often returned from her journeys feeling undone, as though she'd failed or messed up in one way or another. But as you already know, she had hundreds of successes and very few failures. It will be the same with you. Her wall of images is like a shelf filled with books. Incredible stories authored and known in detail, only by her. Some she shared, but others were painful remembrances that were better left locked away.

"I could always read her like a book, knowing right away by looking into her eyes that something in her journey had taken her joy hostage. I see that same grief in you. Something happened that's making you feel unfulfilled or like you didn't accomplish all that you wanted to in some way, but you'll come to find out that everything is going to be alright. The main thing you need to consider is whether or not you completed the task that you were meant to complete. Remember, you are simply human and an instrument of a divine calling. You know what they say about an instrument, right?" He picked up a scalpel off of the tray and held it in his hands. "An instrument is only as good as the hand that's holding it. All you need to do is be willing and trust."

I wanted so badly to scream out, "How *will* I ever know? How will I ever know that it wasn't a complete waste of time?"

I just laid there, once again weeping as he held my hand.

"Beni, I can already tell you that this journey was successful."

I turned my face away from him to both hide my tears, and the slightly disrespectful roll of my eyes at his speculative position on the matter. He was only trying to make me feel better, yet he had no way of knowing. How dare he say anything to me about it! There's no way he could know. There was no way that *I* could know.

"Look at me, Beni!"

I didn't want to! Actually, I didn't want to see anyone at this point. I just wanted to be alone.

He proceeded to speak to me in a manner that was both caring and firm. He knew as well as I did that I had begun a downward spiral that needed to be stopped or I might never recover.

"Beni girl, I have some insight to share with you that you obviously don't know. So why don't you give me your attention!"

Reluctantly I heeded his request and glared at him in a most insolent manner. He walked over to the door and picked up the Tempus Vector that was leaning against the wall. He held it up and brushed off the dried mud.

"Now, let's see here. Ooh wee! This thing has really been through the mill! Yep, yep, you did good alright!"

His babbling about that stupid frame was really annoying me, and I wasn't hearing one ounce of wisdom coming out of his mouth. He just kept talking and cleaning the frame as he spoke.

"You know, I used to spend endless hours with Adina, Killen, and Mari, just talkin' and enjoying each other's company. Believe it or not, out of all of the great spaces in this house, we spent most of our time in the sewing room. Adina would always have fresh brewed iced tea and cheesecake. Do you know why we always chose that area? I mean other than the fact that it was home to my favorite chair. You know the one? Navy blue recliner with worn arms? But really, every last one of us chose that room because being there meant witnessing firsthand the incredible stories of her journeys. Her accomplishments would confirm to each of us who were giving so much of ourselves, that we were achieving something bigger than what we would ever see. Each time she pulled a frame from the wall, we would return with her to that place in time … it was far better than goin' to the movie house. The pictures were nothing special to us in and of themselves, that is until the details brought them to life."

I really had no idea why Dr. Dean was telling me all of this. I soon discovered, however, that amongst those photos and all of the stories they paralleled, there was one that was not only significant to him but that he believed would benefit m

Chapter 3

The Symbol Marker

"She explained that, for her, the picture had always been the starting place, and sometimes the ending place, but it was always there from the beginning; always the symbol marker of her journey." ~Dr. Ray Dean~

"There's one particular photo that I would like to tell you about, Beni, if you can humor me for just a little bit. I know I won't be able to tell it the way Adina did, but maybe, just maybe, it will help you. I don't know if you've ever really noticed it before but intermingled among the myriad of photos on Adina's wall is an image of a fencepost covered in barbed wire, seemingly swallowed up by overgrown brush. Quite honestly, no one in their right mind would ever hang such an unattractive picture, but believe it or not, that one black and white photo was my favorite of all of her stories. I had such a deep connection to this adventure that Adina would always ask my permission before telling the tale.

"She had been traveling for several years at this point and experienced many things both good and bad. However, she would say in regard to this particular journey, that it started and ended as though she was looking into a hazy mirror. Like you, when this journey ended she was both confused and disappointed in the outcome. It wasn't until years later that she was able to see the reflection clearly. Only then were her eyes opened to the great success that came from it.

"Now the reason this particular journey left her so confounded was because her destination was identified by a fencepost in Sauk City, Wisconsin in the middle of nowhere. Generally, she would land in a town or city denoted by a particular person or building of some sort ... but never a fencepost. Even though she thought it odd, she walked out of the third story door and found herself in a wide-open space in the middle of nowhere. As she stood quietly studying the area, she quickly realized that there was no fencepost, but only an old, whitewashed, wood-framed house with a large white barn behind it. Off to the side was another wooden house, but shorter in height than the other with a bountiful field of corn rising up behind it. The entire property had obviously been around for many years as it was weathered, but well-kept just the same. Fencing ran for miles around the property which boarded hundreds of cows happily grazing on the green grasses. The sign sitting on the dirt road was labeled 'Chesney Dairy Co.' On the opposite side of the house was a hill that was high enough to view great distances in all directions. In hopes of spotting the mysterious post, she climbed to the top and surveyed the land, but saw no sign of anything like it. She explained that, for her, the picture had always been the starting place and sometimes the ending place, but it was always there from the beginning; always the symbol marker of her journey. And yet all that she could see for miles were green rolling hills. Nothing even vaguely resembling dead grasses and an old post covered in barbed wire.

"She stumbled back down the hill as it kept grabbing hold of her heels and began walking towards the white house. It was the only structure for miles around, and the only reasonable place to go. Like many times before, when plagued by uncertainty she moved forward in faith to see where it would lead. As Adina recalled how the swift breeze of that summer's day practically nudged her right through the rusty gate and up the walkway toward the main house, she was amazed by the unfailing faithfulness and power of her calling.

"She thought it unusual that no one was around, except of course, the cows. Suddenly, in the distance she could hear the rising echoes of chatter along with a rapid scuffling of feet. She stood completely still as the now quiet group of people spotted this out of place stranger standing on their property. She was far outnumbered and hoped that they were the friendly sort. Their comfortable conversation quickly turned guarded and solemn.

"Two men led the pack, and with outstretched gestures cautioned the others to stay where they were. The duo cautiously approached Adina. They were similar in many ways, both middle-aged, dressed in overalls, each with a shotgun resting on one shoulder. One was fair skinned and the other darker, but it was easy to see that they were close, the best of friends. Their wives and children, who stayed behind as instructed, expressed great care and concern for one another and for the well-being of their patriarchs. Although each family was different in complexion, they were by all means a strong family unit who had obvious respect for one another. The two younger girls and the teenage boy lagged further behind the others as they skipped rocks across the meadows, while the twin girls, probably around nine years of age, walked with their noses stuck in books. When they saw Adina standing there holding her suitcase, they too stopped in their tracks and stared at her in fear.

"Both men continued toward her with kind but stern faces. The white gentleman asked if he could help her, and how in the world did she get this far out of town, especially wearing those shoes? As she had done so many times before, she told her story, which was simply that she was seeking employment and was told that the Chesney Dairy might be hiring help. As far as how she got there, she would always rely on the pretext of 'a stranger in a black truck gave her a ride.' She would laugh as she told this part of the story, stating that 'no one ever seemed to question a stranger in a black truck!'

"Well, they both sized her up and came to the conclusion that she had never milked a cow before, or even seen a day's hard work at that. Many times, throughout her journeys, Adina was able to use knowledge of things that she forgot she even knew. Although her childhood was difficult, she was thankful for the many things that she was forced to learn, such as milking a cow, which she had done many times before in order to have milk for her brothers and sisters. The grocer in Belin had had a couple of Jersey cows in a barn behind his store, and if Adina brought her own bucket, he would allow her to take all the milk she could carry home. It was certainly not her favorite thing to do, but nonetheless, she knew how to do it.

"After she convinced the two that she was fully capable of milking a cow, but more importantly an extremely hard worker and an excellent seamstress, they agreed to let her stay, telling her that they could only pay her in food and shelter, which she gratefully accepted.

"As the rest of the family approached, Adina could tell that they were notably grieved over something. Upon entering the humble but efficient-running home, Ma Chesney showed her the room where she would be staying and supplied her with appropriate work clothes. As she usually did on her journeys, Adina had worn a navy-blue suit, yet it certainly wouldn't do for this kind of work. So, before she went back downstairs, she slipped on the oversized work pants, button down shirt, and boots that had been provided for her.

"When Adina entered the dining area, she found each member of the family sitting at a long table, praying before they ate lunch. One by one their prayers were similar, all begging for help and mercy in finding a lost *someone* called Sam. She couldn't help but become emotional right along with them, but the words of Moses, Sam's father, were strong and full of faith. He believed and was confident that the God of all gods would hear and answer their prayers and bring his boy back. But amidst his strength, his voice broke and the family around him wept at the sight of one so strong falling to pieces. As Adina sat at the table with that blended group who were evidently tighter than most families, she discovered that they, and their people before them, had remained a close-knit family since the Civil War days. Together these two families from different parts of the world, had an astounding and uncommon history that all began with the arrival of two Hungarian immigrants.

"In 1849, Odi and Hajan Czasni immigrated from a war-torn Hungary to a place they believed could give them a new start in a free land. All that Odi knew was dairy farming. His family had provided the best milk, cream, and cheese to their community until their world crumbled, forcing them to leave. Both sets of parents bestowed everything they had on the young couple, and then sadly sent them off to America hoping that at least *they* would have a future and carry on the Czasni name.

"With every last penny, the newlyweds bought Wisconsin land, built a small house, and purchased two cows. Visions of hope and freedom were brutally replaced by the sting of prejudice, as they soon realized that 'their kind' was not welcome. Unfortunately, they were surrounded by those who had forgotten that they too were once foreigners in a melting pot, unable to see past the Hungarians who talked 'funny' and spoke very little English. Although it was difficult, Odi and Hajan persevered, knowing that giving up was not an option. This was now their home.

"Day after day, Odi would push his cart filled with fresh milk, butter, and cheese into town. At first no one would buy from the Czasni Dairy Cart. He was a stranger, and strangers (especially immigrants) were not warmly received. Trying to remain positive, he would return home with his cart still full and no money in his pocket, and every night they would pray that God would help them and show them what to do.

"After many days of hopeless despair, God answered their prayers by giving Hajan a brilliant idea. First, even though Odi didn't like the notion, they changed the spelling of their name from Czasni to Chesney in hopes of creating a brand that sounded more American. Next, Hajan stayed up all night repainting the name on the cart, and she also made Hungarian bread and sugar cookies to prompt the townspeople to try their dairy products. The following day she traveled to town alongside Odi. As the shoppers walked by, she sliced the bread, then smeared on sweet butter and thin slices of cheese, serving the community free of charge. As children passed by, she would give them a cookie and a ladle full of milk. Their quality of milk, butter, and cheese soon captured the hearts and taste buds of the entire community, and within a few years Chesney Dairy served the residents of their town, as well as the surrounding communities.

"Now as time went on, between their dairy business and their growing family, Odi and Hajan became overwhelmingly busy and were desperate for help. They were told that slaves were the answer to their dilemma, given instructions on how and where to purchase them, and assured that after a one-time investment they would enjoy free labor from that point on. From the very beginning, the idea of slavery did not sit well with them at all as they did not agree that any man should be in bondage to another, no matter their color. They knew that God had blessed them in their new home and taking on slave labor would be like slapping Him in the face, knowing that He too despised slavery.

"One day as Odi and Hajan traveled down to Illinois, they were appalled as they witnessed a slave auction occurring in the town square. Many had been bought and sold on this stage, but as they neared the square, they watched in horror as an entire family was herded onto the platform - mother, father, three teenage boys, and two girls standing there chained together as one. Both Odi and Hajan followed their urge to purchase the entire family, knowing that they would otherwise be sold off separately. After finishing Odi's business in town, they all left together.

"Over the many years of slavery that consumed the United States, and through the perils of the Civil War, Odi and Hajan made this family part of their own. Odi worked side by side with Moses to build his family their very own home on the Wisconsin property, and paid them fair wages for working in the dairy. Moses also planted fields of corn behind his house that would also help to support his family. They did something in that day that was practically unheard of. They came together as one family that stood strong when many crumbled. Moses and Sarah grieved over the persecution of their brothers and sisters who were in bondage and risked their lives to aid a new freedom movement. They all knew that no matter the consequences, they had to step up and help. To the north of the property, they dug a tunnel that became a depot used as a stopping point for slaves escaping into Canada by means of the underground railroad. As with everything else, Odi and Hajan came alongside and helped Moses and Sarah in any way that they could. The legacy of love and devotion that began with these two families carried on to their children and their children's children and so on. But back to Adina's story.

"At the table, Adina sat next to the youngest Chesney girl, named Mary, who was somewhere around eight years old. She had beautiful long blond hair, and hazel eyes. Once the prayer was finished, everyone began eating, except Mary. Come to find out, Sam was her best friend and they spent almost every waking moment together, so she couldn't stand the thought of eating when he was still lost.

"Mary jumped up from the table and ran outside. Everyone continued eating, but Adina excused herself and followed her. She found her sitting on a swing that hung from the high branches of a shade tree. Obviously, she could tell that this little girl had a lot of spunk and hated injustice. In her mind, a great unfairness was being committed by her family enjoying a meal while Samuel was missing. Finding a sympathetic friend in Adina, Mary poured out the story that was weighing heavily on her heart.

"Apparently, Samuel had been scolded for skimming all the cream off of the top of the milk that was supposed to be used for butter and cheese. His daddy got a switch from the tree and whipped him on the backside for it. Sam got so mad that he ran away and had now been gone for two days. This was not the first time Samuel's temper had prompted him to run away, but in the past, he had always returned before supper. This time was different. Adina questioned Mary, asking her where he might go, but she assured her that they had checked all of his normal hiding places. When Sam never turned up, his family searched to no avail. As time passed, they all became overwrought with worry, but didn't know where else to hunt for him.

"Over the next few days together, Mary and Adina became very close, mainly because Adina remained her constant ally in the search for Samuel. When Mary would get a hunch about where he might be, Adina was always available to go with her. She just *knew* that he was still alive, she could feel it in her soul.

"With each passing hour, Adina felt constant turmoil, continually wondering exactly why she was there. At night, in the secrecy of her room, she would remove the frame from her suitcase and examine and study the picture of the mysterious and hidden fencepost covered in barbed wire, hoping she would discover some kind of clue that would direct her. One night as she was sleeping, Adina awoke in a panic to a distinct scream for help. Most disturbing was that the shriek was that of a child. Covered in sweat, with every inch of her body pulsating in fear, she sprang out of the bed. The overwhelming jolt that woke her was in truth a revelation, and the enigma of the fencepost became very clear. She not only knew the purpose of the seemingly insignificant photograph but knew that wherever *it* was located, Samuel was there.

"She ran into Mary's room and woke her up, showing her the picture and asking if she had ever seen the fencepost, or if she knew the general area of its location. After wiping her eyes and trying to focus, Mary nodded. She knew exactly where it was! Yes, she knew the area well. But unfortunately, along with Samuel and all of the other children, she had been warned to never go there. Frightened and taken aback, she asked Adina why she had a picture of that terrifying place.

"Adina didn't understand Mary's fear, but with a resolved sense of urgency she insisted that she get up, telling her that wherever this fencepost was, Samuel was there and if they didn't hurry it would be too late to save him. Mary hastily explained that this was not just a post, but a warning marker noted by two arrows striking one another. The symbol marked the entrance to an ancient Indian burial ground where the spirits of a slaughtered Indian tribe had been laid to rest. Entering this evil but sacred ground would mean certain death for whoever set foot in it. Mary couldn't believe that Samuel would go there after so many warnings to stay clear. To add to her fear, she now distrusted Adina. This stranger, who held a photo of such a wicked place and claimed that it held her Samuel captive, bothered her greatly. Mary wanted to go and tell her folks all about it, but knew if she did, they would never allow her to go to that forbidden place. She didn't even know if she really believed Adina, but she was willing to do anything for Sam.

"Reluctantly, at the crack of dawn Mary led the way to the forbidden burial ground. With suitcase and frame in hand, Adina left the Chesney house thoroughly prepared to return home. However, the further they moved away from the property, the more unsure Adina became. Although she knew that this post would lead to the missing boy, like so many times before, she wasn't sure what else she would find once they arrived.

"Mary was uncharacteristically quiet for the entire journey. She had no idea if she could trust this stranger who had stepped into their lives holding such a picture and was now taking her to a forbidden place. After a few hours of walking, and afraid to go any further, she stopped and pointed to the graveyard in the distance, but Adina kept moving forward. Apprehensive and hesitant, Mary followed cautiously. As they got closer, the exact image of what the Tempus Vector had revealed was standing before her. Just as Mary had said, it was an old Indian burial ground that was overgrown, and it appeared as if no one had walked there for over a hundred years.

"Out of the corner of her eye, Adina saw a small red knapsack sitting atop the dried-up grasses. Mary excitedly confirmed that it did indeed belong to Sam.

"To the side of one of the ancient grave markers was a wooden door that seemed to have once been hidden by a blanket of sod. Adina asked Mary if she knew where the old entrance led. At first, she shook her head no, but then paused, and Adina could tell that she remembered something. In fact, she had remembered an old ballad that Sam's grandpa used to sing about salvation, and that 'it was comin' through the burial of the saint, in the place where no one ain't!'"

As I watched Dr. Dean recall the story, the song flowed from his mouth as if he had heard it many times before.

"'Oh Lord, take me, take me, take me to the burial ground. Salvation's comin' through the burial of the saint, in the place where no one ain't. Take me, take me, take me to the burial ground, and let me lay down this burden, let me lay down in the burial ground.'"

As he finished the low-pitched melody, he continued with his story.

"Mary told Adina that she wasn't sure, but it was perhaps a depot or waiting place, where slaves would hide - part of the Underground Railroad. She had always heard about it, but never knew if it was true, and definitely didn't know that it had been hidden in the old Indian burial ground. Cleverly, it was made out to be so evil and terrifying, but in fact, the opposite was true. This was a haven that had kept hundreds of slaves safe for a night, in a refuge protected among the city of the dead.

"Adina hurried and began opening the wooden door, but before she could get it completely open, Mary ran in front of her and stepped into the dark tunnel screaming Sam's name. The last thing Adina heard was, 'He's dead, I think he's dead!'

"At that very instant, Adina was called to return. She said when she arrived back home, all she could hear over and over again was, 'He's dead!' In her mind she had failed greatly. She was sent there to save that boy's life, and she failed. To make things worse, she left Mary there alone, and the family wondering why she left without saying goodbye after they had shown her such kindness and generosity."

I didn't really know if Dr. Dean told me this to make me feel better about failing in my task. Perhaps it was a blessing that I couldn't speak. But this story still did not answer the question of how he could possibly know if my journey was successful or not.

"Now listen here, Beni. I'm no psychic, but I do know that just as Adina was successful in her task, so were you."

He just sat there staring at me, and I at him. Then he gave the frame one last brush and turned it around. There in the frame was the picture of the bakery. It was the bakery that I saw the moment I stepped out onto the streets of Friedlich. I shook my head and shrugged my shoulders with my rude body language saying, *"Okay? Why are you showing me that?"*

With a big grin on his face and clutching the frame, he held it up to the side of his face like a giddy schoolboy at show-and-tell, continuing to point at the picture with his eyes.

"Beni, don't you get it? You of all people should understand this. The reason the picture still remains in this frame is *only* because your journey was successful, and you carried out what you were meant to accomplish, otherwise it would be gone. Just like Adina's picture of the old post wrapped in barbed wire. The picture was there, she was successful. And here, right here is the picture of the bakery. You didn't fail."

I sat there in a daze of disbelief.

"It's true, Beni. I'm telling you the truth. The empty frames are the regrets, the failures. The others are successes."

Relieved by his revelation, I didn't realize that if, and only if, the picture remained in the Tempus Vector, did that mean that the Carrier was successful. Although I didn't understand how my journey would have possibly been a triumph, I, like Adina was still gazing into a foggy mirror. Everything had left me exhausted, and I was hurting so badly that I could hardly see straight. I watched as Dr. Dean injected something into my IV.

"Sleep, Beni, it's time to rest. When you wake up, you'll feel much better!"

Chapter 4

Axiom

"But when Carig walked into my life, even though just a
boy, he was somehow in tune with my hurt, maybe because it was
not unlike his own."
~Benidette Hammel~

I woke to the familiar sound of the ocean lapping at the shore, which for some reason always seemed to be louder and more restless-sounding in my room. I was no longer lying on the gurney in the third story, but in my own bedroom. I could tell by the sliver of light that broke through the window that it was very early in the morning. If I was remembering correctly, I had been asleep for an entire 24 hours.

I tried calling out for Carig with only a trace of a voice. Although my shoulder still throbbed, Dr. Dean was right, I felt so much better than I had a day ago. Whatever healing serum he put in my IV seemed to work like magic. Of course, getting back to normal would take time, but I felt like a new person. Mainly, I was so relieved to finally be home with my husband. However, still gnawing in the back of my mind were all of those who I had left behind. Perhaps in order to survive all of this I needed to learn how to turn off my affections and feelings for others … just use them to get what I needed, and then get out? With this one unpleasant thought, that spoke against everything I believed in, I could feel a tangible bitterness within me. One that I had never known until now.

The only thing that would make this better was to see Carig. With both excitement and frustration, I pulled out the IV, grabbed my robe off the wardrobe hook, and set off to find him. Finding my husband seemed like a grand idea until I passed by a mirror and took a shocking gander at myself. I was appalled at my reflection! My hair was dirty and disheveled like a rat's nest, and for that matter, I smelled like a rat's nest. I didn't care if I got my bandage wet, I was taking a bath.

While I waited for the tub to fill, I pulled the bandage from my shoulder. With a quick glance in the mirror, I gasped at the sight and severity of my wound. A gunshot wound? I still didn't remember getting shot, or who did it. My best guess was Halag, but on the other hand, I remembered knocking him out with the wooden shoe box. Oh my gosh, the wooden box! On top of everything else, had I left the box there? I know I tried to grab it, but did I? If I left it behind, it surely led them to Malachi. I had to keep reminding myself that Dr. Dean showed me the picture in the Tempus Vector. The picture, the picture! That means my journey was successful. So why did I have this horrible feeling that it wasn't? Why did I feel that I had only made matters worse?

As I lowered myself into Adina's iron tub that was filled to the top with steamy water and rose petals, I knew I was home. The fragrant water felt so blissful that I pondered the idea of staying there forever. But once my toes and fingers began shriveling like raisins, I stepped out, mentally trying to relinquish all of my concerns into the filth that I had just washed off, and hopefully rise up from this place and take up where I had left off prior to my journey.

Slipping on my jeans that were a bit baggier than normal, and my favorite sweatshirt, I went to find Carig. As I walked up to the third story, I was surprised to see that everything there had been cleaned up and restored to its normal order. Lured by the tantalizing aroma of fresh coffee brewing downstairs, I made my way to the kitchen, hoping that I would see Carig sitting at the table waiting for me - but still, he was nowhere to be found. In an effort to soothe the dry stinging sensation in my throat, I poured myself a cup, and grabbed my fluffy cashmere blanket as I collapsed into the safe and comforting arms of my favorite easy chair. I loved this house, this room, this place, and I didn't realize how much until this very moment. I was just on the verge of giving in to the peacefulness of it all when I was distracted by an image on the computer screen.

I reluctantly crept closer to get a better look, and a feeling of dread washed over me as I noticed a picture that I never dreamed Carig would see; that I never thought *I* would see. To my dismay, it was a photo of Alrik and me, together on our wedding day. Our wedding day! This was so weird; it wasn't real. It was a journey gone sideways. Where in the world did this come from, and how could he have known about Alrik Richter?

I was quickly reminded of the vast possibilities of the internet as I began reading all about this man whom I had recently visited. But the question remained of how Carig could possibly know to search him out in the first place. I mean really, out of all of the people in all of history, he chose to research this man. As I scrolled once again to the photo and studied it in more detail, my heart became sickened. I could only imagine what Carig must be thinking. It was not just a photo of the two of us standing together side by side, but our gaze spoke of an impassioned tale. If I didn't know better, I would believe that these two people in 1940 Germany were passionate lovers ... exhibiting an intimate display and hunger for one another. But I remembered that moment distinctly. It wasn't romance on my part at all, but excitement at discovering that the Tempus Vector had not been destroyed and I was going home. I did care for Alrik, but not like that. The passion in my eyes was not for this man, but for the only man that I have ever loved and knowing that I would soon be home with him.

I knew the truth of my heart, but did Carig? All I knew is that Carig was upset, I could feel it. He promised me that when I returned he would be there waiting for me, yet so far he had been completely absent. We had to talk about this - I had to make it right. I looked out the front door and could see tracks leading to the lighthouse]. It didn't matter how cold it was, I had to go to him and try to explain. Hopefully, he would understand.

All of Bar Rousse as far as I could see was covered in a blanket of white, similar to a Christmas card, sparkles and all. Everything felt fresh and new. By the looks of the heavy covering, this storm must have been raging for days. Even though I wasn't quite up to it, I threw on my cold weather gear, including Carig's favorite parka, and walked down to the lighthouse.

The frigid air burned my raw throat, but I didn't care. I had thought about the moment I would see him again for days now, but my expectation of us reuniting did not include the burden of another man. Feeling as though my legs weighed a hundred pounds each, I trudged up the stairs of the great tower until I arrived at the glass door. Finally, there he was, staring out at the sea like he did so often. I couldn't see his face, but I could tell by his hunched-over demeanor that he was weary. I slowly opened the door, and walked up behind him, wrapping my arms tightly around his body. At first, he didn't move or return the embrace, and my heart sank. But then, he turned, encircling his arms around me as well. I didn't know what to say, and it seemed that he didn't either.

"Let's go inside, lass. This cold air can't be good for ye!"

He took my hand and walked me down the stairs to the living quarters.

"Did ye wear that parka just for me, Beni?"

Oh good, at least he hasn't lost his sense of humor.

"Have a seat. Can I get ye anything?"

I shook my head *no*. I could tell by his downcast expression, that the internet photo had hurt him deeply, but I still had no voice and I couldn't explain.

"I'm glad you're back, Beni. I honestly didn't know if I'd ever see you again. I didn't really think I could feel more pain than the thought of you not comin' back, but then I saw ... Beni I don't know what exactly happened there, except maybe you fell in love with that man? I don't know. I've tried to convince myself that it wasn't true, that you didn't give yourself to him ... but I don't really know. I don't know, and it's killin' me inside!"

Exactly what I *didn't* want to do to him, I had done. I had to tell him what happened; this was not the time to stay quiet. I didn't care what it sounded like or how it felt, I needed to speak up and I needed to do it now. I went over to where he was sitting, and in only a whisper, I poured out my heart.

"Please know, from the moment I arrived there all I wanted to do was come back to you. I'm not sure what you know, or even how you know, but I have no intention of telling you anything but the truth."

I held his face in my hands, making his eyes meet mine.

I furiously began spilling the details of my journey, beginning with my encounter with the very young and beautiful Adina, and that it was me who pointed her to Malachi's door.

Just the mention of Malachi's name grieved me, and my breathy murmurs turned into quiet sobs.

"Everything was going so well at first. I mean, after a pretty rocky start, Malachi figured out who I was. After that, it was like we'd known each other for a lifetime. His gentle eyes were filled with such reassurance. So much so that I believed that my journey had begun and would end right there in his shoe store, but I was wrong. The next thing I knew, I was being taken against my will by hard-core Nazis. Nazis, Carig! When it was all happening, I hardly believed it myself. But I knew that no matter what, my first priority was to protect the Tempus Vector, and the only way I could do that was to leave it behind with Malachi. This might be difficult to fathom, but as I sat in back of that car, guarded on each side, I resigned myself to the very real possibility that I would either die or be stranded in that place for the rest of my life, and that my first journey would be my last. From that point on, my journey turned into a catch-22. Because I didn't have the frame with me, I would have to be very careful what insight I would offer. If I had fulfilled my task absent from the Tempus Vector, I would have been trapped there, forever."

I had to stop. My throat was on fire and my grief was overwhelming. Carig could see the pain on my face and told me not to talk. When I insisted on forging ahead in spite of my discomfort, he first made me sip on a cup of hot lemonade and honey whisky that burned all the way down. He was trying to be understanding, but at the same time was more concerned about my encounter with Alrik than thankful that I had returned. I could feel myself growing more and more irritated with his one-track attitude. I only hoped that my efforts were not in vain, and that these sordid details would help, not make matters worse.

"Okay, Carig, here it is! I was taken directly to the estate of the Field Marshal of Germany. From the moment I walked into Alrik's house, he wanted me. Every part of me. Is that what you wanted to hear? I went along with his advances only to survive, but I never gave myself to him. Still believing that my journey was all about warning Malachi, my goal was to get back to Friedlich and the Tempus Vector, and then leave."

"So why didn't you, Beni? Why did you stay there so long?"

"You act as though I had a choice in this. I was guarded day and night and made a prisoner in that house. There was a maniac there that hated me. For the first three days I was unconscious after Alrik's cousin, Halag, tried to strangle me to death."

I could tell as Carig once again cringed at the bruises on my neck, that he was ashamed for his lack of sympathy.

"Everything that could have gone wrong, did. When I finally escaped and made it back to Friedlich, I discovered that the frame was no longer there, but had secretly been sent to me at the Richter Estate. I had two choices at that point: stay in Friedlich in 1940 Germany forever and never come back to you, or go back to Alrik's house, face the consequences, and get my hands on the Tempus Vector.

"When I returned, what little freedom I had before was completely stripped away. I was then told that the box which I sought, the one that held the frame, had been incinerated with the other trash. I was devastated. The gavel of finality had slammed down and issued my life sentence apart from you. That was horrible in itself, but to make matters worse, Alrik was furious with me for running away, and told me that we were to be married that Saturday. So, there I was, believing that the Tempus Vector had been destroyed and I was stuck there forever. What choice did I have? What would you have done?"

Carig just sat there with his head in his hands, listening but not looking at me.

"I don't know, Beni!"

"You don't know? You don't have any idea, because you weren't there! Until the day that we were going to marry, I didn't know that the frame actually had *not* been destroyed. Once I found out, I didn't marry him, did I? I went along and pretended I would but didn't. I would have rather died than marry anyone but you! I ran away and was almost killed trying to escape! Now tell me this, does that sound like someone who wanted to stay there? If I cared for him the way you think I did and wanted to stay, believe me, it would have been so easy. But I didn't because *I love you, and only you*. All I wanted and thought about the entire time that I was there, was getting back to you. It's always been you, Carig. It will always be you! It's just a shame that you have such little faith in me. Through it all, through all of the never-ending pursuing, groping, and words of passion that he spoke to me, I didn't give in and give myself to him. It was a difficult place to be, but always, *always*, I thought about you! It was my undying devotion for my husband that saw me back here, that gave me strength when I had none!

"You have made this whole thing about yourself, when it wasn't about you at all. The fact of the matter is that in the time spent there, I failed. Carson died. Malachi, Lavi, Ira, and Estee died, and the journey was all for nothing. I have to live with that! But you go ahead and keep thinking I betrayed you, when I didn't. You know what? Forget it! I knew it! I knew from the very beginning that this wouldn't work. We shouldn't have gotten married. I'm sorry that I said yes - I should have never said yes!"

By the time I was done talking, Carig was obviously ashamed of himself, but made no attempts to stop me as I walked right past him and out the door.

It was colder than when I first came. Clouds were rolling in, covering the vibrant sun with their darkness as I made my way back to the house. I had hoped that it wouldn't come to this, but nothing I said seemed to help. Saddled atop his Scottish high horse, Carig showed no signs of dismounting his throne of stubbornness.

Although the day had just begun, I was already exhausted, mostly due to our extremely unpleasant interaction. I wasn't exactly sure what I had expected once I returned home from my journey, but I would have never imagined that Carig and I would be fighting. To compound matters, my body and throat were hurting along with my heart, and if I were to be perfectly honest, all I wanted to do was go back to bed and try to forget everything. Digging deep into my well of understanding, I tried to find empathy and insight into Carig's perspective, but his total lack of consideration for what I had been through left me greatly disappointed. He'd made me feel like an unwelcome stranger in my own home, and for the first time in my life I wasn't sure where I belonged. I wasn't certain about anything except my struggle of overwhelming grief.

Rising up like a beast from the depths of the ocean was a familiar wave of hurt and discouragement that crashed down upon me. As a young girl, it was forever hovering above me with its icy threats raining down reminders that it was there, ready to strike. Inevitably, it was prompted by an unkind word or bitter stare from the only man who had held my heart until Carig. The ultimate goal of this mighty wall of unhappiness was to consume me. It surely would have if not for Adina, who rescued me. But Adina was no longer here, and I was alone.

When Carig walked into my life, even though just a boy, he was somehow in tune with my hurt, maybe because it was not unlike his own. From the get-go he battled away at my ever-present foe with his caring spirit. His love for me was always greater and fiercer than the attempts of the enemy. I'll never forget how he carved a sword out of wood, a magical sword he called it, that had the power to slash away any and all sad thoughts, destroying them once and for all. His chivalrous gestures of waving the timbered blade would inevitably lead to uncontrollable laughter when he zealously threatened to cut off every last bit of sadness, until none remained. I would smile so big and agree to it as long as he left my head intact. Then, as we would sit there together, he promised that he would never let anyone hurt me again. Although childish, he would make the rejection by my father somehow disappear.

Now I fell victim once again to this raging storm of thoughts and feelings. Carig's unemotional response reminded me of my father, and I couldn't stand it. He promised to protect me from that wave, not be the one responsible for bringing it about. I felt betrayed, aching from the inside out.

As if anything else could go wrong, I suddenly felt uncomfortable and clammy. Blood had begun dripping down my back, seeping onto my favorite sweatshirt. My stitches had come undone. Trying not to panic, I ran into the bathroom and pulled off my shirt and wasn't quite sure how I would manage the bleeding on my own. While straining to get a better look in the mirror, I saw Carig in the reflection, watching me.

"Let me help you, Beni!"

"No, that's okay. I've got this!"

"Stop bein' so damn stubborn, lass, and let me help you!"

"I'm the stubborn one? Okay, fine, but only because I can't reach it. Otherwise, I wouldn't need your help!"

In a frustrated voice, Carig began speaking obscure words in his native tongue. I was just as frustrated with him as he was with me, and I wasn't just going to stand there and take it. I realized that he was upset, but he needed to get over it and understand that I did the best I could.

"I'm sorry, what's that? Do you have something to say to me?"

"Na, nothin'!"

I held my hair up off my back as he firmly pressed a folded piece of gauze onto my wound, trying to stop the flow.

"Aw, Beni! I'd better call Dr. Dean - he probably needs to see to this. Ye shouldn' a got this wet ye know!"

I was getting more and more irritated at him as he continued scolding me, until I couldn't stand it anymore.

"The bleedin' has slowed down, but I'm gonna need to clean it, and then I'll put on a new bandage. It should be okay until he can get here."

"You gonna give me a hard time over this too? Maybe I should have ducked a little better, and then maybe I could have avoided getting shot?"

Without hesitation, and before I could get the last word out of my mouth, Carig splashed alcohol onto the open area causing me to wince and gasp for breath while clinging onto the edge of the sink. The stinging was so painful that I couldn't breathe, let alone speak, which I'm sure suited him just fine.

"Beni, I'm sorry, lass!"

To ease the sting, he lightly blew on the wound as I leaned over the vanity. After a few minutes, the pain subsided a bit, and all I could feel was his soothing breath on my skin. I would have never admitted it in a million years, but right then and there my body burned for his, and I could tell by the gentleness of his touch as he applied the bandages with his fingers skimming beyond the tape and onto my skin, that he wanted me too. I turned around and stared at him deeply, moving closer, and then closer, until our bodies touched, and my hands caressed his chest. But to my surprise, rather than returning my advances, he stopped me.

"Beni, I don't think this is a good idea. I don't wanna hurt you, lass ... we need to be careful and not do anything that might start you bleedin' again!"

I could take his rejection one of two ways. The first, that he was being considerate in not wanting to hurt me, or the second, that he just wasn't interested. Because I chose the latter, I was hurt and my ego severely battered. I knew Carig well enough to understand that there was no stopping him when he wanted something bad enough, he just didn't want me. I resolved not to ever let this happen again, and from this point forward it would have to be him that pursues me. He had created a path of scorn where no man would rationally choose to go.

I backed away from him, half naked, dressed only in my button-up jeans, and simply stood there, purposefully letting him take a good hard look at what was just about to walk away. Then my wounded pride conjured up a declaration that was aimed at stinging him back.

"Well, that's too bad then, because the things that I wanted to do to you wouldn't have hurt me but would have been intoxicating for you. I'm a little disappointed that I won't be able to live out the fantasies that have been churning through my mind in the last week. Believe me, I would have been fine, but even so, I would have been more than happy to risk it."

I walked over to the wardrobe and pulled out another shirt and put it on while Carig stood there speechless, and then walked over to the door to leave. For a moment I felt half guilty over my shrewd reaction. What I really wanted was for him to speak up, tell me what was weighing so heavily on his mind, and fight for me.

"I'll go make up some lunch while you finish gettin' dressed. I think maybe it might be a good idea if we talked - there are things to say. Ye know lass, you're not the only one who's struggling and has had a hell of a week."

His statement was not cutting or profound like mine, but even still, it pierced my soul. He was right. At this moment, we were on two separate planes of thought, each consumed with our own scars left from our first journey together.

Chapter 5

Together Parted

"Don't lose yourself, Beni. Be present among the living, the here and now.
Let the things of the past, remain in the past!"
~Adina York~

Carig and I were together in the same room, but it felt as though we were separated by an indiscernible barrier, like bein on opposite sides of a closed window. I could see him, but was deaf to his voice, and numb to his touch. Our senses, which were normally invigorated and intense in one another's presence, felt empty and hollow. Even more troubling was that the life from which I had just returned felt more tangible than this one. I knew I shouldn't feel this way, but I did. Perhaps it was all in my mind. I reminded myself that Adina experienced these same kinds of feelings, so much so that she warned me about them in her journal. I could almost hear her voice reciting words of life to me.

"Don't lose yourself, Beni. Be present among the living, the here and now. Let the things of the past, remain in the past!"

Through my own life experiences and travels, I understood that long journeys, filled with excitement and intrigue, often generate uneasy restlessness, even depression, upon return. My personal encounter, journeying and returning at the will of the Tempus Vector, had far surpassed any feelings of melancholy that had ever plagued me before. Even through the many years of being forced to leave Adina, and then returning back to a loveless home with my father, I had never experienced as much turmoil as I was sensing at this very moment.

Carig and I tried to act normally by making meaningless small talk, acting like nothing had happened, but even that didn't really help. There was no denying that it felt strained even being in the same room. Both of us were on edge, acting more like strangers than lovers, and unsure of how to behave with one another. Our relationship, our marriage, and the immediate trial that we encountered had turned into our first great test, and I feared that we were failing miserably. Over the years our friendship had been tested many times, but *this* went much further, landing us in a deep valley separated by a veil of darkness.

We both knew that our lives together would never be typical, and I suppose that nothing could have prepared us for what was coming. Because my first journey turned out to be exceptional and uncommon, "a practically-everything-gone-wrong sort of experience," we were both struggling to make sense of any of it. I concluded by Carig's actions, that he realized marrying me was a mistake and he now felt stuck. Was that why he was being so quiet and unresponsive, or why he didn't want to be with me? I knew that these strange feelings that were torturing me were somewhat normal considering what I had been through, but what I didn't understand was how Carig was acting. It was apparent that something intense was troubling him, but for some reason he chose to stay quiet and keep whatever it was to himself.

He stood at the stove, staring into the pan with his back to me, seeming quite content to perpetually stir the soup. He had mentioned that we should talk, yet he remained completely silent. The awkward silence, or should I say the elephant in the room, was too much to bear. Fed up with the deafening silence, I decided to start a conversation.

The second I opened my mouth, Carig's phone rang. *Saved* by Uncle Wil's ringtone of "Do Not Forsake Me, Oh My Darlin'!" He talked and ladled soup simultaneously, focusing mainly on the call. As he set the bowl down in front of me, then walked away, I felt as if I was being served by a stranger.

"Hey, ye Wil. How are ye? Oh, we're doing okay. Ya, Beni's okay. Just a little under the weather. What was that?"

Whatever Wil had just asked him, he didn't seem to know what to say back.

"Yes sir, no, you're right, I know. I know you didn't. Oh, that was very thoughtful of ye. Ya, me too! Haven't had much time for that. Oh, that's tomorrow already! Ya, what time? What can we bring? No, no, it's tradition. I'll be there! Okay, that'll be fine. I'll see you in an hour or so. Alright, bye then!"

After hanging up the phone, he mindlessly stared out the kitchen door as he spoke to me.

"I guess tomorrow is Thanksgiving Day. I didn't even know. I've totally lost … lost track of time. It's been Wil's and my tradition for the past few years to go huntin' for the Thanksgiving turkey. He said he hadn't called all week trying to just let us be alone - just be married without anyone interferin'. I would have told him I couldn't go, but I realized that he's gonna be missin' Adina this Thanksgiving."

"What else was he saying to you? I mean, it sounded like he was upset about something."

"Aye, he told me that he had a horrible dream about you and was askin' if ye were okay. And then ..."

"And then what?"

"He asked me if you had taken up where Adina left off."

"He knows? He knows about what Adina did?"

"Ya, he does, but he never liked any of it too much. She didn't tell him about you before she died, that you would take her place. Probably couldn't bring herself to tell um. He saw how hard it was on her, and he just couldn't stand it. They were best friends their entire lives, but that was one thing they could never see eye to eye on. I guess she had asked him years ago to be the one to be there for her when she would get back, and he said no. He said that his heart would never survive it. Somehow, he knew that it was you that had taken her place, but he's not too happy about it."

"Is that how you feel, Carig? Can your heart not take it either? Do you wish that you never married me?"

He didn't answer me, but just continued staring out the door.

"Anyway, we're invited over to their house tomorrow at twelve for Thanksgiving dinner. I guess Dr. Dean and his wife will be there as well. Their son is stationed in China right now, so they're alone. Maybe he can tend to your back while we're there."

His avoidance of my question spoke volumes. He had answered me without saying a word.

"Listen, Beni, I didn't mean to ..."

"Don't worry about it, Carig. It's very clear to me what's wrong with you, and I don't really know how to make it better. But if you don't want to be married to me anymore because it will be too difficult to always be here waiting for me, I just need to hear you say it. I need to hear you tell me that you don't love me anymore."

With a grieved expression on his face, he spun around and stared icily.

"I'll be back later, Beni. Why don't you go and rest?"

I didn't answer, but just sat there, feeling numb as he grabbed his coat and hat and walked out the door.

After that *empty* exchange, I needed to unwind. If only I could go and walk along the beach. But everything was covered with snow, and I was stuck in this house. What had I done to make Carig behave this way? What was he not telling me? I decided to go and sit where he had sat all week waiting for me to come back. Since he'd chosen to be closed-mouthed about how he was feeling, perhaps I could discover on my own what was going on.

I could smell his scent on the chair which didn't help the brokenness I felt inside. Stacked on the table beside the chair were two books. The one on top was Malachi's journal with a strap of leather marking a page. Below it was a Gideon Bible labeled with a sticker that read "Portland Moose Inn, Portland Maine." It also had a page marked, but with a business card from the inn, listing the proprietors' names, George and Sharol Maple. As I opened the Bible to the flagged page, underlined in pencil was Hebrews 11:5 - "By faith Enoch was taken away so that he did not see death, and was not found, because God had taken him." I read this verse over and over again, trying to figure out why Carig had it underlined, and why he drove all the way to an inn in Portland, and why he brought a Bible back with him.

Opening up Malachi's journal, and turning to the page marked by the leather strap, I noticed that it was the end of an entry. After turning back several pages, I began reading. Incredibly, he wasn't talking about himself, but about me. He referred to the day I walked into his store, how I was taken, and who I was with. He was very thorough with his particulars, even down to news heard throughout Friedlich that the Field Marshal was getting married to an American girl and they appeared to be quite smitten. Malachi grieved for me in his notes, hoping that I had not forgotten who I was and my purpose for being there.

As I sat there in this big room all alone, I understood a bit more about Carig's journey that had paralleled mine. There was no doubt that these words of Malachi's left my husband wondering if I had fallen for another man in another time, and even worse, if I was ever coming back. All at once, the pieces of the puzzle began falling into place. The wedding photo on the computer was probably the beginning of Carig's search for historical information about this curious man who had invaded my path. At the time, it was his only link to me. What else was he to do? Once hours and days passed without my return, he began reading through Malachi's journal. I couldn't even imagine how devastating it all must have been for him. When he saw that photograph, he must have believed that I would never return.

I hurried downstairs to the computer and saw that everything, including the picture, was gone from the screen. Clicking into the history of where Carig had searched, I discovered one chronicle after another displaying descriptions and accounts of Alrik, as well as recurrent photos and stories about Caprice Richter. There was so much information about this man that I had come to know quite well, including his well-known good looks and reputation as a womanizer after his wife had died. Strangely, I had just seen him a few days ago, even spoke with him, but in reality he had been dead now for seventeen years. According to this article, Alrik and his daughter, Annaliese, disappeared from Friedlich in October of 1942, and because of that, he was considered a traitor to the Third Reich. In another article that was based on conspiracy theories, it was said that Alrik had secretly been given a large share of Hitler's gold in the form of 500-gram bullion bars in order to finance escape routes for German war criminals and help create and instigate the rise of the Fourth Reich. The article went on to say that he, along with other missing Nazis, were hiding on a secret island in the Pacific with the goal of generating the next uprising that would far surpass that of the last three.

As I scrolled down, I found the picture that Carig had seen earlier, of Alrik and me sitting together on Atlas. To say the least, this revealing snapshot made it appear that I adored the man. My gestures were not flamboyant, but intimate, as I was pulling his lips towards mine. I remembered that moment, and whether Carig believed me or not, it was all an act. This piece of hard evidence against me had become the source of his fury.

Toward the bottom of the page there was another photograph of me standing alone, paired with one of Annaliese sitting on my lap clinging to her favorite doll. I was thankful that these were the only other pictures displayed, as so many more were taken on that day and it would have been heartbreaking for Carig to see them. According to this false piece of writing, *Alrik married the unknown*

American, who would later be blamed for his unexpected defection. For whatever reason, it failed to mention that the union never happened and that I was never seen again after that day.

The vast amount of information regarding Field Marshal Richter, who hailed from one of the most well-known families in German history, was overwhelming. Most shocking, and enlightening at the same time, was the final blurb regarding his death. It stated that he had passed away at his home in *Portland, Maine,* survived only by his daughter, Annaliese Richter. Portland! That answered the question as to why Carig had gone there. His mysterious outing that included the inn, and the Gideon Bible, was all about finding Annaliese. This incredible newfound information about Alrik and his daughter was no coincidence, but somehow an extension of my journey.

The uneasiness in my soul made me question Doctor Dean's conclusion of the trip's success. I had returned home, but my task felt incomplete, like an open book waiting to be read. Trying to make sense of any of it was like piecing together a blank puzzle. I was missing something, but that something was leading me once again to the door of the Richter Estate. It seemed crazy, but I had to see Annaliese. No doubt, it would be awkward, trying to explain my youthful appearance after all these years, but I was determined to go and face whatever would come. Since I would be traveling all the way to Portland, I decided that my first stop would be the Portland Moose Inn. I understood why Carig would seek out Annaliese, but I had no idea of the significance of the inn.

The day, and the opportunity to discover all of the unknowns, was quickly passing. Knowing that the 2:00 train was the one that I needed to catch, and time was of the essence, I called a cab before I did anything else. I packed a bag with a few personal items just in case I couldn't get home by nightfall, and of course Malachi's journal and the Gideon Bible. As I was packing, it occurred to me that I had lost everything that I had taken on my journey. It had all been left behind. Malachi's suitcase, Adina's butterfly brooch, and the aquamarine and pearl pendant were forever gone. At the same time, I realized that I had returned with precious items that were not mine - the ruby ring and the pearl choker that had been Caprice Richter's, and now rightly belonged to Annaliese. After fetching them from the table in the third story room, I safely tucked them in my bag. If I accomplished nothing else, I would at least return them to their rightful owner. I knew that Carig would most likely arrive home before I returned, but he would probably be relieved that I wasn't here.

The old vintage train station reminded me of my adventures to New York with Adina. The cold fog rising up from beneath the wooden platform brought back memories of that frigid day when I had my first encounter with Alrik Richter. Among the first stops after departing Bar Rousse was Portland, the place where he and his daughter found asylum so many years ago. Until today, I never really paid much attention to this quaint town. But now, it held great interest for me. I was perplexed by the idea that he had known who I was as a child and sought me out. How did he know that I would become the woman whom he would love and almost marry in 1940? For that matter, out of all the places in the world, how was it that he ended up in the next county over? And where did Adina fit into all of this? She obviously knew him well.

So consuming were these unanswered questions, that the ride into Portland seemed a quick jaunt and a complete blur. As the train slowed to a halt, I found myself growing more fearful and apprehensive about my visit to see Annaliese. For the next few moments, I remained seated, debating on whether to stay or go. What would I say to her as we would stand face to face? How would I explain my unchanged appearance? Perhaps it would be in both of our best interests if I lied and told her that the one she knew as Beni was my grandmother.

Although surrounded by dozens of cheerful faces and merry travelers on their way to see loved ones, their joy and enthusiasm were no match for my anxious heart. With the blow of the whistle and a cold gust of wind, the door opened, and I stepped down the frosty metal steps onto the platform. I couldn't help but second-guess myself and my motives, wondering if this was such a good idea after all. But then I looked up and noticed the familiar terminal that seemed more like a dream than reality.

Along with the echoing toll from the oversized antique station clock, were age-old buildings covered in unrefined brick, as smoky gray in color as the sky above. The large wooden beams stretching across the gusty breezeway were home to metal signs that clapped in the wind like sheets of thunder.

As I stood in the throng of holiday travelers, Alrik's face suddenly flashed in the midst of the crowd. In a frenzied instant, I sprinted after him, pushing my way through the hordes of oblivious strangers only to discover that he was nowhere to be found. Had it been a figment of my imagination? Of course, he wasn't there! How could he be?

Ironically, my fruitless ghostly pursuit had led me here - to the very platform of our first encounter.

Ashen clouds covered the sky while a thick layer of glacial air settled over Portland, somewhat resembling a shadowy veil. I soon realized that another storm was moving into the area, and residents were being advised to get indoors before it arrived.

Because of the sense of urgency felt by all to beat the tempest, finding an available cab was no easy task. After several attempts, I finally hailed down one of the last few.

"Where to, miss?"

I pulled out the business card from the inn and flashed it at the driver.

"Do you know this place? The Portland Moose Inn?"

"Yep, sure do! It'll be about a ten-minute drive, give or take a few."

"Okay, great. Can you please take me there?"

"Yep! You staying with the Maples for Thanksgiving?"

"The Maples? I'm afraid I don't know who you're talking about."

"Well, that's whose inn you're goin' to, right? That's their names, right there on the front."

"Oh, yes, the Maples. Well, I've never actually been there before."

Chapter 6

Wishbone

*"By the end of her life, her fingerprint will be in hundreds of places in history,
and she can't do any of it without you!"*
~Wil Crawford~

"Son, what's goin on? I can tell your heart's not in the hunt!"

Wil was very in tune with Carig and could tell that he was greatly bothered. He had seen him upset before but could tell that this was different. His struggle cut into the depths of his heart, and he knew from times past that there was only one person that could inflict such pain. Without hesitation, everything that the groom of recent had been holding inside, spilled out through tears of frustration. Wil had a way of bringing things to the surface simply by his caring spirit and his willingness to listen. He was just plain sincere, and never judgmental. In addition to viewing him like a father, Carig knew that he was a man of wisdom, and his mere presence and kindred spirit were the glue that bonded their relationship. Even though no details had been revealed, Carig experienced a welcomed sense of relief.

Overflowing happiness and blissful contentment were Wil's expectations of Beni and Carig's first week of marriage. But instead he found himself staring at a shell of a man who was carrying the weight of the world on his shoulders. Carig was not only bearing an overwhelming burden but his cheerless demeanor exposed the broken heart that he wore on his sleeve. Wil couldn't even fathom what had happened. Last time he saw the two, they were giddy and love-struck. Thankfully, he had a powerful gift of discernment and quickly went at it, trying to nail down the problem. It was Wil who came along after Carig's grandparents died within six months of one another and helped him through the terrible ordeal. His was the quiet voice of reason, reminding Carig that this life was not the end, and he would someday see them again. That, along with his sense of humor that brought light even to the darkest situations, was always a breath of fresh air.

He first put his arm around Carig's shoulders and stared him straight in the eye. His clear blue eyes alone would penetrate through the heaviness of any burden and somehow replace it with hope. Wil could tell by Carig's still-defeated appearance and lack of fortitude to move forward, that he was in need of a little more time in this whitewashed paradise. When the time was right, they would talk.

A choice counseling spot of Wil's was an old picnic table tucked beneath the oldest and grandest oak in Bar Rousse. The two-hundred year old roots that reached deep into the earth were to him, a perfectly sculpted picture of godly wisdom. Like the roots, although they now lay dormant beneath a cold layer of winter, it was his desire to stand strong and firm, unwavering in the advice that he would now give Carig.

After brushing the snow from the seat, and instructing Carig to sit down, it was time to talk this through and get to the bottom of it. When Carig began to argue that the window to hunt was short, Wil assured him that "the old wishbone" could wait. This was far more important.

Wil always referred to the Thanksgiving fowl as the "wishbone," simply because the breaking of the bone was his favorite tradition of that holiday. Each year as he would carve away at the bird, his utmost goal was to retrieve the wishing bone from the carcass. He would always tell Carig and Beni when they were kids that there was real juju in the wishing bone that lay like a genie's lamp within the heart of the Thanksgiving bird. For two days he would set the forked charm out to dry, and then bring the two of them together to break it apart, but not until they had each searched their hearts and created the ultimate wish. By the way Wil prepared for this event, one would have believed that it was truth rather than fantasy. He made it so exciting that it soon became everyone's favorite tradition.

"Only one may win!" he would say as he stood atop a soda crate in his grocery market. "It's not possible for it to break equally … one winner, one wish!"

He instructed each child to hold their side of the wishbone as their elbows rested on the counter, so that neither would have an advantage over the other.

"Close your eyes, both of you. No peekin'! Now think of the deepest, most eager wish of your heart, and then focus on that one thing - nothin' else - and then never, never tell a single soul until it comes true! You'll see, it'll come true!"

Without fail, Wil made the simplest things the most fun. Carig believed wholeheartedly that Beni's wish was career driven, to become a professor of literature at a significant university, preferably ivy league. That was always what she insinuated, but not what she actually wished for. Carig's wish, however, had nothing to do with a career. The utmost desire of his heart, his greatest wish, was to marry Beni.

Wil would then count to five and yell out "pull!" Carig inevitably cheated, each time ending up with the bigger side. All he knew is that he wanted to marry Beni, and if gettin' the bigger part of the bone would make his wish come true, he was damn well gonna win. Then and now, Beni was his life's pursuit.

As Carig and Wil began talking, it wasn't long before the biting chill of the next unfriendly storm began seeping into their bones. Like the unusual bombardment of frigid temperatures and snowfall that had recently hit, life too felt uncommonly cold and peculiar for Carig.

"Talk to me, son. What's goin' on?"

"I don't wanna burden ye, Uncle Wil. Let's just find the wishbone and get back. It's gettin' real cold!"

"Naa! This is nothin'. I'm concerned about you, and it won't burden me. Maybe I can help. How's married life? Is everything okay with you and Beni?"

He could tell that everything was *not* okay with the newlyweds as Carig avoided eye contact, actually looking in the opposite direction.

"I see. Why don't you start from the beginning?"

"Well, everything started out just grand, but then ..."

"But then? The Tempus Vector?"

"Yea! That next day it happened. I don't know why, but right when we found out that she was leavin', I had a bad feelin' that somethin' would go wrong."

"What happened? What went wrong? Is she okay?"

"Well first of all, she just got back. She's been gone this whole week, and when she wasn't back right away, I didn't know what had happened to her or how to find out. She was just gone and there was nothin' I could do about it! But then I found her, well I found her in the pages of Malachi's journal. She'd been captured and held against her will. Nothin' could be done except to wait it out. I felt so helpless. Quite honestly, Malachi's journal was both a blessin' and a curse. In it was written the name of her abductor. I got desperate ya know, so I researched 'im. I thought maybe I could find out somethin' about what had happened to her. I found both him and her - pictures of her with the bastard on their weddin' day."

"Hold up! Wedding day? Beni married another man?"

"Well, no. She was doin' what needed to be done to get back. It went as far as the photos, but she didn't marry him."

"So, what's botherin' ya, boy? It sounds like she was doin' her best!"

"Well, that's not all. Through the research, I found out that this man's daughter lives in Portland, so I went and saw her. She had a box filled with pictures of Beni with him. There she was, plain as day, happy, and sweet on the German bastard. Now I can't even close my eyes without seein' them together."

"Carig, son, it wasn't real. Unfortunately, you had to read about it and see pictures of it. But it was a means to an end, not real, an act. It will probably not be the last time she has to do something like that."

"So, if you were to see Angelina lookin' at another man like that, you'd be okay?"

"Hell no, I wouldn't. But, Angelina wasn't chosen to be the Carrier of the Tempus Vector! Did you talk to her about it?"

"Aye."

"And?"

"She told me I was thinkin' all wrong about the whole thing. If that woulda' been the case, she could've stayed, but it was me who held her heart, and she woulda' done anythin' to get home to me."

Wil looked hard and long at Carig, taking a deep breath before he lowered the boom.

"Good Lord, son! So, let me make sure I understand what you're saying. You talked to her about this, and she told you that she was trying to get back to you and had to pretend to agree to marry him, but didn't, and could have?"

"Aye!"

"So exactly why are you so upset?"

Carig remained silent. He didn't really know how to answer

that question.

"Was she unfaithful to you?"

"Na, I asked her, and she said no. She said that she only did what she did so that she could get back to me."

"Do you believe her?"

"Aye, with everything within me!"

"Hmm? Is there anything else?"

"Nothin' else, well, except …"

"Except what?"

"She came back with bruises all over her neck. Someone had tried to strangle her to death *and…*"

"And what?"

"She'd been shot in the back."

Wil stood up, eyes closed, and lips pursed. He was angry. Carig hadn't seen Wil's anger too many times, but he recognized it in that moment.

"Beni got shot? With a gun? And what part of *any of that* gives you reason to believe that she wanted to stay there? If anything, it sounds to me like she was definitely bucking the system and trying to get the hell outta there. Am I right?"

"Aye"

"Carig, I'm gonna tell you a little secret that I promised Beni I would never reveal. Each year when the two of you broke the wishbone, she wished every time that someday she would marry you. She told me never to tell you, because then it wouldn't come true. She loves you, son. She always has! Think about it! Beni is an extremely beautiful and smart girl, and she would never … ever do anything to hurt you! Do you think that she never had a serious boyfriend or relationship with anyone because they didn't try? When she came here on her breaks, without fail I would always ask if she had a beau. Each time she would just say, 'Oh, Uncle Wil, you already know who I'm waiting for.' And she was right, I did know. It was you."

"She loved me? I didn't know … she never showed her feelin's outwardly."

"Well, she's a little bit of a hard nut to crack. But one thing about Beni is that she always knew what she wanted. This damn journeying that Adina did for most of her life, I used to hate it. But then over the years, I would hear her stories of change. Horrid events that were transformed to good because of what she did. Now that it has been passed on to Beni, you have to realize that it will never be easy, but I can promise you that it'll be impossible if you don't trust one another. You're going to have to think of the circumstances in more normal terms. Even if she wasn't doing this, there are many times in a relationship when you will be parted for a time. Things in life, like work or family, sometimes create occasions that will keep us apart. Yet even when you're apart, you trust and have faith in one another. Carig, you must think in those terms or you'll make yourself crazy getting caught up in the 'what-ifs' that you have no control over. For example, when Angelina and I are away from each other, we are thinking the best, not the worst."

"I guess those pictures and her bein' gone so long, just made me imagine the worst."

"You gotta let those pictures go, and if this ever happens again, don't search the world over trying to figure it all out. Was it your search that brought her back?"

"Na."

"Listen, I understand that your situation is highly irregular, but at the same time, it's invaluable! What the two of you are doing is making a mark, an alteration of what has already been. Her presence there is just tweaking a flaw that is ultimately metamorphic. By the end of her life, her fingerprint will be in hundreds of places in history, and she can't do any of it without you!"

Carig sat there with his head in his hands. He knew that Wil was right, about everything. What he didn't tell Wil was the story of when Adina almost remained in another time to marry a man who had captured her heart. He became fearful that Beni might have done the same. And yet it wasn't the same. If Carson would have still been alive, Adina would have never been unfaithful, but then neither would Beni.

"You're right, Wil. Everythin' you said is right. I feel ashamed of how I treated her. You should've seen her. I didn't think she was gonna make it. When I found her, she was a mess. She's been through so much, and I was so unkind to her. I gotta make it right! Let's find our bird, and then I'll go back."

"Why don't you go back now, son, and I'll take care of the bird. We'll see you tomorrow for supper."

"Will you be okay out here? It's awfully cold, and a storm's comin'!"

"Are you kiddin' me? I'm wearin my Sorels, and frankly, I know exactly where that meaty wishbone went. I've been spying on 'er for months. You go home to Beni and make things right!"

Carig felt grateful relief as he got into the truck, and haphazardly spun away through the snow. As a matter of fact, he felt like a new man. Wil's gift, one of his many, was putting things that seemed overwhelming into perspective. His renewed desire to see Beni consumed his thoughts as he sped over the icy roads. He had been harsh towards her and hoped and prayed all the way home that she'd forgive him. He began reviewing the things he had said as well as the things he didn't say and cursed his stupidity.

"You're such an idiot! Wha'd ye have to be such a daft prick for?"

If she only knew how hard it was to act uninterested in her advances this morning. In all honesty, he wanted her so badly that it took everything within him to turn away from her. His guilty conscience replayed Beni's sorrowful and rejected expression as she walked away from him that morning, over and over again in his mind.

As he drove up to the house, he was initially distracted as he watched the icy fog settling over the sea, and the outdoor thermometer that wasn't even registering. It would be a perfect evening to spend with Beni in front of a warm crackling fire. To his dismay, he ran through the front door calling out her name but received no response.

"Beni, Beni, where are ye, lass?"

One after the other, he began searching each room, and panicked when she was nowhere to be found. His first thought was that she had left on another journey but hoped that she would never leave without saying goodbye, even if they had been quarreling. In the back of his mind he was fairly sure that she was still there. He read in one of the journals that Adina was never called to go again when she was still recovering, and he knew that Beni was in no shape to travel. If that was the case, where had she gone? He checked to see if her car was still there, and then headed up to the third story room. A sigh of relief escaped his lips as he saw the Tempus Vector still sitting there with the picture of the bakery in the center. This would be the first photo that would begin Beni's walls of travels, and hopefully an adventure that they would someday laugh about.

He was tired and cold and decided to sit down for a few minutes but couldn't help wondering if Beni was so upset with him that she'd left for good. Leaning his head back on the chair, like he had so many times in the last week, he closed his burning eyes and took a deep breath.

"Where are you, lass?"

When his eyes reopened, he noticed that Malachi's journal and the Gideon Bible were missing from the side table. Panicking, he jumped up and began searching every corner, making sure that he hadn't set them somewhere else. When he saw that the ruby ring and choker of pearls were also gone, he knew exactly where she was headed. She had discovered the whereabouts of Annaliese and was on her way to Portland. Fear gripped his soul as he recalled what a loose cannon Ms. Richter had proven to be, and his gut instinct told him that she was not to be trusted.

"The computer!"

He ran down to the computer to see if she had followed the same pathway of information that he had. With one click, he realized that she had indeed discovered that Annaliese was alive, and she was now aware of everything he found earlier but chose not to tell her.

The last site that Beni searched was Bar Rousse Cab Company. Without wasting another minute, he called the number that was listed to find out where the taxi had taken her. Confirming that she had been dropped off at the train station at 1:30, he knew that she had made her way to Portland. It was almost 5:30, getting dark outside, and very soon the wild tempest that was sitting offshore would be moving in. He tried calling, but her phone, which she had left on the desk, began buzzing. There were no two ways about it, he was going after her. Whatever they would find out from this point on, they'd find together. Carig was so angry at himself! Her leaving was his fault. All she wanted was to be with him, and he practically pushed her out the door.

The drive into Portland was brutal. With all of the holiday travelers and the blistering winds that caused slippery skids, dangerous accidents, and roadblocks, it seemed to take forever to get there. Finally, after making it through, Carig arrived at the wrought iron gate of the Richter Estate. The driveway leading to the house was long and packed waist-high with mountains of snow. There was absolutely no way that *any vehicle* might make it through these deep drifts. The only way to get up to the main house was on foot, and even that would be difficult. He couldn't imagine that Beni would attempt to do so, but he would check it out himself just in case she was there.

The entire place was even eerier at night, and his spirit was distressed by an atmosphere of evil as he slowly plodded through the packed snowdrifts. It was so cold and seemed such a long stretch, but he continued moving forward.

Other than a faint light coming from the front room, the house was completely dark. As he walked along, he began shining his flashlight over the surrounding snow for any evidence that Beni might be there, but everything around him was smooth and untouched - not one footprint. As a matter of fact, it appeared as though no one had come in or out for days. Finally arriving at the porch stairs, he stepped up, at last free from the clutches of the frigid void. Although he felt a powerful uneasiness about being there, he refused to leave until assured of Beni's safety, even if it meant dealing once again with Annaliese.

He lightly knocked on the front door and stood back attentively, waiting for it to open. He was somewhat relieved at the prolonged silence, half hoping that he wouldn't have to see those pale lifeless eyes again. At the same time, he could tell by the smoky incense pouring from the chimney that someone was, in fact, there. The second attempt was an impatient hammering of his clenched fist against the heavy mahogany door. The explosion of banging set in motion the sound of nervous footsteps scurrying on the other side, but still, the entrance remained closed. The single light abruptly switched off, leaving only the flicker of a modest fire peeking from the window.

"Annaliese, are you in there?"

There was no reply, only the sound of a little girl humming, followed by the rustling of a body sliding down the door and onto the floor.

"Annaliese, it's me, Carig Hammel, from the other day. Is Beni in there with you?"

All at once the humming stopped, and he heard shuffling and heavy breathing as she turned around and pressed her mouth against the door, causing an odd noise like that of an animal that was wildly panting in and out, followed by strange wailing moans. Slowly backing away from the door, he then heard the same child-like voice calling out Beni's name in a demented and painfully drawn-out singsong tone. He instantly realized that it wasn't a child at all, but the spine-chilling impersonation from the old woman, Annaliese.

"Bennnnnnni … Bennnnnnni, where have you gone? The man with blood on his hands has come to take you away … She's not here, she's dead!"

"Just tell me if she came here to see you today!"

In frustration with this complete nonsense, he pounded once again on the door.

"Did Beni … did *anyone* come here to see you today other than me?"

"No one comes here. She left long ago and was buried with my father. When he died, she died! When he died, she died!"

She began wildly carrying on and laughing maniacally while still facing the door, then stopped, and began spewing out nonsensical riddles that infuriated Carig. Her voice was like screeching nails on a chalkboard.

"Leave now, Rot Krieger! Do you come here to shed blood, Tribe of David?"

"What in the hell is the batty lass talkin' about?"

Carig was speechless at her unhinged maze of ramblings. This whole encounter had turned entirely weird, and he was finished dealing with her. As he hurried through the cold of night, all he wanted to do was escape from this place and any memory of it. For the umpteenth time this week, he felt the weight of the world tumbling down on his shoulders. Not only was he still unsure as to Beni's whereabouts but something strange occurred to him. Although it was he who invaded the twisted dominion of Annaliese Richter, he felt as though her final words were confusingly prophetic. A bitter pill that he would soon be forced to swallow. She was crazy to be certain, but the matters she had previously disclosed had turned out to be true and correct. Somehow, she knew things that were impossible to know. This entire situation was upsetting, and he felt himself suddenly filled with a fire-like anger as he got into the truck and slammed the door shut. He didn't know what to do … there was nothing else *to* do at this point except go back home and pray that Beni was there.

Like everything else as of late, the storm was out of control, blasting viciously in all directions, leaving Carig blinded to the road ahead. As much as he wanted to get home, he knew that he would never make it in this mess and had no choice but to stop somewhere for the night, or at least until the storm passed. As he slowly drove down the snow-filled highway, he was relieved to spot a familiar haven that was hidden amongst a forest of trees. The white lights that encircled each trunk illuminated the entire pocket of land, creating a beacon of deliverance for this weary and half-frozen traveler. Although unfamiliar with the town of Portland, he knew this place and was relieved to be there.

The parking lot was filled to the brim with cars that were already buried in snow. He pulled into the only available spot, right up front, beneath the portico, *Home of Portland Moose Inn* sign.

Chapter 7

Portland Moose Inn

"Follow me, Red. I'll show you to your room, or rather the
storage closet ...
maybe closer to a broom closet. But it's clean and warm,
by golly,
and smells like pine cleaner. I have to warn you,
one roll-over in the night will land you straight in the arms
of that old water heater.
She's friendly though! Don't be alarmed by her sputtering
and humming.
It's kinda like bein cozied up next to Sharol."
~George Maple~

Carig had no idea in what manner he would be greeted by the proprietors, Sharol and George Maple, considering their strange encounter with him a few days back. When he literally drifted in with a mighty gust, George nearly jumped out of his boots with fear as if he had seen a ghost.

"Well, lookee what the wind blew in! Welcome back, Red! What brings you here? Wait, let me guess!"

He began making funny faces and gestures with his hands in the shape of a basic rectangle, trying to generate a response to his own question.

"Another Bible perhaps? Me and the missus were just talkin' about you. What can I do ya for?"

Carig smiled at his attempt at a joke, but in fact was a bit embarrassed that he and Sharol were still talking about him. They must have believed him to be a complete loon!

"Na, not here for another Bible, but I could use a room for the night, and a phone that works. I'm not gettin' any service on my cell."

George began clicking on the computer keys to see what might be available, and then turned around and opened a large cabinet filled with empty hooks except for some old skeleton keys that were hanging towards the bottom, appearing as though they had been untouched for decades.

"Hmmm? Well, I've got some good news, and some bad news. We're booked solid! Ain't got even one room left, and the phone lines are down. Between the storm and a wedding this afternoon, every nook and cranny of this place is taken."

Carig was obviously confused by the proprietor's brain-twisting statement.

"So, Mr. Maple, what's the good news?"

"Well, Red, the wedding party is still going on and probably will all night. Since the band got stranded here along with everyone else, you can enjoy good music and good food till the sun decides to come up. I'll tell you what, we got a small room right next door to the storage closet with a pretty comfy cot that you can use for the night. Sharol makes me go there when my snoring revs up to 10."

Slyly glancing in all directions to make sure that Sharol wasn't anywhere near, George gestured for Carig to come closer so that he could tell him something he didn't necessarily want his wife to hear. Reluctantly, Carig obliged, and moved in.

"Between you and me, there are a lot of single beauties here that have been downin' bubbly since four and would be mighty happy to see one as good-lookin' as you walkin' in!"

Carig smiled politely and thanked him for the invite but was in no mood to celebrate.

"So, where might that cot be, Mr. Maple?"

"George, call me George! It's this way, follow me."

Just then Sharol, George's wife who had obviously been plucking the feathers from a turkey, came out to the desk slightly covered in fluff.

"Well, hello there! What a coincidence. We were just talking about you not 15 minutes ago. We were reminded of you when a …"

At the clanging sound of a metal pan falling, Sharol's train of thought was derailed as she thundered into the kitchen to find out what all the ruckus was about.

George could tell that the overflow of guests and partygoers was taking a toll on his already high-strung bride. That, along with unfinished preparations for the "Five-Star Portland Moose Inn Thanksgiving Dinner Extravaganza" (an unbreakable Portland tradition), was destined to cause a slight breakdown somewhere between the oyster stuffing and flaming rum punch. Her rantings, that could be heard all the way into Bar Rousse, were George's cue to step in and carry some of the burden rather than pretending to be busy at the front counter.

"Follow me, Red, I'll show you to your room, or rather the storage closet … maybe closer to a broom closet. But it's clean and warm, by golly, and smells like pine cleaner. I have to warn you, one roll-over in the night will land you straight in the arms of that old water heater. She's friendly though! Don't be alarmed by her sputtering and humming, it's kinda like bein cozied up next to Sharol."

George was a funny man who laughed out loud at his own humorous antics. Carig couldn't help but appreciate his sense of humor.

"Thank you, George, and thank ye for the room. Also, just so ye know, I don't generally go around takin' Bibles from hotels."

"No worries, son, there are worse things you could do. Hey by the way, I see you're wearin' a wedding ring. Where's your better half? I mean, why are ya here alone the night before Thanksgiving?"

Carig felt greatly saddened by his question, not knowing exactly how to answer. George could tell that something was up and decided that this young man seemed to need a friend more than Sharol needed another kitchen worker.

"It's Carig, right?"

"Yes sir."

"What's your surname, Carig?"

"Hammel."

"Hammel, hmm? Where have I heard that name before?"

He thought for a moment, and then absentmindedly shook his head.

"Can't remember nothin' these days! I'll tell you what, how about you and me go chow down on some roast beef and mashed potatoes compliments of the bride and groom? I'll even buy ya a drink. You seem like a Scotch whiskey man to me!"

Carig took a deep breath and agreed. He couldn't even remember the last time he ate, and he was starving. Although he didn't make it a habit of drinking the robust elixir of his ancestors, the thought of numbing his affliction sounded like a brilliant idea.

"Aye! Tha'd be great, but can we make it a whole bottle?"

"Will do!"

For the next several hours, Carig ate and drank more than he would normally ever allow himself. Along with every glass of GlenDronach, he poured out his story, minus classified facts such as The Tempus Vector. The comforting food and drink warmed him inside and out while greatly improving his mood and elevating his Scottish brogue. It was the first time in a long time that he was able to relax and just talk about anything and everything like he used to do with his Gran. He shared bits and pieces of his life beginning with the day that he arrived in America. But ultimately, Carig's story revolved around Beni. How they grew up together, the fact that he had always loved her, their perfect and rather unexpected ceremony just a week ago, and finally, how she had to leave the very next day. He explained that through a series of misunderstandings, they had argued and then parted in anger earlier that day. His search for her whereabouts led him back to the Portland Moose Inn. The more details that Carig revealed about his new wife, Beni his beloved, with her silky brown hair, blue eyes like the sea, and the hottest body he'd ever seen, George listened intently, and all of a sudden had a revelation that unlocked his earlier forgetfulness.

"Is Beni her whole name?"

"Na! Beni's short for Benidette."

"Hmm? You don't hear that name too often."

"She's the only Beni in the whole wide world, and I've lost her! What if I've lost her forever?"

George felt rather sympathetic and warm-hearted towards Carig, and he quickly realized that he had met *"Carig's Beni"* earlier that afternoon. All of the details from Carig's saga began to add up into one incredible truth. She was here at the inn, but her rather addled husband had no idea.

George now remembered checking *Benidette Hammel* into a room just an hour or so before Carig showed up. She came looking for answers as to why the man they could only describe as having "red hippie hair" (as George called it), would take a Bible from the inn. George and Sharol didn't know any more than she did about the whereabouts of the man, but afterward they felt rather strange about her inquiry.

By the time they were done discussing the cryptic mystery surrounding The Holy Book, the storm had moved in and Beni had no choice but to stay. Even her cab driver became a lodger of the inn for the night. When Carig walked in shortly after, the coincidence of him showing up from out of the blue frightened George. But now, he could see that it wasn't a coincidence at all, but providence.

Nearly jumping out of his skin with excitement, George stopped himself before spouting out his inside intelligence regarding Beni. As the information hovered on the tip of his tongue, he calmly sat back in his chair with an ornery but satisfied grin. His mind began spinning with daring ideas of how to covertly bring the twosome together. He could tell that there was a fierce devotion between the couple, they just needed a little jump start. After all, the best way to light a fire is with a little spark. As The Love Doctor finally decided on his course of action, he stood up and told Carig that he'd better go and give the wife a hand. Carig stood up as well, and asked if they needed any help

"As a matter of fact, Red, we're a little short on staff for the night, and I just remembered that room 222 ordered champagne and blueberries to be sent up at 9:00. That's in a few minutes. Before you call it a night, would you mind delivering it for me?"

Carig was happy to help but was struggling just a bit to walk in a straight line. Both George and he slightly staggered into the kitchen where Sharol was scrambling at top speed, running circles around the two and shooing George out of her way. George grabbed a bottle of their "finest" out of the cooler and placed it in a bucket on a tray, along with two glasses and a silver bowl filled with blueberries.

"Okay now, remember, take this upstairs to room 222 right now. They're waiting. When you knock on the door, tell them that it's room service with their order ... got it?"

"Aye, I'm on it, George! Hey, thank you for everything!"

"Wait a minute, George! Sharol piped up. Where's that going? I don't remember any order for champagne to be delivered anywhere! Everyone's pretty much downstairs."

"The order came in while you were gone."

With an open mouth, George gave Sharol an over exaggerated wink, so that she would go along with his story.

"What in the hell is wrong with your face, I haven't gone anywhere!"

George awkwardly smiled at Carig, then grabbed hold of Sharol's shoulders, and guided her into the freezer room.

"Hang on, Red, we'll be right back."

Carig stood there feeling a bit dizzy and was anxious to lay down and go to sleep. It had been a long day, and he was whipped.

A few minutes later, Sharol and George came out of the freezer, Sharol with a rather large grin on her face.

"Ya know, with the business of the day, I totally forgot about that 222 room service order. I really appreciate the help. Now for once today, George can stop hangin' around here like he owns the place, and get some work done!"

"But, Shar Bear, I do own the place!"

"Don't you 'Shar Bear' me! Start peelin' those spuds before I peel you!"

George rolled his eyes while Carig grabbed the tray and headed for the elevator.

The elevator was old and slow, but after finishing off the bottle of GlenDronach, almost by himself, it seemed like a better idea than the stairs. He could hear it revving up at the second floor, struggling its way down. At this rate, he thought, he could have delivered the champagne five times over before it finally made its way down.

Chapter 8

Juxtaposed

*"How about I take over here, sweetheart? You're as pale
as a sheet and looks like you could use something to eat. You see
that table over there, the only one with a candle still burning?
Take this plate and make yourself comfortable.
I'll be there in a minute with something to wet your
whistle."*
~Sharol Maple~

It seemed everything I sought to accomplish was ruined in
one way or another by circumstances beyond my control. Seeking
one piece of information that could be found at the inn, and then
moving on to see Annaliese were my intentions, but the imminent
thundersnow arrived and was the deciding factor to stay at the inn
for the night. By now, I imagined that Carig was more than likely
home and discovered that I wasn't there. Based on the way he was
behaving when he left, I would say that he probably didn't really
care where I was anyway. It made me sad to think about what had
happened to us and how our first, although quite significant, marital
issue caused him to become so indifferent towards me. I had no
doubt that he was guarding his wounded heart, but at some point, he
was gonna have to get over it.

It had been such a long day, and I dreaded the idea of
spending one more night away from him. I wasn't tired, and the last
thing I wanted to do was to be cooped up in this room all alone. Even
though I'd been surrounded by people all week, I felt as though I
had been stranded on a desert island, alone. It was Carig who I
wanted to be with, but he didn't feel the same, and I didn't know
how to fix it. I knew for a fact that if Adina was here, she would tell
me to put on my prettiest party dress and go down and kick up my
heels, which was exactly what I would do. Well, minus the party
dress. More like a very un-party turtleneck sweater that would cover
the bruises on my neck, and Converse sneakers. The owners had told
me when I checked in that I could come down and join the party any
time. Anything was better than this.

After freshening up a bit, I headed out the door. Just as I was about to push the elevator button, I heard it creaking and whistling as it inched up towards the second floor. Rather than taking my chances with the human dumbwaiter, I opted to take the stairs.

From the top of the stairs, my eyes were immediately drawn to the large window above the double doors that overlooked the parking area. The battle of elements raged wildly, pelting fiercely against the glass. Not even the roaring music that rose up from the all-nighter compared to the howling wind and the booming thunder. Every car was completely buried beneath thick layers of snow, yet the inn, full of partygoers, appeared oblivious to the nor'easter blizzard that was swallowing up everything in sight.

If no one else was concerned, why should I be? I took a deep breath, tousled my hair, and thought to myself, *Hang it all!* I was so sick and tired of being afraid of things I couldn't control. Staring out the window and worrying that it might break through at any moment would certainly not stop it from happening. I would go downstairs, have a great time, and let the storm do what it was gonna do.

I followed the Dixieland sound of upbeat jazz, cheerful people, and most importantly, the mouthwatering aroma of food that was calling my name. About halfway down the stairs, I was startled by a loud explosion-like pop, and then everything went dark; the entire place had lost all power. Most would have panicked in this situation, and by the resounding screams that instantly replaced the music, fear had taken over. Call it crazy, but in the midst of the chaos, I sat down on a step and began to laugh. Perhaps, after the week I'd had, this little ripple didn't faze me. Compared to dealing with Nazis and almost dying twice, I was unmoved by the blackout. What did bother me was the overwhelming sense that wherever I went, trouble was close by, nipping at my heels, and *this* was just one more thing. I could either laugh, cry, or worry myself into a lather, so I chose the best of the three.

Then all at once, the back-up lighting and bullhorn siren startled the room into silence. Once George had the crowd's attention, he began trumpeting out emergency protocol instructions, which was slightly comical considering the half-bashed audience. I was thankful to be observing the bedlam from afar rather than being in the center of it.

"Listen up, all! Listen now! Eyes on me, everyone! Now then. The main thing is to calm down! This is nothing that can't be fixed. We lost power a couple of nights ago and it was up and runnin' by mornin'. Everything will be fine! The main thing is *not to panic*! Now listen carefully! Three stations are being set up: one with lanterns, one with water, and this last one here, with food packs. Now line up, get your supplies, head on back to your rooms, and stay warm. We'll keep you posted about the latest storm information."

I stood up and headed to the banquet room to grab my emergency supplies and hopefully a bottle of champagne - not in that order! But when I noticed George Maple standing at station one handing out lanterns, he reminded me of Wil, and it was apparent that he could use a helping hand. I walked over to his table, and lightly tapped him on the shoulder.

"Mr. Maple, is there something I can do to help?"

Without considering who I was, only paying attention to the oncoming patrons, he told me to grab the box cutter and open up another container of lanterns. I did as he asked, and then began setting them out on the table.

"Thanks, kiddo! You think you could take over? We've got someone stuck in the elevator, and I've gotta go grab a crowbar or axe ... somethin to pry the damn doors open."

"Sure, I'd be happy to!"

George turned and gaped at me in the most peculiar fashion, like he was staring at a long-lost friend, yet we had just met earlier that day.

"Beni?"

"Yes!"

"Where's your husband? Where's Carig?"

"Carig? I'm pretty sure that he's at home. Wait, how did you know that Carig was my husband?"

George's blinking tick suddenly flared up along with concerning confusion most likely brought on by the stress of the situation.

"Well, uh uh, you told me about him this afternoon. Don't you remember?"

"No, I don't believe that there was any mention about my husband, Carig!"

"Well, that settles it then! You take care of the lanterns, and I'll be back as soon as the elevator issue is all taken care of."

"But wait! Mr. Maple!"

Marking *that* as one of the most ridiculous conversations that I had ever had, I tried to ignore how weird the vague exchange between Mr. Maple and myself made me feel. Instead, I tried to focus on the task he had left me - bringing light to the guests of the Portland Moose Inn.

Within a few minutes, everyone began to calm down and the lines started moving smoothly. I felt sorry for the bride and her faithful attendants who stood behind her. They were doing all they could to make the best of this horrible situation. Only hours before, each a picture of perfection with their flawless forms and rosy complexions, covered from head to toe in silk and tulle, walked down the aisle beaming with excitement that the moment they had anticipated for months had finally arrived. And now they stood at my station, barefoot and drunk, with mascara rings beneath their eyes, and filthy and tattered hems.

But then I watched as the groom walked up behind his precious bride, placed his hands over her eyes, and asked her to *Guess Who!* He whispered in her ear that he was the luckiest man in the world, and then he embraced her. Even better, to curb the inevitable disappointment that he knew she felt, he assured her that this had been the perfect day that they would someday brag about to their children. With those words warming her heart, he whisked her up in his arms and told everyone to *Make way! The honeymoon is about to begin!* It was the sweetest thing I'd ever seen and reminded me that no matter who you are or what journey stands ahead, storms will come. They were perfectly okay amidst the whirlwind of the day that could have very well robbed all joy, as long as they had each other.

Seeing them together made me miss Carig even more. Our situation may have been far more trying than winter storms and loss of electricity, but I didn't care what had happened or what would come. Every fiber of my being was committed to him today and always. I couldn't wait to see him again so that I could tell him so, face to face.

Apparently, while en route to the elevator mishap, George had recruited every able-bodied man along the way to assist in the rescue. Talk around the room revealed that it was one poor soul stranded between floors, and there would be nothing easy about springing him from that old rust bucket. I hoped for his sake that he wasn't claustrophobic, as the whole ordeal was taking longer than anticipated. Either way, it looked as if I might be filling in for George for a while longer.

After a good hour or so, cheers rang out from the second floor, as the victim was successfully pulled from the hatch. Everyone was thankful and relieved. I didn't see any signs of George coming back, but from behind, I felt a hand on my shoulder. It was Sharol Maple, my angel of mercy, holding a plate of food.

"How about I take over here, sweetheart? You're as pale as a sheet and looks like you could use something to eat. You see that table over there, the only one with a candle still burning? Take this plate and make yourself comfortable. I'll be there in a minute with something to wet your whistle."

Even though the food was overcooked and now lukewarm, it hit the spot, along with a large glass of champagne that was filled to the brim. My stomach was so empty, that I could feel the dry path that was rapidly and most wonderfully being quenched by the liquid bubbles.

As I sat back in my chair utterly satisfied, I was head-on distracted by a familiar fragrance. At first, I felt silly even noticing such a thing. With all of the guests who still remained in the hall, there was a vast array of perfumes swirling all about the room, most of which would never appeal to me or catch my attention. But this aroma was different, unique, one that I was intimately acquainted with. It had the power to stimulate all of my senses, beginning at the nape of my neck, and meandering all the way down to my toes. I spun around to find the origin of this spicy incense, but no one was there. To my great dismay, *he* wasn't there. The perfect mixture reminded me of the day I married Carig. I smelled Adina's scent and felt her presence so vividly that day, that I knew she must be there, standing by my side. Maybe this too was my imagination playing tricks on me, but it was somehow different. The aroma was not just from a bottle that could be doused on, but a particular combination of Carig's natural scent intermingled with his aromatic cologne. The fusion of the two was altogether sexy and drove me crazy.

Turning around once again in my chair, this time rising up to my knees, I began scouring the room. The aroma became more intense and overpowered my senses. For a moment, I was certain that I was losing my mind; my palms, clammy and face, hot. As I put my cold hands onto my cheeks, I felt slightly tortured as he seemed so close, but beyond my reach. Lightly spreading my fingers over my nose and my mouth, I inhaled deeply. This one-of-a-kind combination that paralleled Carig was now all over my hands. What was this? What was going on? Although completely impossible, the answer was right at my fingertips, actually hanging from the back of my chair. Like some kind of cruel magic trick, Carig's soft down jacket had been sitting there the entire time with the scent of him rising up like a burnt offering. Not unlike Adina's presence, his jacket manifesting itself was impossible. Even if it was all in my head, I grabbed it and wrapped it around me. Whether real or fantasy, I hugged myself tightly within his coat, pretending that I was nestled in his arms. I was overwhelmed with emotion, and it was all I could do not to stand there and cry.

I'm not exactly sure how long I stood there. The noise of the crowd died down as I buried my head in his jacket. When finally I peered upward, I saw him standing in the doorway! As my face emerged, his eyes caught mine, and he strode over to where I stood.

Chapter 9

Kristall Himmel

"Awkwardly, George continued standing at the door as if he wanted to be invited in, until Sharol grabbed hold of his shirt and began dragging him down the hallway, reminding him that there was much to be done, and to wipe that ridiculous smile off his face."
~Benidette Hammel~

With focused anticipation, he swiftly maneuvered through a maze of people, chairs, and tables, until finally he stood only inches away, breathless. At first, we were both taken aback by the sight of one another, half afraid that the image before our eyes was merely a figment of our imaginations. Lacking faith that he was truly there, I reached forward, placing my hand on his chest. His heart along with mine, was pounding wildly. I didn't know how or why he could possibly be standing right in front of me, but the world seemed right simply because he was there. Within those few moments, I realized that my flawed understanding about love and devotion went completely out the window. Apart from Carig, I had functioned my entire life as half a person. So, this is love. The Adina and Carson kind of love that lives on, even in death. The kind everyone strives to find, but rarely does.

Gently, he cupped my face in his hands, holding it like a fragile piece of china, tenderly caressing every curve and every line with the tips of his fingers. In one swift movement, he pulled me close and held me so tight, as if we had been parted forever. His inviting brogue was like music to my weary soul.

"Beni, don't ever leave me again!"

"Never! I'll never leave you!"

There in the midst of strangers, he recklessly began kissing me. Although his enthusiasm was familiar, this medley of furious passion that was sweeping over my lips was new and different. He was altogether unconcerned about our lack of privacy, paying no attention to the fact that we were surrounded by patrons of the inn, completely uninterested in *anything* except for me. In a moment's gap, I gazed into his eyes and could see that he wasn't himself.

Maybe it was the stress of everything that we'd gone through, or the relief of finding me. All I knew was that the normal sage-colored twinkle in his eye now appeared like a sea of flames, and the ballad of affections that flowed from his lips both concerned and intoxicated me.

"Do you have the faintest idea what ye do to me? Mo ghaol, when I saw ye from across the room, a fire was set ablaze within me. Don't make me wait another minute without feelin' your skin against mine. Where's your room, lass?"

Words were no longer necessary as I took hold of his hand and pulled him with me.

The earlier curse of darkness was redeemed by an atmosphere of romance. Our ascent up the stairs was slow moving, like a dance we delighted in every stride. Others were running circles around us, but he stood behind, holding me tightly as we climbed one stair at a time - connected - our bodies moving as one. When finally, we arrived at the room, Carig noticed the number posted on the door and laughed.

"222? This is yer room?"

"Yeah. Why is that funny?"

"Aw, nothin'. It's just that I think I heard that the poor lad who was stuck in the elevator was deliverin' champagne to this room."

"Really? I wonder why?"

"Dunno. Maybe he'll still show up."

Still smirking, and uninhibited, Carig pushed his body against mine and aggressively began kissing me. He was filled with an unstoppable eagerness that I had not yet seen; completely different than the broken man I had encountered that morning.

"I'll just say this lass, we were destined to be here together in this exact time and place. The route may have been roundabout, but believe me, the wait will surely be worth it. That, I can promise ye!"

He caressed his hands slowly over each pocket of my jeans until finally discovering the room key, and while still holding me in his arms, unlocked the door in one swift move. Once inside, we both stood there studying one another. I think for each of us, it was difficult to fathom that we were finally together with no obstacles, no agenda, just he and I. I slowly slipped my hands beneath his sweater, pulling it off with his full cooperation - and I was happy to return the favor. With each garment that fell, I was able to partake in the glorious fragrance that belonged only to him. Finally, in that small dark sanctuary on the second floor of the Portland Moose Inn, with the song of snow tapping on the window, our world began to slow down.

"Say it to me again, I want to hear ye say it!"

"What? Say what?"

"What you said to me this morning, lass!"

"I said a lot of things this morning."

One by one, he kissed the tips of my fingers, and then with a flirtatious grin, he initiated a playful exchange.

"Well, let me see. You were mad to be sure, but those words ye spoke have been soundin' through my head all day. Somethin' to the effect of liberatin' your fantasies, and things ye wanted to do to me. And then ye said somethin' about intoxicating! I'm not exactly sure what all that means, but I'm more than willin' to find out."

He stepped behind me and softly kissed my bandaged shoulder.

"I'm so sorry for what ya been through, lass, and I know I didn't help one bit with my attitude. Please forgive me, Beni!"

"I'm sorry too! I know this has been hard for you. I'm sure I don't even know half of what you've been through!"

He smiled and moved toward me with unbridled passion. That outpouring of awe-inspiring fervor, and the feel of his body next to mine, was what fueled my determination to return from my journey. I couldn't imagine living a life without Carig in it.

"Beni, I never meant to hurt ye. I would never! You're my life!"

I stared up at this tall god-like man who peered back at me through glassy eyes, conveying volumes of unspeakable sentiments that warmed my heart. Oh Lord, how could I have stayed away from him for so long? How could I have been so blind? An unquenchable fire spontaneously stirred between us. If I were to be honest, a flame had always lingered, but now had been fanned into a roaring inferno. We had an insatiable gift of becoming lost in one another's presence. At that moment, nothing could have distracted us.

Well, nothing that is until a pounding knock sounded from the other side of the door. Carig wanted to ignore it, but when it happened a second time and we could hear Sharol and George bickering from the hallway, we hurriedly wrapped ourselves in hotel robes and opened the door.

"Well, I see you two love birds found each other!"

Apparently, George and Sharol had been watching our reunion from afar and were bursting with satisfaction at the part they had played in our reconciliation. Sharol stood on the other side of the hallway, holding an oversized lantern that illuminated her flutters, waves, and winks of good cheer. George stood at the threshold with a big smile, holding an even larger bottle of champagne marked with a label that congratulated Mr. and Mrs. Sandstone, the happy couple married earlier that day. Along with the confiscated bubbly, he brought in a silver tureen filled with shrimp cocktail, clearly *another* leftover wedding freebie. He laughed out loud and told us it was "on the house."

"You two enjoy. Ya might as well get comfortable. This storm ain't leavin' any time soon."

Awkwardly, George continued standing at the door as if he wanted to be invited in, until Sharol grabbed hold of his shirt and began dragging him down the hallway, reminding him that there was much to be done, and to wipe that ridiculous smile off his face. Even after the door closed, we couldn't help but laugh and shake our heads as she relentlessly chewed on his ear all the way down the hallway.

I think we both knew that this life of unpredictable journeys would never be easy, but rather an uncomfortable lot driven by a divine sanction. But for the time being, this little room became our sanctuary, allowing us to check our cares at the door and enter into a much-needed intermission.

Neither of us were generally too keen on drinking. Between all of the stories of my alcoholic grandfather, Roy, and Carig's spirituous and hot-headed father, we just chose not to go down that road. However, tonight we didn't care, nor did we hold back, allowing each glass to wash away the reality of our lives, even if just for a few hours. Supposedly, Carig fell off that sobriety wagon hours prior, as he admitted to earlier baptizing his sorrows in a full portion of Scotch whiskey.

The more we drank, the more reckless and carefree we became. I watched as Carig plunged into the oversized chair that sat next to the window. He solicited my presence to join him with a provoking stare and come-hither pat on his knee. After pouring one more glass and consuming every last drop like it was water, I surrendered myself to his invite. Inching towards him, face to face, I wrapped my arms around his neck and combed my fingers through his hair, as he without further hesitation pulled me into his world. Although a bit slurred, he whispered in my ear, burying his face in my hair.

"Ah Beni, my body is burnin' for you right now! But I don't wanna hurt ye, lass. I'll tell ye what, I'll be extra careful with you, but don't ye be worryin' a bit about hurtin' me!"

For a moment I forgot where we were as he brushed his lips on the nape of my neck while Gaelic verses poured from his mouth. I had no idea what he was saying, and frankly, I didn't care.

"Tha gaol agam ort!"

He knew very well that his exotic speech braided with his gentle tone, drove me crazy.

"Just stay still … don't move … close your eyes, Beni. Please!"

There was no denying his request as he was extremely eager to reacquaint himself with every curve of my body. I found myself lost in his caresses and was blissfully reminded of his rare ability to transform a mere touch into an intoxicating experience.

Whether he realized it or not, he had been my strength from afar. Like the lighthouse platform where he stood so often, he became my beacon of hope, the refuge where I longed to be. There were countless moments in my journey when I felt as though all was lost, including myself. But somehow, there was always a faithful flickering of light, assuring me that I would make it home.

Everything about Carig was sensuous and enticing. Beginning with his auburn locks that practically begged to be fondled, all the way down to his strong but shapely legs that he claimed grew weak whenever I was near. We had been married for such a short time, but the one night we were together was powerful. Since then, images of my husband were set afire in my mind like the flames that danced on the walls of the bothy.

My soft breathy whisper that nuzzled against his ear prompted him to hold me even tighter and made his heart beat so quickly that I could feel it pounding through his flesh. Just for fun, I uttered broken French verses that I had learned so long ago, and probably made no sense at all. Nonetheless, my attempt to tell him how sexy he was, and something about my appetite, sounded good anyway. The main thing was that Carig greatly appreciated my unexpected poetry.

"Tu es tellement sexy! J'ai faim pour toi!"

"Mrs. Hammel! What was that?"

"Does it really matter?"

"No, not really! I have no idea what you said, but I like how it sounded!"

In a million years, I never thought I would say such things to anyone, but when it came to Carig, poetry easily flowed from my mouth. He inspired me.

"Well, if I must … I was just telling you how incredibly sexy and intoxicating you are, and thoughts of our first night together only whet my appetite for more."

I could tell by the gleam in his eye and the ornery grin on his face, that he was pleased with what I had to say and paused to see if there was more.

"Fais-moi l'amour, s'il vous plait!"

Carig laughed at my attempt to woo him with a French lyric.

"Was that funny?"

"Na, not at all! It's mesmerizin'! I was just thinkin', you could be sayin' anythin' to me Beni, and I wouldn't care. Every word you speak is like honey on your lips."

For the first time, hours, minutes, and seconds seemed to pause - a gift of opportunity perhaps to claim back the span of time that was seized from us.

As far as we were concerned, sleep was a waste of time. We had both learned as of late, that while following this decree that had now become our calling, we would need to seize every moment. Throughout the night, we talked about anything and everything, but were also completely content saying nothing at all. Without a doubt, being wrapped in his arms was my favorite place to be. I felt safe, not having to think about anything, or make any decisions or choices. I only had to be present in the here and now.

Finally, in the early hours of the morning, when neither of us could keep our eyes open for another second, I fell into a deep sleep that led to a most frightening dream.

I found myself back on the bridge of my journey, the pathway that spanned from the third story balcony to the doorway of Friedlich. The overpass was shaky and unstable, which made me stop and hold tightly to the side rails. From below, there were deafening echoes of anger and unrestrained chaos rising from the darkness that was grasping at my heels with claws of ice. From all sides, a foreboding vapor rose up from beneath, making me cringe in fear. I crouched down, and then fell to my knees, squeezed my eyes shut, and placed my hands over my ears, trying to block out the noise.

At first the uproar only rose in volume, and then without warning, stopped. The ear-piercing confusion was replaced by an eerie silence. I stood up, more determined than ever to once again return home, but found myself physically unable to turn back. Continuing forward was my only alternative. I didn't want to go back to that place that nearly captured me forever, so I waited and watched.

From the other side of the bridge, the door flung open, revealing the familiar city from which I had narrowly escaped but a few days ago. Although recognizable by its weathered buildings and cobblestone streets, it was now covered by the shadow of night. Two images rose up from the dusk at the corner of the opening. At first, I squinted and strained, trying to make out the faces that were camouflaged by frosted sheets of glass. When their faces were finally revealed, I was shocked at the appearance of these two men whose gazes were fixated on me. It was obvious that they could see me clearly and knew who I was. Although they wore horrifying veils of death with eyes that were hollow and empty, I could see that it was Carson and Malachi. They were but shells of the exuberant men who I had previously met. On the other side of the door stood Alrik with his eyes fixed on another ... like the portrait that hung in his family gallery. Unlike Carson and Malachi, he was completely oblivious of me and the other two observers in his midst.

I watched as he walked into a shallow blue lake where a woman wearing a white dress stood. Without hesitation, he lovingly wrapped his arms around her. As she turned around, I could instantly tell that the woman was me. He swept her up, or rather, he swept me up in his arms. The initial moment for the two was sweet, but then turned peculiar as he delivered her over to where Carson *and Malachi stood. The moment her feet hit the ground, she became like them, also shrouded in a deathlike appearance. As he stepped back into the lake, a powerful wind swept beneath his feet, parching every last drop of water, until the ground turned to ash. Before my very eyes, every inkling of beauty and light disappeared with the water.*

Not only was I astounded by what I saw next, but I was simultaneously consumed with that gut-wrenching call of the Tempus Vector. The pain was unbearable, far worse than what I had previously experienced. Once again, I dropped to my knees, trying to catch my breath. I knew that I didn't belong there, but I didn't know how to escape. The more I tried to walk away and close my eyes to the show of misfortunes, the greater the discomfort became. It was only when I turned back around and continued watching that the pain subsided along with the image of Alrik Richter.

In his place now stood Halag Sauer, the most evil man I had ever encountered. Halag stood in the center of the ashen cemetery strewn with massive headstones, one of which was more worn than the others, covered in cobwebs and a thick layer of dust, bearing the initials HS, similar to the engraving on his cigarette case.

As if the sky was falling, a great rumbling began shaking the earth, resounding like thunder. Through the open cavities of earth, rose four shiny black pillars. With great command they continued upward, breaking through the clouds. Not even the heavens suppressed their force. As the pillars ascended higher, he raised his left hand toward the sky, and when he did, blood poured from it and down his arm until he was completely covered in scarlet. With the drop of his head, his eyes caught mine, and turned to flames. Like a rabid dog, he burst through the door and began running toward me. The closer he came, the larger his stature. To make things worse, I was paralyzed there in the middle of the bridge. All I could do was watch him move closer, allowing him to destroy me once and for all.

As his arm stretched forth with his hand only inches from my face, the door leading to the third story room exploded open with a thunderous noise and a blinding light. So brilliant was the glow, that I was forced to shield my eyes. Through my webbed fingers, I could scarcely make out a larger-than-life silhouette of what seemed to be a mighty warrior. With powerful wings, he landed instantly at my side, covering and shielding me with his body while at the same time raising his right hand, crushing Halag to the ground.

I was so relieved, until Halag once again rose up and began to battle back. The war between the two was fought with blades of steel and storming rage. For some reason I couldn't see the conflict, but I could hear it.

With a grunt of victory, the warrior struck Halag once and for all, casting him from the bridge into a black abyss. I could hear his cutting screech as he plummeted into a bottomless ruin.

As my protector lifted the mask from his face to reveal his identity, I woke in a lather of sweat and blood.

It was still dark outside, and Carig was lying there so peacefully that I didn't want to wake him. Somehow between the romance of the night and my brutal dream, my stitches tore just enough to bleed all over my pillow. After taking care of the mess as best I could, I decided to go downstairs and see if the snow had subsided, and if there happened to be any coffee on the horizon. Due to the wildness of the "Almost All-Nighter" party that had been raging since early yesterday afternoon, all of the guests were sound asleep. By the looks of the neon sign once again glowing from outside the front window, the electricity had been restored.

I started to go back to the room when I heard the rattling of pans from the kitchen. It was still quite cold, so I clenched my sweatshirt tightly and pushed on the door that led into the cooking area. With all the ovens and burners blazing non-stop throughout the night, the kitchen was toasty. It reminded me of when I was a little girl. Adina used to keep the oven door open while broiling cinnamon toast. To me that was the normal way of staying warm on cold winter mornings.

Mrs. Maple was busy peeling the last of the potatoes. Sitting on the large stainless-steel counter were dozens of pumpkin and pecan pies, and on the next counter were several turkeys still waiting to be cooked. She was in her own world, busy at work, so when I said good morning, she nearly jumped out of her skin.

"Good Lord Almighty! You nearly scared me to my very death!"

Once she caught her breath and realized that she may have come across a bit rude, she calmed down.

"I am so sorry, I didn't mean to snap! I've been up all night preparing this damn dinner. Every year I say that it'll be my last year doing this, but it's kind of like having a baby. You tell yourself that you will *never* do it again, and lo and behold, one quickie in the broom closet, and nine months later your poppin' out another one."

I couldn't help but laugh. I thought *I* was a nervous talker, but she was wound up as tight as a watch.

"Anyway, sorry. Didn't mean to ramble on. I really am almost done. Just a half hour ago I let George and the staff go get some shut-eye while I finished peeling these potatoes."

Poor thing. I could tell that she was exhausted and could use some fresh help.

"Mrs. Maple, would you like me to finish those for you?"

"No, it's fine. Besides, I'm expecting a delivery of oysters. My turkey stuffing is famous all throughout Maine, but without Taggart's 'special' oysters as the backbone of my herbed crumbs, it won't be famous for long. Nobody has oysters like his, tender and meaty … I have to have them, or my dressing will be ruined. I'm a little worried though. Joseph Taggart died a few months back. His boys took over the business, but they've had an awfully hard go of it since then. Heaven forbid if one of them doesn't make it. If that's the case, I might as well open up a box of Minute Stuffing!"

"Joe Taggart the fisherman? I hadn't heard that he'd died. What happened to him? Gosh, I haven't seen him in forever!"

The last time I'd seen him, he delivered fish and oysters to our house in Bar Rousse for Mari's soup. He stayed for a long while talking to my Aunt Adina on the front porch swing. When I went out to join them, their conversation was anything but lighthearted and ceased the moment I set foot on the porch. He was always very kind, but never said too much to me. But on *that* day, right before he left, he reached deep into his pocket, pulled something out, and held it behind his back. Then holding out both fists, he told me to choose one. I tapped his right hand, and he opened it, revealing a single pink pearl, and I reached out to grab it.

"Wait now, my girl," he said. "This is no ordinary pearl. Have you ever seen the likes of a pink beauty like this one? Each jewel of the sea tells a story. This one journeyed far and wide to find you. It will give you a wisdom far greater than you knew you ever had inside ye, and a love that will never fail, no matter what. Don't lose it … it is as rare as you. There's not another quite like it."

Before he walked away, he closed my hand tightly around the pearl, and then clenched my small fist within his own. With a stern gaze, but soft words, he spoke proverbs that seemed silly to a little girl, but as a woman, became quite meaningful.

"Beni, hold tightly to wisdom as if it were a precious and most valuable pearl. If you do so, you will surely never falter!"

I hadn't really given him, or that pink sea jewel, much thought over the years. Like most kids, I treasured it for a few days and then put it on my shelf. Adina surprised me that next Christmas with a teardrop-shaped crystal ornament that held the pink pearl. Each year when I hung it on the tree, she would remind me that great wisdom and unending love was far more valuable than all of the pearls of the sea.

My remembrance of Joseph seemed to grieve Sharol. She neither wanted to talk about what had happened to him, nor of my past remembrances, and quickly changed the subject.

"Quite honestly, I have no idea how those boys fish for oysters in this weather, nor do I care, as long as they bring me at least four pounds! Through hell or high water, the Taggarts have never failed me yet."

"Sharol, I'd be more than happy to finish these potatoes. There aren't that many ... and I'll wait for him. Why don't you go and get some rest!"

Mrs. Maple finally agreed and happily went off to bed. For the next hour, I washed and peeled potatoes, and when I was finished, sat down and had a cup of coffee, one of my all-time favorite things.

My dream left me so burdened that I could hardly think of anything else. I even prayed as I sat there, that the Lord would capture my thoughts and stop this war that was raging within my spirit. But still, I couldn't turn off the haunting recollection.

As hard as I tried to focus on the many blessings of my life, my mind returned to the scattered pieces of my nightmare. I never thought too much about such visions or their underlying meanings, but this one was different. Even though I tried to *not* think about it, it continued to rear its ugly head. The sight of myself standing with Carson and Malachi beneath a veil of death was unnerving. Like my two friends of old, perhaps it was my destiny, maybe even my near future, to be where they are. Why else would I have dreamed such a thing? None of it made sense. And then the vision of Halag running after me stirred up memories that were better left forgotten. The entire episode bothered me greatly.

Thankfully, I was saved from any further thoughts on the matter by a loud knock on the back door. Although my heart was already racing, the sudden pounding stirred my adrenaline. Not thinking that he was no longer with us, I expected to see Joseph Taggart, Maine's foremost huntsman of shelled delicacies standing there, but instead, it was his son, Ivan. Ivan was the youngest of seven brothers who had always been extremely smart and knew it, graduating valedictorian of his class, and always excelling at whatever he attempted. Regardless of his genius status, he chose to stay in Bar Rousse and help run the family business rather than going off to college. He was both cocky and cool, never letting his short stature hold him back. Even though he now stood in the doorway with his dusty brown hair wildly sticking out from beneath his most hilarious fur-lined aviator hat, he brimmed with confidence.

"Mornin', beautiful! Long time no see!"

Just as I remembered, smooth as glass in the art of womanizing. At the same time, always likeable. Although Ivan was a few years older, he and Carig went to school together, but Carig never cared too much for this arrogant Taggart who relentlessly made fun of his Scottish brogue and red hair. Always referring to him as a "wickie," the ancient branding of a lighthouse keeper. Somehow Ivan demoralized the occupation with his constant insults. For the most part, Carig ignored the insults from the "wee lad" who was half his size, but something happened the summer before I left for college that caused a major brawl between the two, leaving Ivan pretty beat up and his six brothers showing up at the Hammel door.

"Ivan, how are you? Come in! Oh my gosh, it is freezing!"

"I'm good. Yeah right? That was some storm, and lucky me, I drew the short straw. So here I am. Is Mrs. Maple here?"

"She's sleeping. I told her that I'd wait for you to come."

"So, Beni, you work here?"

"No, I kind of got stuck here for the night."

"Hmm? Kind of a long way from home, aren't ya? Hey, by the way, congrats! I heard through the grapevine that you and … Carig got hitched."

"Yes, we did. Who'd've thought? Even now, I can't believe it really."

Ivan's intense stare made me feel uncomfortable.

"Why are you looking at me that way?"

"Just hopin' that the whole married thing is agreeing with you."

"What would make you say that?"

"Well, to be honest, new brides are normally glowing. You on the other hand, seem a bit worn out."

As hard as I tried not to be insulted by his honesty, I obviously appeared as weary as I felt. Ivan set the large box of oysters on the table and then, most unexpectedly, he took hold of my hands and began examining both sides. He then studied the gnarly bruises on my neck that I had forgotten to cover.

"Have a seat, Miss Beni. It's time you and I had a talk."

I realized that the people in this town were friendly and caring, and it was common for them to be thick as thieves in one another's business, but his comment made me feel as though he had somehow been *waiting* to have a one-on-one with me. His intense regard mingled with his crooked smile was just flat out comical and made me laugh nervously.

"I didn't mean to be disrespectful, Beni, but I'd be lying if I said differently. I see your weariness on the outside, but lyin' deep inside of you as well. My dad and Adina were good friends as long as I can remember. He was always a wise sounding board when she would get overwhelmed. You probably remember, my pop was the quiet sort, real good at listening. When he would talk, people would stop and take note. Like you, Adina was independent and what my dad would call an overachiever. When their conversations were done and over, he would always ask her the same exact question. Until this very moment, I had no idea what he meant by it, but he told me that someday I would."

He was clearly overjoyed by this revelatory encounter, but at the same time was making me feel very strange, and for heaven's sake, what question was he talking about? Obviously, there was something wrong with him. He and I hadn't seen each other for years, yet he was getting all philosophical on me. He wasn't that much older than me, but he was speaking as if he were my much older and wiser elder. The whole thing was strange, and then he blurted out the mysterious question that had been passed down from his father.

"How long will you take counsel in your own soul?"

"Excuse me?"

He eagerly sat there, waiting for a reply.

I knew that I had been through a lot, but somehow this swaggering Don Juan of yesteryear seemed to stare right through me, like the burden of my heart was open for him to see.

"What is it, Beni? Tell me, what's eating away at your soul?"

"I … I had a dream last night that's haunting me. I know it was a dream, but yet it was so real, or *they* were real. I don't know, I just can't stop thinking about it, that's all."

The instant I revealed information of a dream, his entire demeanor changed, and he became obsessed with learning of its every detail.

"Tell me all of it, leave nothing out!"

At first, I wondered why he was so interested, but before I knew it I had divulged every sordid detail from start to finish. With each syllable, he sat back in his chair and closed his eyes soaking in all of the twists and turns of my story. However, at the mention of the four black pillars rising from the water, he cringed almost as if it brought him great pain. Suddenly, his eyes opened wide and he sat straight up repeating certain phrases.

After divulging my dream, I felt rather relieved, but he on the other hand, seemed abundantly worried. It appeared that he had taken the burden upon himself. He stood up and walked over to the window, not saying a word about what I had just told him.

"Ivan, what is it? "

Still he said nothing.

"You know what, don't worry about it! It was just a stupid dream - it doesn't mean anything!"

He slowly turned around and stared intently into my eyes.

"That's where you're wrong, *Carrier of the Tempus Vector*!"

Chapter 10

The Dream

"How long will you take counsel in your own soul?"
~Ivan Taggart~

I took a step back. Not only did his comment leave me completely speechless but I shuddered at his unexpected insight into my dream-story. Somehow, my morsels of gibberish became a foundation of evidence that revealed to him the calling of my life. How much did he really know, and by what authority was he allowed to enter my world? This young sea man with hands as rough as sandpaper was mysterious to be certain, but what I didn't know is whether he was good or evil, and how he so instantaneously wove his life into mine. His countenance had changed dramatically from the moment he knocked until now. He had the appearance of a young man, but a soul of aged foresight and wisdom that went far beyond his years. Whatever this was, he frightened me with his powerful and commanding stare as he peered into my deepest thoughts. Like a facade, his tanned skin camouflaged his bronze-toned eyes. He could obviously tell that I was struggling to make sense of this odd relationship that had now come to life.

To break the awkward tension that stood between us, he removed his coat and hat and hung them on an apron hook. Once again, he sat down, this time making himself comfortable. He had not come simply to deliver oysters but was obviously an important player in my life. He reached into his pocket, pulled out a brandy pipe and small pouch of tobacco, and then stuffed the chamber until it overflowed. After igniting the fragrant weed, he clinched the bit in his teeth, and then like a ship gliding into a cove, it slipped into the corner of his mouth. It was comical to see one so young possessing such an old-school piece, but like all the other men in his family, it was more common than not to see a pipe between his lips. As he held up the matchstick to the bursting chamber, I noticed a familiar marking on the inside of his wrist. At first glance it resembled the name "Jon," but in a peculiar sort of way. The J was upside down, the O was oddly shaped with two dots below it, and the N broken at the top, crowned with another period-like dot.

He saw my attention drawn to his small black tattoo and laid his arm in front of me so that I could see it better. I ran my fingers over the Middle Eastern-type writing.

"I recognize this. Where have I seen it before?"

"My guess would be, on my father's wrist."

He was exactly right. On that day when his father flipped over his closed fists and revealed my pearl, he too bore the same symbol.

"This might be hard to believe, Beni, but after he passed, the craziest thing happened. Right before my eyes, the consecrated marking dissolved from his arm and appeared, burning like fire, on mine."

I could tell that he believed what he was saying, but I had heard enough. Poor Ivan. Somewhere along the way, he had completely lost his mind.

"Well, thanks Ivan. It was great seeing you! I'll make sure Mrs. M gets her oysters. Happy Thanksgiving!"

I walked to the door and opened it wide. I didn't care that frigid wind was filling the kitchen, I just wanted him to leave, and he knew it too. But he just sat there, with no intention of moving.

"Don't you want to know the meaning of your dream, Miss Beni?"

"I don't ... no! I just think that you should leave. Why should I trust you or believe anything you have to say? You don't know me, or anything about me."

"But I do, miss. Each and every time my father and I watched you runnin' on the shores of Bar Rousse, he would tell me that someday those same feet that carried you through the watery sand would also carry you into other worlds. I didn't know it at the time, but every word he spoke to me was preparing me for this very moment, here, now, with you."

"What do you mean? How could he have possibly known that?"

Incredibly, this man whom I had only known as self-absorbed and flirty, stopped me cold in my tracks with a knowledge as abundant as the vapors of smoke that spilled from his mouth. He told me that even before I was born, Adina knew that I was bound as her successor. Of course, that information was nothing new to me, as I had read Adina's early diary notations "To One Called Beni."

She was given my name years before I was born. What I didn't yet understand, was how *he* knew these things.

He could tell by my worried expression, that I was growing more and more antsy at his familiarity with my life events. It was just strange to think that I had been the object of observation since I was a little girl. No wonder I always felt like I was being watched - I was.

"You miss, have been blessed with the gift of wisdom from the Tribe of Solomon. Like you, I have also been given an unexpected faring. The wellspring of *my* calling, also rooted in the lost tribes, and hails from the bloodline of Yosef. The badge on my arm is the mark of this tribe. I know it sounds crazy, especially because it's me. You and everyone else in these parts remember me as a know-it-all donkey rear. I never really deserved it, but I always had a God-given intelligence and understanding that I didn't use for good, but to *my* advantage. It just took me a few years and the tragic death of my father to wise up and channel it in the right direction. You could call me the smartest *stupid* person that has ever walked this planet. Believe it or not, the calling of my life is the gift of interpretation, well, wisdom within interpretation. Until the time comes that I see my father again, I'll be here to help you, just like he helped your aunt. Believe me, Benidette Hammel, I know *much* about you and your calling. My life from the very beginning has been one learning lesson after another. Like strategically placed blocks, one upon the other. The truth is, I've stumbled more times than I'd like to admit, but that rocky path was part of the instruction that led me here. For years, as you probably remember, I was stupid and rebellious. The more my father counseled me, the more defiant I became. I thought I knew it all. It didn't help that my brothers viewed me as my father's favorite, and as ashamed as they might be to admit it, they came real close to launching me off in a boat with no paddles. He would make them do my share of work so that he could ground and instruct me in the things I didn't even care about at the time. They resented me. But deep inside, I knew that I had a gift, one that I kept bottled up. Did you ever feel the same way? Like you were destined for something far greater than yourself?"

I knew exactly what he meant. Perhaps that's what drove me, or why I excelled in school and my career, rising quicker than others my age. It was practically unheard of for someone of my age and experience to become a Professor of Literature and Department Chair. I was surrounded by individuals far more accomplished than myself, but I worked harder and was far more driven than my competition. Funny that he mentioned a lack of satisfaction or fulfillment. Even with all of my accomplishments, I found myself empty. As much as I adored literature and enjoyed teaching it at the highest level, I would often look out at the faces of my students and wonder what I was even doing there.

But my new calling was different. Even though I started out a bit shaky, and thus far felt ill-prepared, I felt an uncanny peace. One that I had never experienced before now. This extraordinary journey was my destiny, and like Adina, I would spend the rest of my life as the Carrier of the Tempus Vector. As I continued listening to his fast-paced story about his own personal journey, I gave a small grin in agreement.

"I know what you mean, I've experienced the same thing! But I can't say that I've ever really had an unusual ability that I kept hidden. As a matter of fact, this whole wisdom thing leaves me feeling as though they chose the wrong person. I mean, I don't think I'm wise at all."

"You have far more wisdom than you realize. Like anything new, you'll grow with experience. I did. At first, I only dreamed dreams. Some were really good, but some were so weird, and it took time for me to learn what they meant, but more importantly, who to share them with and how. In my more foolish years, I told my brothers a dream that I never should have shared, even if it was truth. I won't go into it too much, but being that we are all fishermen, I basically told them that success, like pearls, would always fill my vessel, and theirs would be empty in comparison."

He hung his head in remembrance of past sins that now haunted him.

"Beni, do you remember that time when Carig came and beat me up somethin' fierce?"

"I do. It was right before I went away to college."

"That whole thing was my fault. I was bein' a complete idiot! I, well, I had a serious crush on you, but I knew, well, everyone knew that Carig was crazy in love with you. So anyway, I had a dream that involved you, that if not interpreted correctly could definitely make, well let's just say, 'make a statement.'"

I could tell that he was uncomfortable telling me his dream, but he did so anyway.

"It began with me standing in the front of a church, alone. I heard the congregation rise in unison, and music build as the bride entered. Yet, when I surveyed the church, it was completely empty, not even a pastor was present to officiate. I curiously watched as the bride approached me, wondering who it was beneath the sheer veil. To my great surprise, it was you. As you got nearer, a large gold circle appeared on the floor in front of us. Somehow, in the dream, it made sense and we knew what we were doing, as we together, stepped into the glowing golden circle. As we stood there, immersed in one another, I lifted the veil. It was still you, but your face had grown old. And then I woke up. Now, at that time, I wanted to believe that you and I would someday marry, but I knew it wasn't meant to be, and was absolutely not the revelation of my dream.

"Just for fun, I used my privileged insight to get under Carig's skin, telling him only parts that I knew would bother him most. I not only bragged and gloated non-stop but I emphasized the fact that my visions *always* came to pass. Well, the rest is history, and I have two caps on my front teeth to prove it.

"The real meaning of my dream was this. You and I were never to marry, which is probably good news since you're already married to Carig. The absence of a preacher and witnesses confirmed that it was a bond of friendship that needed no witnesses. The ring in which we stepped together, represented an unbreakable, deeply-rooted alliance, and your face of age symbolized length of days. My dream's proclamation showed that our callings would parallel one another, but also continue on for many years. Beni, the dawning of our alliance has now begun. I'm here for you.

"As time has gone by, my dreams are fewer. Please don't take this as bragging, but I now have an incredible and quite accurate God-given ability to interpret. Before my dad died, I discovered that he too had this gift. I was with him only moments before he died, scarcely giving him time to bless me; it was all he cared about. Beni, I was meant to come here this morning. I thought drawing the short straw was just plain bad luck, but it was preordained so that I could see you. If I've learned nothing else thus far, I've discovered that nothing happens by accident!"

"This just can't be possible!"

"Why would you say that? I have no doubt that you've already seen enough to know that all of this is absolutely possible. Indeed, you were told that we are a tribe of ten, were you not? Did you really think that you would, or could, do such a task all alone? Did you think Adina was alone?"

"No. I knew that she had Killen!"

"She did for sure, but he was only a small part. You must understand. Among all of the tribes, the Carrier of the Tempus Vector is the highest authority and power, but the gifts of the nine are paramount to the success of your journeys. So again, I ask you, miss, 'How long will you take counsel in yer own soul?'"

I knew what he was asking. He was implying that wisdom comes in numbers, the counsel of many, not just myself. I was reminded of what both Adina and Malachi had stated many times over, I would never be alone. The power, gifts, encouragement and insight of the nine others were what they spoke of. I'm not sure why I hadn't fully comprehended their existence before now. Perhaps I just lacked enough faith in a divine masterpiece or refused to believe what I couldn't see or touch. I was ashamed of myself for not opening my eyes to a truth that was given to me. I now realized that there would come a day, in another time and place, when I would be faced with other incredible dilemmas, and like me, an ordinary person with an impossible gift would rise up from the shadows.

I didn't really know what to say. It seemed as though the events of my life were moving along so rapidly as if there was an agenda to maintain. One moment I was alone, and the next I was married. And now, one by one, I would be met by gifted strangers who would know me before I would know them, Ivan being the first. Because we had known each other as children, he was working double time to convince me of his abilities which were powerfully revealed as he dismantled my dream.

With each tangled detail his grim reactions were unconcealable. His senses were awakened with every daunting symbol that obviously spoke of dark and chilling events that were yet to come. To most, the whole thing would seem far-fetched, but he was not like most, having the keen ability to decipher its clouded meaning. As far as I was concerned, his gift was double-edged. I needed to know the truths that were hidden within my subconscious, but to be honest, I was a bit unhinged at the thought of hearing him reveal the realities of my nightmare.

"Miss Beni, through the years my father shared many strange accounts, but your words are like none that I have heard. Before I begin, however, let this account awaken your fortitude, not your fears. Darkness has already been defeated, but unfortunately, we are still poked and prodded by an invisible enemy. Adina's season as the Carrier was also lanced with darkness, but this time that we live in is changing, and is even more tainted by a beastly evil. Past journeys did not often require the powers of my tribe.

"Now, your dream. Faces shrouded in death, doesn't mean that they will die, it means they have already passed to the other side. Malachi and Carson were shown to you in their deathlike state for a twofold purpose. First, saving their lives was not your journey's objective. Secondly, their hour of demise was perfect timing and not to be meddled with. Nothing you could have done would have saved them. Find peace knowing that truth."

"That makes no sense. I mean, I had a shroud over me, and I'm not dead. I don't understand!"

He smiled at me, "Let me finish, miss."

"Everyone will die, but your time is not yet. Because you were both vibrant and shrouded, this part also has two meanings. When you journey as you did, you leave a part of yourself there in that place. What you saw were the fragments of your heart and mind that remained in that time ... that died there with those you cared about. At the same time, the part of you that grew and changed while there, returned - still spirited, still alive. A bit of every individual you meet will return with you; good, bad, or indifferent, they will always be a part of you.

"Now, this next piece is going to be more difficult to hear. This evil player, Halag Sauer, who stands in the yard filled with graves, was destined to die. He should have died on that day of your return. The stone that revealed his name was a symbol of his death, but the dust and cobwebs that consumed it, represent the passing of time. I must warn you Beni, even now, he lives. It is with great regret and tragedy that he marked history with violence and death while cleverly remaining amongst abandoned shadows, unmonitored. The left hand raised signifies an unknown weakness. However, an entire body covered in scarlet means that death pours forth from every part of his being."

For a moment he sat quietly with his head bowed, trying to steady his elevated breathing … inhaling and exhaling ... in and out.

"The four pillars are a foundation of an empire, perfectly balanced. Stones such as these are immovable. This dark force that rises behind him was forged by absolute power, an evil that will rise with a vengeance. Because the pillars exploded through the heavens, once unleashed, the power will be unstoppable ... too late!"

As he trudged through the scattered details, he became wearier, but I didn't know how to help him, until finally he finished. As it ended up, the horrid revelation of it all wasn't the worst part, and I never would have expected in a million years what would come next.

"Miss Beni, I have not only come to walk you through the valley of your dream but to tell you something that will be difficult to hear. Like a rat plagued with disease that narrowly escapes a murky trench and skillfully infects and destroys too many to count, so Halag Sauer emerged from a fated death. The destruction, the evil done throughout his lifetime is vast, but not unfinished. Beni, I'm sorry, I'm so very sorry!"

"Sorry about what? Why are you sorry?"

"You must go back! Until you do, your life will be paralyzed. You have to go back and make certain that there is no breath in his lungs before you return. But here is your encouragement."

If Ivan learned nothing else from the years spent with his father, he learned to commission every revelation with light. Where God was present, there would always be light.

"Beni, look at me!"

I felt broken in half, unable to even lift my eyes in his direction.

"Look at me now! The warrior! You won't be alone in this! I don't know how, or when, but at the most crucial time when all seems lost, a help of titanic proportion, a 'right hand' will rise up from the gloom!"

Chapter 11

The Furthermost

"Without a doubt, I'd rather live the most unordinary and crazed life by your side, with all of the ups and downs that are sure to come, than to have normal without ye!
I adore ye, no matter what! No matter what! That will never change!"
~ Carig Hammel~

I heard his distressing words echo through my mind, but I couldn't fathom that there was any truth to the absurdity. Please Lord, let this be a joke! I could tell, however, by his tense expression, that he was dead serious. With a grief-stricken and panicked cry, I shot up so abruptly that the metal chair tumbled backwards, causing a loud clang as it bounced on the tile floor. Creating a duet of bedlam, Carig exploded through the kitchen doorway, practically ripping the swinging door from its hinges as it side-swiped a large rack of cast iron pans. When my eyes caught his, a swell of emotions flooded over me as I was confronted with the agonizing prospect of returning to Friedlich. The thought of it was killing me, and I knew it would be just as difficult for Carig. My soul ached as if a knife were cutting straight through it, causing me to double over in pain. It was not unlike the summoning misery brought about by the Tempus Vector.

"No Lord, please, I can't go back. I *won't* go back!"

I needed air and had to get out or I would surely keel over and die right in the middle of Mrs. Maple's kitchen. Who cared that my clothes were unsuitable for the frigid temperatures. My holey jeans, sweatshirt, and old Vans tennis shoes would have to do as I raced out the back door. Carig yelled out my name and began running after me, but not before pointing straight at Ivan as if he were about to grab hold of his neck while threatening him not to move from that spot until he could deal with whatever this was. The moment Carig ran out the door, Ivan grabbed his coat and escaped through the front. He'd seen that fury in Carig's eyes before and had no intention of losing any more teeth.

Ivan's calling was unique, but if made known would be

highly sought after, like any great calling. Similar to the Tempus Vector, he would need to take every precaution to keep it safely hidden. His function within the Ten Lost Tribes included the ability to interpret, but also to catch short glimpses of the future. Just recently, many began to judge his quietness, labeling it as rudeness, yet nothing was further from the truth. Most who were well acquainted with Ivan's normal and incessant babbling believed that his uncharacteristic silence was brought about by the overwhelming grief of losing his father. In a way it was. The years spent preparing Ivan to take up where his father would leave off, switched on like a light with the final handful of soil tossed upon the casket. For the well-being of the power to possess unfathomable knowledge, he found that keeping his mouth closed more than opened, served a greater good to a higher purpose. What he didn't expect, and found quite difficult, something his father failed to cover, was the enormous burden that he would bear alongside the Carrier. Perhaps his father knew that nothing except time and experience would prepare him for this particular element of his charge.

Part of what weighed so heavily on Ivan's heart and mind was how his words had upset me, but he also knew that it couldn't be helped. Whether I realized it or not, this so-called stirring of the pot was a necessary evil that would prompt me to move in the right direction. As he drove away, he could see even more vividly his dream involving me coming to life, and he knew that until he someday joined his father, he and I would be bound together within an unbreakable circle of gold.

The snow was waist-deep, and I didn't get very far. The cold air burned as I inhaled, but anything was better than that stuffy kitchen. The fresh crispness of the day eased my agony. Even before I could hear Carig's footsteps crushing through the white powder, I could feel his concern and sense his curiosity of "what now?"

"What's happened, lass? What in the hell was Taggart doing here? What did he say that upset you? I swear I'm gonna kill 'um!"

How would I even begin to tell him what had happened?

"Beni, let's go inside, lass. We're both gonna catch our death!"

I turned around and faced him with tears streaming down my face.

"Carig, are you sorry?"

"Sorry for what, Beni?"

"I … I can do anything … all of this, as long as I know that you're with me. This, our life, everything, is never going to be easy, never! Are you sorry that you married me and that our life will never be ordinary?"

"Without a doubt, I'd rather live the most unordinary and crazed life by your side, with all of the ups and downs that are sure to come, than to have normal without ye! I adore ye, no matter what! No matter what! *That* will never change!"

For those few moments standing together, waist-deep in snow, I felt warm and secure. It was a beautiful reminder that even though surrounded by the harshest conditions, Carig made me feel safe.

"Now lass, let's get inside before everythin' on my lower half completely freezes off!"

When we walked back inside the kitchen, Sharol and George were busy at work preparing the Portland Moose Inn Thanksgiving Feast. Although Sharol was thrilled with her meaty oysters, she and George had clearly been concerned with the earlier kitchen racket that woke them out of a dead sleep, I could tell that they wanted to know what happened but chose not to ask.

"Thank you for takin' in the delivery … and for doin' the potatoes too!"

"You're welcome."

George took one more shot at trying to engage us in conversation as we walked out.

"Hey, you two, breakfast is served in the dining hall between seven and nine! Pumpkin pancakes with Ma Maple's vanilla cinnamon syrup, cottage potatoes, and thick-sliced bacon. We'll see you then!"

Carig took my hand and we headed back upstairs. There was one thing that I knew. If he and I were going to survive all of this, we had to be able to tell one another everything - no secrets! As the door shut behind us, I could tell that he was completely perplexed over what had just happened. I felt the same way. I should have just stayed in bed this morning, discarded my dream as nonsense, and ignored the whole thing. But the idea of hiding my head in the sand was utterly ridiculous. None of this would go away on its own.

The moment we walked in, he held me tightly in his arms,

and spoke softly in my ear.

"I saw the blood on yer pillow … I'm so sorry if I hurt ye, Beni! And then when you weren't there, I was worried!"

"You didn't hurt me at all. Last night was the best, you're the best!"

Carig was concerned. Neither of us wanted any more barriers between us. That was an agreement that we had committed to during the night … no matter how difficult the obstacle, we would face it together. Right now, explaining what I had just discovered would definitely put it to the test.

"Beni, tell me what's goin' on. I have to say that I would have been less shocked to see a room full of leprechauns than Ivan Taggart sittin' there with ye. But then after putting two and two together, I just marked it up to him makin' a delivery for Miss Maple. But there's more, I saw it in your faces. Tell me then, what happened between the two of ye? What is all this?"

He sat down in the chair by the window (the one we had grown fond of in such a short amount of time), once again patting his knee to come and join him. For the next couple of hours we sat there together as I spilled every last detail of my dream, who Ivan had become, and that from this point forward he would be a part of our lives. I struggled to tell Carig the final revelation of my dream. I knew myself well enough to know that until I said it out loud to him, it didn't have to be real. I didn't want to tell him. I didn't want it to be real.

"Is that it then?"

"No, there's one more thing that I can't even believe myself, and I can't hardly stand to say out loud … I don't know if I even can!"

"What could be so bad, Beni? So bad that ye don't wanna tell me?"

I closed my eyes, and leaned my forehead on his, taking one last deep breath.

"I have to go back!"

"Go back where?"

"I have to return to Friedlich, back to that time!"

"Like bloody hell you will! What is this, some kind of joke? I don't trust that … I don't trust him, Beni. All these years he's been a liar and conniver, and now all of a bloody sudden we're gonna believe anything he has to say? No! It's not gonna happen! Why? Why in God's name would you need to go back? Well, Beni? Why?"

My eyes welled up with tears. This was hard enough for me to swallow. I just didn't want to deal with him being angry over something we couldn't change. To make matters worse, the reason I had to return, and how I could possibly accomplish such a thing, swept over me like a tidal wave.

"Tell me!"

"Alrik's cousin, Halag Sauer, the one who gave me these bruises and most likely shot me in the back …"

"What? What about him?"

"I … I have to!"

"Beni, calm down, what do you have to do?"

"He was supposed to die. I have to go back and kill him!"

At first Carig was speechless, and then he began laughing.

"I know that there's nothin' ye can't do, Beni, but I also know ye can't even step on a bug without feelin' guilty. How in the hell are ye gonna kill someone?"

I sat there holding my head in my hands. He was right. I was not a killer. How could I even fathom taking a life, even one as horrid as Halag's?

"Oh Beni, I'm so sorry, lass. Are you sure? Is he sure? Listen, this is what we're gonna do. There's gotta be some mistake here! We're gonna talk to Dr. Dean. He was around Adina and my Gran for years and will know what to do. Don't worry lass, we're gonna figure this out. There's gotta be another way."

He was right. It was one thing to return to Friedlich, but an entirely different situation to kill someone. Dr. Dean was wise and would know what to do.

"Okay, okay. Dr. Dean will know! We'll talk to him after dinner. But what about seeing Annaliese before we leave Portland?"

"Really, Beni? Don't ye think we have enough to deal with right now?"

"Carig, Ivan also told me that Halag is still alive. Somehow, even though he's gotta be ancient by now, he, and possibly Annaliese, are behind the rising of the four pillars that were in my dream, and I'm supposed to see her. She is somehow connected to all of this!"

I went on to explain that the desire to see her was not just a passing fancy in order to return the ruby ring and pearl necklace. Those two trinkets were simply a means to an end. There was a powerful undertone that was summoning me to the Richter Estate, one that I couldn't explain. I told him about Alrik meeting me at the train station when I was a little girl, and that I couldn't help but feel that there was more to it than him just giving me a white wooden horse. He was trying to tell me something. I was caught up in a cloak-and-dagger mindset, and when I said Alrik's name out loud, I could tell that it bothered Carig. Just the sound of his name obviously made his skin crawl.

As he sat there with his head leaning back on the chair and his eyes closed, I wrapped myself around him. It was time to stop with all the talk, everything else could wait.

"You, my love, are my priority, my everything! Don't ever forget it!"

Chapter 12

"Inn" Disguise

"As my eyes moved from one photograph to another, the images came to life - I was once again riding across the meadows, seeing it all for the first time. The dense edge of the Black Forest, swaying grasses filled with wildflowers of every color, and of course, the vast blue waters of the Crystal Himmel, spread from one edge of the glossy paper to the other."
~Benidette Hammel~

The dining room was simple but pleasant, with a long family-style table covered in a sharply pressed cloth, and a cheerful display of pumpkins and fall leaves running down the center. The outer edge of the room was lined with small cafe tables for two, for those of us who wanted a more intimate dining experience away from the gathering. Dividing the lobby from the eating area was an old brick fireplace exploding with colorful flames that danced and crackled. This clever setup provided heat to both sides, which set a warm and welcoming mood after such a cold and blustery evening. There was no need for a breakfast bell, as the glorious fragrance of coffee and pumpkin spice flapjacks permeated every nook and cranny, trumpeting a call to dine.

What with the incoming storm and the darkness of night, I hadn't noticed the vast property that sat behind the inn. Now that daylight had emerged, I could clearly see the glistening snow-covered trees through a remarkable glass wall that ran floor to ceiling. Apparently, this room was only the beginning of the glass curtain expanse. To showcase the exquisite property, including the thick forest of trees, the entire rear side of the inn was made entirely of glass. I was amazed by the complexity of this hokey-titled inn, that was, in fact, a hidden treasure in the middle of nowhere. It was one of those places that most would drive by after perceiving it to be a hole in the wall. In actuality, nothing could be further from the truth.

Sharol was so proud of her venue that she nearly busted the buttons off of her slightly gaudy Thanksgiving sweater and couldn't help but join me in my admiration.

"Beautiful, isn't it? You haven't seen anything until you've seen it in the springtime and summer … glorious, that's what it is! What's even more spectacular is what's beyond the trees. There's a huge grassy pasture, and then beyond that is a crystal blue lake. Once you make your way through the forest, it's like stepping into heaven. Nestled within the trees is our wedding chapel that's notably unique. As far as I know, there's nothing anywhere in the world quite like it. It's a hidden haven to be sure. That's what our brochure says anyway."

"Your brochure?"

"Oh yes, we do weddings and special events here. This is the most sought-after wedding venue on the east coast. We're booked three years out!"

I stood right next to the frozen glass and stared out at the trees. Strangely, the view was familiar, and reminded me of the forest outside of Alrik's property in Germany - one side leading to Friedlich, and the other to the unforgettable crystal blue lake with silver lights showering from the trees.

Sharol returned a few minutes later with a stack of matrimonial literature. On the front of the pamphlet, in scrolled baby blue lettering, was their "Happily Ever After" call to wed.

"Begin Your Tomorrows at Kristall Himmel."

Their gold star promise was to provide a dream-come-true ceremony, commencing with the unique and most coveted bridal extravaganza. The celebrated tradition would begin upon the back of a white stallion. A hushed silence falls over the crowds at the anticipated moment when satin and lace emerged through the brushes of the famous Wilblumen Woods, carpeted in brilliant and colorful wildflowers.

While the grounds were described as something to behold, the chapel was, without a doubt, the crowning jewel of it all. There was a valid reason why this place was booked solid three years out, to primarily daughters of senators and the rich and the famous. It was a meaningful old-world experience where patrons claimed to have been transformed through the sheer beauty that surrounded them on every side. Their experience would begin as they walked through the heavy double doors, serving as transport into the heavenly sanctuary. There were no pictures on the brochure, but it was described as a unique combination of a museum filled with aged portraits framed in gold, whimsical statues dotted throughout the room, and windows of topaz illuminating the black and white checkerboard floor. It boasted of the elegant and unique characteristics that stood on their own, requiring no additional decorations. The inside of the brochure revealed an anonymous and romantic quote engraved on a bronze plate that was attached to a stone pillar centered between the two doors. As tradition dictated, to assure the bride and groom a happy and prosperous life together, they would touch the bronzed sign as they entered. The words written were both romantic and charming to those who brushed their finger across the inscription.

As I began reading this haunting reminder of a man whose grief-stricken life had somehow intertwined with mine, the wedding brochure slipped out of my hands and fell to the floor. Would I ever be free of him? Even though he wasn't here, our lives were somehow entangled and knotted. He was connected to my every pathway, every bend, including this place. I had felt relief upon my return from the land where he dwelt, but now I was faced with the reality of seeing him once again.

Carig picked up the brochure and began reading.

"To the captor of my heart, In life you gave it perfect cadence, but in death it ceased and has refused to endure apart from its cherished companion. When we meet again, my lovely Caprice, if I should be allowed to be with ye again where the angels dwell, I beg you bring life once again to my heart. Nonetheless, it will always belong to you."

Judging by the confused expression on Carig's face, he was troubled by the heartbreaking score.

"Aye, right! That's kind of an odd thing they picked to put on the keystone of the weddin' chapel. It's more like a tragic Romeo and Juliet saga love story where everyone dies, rather than a new life together ... I'd be feelin' cursed from the beginnin' if I got married here!"

IT *WAS* INDEED A TERRIBLY SAD ACCOUNT! Although born into privilege, and provided with endless amounts of money and power, Alrik was forever desperate and alone. How utterly strange it was that a reminder of his personal tragedy so curiously appeared in the most unlikely of places. Whether I liked it or not, his life had permanently connected with mine, and to be perfectly honest, I cared very deeply for him. History books, rumors, and the internet were wrong. Alrik Richter was far more than his vast affluence and abundant possessions. He was smart and passionate, but unfortunately misled by the swastika-saluting Halag Sauers of the world. His now hollow legacy weighed heavily upon my heart.

"Beni ... Beni! Are you okay, lass?"

"Yes, sorry. I guess I'm just tired."

I was Carig's main concern. He discarded the brochure and just held me tightly.

"Yer *my* everythin', Beni! Ye know, whoever it was that wrote that, lived for Caprice like I live for ye. If anything, ever happened to you, my heart would stop as well, and I'd spend the rest of my days longin' to see ye again."

Within the haunting words of despair, Carig was obviously touched by Alrik's pain intertwined with his own worry. Little did he know that both he and I were familiar with the author. But I didn't dare tell him. All of it was a terrible reminder of my past and future journeys.

As the last syllable of her name fell from his lips, his anxious brow furrowed.

"Caprice? Where have I heard that name?"

I wasn't quite sure how to respond as I watched him probe the corners of his mind for an explanation of his recollection. More than likely her name had been tucked within the pages of his exhaustive Google search. He was so preoccupied with Alrik and the unfortunate images of the two of us, that Caprice seemed to slip his mind. For now, I hoped that he wouldn't make the connection. If he realized that the spirit of Alrik Richter was meeting us at every turn, he would most certainly snap.

Just in time to redeem the moment, shafts of sunlight unexpectedly exploded through the massive wall of glass and curiously roused Carig to *come and see*. The beautiful distraction of glistening alabaster that covered the grounds was a welcomed diversion. Whether the stormy ocean, radiant beams raining from darkened clouds, or the vibrant snow-covered ground, Carig's soul couldn't help but be moved by the wonder of God's hand.

"I'm not sure how ye do it, Beni."

"How I do what?"

"Become the core of everything that's beautiful. All of it, everything that's lovely makes me think of you, lass. It always has!"

I was bewitched by his poetic sincerity. He didn't say such things simply to elicit a reaction but meant them wholeheartedly.

As I wrapped my arms tightly around him and began admiring the vast property that surrounded the inn, I almost fell over in disbelief. Although covered in thick snow, it was a near perfect replica of the forest, meadowlands, and lake that was located on the outskirts of the Richter Estate. At first glance I felt like I was losing my mind or maybe the sunlight was playing tricks on my eyes, but then I realized that it was real. For that matter, it was too real and exact to be a coincidence. Keeping my composure was no easy task as I turned around and looked at Sharol in disbelief. She had to know something, but I couldn't yet determine if she was a pawn or a key player in this twisted game.

"Crystal Heaven ... wildflowers?"

Sharol was both surprised and curious at my insight.

"That's right! You speak German?"

"No, not really. I mean just a little! So, Mrs. Maple, I noticed that there aren't any pictures in your brochure. That's kind of odd for a promotional flyer."

"True. But there's a reason. Pictures don't do it justice. Our descriptions are thought-provoking. You have to see it to believe it. A perfect example is how your senses seemed to awaken the moment you looked out the window. But if you insist, Benidette, right over there, on the side table, are a few photos of the venue that somewhat capture the magic."

As my eyes moved from one photograph to another, the images came to life - I was once again riding across the meadows, seeing it all for the first time. The dense edge of the Black Forest, swaying grasses filled with wildflowers of every color, and of course, the vast blue waters of the Crystal Himmel, spread from one edge of the glossy paper to the other.

"Are you okay, Beni? You look a bit pale, lass."

This impossibility had to be some kind of a joke. I frantically bolted past my concerned husband and glared in disbelief at the innkeeper's wife. A million thoughts raced through my mind, yet I had no idea of what to say.

Her eyes connected with mine, and I was set aback by her uncharacteristic silence and strange expression. The voice that could bring sense to my confusion, was now under lock and key, as she turned and walked away. For now, this place and what it all meant, would remain a mystery.

Poor Carig was even more confused than I.

"Take me home, Carig … take me away from this place."

"Aye."

Chapter 13

The Good Doctor

"As the years go by, Beni, you will find that there are two kinds of people in this world, those with a wishbone and those with a backbone. Those who are never satisfied, and those who stand for what is right. If the Tribe of Yosef said it, it's truth and must be carried out."
~Dr. Dean~

The ravages of time had literally taken a toll on both of us. That, along with the strange perplexities of the morning, compelled us to leave. Portland and wait for a different day to fall victim to the eccentricities of Annaliese Richter. I knew that I was destined to see her but dreaded the moment.

The ride home proved to be anything but boring as Carig spilled every detail about his bizarre encounter with the "fair-eyed demon." It pained him greatly to reflect on the box filled with wedding photos, not to mention the deep sorrow he felt on hearing that I was dead. Although difficult, he was thankful that her crazy story of my disappearance was, in reality, a vital clue that I had returned home. Even after Carig had nothing left to say, we kept the conversation going with talk of everything and nothing. Anything was better than discussing the one topic that neither of us wanted to talk about.

I was anxious to speak with Dr. Dean about my conversation with Ivan. At this point, I wasn't real clear about Dr. Dean's connection to Adina, and now me. Whatever part he played in all of this, I felt confident in his wisdom and knowledge. I couldn't fathom the idea of returning to Friedlich and prayed that it was all just a big misunderstanding.

Thanksgiving was already upon us. Although Carig and I had spent many a holiday together, this would mark our first Thanksgiving celebration as a married couple. Even if just for a few moments, we both tried to pretend that our lives were normal. And yet, the still discolored, swollen contusions, and a gunshot wound that refused to stop bleeding were constant reminders that there was nothing normal about my situation.

So, not wanting to upset anyone with the alarming bruises on my neck, I wore one of Adina's turtleneck sweaters to hide the black and blue hand prints that were haunting reminders of Halag's madness. No matter how hard I tried, I couldn't seem to get that man's spiteful accusations and incriminations, nor his raging fury, out of my head. I still had no idea why he detested me so vehemently. Even though he couldn't be too much of a threat at this point, the thought of him still being alive unnerved me. The vision of his wretched face, along with my own disturbing reflection in the mirror, was disheartening.

While Carig was getting ready, I went up to the third story room. I wanted to see the Tempus Vector. This was all new to me. Would there be some kind of message telling me that I had to go back? A different picture? Date? From a distance, I saw it sitting there. It was nothing special really. As a matter of fact, it reminded me of an old piece of kindling that would be better off used as firewood. Holding it in my hands, I noticed that nothing was different - the photo was still the same, except something *had* drastically changed. When I tried to pull out the picture to check the date on the back, I discovered that the photo of Ira's Bakery and the backing of the frame had fused into one solid piece of porcelain. The normal evolution of the Tempus Vector had ceased, unwilling to move until its will had been carried out.

From downstairs, Carig called up to me that it was time to go. Although confused, I set the frame down and begin to walk away, all the while experiencing a cutting feeling sear right through me. Even though I didn't want to admit it, I knew that the pain was but a small reminder that my journey in Friedlich was not yet finished.

As we arrived at Uncle Wil's and Aunt Angelina's house, the notably delicious aroma of turkey, dressing, and pecan pie filled the room. There was just something about walking into their company that made everything seem okay. Sweet Angelina. Her warm smile and open arms made even a stranger feel completely at home. With arms opened wide, she gave us both a great big hug and kiss. It didn't matter that she had worked since the wee hours to prepare such a wonderful dinner, she was ready to serve any and all. Angelina was the quiet spirit that made a huge impact in everyone's life. Even though she had practically put the entire dinner together by herself, it was her deepest desire to take care of everyone else's needs. Like always, she was so beautiful and full of life. Her generous heart shined through in everything she did. Honestly, she was the kind of person inside and out that everyone aspired to be.

Glued to the black-and-yellow versus red-and-white football game on the big screen, I heard Wil and Dr. Dean excitedly screaming out what a horrible call the ref had just made, and then coached the sideline on what the next "smart move" would be.

"Hey, Jaybird! Happy Thanksgiving!"

"Happy Thanksgiving, Wil. Thank you for having us!"

Dr. Dean stood up and walked over to where we were, giving me a gentle hug and Carig a firm handshake.

"Well, you two look like you're doin' a little better than the last time I saw you."

"Yeah, we're doin' better, but Beni's shoulder needs some attendin' to!"

From behind the doctor, a blonde-haired woman with brown smiling eyes, wearing blue jeans and a white t-shirt covered with an autumn-colored apron, walked towards us.

"Ah, Carig and Beni, this is my sweetheart, Mary."

"Hi, you two. So nice to meet you! Sam has told me all about you. Congratulations on your marriage. You have definitely inspired us! Sam and I are thinking about getting married ourselves!"

They embraced one another tightly as they kissed and laughed at their romantic banter.

"Are you kiddin' me? I snatched this beauty up forty years ago and never looked back!"

Both Carig and I just stood there looking at them both with perplexed expressions on our faces, not knowing who this "Sam" was that she was going on about.

"Excuse me, did you say Sam?"

"Yes, Dr. Dean - my Sam!"

Still looking at her in a confused way, Dr. Dean grabbed his bag and pointed me in the direction of the washroom.

"Beni, why don't we go and see how that shoulder of yours is doing?"

Carig grabbed my hand to go with me. He knew that now was the time to seek advice about what Ivan had told me, and what we should do.

"Son, do me a favor, and give me a few minutes alone with Beni. You and I can talk later."

I could tell that Carig wanted to join us, but I reassured him that everything would be just fine, and that I knew what needed to be said.

On our way down the hallway, Dr. Dean opened the cupboard and grabbed a towel.

"Go on in the washroom, take off your shirt, and wrap this towel around you. Holler at me when you're ready!"

He entered the room holding his black leather medical bag. One after the other, he began pulling from it each needed instrument, carefully placing them on the vanity.

"Let's first take a look at your throat."

After a lengthy examination with a small light, he gently rubbed his fingers over the bruises on my neck.

"Well, kiddo, I know it's still uncomfortable, but I'm very pleased with your progress. This kind of thing takes time, but you're comin' right along."

As he was only inches from my face, I stared at him in deep contemplation.

"Dr. Dean, I'm confused about something. I thought your name was Ray?"

"It is, Beni. Raymond Samuel Dean."

After he spoke the first, middle and last, he took a step back and watched as the clues unfolded.

"Are you ...?"

"Am I who, Beni?"

"Are you the little boy in Adina's story? Are you Samuel? Lost Samuel, that she failed?"

"Yes, I am Samuel, and Adina didn't fail me, but saved my life when I was nine years old!"

"But I thought the last thing that she heard before she left that journey was Mary yelling out that you were dead. Wait ... Mary ... Mary from the story, you married her!"

"I certainly did. She and I grew up together - we were always meant to be together. Kinda like you and Carig!"

"Oh my gosh, this is remarkable! But tell me, what happened to you in that old Indian graveyard? How in the world did you escape alive?"

"There is far more to this story, to your story, than you even know. Probably even more than you'll be able to comprehend at this moment. I've been waiting for just the right time to tell you. I started to the other day, but you just weren't in the right mindset to hear it."

I could tell that whatever Dr. Dean needed to tell me, was monumental. He was generally a confident, straightforward kind of man, and I could see that he was struggling to get this out. He leaned against the wall, and not only told me the rest of *his* story but a different beginning to mine.

"You see, Beni, when Adina found me, I had crawled into an old abandoned tunnel that was used during the Underground Railroad Movement. I went to the one place my daddy told me to never go because I was so mad at him for takin' the switch to me. The whole way to that graveyard, I mocked the evil spirits that he said lived there, sayin', 'I'd rather live in that old graveyard with a bunch of old dead Indians, than with the meanest dad in the world.'"

He laughed at himself and shook his head, remembering how stubborn he was.

"Yep, I had it all figured out and didn't need nobody! I had my knapsack filled with two apple fritters and a canteen of milk, swearin' that I would rather die than go back home. I wasn't that scared, that is, in the daylight. But when the sun went down and wind began to howl, my nine-year-old eyes started seein' Indian ghost spirits roamin' around those plots. Quicker than a jackrabbit, I opened up the tunnel door and crawled in. If my presence didn't wake up the dead, the sound of my chattering teeth sure did. I fell asleep in that cold tunnel, praying that if the Lord would save me from all the bugaboos, I'd go straight home at sunrise and apologize to my daddy.

"Slivers of light breaking through the wood door above me only confirmed that my time in this world was short, because to my great dismay, they illuminated the floor around me which was moving in all directions. Over and again I squeezed my eyes shut hoping that the stirring before me wasn't real, but it was. Snakes! Everywhere, all around me were snakes! The floor was winding and twisting into an entanglement of fang-filled knots. I couldn't believe that I was sittin' in the middle of a bunch of rattlers. They were crawlin' up all over me, and I dared not move. I don't know how long I sat there, not even movin' a finger! Completely ensnared by the wriggling demons that were slitherin' all over me, I wet myself, but I didn't care. I said every prayer that I knew, hopin' that I would somehow get out of that tunnel alive. As day turned into night, all I could do was wait. There was no yellin' for help, no out of the ordinary movements or gestures. If I even blinked, I'd be a goner. I was convinced without a doubt, that I would die there, and all I could do was pray.

"Now the next morning it was so cold that the snakes were very still. I decided that no matter what, I had to try to get out of there. While they were dormant was the time to make my escape. Slowly, like a snail on a tomato plant, I moved my hands up towards the door in order to push it open. I thought I was home free, doin' okay until I sneezed. I couldn't hold it in! After letting out an unstoppable sputtering breath of air, several of my slithering guards arched up and struck me with the fierceness of fire. Unbeknownst to me, I had been bitten five times, and it was *only* by the grace of God that I didn't die within a few minutes.

"The next thing I remember, an old man of foreign origin, like from Arabia or something, was carrying me home with Mary by his side. You see, when Adina disappeared, this man showed up and approached my very upset Mary, who was yelling for help. Mary believed that all hope was lost when she saw the massive knot of snakes. She knew that there was no way to help without putting herself in grave danger. Suddenly, from out of nowhere, she watched as this old man walked right down into the pit of snakes, grabbed me up, and pulled me out. At that point, she was hysterical, and kept asking him if I was dead. All he told her was not to fear, that I was only sleeping. Then she watched in awe as he laid his hands on the swollen bite marks and chanted words under his breath with head bowed. All I remembered feeling was a rustling warm wind encircling my arms and legs."

Lifting up his shirt sleeves and pant leg, he showed me the scars that still served as reminders of his brush with death. They resembled marks of a burn victim.

"So, wait, Adina found you, but this man really saved your life, right?"

"Right! But that's only the *beginning* of the beginning of my story. Afterwards, I was inspired to become a doctor ... to heal and help people. My folks couldn't afford to send me to the university, so I joined the military like my daddy, but I chose the Navy because they offered to put me through medical school. It was, and still is, my life's passion to help and heal. Even before I was done with my schoolin', I received orders to report to a city in Vietnam, called Saigon. They had a shortage of doctors, and anyone with a pulse and some medical training was forced to go. Talk about bein' baptized by fire! Day and night, we worked in the worst conditions, seein' things that I'll never forget.

"One day, our canvas hospital was bombed and attacked. Within seconds, it was reduced to a bloodied mass of wounded, with legs and arms blown completely off, and I laid among them. The enemy barreled through, stabbing both disabled and dead alike with their bayonets. There was nothing that anyone could do except lay there and wait for them to come. Completely helpless, I watched as my brothers in arms were being murdered. It was a senseless act of brutality, mankind at its very worst."

Even though this horrible event had occurred so long ago, it remained a source of raw anguish that brought him to tears.

"Screams everywhere ... a gruesome massacre. I remember lying there with my head bleeding, and blood pouring from my leg, thinking once again, this is it! The snakes didn't kill me, but I'm going to die here. For the second time in my life, something extraordinary happened. Similar to the time when I was a little boy in that tunnel, I was rescued. Someone showed up from out of nowhere, grabbed hold of me, and then dragged me out of the tent. Within the hazy dream, I could see men all around me impaled and gushing with blood, faint screams as if they were far away. I could see the enemy looking right at me, but then turning away as if I were invisible, and that was the last thing I remember. Several days later I woke up in a makeshift shelter somewhere in the jungle. As I sat up, I saw a man at the entrance as if he were guarding me. I yelled over to him, asking where I was, and when he turned around and I saw his face, I nearly fell over dead! I remembered him! It was the man who saved me from the pit of snakes when I was a little boy, but he was older of course."

"Wow, that is quite a story, but what part of it has to do with me?"

"Let me ask you something, Beni. When you were first informed about the power of the Tempus Vector, what were you told?"

"Well, Adina's letter from Malachi said that the Tempus Vector was the pinnacle of the Ten Lost Tribes. Mine, Adina's, and Malachi's callings represented the Lost Tribe of King Solomon, the king of wisdom."

"And what else?"

"Let's see, that a photograph would appear at the time and place where the Carrier needed to go in order to correct a flaw in history."

"What else?"

"I don't, I don't know what else. What do you mean?"

"Beni, I know that both Malachi and Adina told you that none of this would be easy, but what did they tell you from the very beginning?"

I didn't know what he wanted me to say, or what he was getting at.

"Beni, think!"

I closed my eyes, trying to concentrate and focus on what he was asking me, and then two words came to the forefront of my mind.

"Never Alone!! They said that I didn't need to be afraid, because I would never be alone! Which I guess is true. Those were among the first words that Malachi ever spoke to me that day at the airport when I was traveling to Bar Rousse. I don't know how, but he was there you know, and he told me that I would never be alone!"

"Right, that's exactly right! Beni, your gift, being the Carrier of the Tempus Vector, is the heartbeat of the Ten Lost Tribes. Without the wisdom you hold, nothing can be accomplished! Every effort from the nine others, begins with you."

"Wait! Are you ...?"

"Listen carefully. The tasks that Malachi, Adina, and those before them accomplished were so pivotal to the welfare of the world and the societies within it ... far more crucial than you'll ever know. What you hold is key. I am one of those that Adina and Malachi spoke of who will be here to help you, that has been given divine gifts and abilities to help in times of trouble."

Somehow, I felt a greater comfort knowing that Dr. Dean was on my side, even more so than the young and inexperienced Ivan. Two of the Ten Lost Tribes had suddenly become tangible.

"Beni, like a single day, take one thing at a time, and the thing you can know for today is that I'm here and *will be* as long as I'm called. Also, just know that there are others who will reveal themselves to you when the right time comes."

I told him that just this morning another of the ten had been revealed to me. Even though he had said others would come, he appeared stunned that it had happened so quickly.

"Who might that be?"

"Well, before I tell you about him, tell me what you are!"

Dr. Dean grinned from ear to ear and laughed at me.

"Beni girl, I'm just flesh and blood, and like you, have been given a task."

"What's your task?"

"Well, remember the man who saved me from the snakes and Vietnam?"

"Yes!"

"He took care of me until I was well enough to leave. But before I did, he placed his hand on my head and recited a blessing over me. He then handed me a stone made of wood and bronze called the Petra-Fero. My calling was assumed from the Lost Tribe of Moses and is only given to one who had the abilities to heal and the heart to help."

Dr. Dean then grabbed ahold of his walking staff. The pendant that was attached at the handle was a petrified piece of dark wood, resembling a crudely shaped heart, covered with tarnished bronze markings that, at first, made no sense - until I got a closer look at it. The bands of gold alloy began as twisted roots of a tree, then exploded into branches. Rising up from the center of the tree was a bronze snake wrapped around a thick shaft, clearly the sign of one who had been given the power to heal and mend.

"My ability is meant to heal those who are hurt, but to also restore what is broken. Sometimes that means a *person* who is sick or hurt, and other times it means restoring or saving *a people* who otherwise would die out. There's something that you need to know … I was there with you, Beni."

"Where? When were you with me?"

"In Germany, I was there after you had been strangled. The moment death called your name, it called mine as well, and I was carried to your side. It was me who came into your room in a gust of wind and healed you to the point that you were able to go forward and finish your task. It was through the wisdom of the Tempus Vector that Adina found me when I was a boy, but the Bearer of the Petra-Fero healed and saved me so that I could be here yesterday, today, and tomorrow to help the Carrier."

"That was you? How come you didn't let me know who you were?"

Again, he smiled.

"You weren't ready, and besides, it would have scared you to death if you had seen me walk into your room."

"I suppose so."

"Now, tell me about this person you've met."

I told him about Ivan Taggart, son of the master trawler and fisherman of the Bar Rousse and Portland communities. Dr. Dean had several encounters with Joseph but didn't know that his calling had been passed down to his youngest and didn't seem all too thrilled about it.

"Well, that oughta be interesting! Are you okay, Beni?"

"Not really. I'm trying to stay positive, but after what I heard today, I'm really struggling."

"What'd you hear?"

His question led straight back to Ivan Taggart, from the Tribe of Yosef, who, after listening to my dream, told me that I must return to Friedlich and kill a man, an evil man, in cold blood.

"Dr. Dean, please tell me that he's wrong and that I don't have to go back! I can't, I just can't do it! I can't kill somebody! That's too much to ask!"

It was obvious that he longed to tell me what I wanted to hear, but that authority didn't belong to him.

The answer to my dilemma would only come from one place, and it was not audible, but physical. At that moment I was suddenly plagued by a wave of agonizing affliction in the pit of my stomach, and I knew that what Ivan had said was true. I would have to go back.

Dean tried to be encouraging, but I was devastated.

"Beni, listen to me. Whatever comes, you will be given the strength and wisdom to deal with it then. You must have faith! Try and focus on the blessings."

"Blessings? I'm not trying to be disrespectful, but I'm

having a hard time seeing blessings in any of this. Honestly, all of it seems more like a curse."

"Beggin' your pardon miss, but the time has come for you to take your eyes off of yourself and buck up. If you do, you'll see more blessings than trials. Do you really believe that you've done all of this alone? Let your eyes be opened to an army of angels that encamp around you. Have faith, Beni! If you don't, *you* will be your worst enemy."

Once again, I asked the doctor if all of this could really be true ... if I had to go back.

"As the years go by Beni, you will find that there are two kinds of people in this world, those with a wishbone and those with a backbone, those who are never satisfied, and those who stand for what is right. If the Tribe of Yosef said it, it's truth, and must be carried out."

"And what if I say no?"

"That unsettling ache that you feel at this very moment will only grow more intense, and with it you will become more unsettled."

"I don't feel anything, so I guess it's not time."

Dr. Dean had been around long enough to know when he was being lied to. Just since we'd been talking, I winced twice, not because of the pain in my shoulder. He knew exactly what was going on and told me that when I was ready to reopen this discussion, he'd be there.

Brimming with excitement over the holiday festivities, Carig burst into the room to let us know that dinner was served. Thanksgiving was his favorite holiday, and I wanted to bring as much joy into his life as he brought into mine, but it seemed that with me came heavy-laden issues.

"Hey you two, Uncle Wil's carvin' the wishbone. He got a beauty!"

As I walked out, Carig gave me a hug and held me tight.

"How's yer shoulder, lass? Did ye ask him about the whole Ivan thing?"

"It's good, he's definitely got a healing touch! There really wasn't a chance to ask, so I'll ask him later. Let's eat! And then you and me ... it's wishbone time!"

Although it didn't come easily at this particular moment, I

tried to do what the doctor had suggested. Stop thinking about myself and what was to come, and to live in the moment and just focus on the blessings of my journey. I had so much to be thankful for. The room was filled with delicious food, and lighthearted joy and laughter from those I loved most in the world. Why was my soul so distraught within me? How would I ever survive this calling if I held on so tightly to every person I encountered and every story I invaded? Aside from returning to Friedlich, thoughts of Alrik and the extraordinary pieces of his life that he had left behind were consuming me. And then there was Annaliese. I half wished that Carig hadn't told me *everything* about her. It was difficult to fathom how such a sweet little girl with such a doting father could go completely off the rails.

Chapter 14

The Blistering Vengeance of Annaliese Richter

"All these years later, up walks a haggis-eating Scot no less, who's supposedly married to your vanishing bride."
~Annaliese Richter~

Although peaceful sleep never came easily to Annaliese, her second scuffle with Carig would throw fuel onto her already-raging insomnia. Uncomfortable tossing and turning, teemed with ceaseless moments of harrowing nightmares, uprooted events that were hidden deep within the recesses of her mind. She woke up in the late hours of the morning to the distressing sound of her papa crying out for Beni, as he often did. She frantically rose from her covers, throwing on her old terry cloth robe while returning whispers of comfort that only she could hear. In haste, she hurried into the kitchen to ignite the kettle for peppermint tea. Tea would always soothe him. Amidst the bustling, she suddenly stopped as she observed his empty chair. Not moving her sights from his sitting area across the table from hers, she once again realized that the echoes of his voice were all in her mind. Her father had been dead for seventeen years now, and as time passed, a ghost of her own making sat faithfully on the opposite side of the kitchen table. At first her conversations were one-sided and irrational. But as of late, the voice of Alrik Richter roamed within each turn, filling every corner of reasoning to insanity.

Reluctantly sitting down, hoping to escape the tomb of memories that endlessly chased her, she began fiddling with the strangely shaped lid that sat upon the silver sugar bowl. Somehow on the journey from Germany, the lid from her mother's set had been bent and never sat quite right. She had attempted many times to restore it, but it only became more contorted. Although small and insignificant, that crooked lid reminded her of herself.

Her mind wandered to the events of last night. She replayed the encounter with Carig over and again, and with it rose an uncontrollable fury. It was *his* fault! His absurd inquisition regarding Beni caused her to spiral out of control. Then her emotional outburst and ugly threats had transformed her into an object of deranged indifference. Even recalling the sickening image of the panicked Scot searching for *her* became a breeding ground for rage. Once again, the person of Beni would mutate her faded and bloodshot stare into a further madness.

From silence to insanity, she belted out an inappropriate laugh. Because Carig returned a second time even after experiencing her wretched and disturbing behavior during their first encounter, she somehow believed that she owned him. He was the horse, Beni was the bit in its mouth, and she was the rider. This red-haired man was just as infatuated as her papa, and it infuriated her. She had watched him closely as he trudged through the snow towards his car, all the while thinking that the only humane thing to do would be to gun him down and put him out of his misery. He was pathetic, just like her father who was ruined by the many years of torment and suffering over losing the same person that Carig now sought.

"Well, Papa, it appears that you were right. Until now, I didn't believe in your insane quest. I still haven't seen her yet though … maybe *he* pursues her just as you did, but in reality, she doesn't even exist at all! Damn you both! I thought I was free of all of this the day you died. That I was finally rid of her and set free from your never-ending search. But all these years later, up walks a haggis-eating Scot no less, who's supposedly married to your vanishing bride.

"Do you think she's really alive? Poor, poor thing! I'd say

he's about the same age that you were when she disappeared, and so handsome too. You must be rolling over in your grave right about now! I'd say … late twenties, wouldn't you? Yes! The exact same age as you were when she destroyed you! Now, assuming that he's not married to a ninety-year-old, it can mean one of two things. Either the girl never ages, or as you always believed, she somehow visited us and then vanished into thin air by means of a power of biblical proportion. I'm not terribly interested in either of them, but *power* such as this would make it all worthwhile, would it not?

"I have one question for you, Papa - one that I never got an answer to. Why were you so devoted to someone who left you hanging? I gave you my whole life, was always here, never left you. I don't understand. She gave you minutes, and then stole your heart leaving only a shell for me to deal with. Yet you chased her with your whole heart. I hate you with every fiber of my being, and I will forever despise her!"

From her pocket, Annaliese pulled out a black and white photograph of her father dressed in the finest uniform of the day, young and handsome. Holding it with both hands, only inches from her face, she stared intensely into his eyes.

"Congratulations, Field Marshal Richter! This is the day that you always hoped for, and the one I have forever dreaded. You are the weakest man I have ever known, allowing your heart to direct your life! We should have never left Germany! You were once a great man, a great German who could have made the difference in the Motherland becoming the world power that it was meant to be, that it will still be. Halag believed that Germany's dominion was foreseeable, but men such as you, a flawed member of a pure bloodline who was selected for greatness, failed miserably!"

Annaliese was so distracted by her one-sided and bitter-filled discussion, that she forgot about the unattended kettle of water on the fire that was now bubbling over and filling the room with steam. With a lack of urgency concerning the murkiness, she casually strolled over to the fire that was blazing on the stove. Her moods varied like the wind, and anxiety quickly replaced her fury, as she had been forced to confront the resurrection of Benidette Crawford.

"Know this, Papa, I will destroy her, just as she did me!"

Glancing down at the gold pendant watch that was hanging from a long chain around her neck, she anxiously became aware of the time, and began making preparations for afternoon tea. She pulled a serving tray from the cupboard and arranged an archaic floral tea set laced in Bavarian gold and crimson red, on the mahogany platter. As she had many times before, she transferred the steaming water from the kettle into the carafe, then tossed in an infuser filled with Ostfriesen leaves. From the tin sitting on the counter, she scooped up the blueberry scones and placed them on a dish, arranging them on her porcelain ensemble. With a wanton and slightly eerie grin on her face, she picked up the heavy tray and slowly headed down the long hallway to the furthest room in the house.

Photographs lined the hallway, mostly of herself riding her prized stallion as a young girl. There was a time when the wall displayed one photo after another of Benidette and her father, but those had been gone for years and had since been replaced by others of Annaliese's choosing. The discarded photographs that now sat in a box stuffed below a chair seat, were not only salvaged from the dumpster after her father's final rampage but were kept only as a chronicle of events, *not* for sentimental reasons. It was difficult to grasp the impact of the faded exposures, and how they had traveled through time to this place, revealing an unnamed ability that somehow stretched across countless years and lives.

Towards the end of the small gallery, there, hanging next to the bedroom door, was a black and white photograph of her Uncle Halag in uniform standing next to a black sedan that was proudly displaying Nazi banners. It revealed a time in his life when he felt that victory was assured and there was nothing that could stop him or the destiny of the Motherland. But he too lay victim to the intrusion of Benidette Crawford.

As Annaliese stared at the staunch image, she recalled a far different version of him, so long ago, lying in a pool of mud, with a bloodied gash in the center of his back. When she approached her wounded uncle and glanced back to see who held the pistol, there were hundreds of gawking guests who turned a blind eye to the horrific scene. Though she tried, she couldn't make out who the shooter might be. She ran to his aid, grabbed his face and turned it out of the mud, using her dress to smear away the muck.

"Are you alive, Uncle?" she cried.

But there was no response, no movement. All she could hear

was her father screaming out for Beni, paying no attention to his fallen cousin. Even Halag's own flesh and blood didn't care.

Everyone hated Halag and only put up with him because of his relation to the Field Marshal of Germany. They were indifferent to his survival, but not Annaliese. The two of them had always shared a loyal connection. His devotion to her was unusual. Halag was always ready to bow out of the grown-up world and enter into hers. During her papa's frequent and extravagant balls, filled to overflowing with adults who objected to her presence, he would grab her up in his arms and dance unashamedly in the center of the ballroom even though causing a scene. He spent more time with her than almost anyone else. As with her mother, he adored spending time with his niece; her sweet smile and beautiful blue eyes reminded him of Caprice. Aside from their amusing duets on the dancefloor, he also taught her the art of riding, which became *one* of the passions of her life.

She never understood how the crowd could turn a blind eye to her most cherished friend and uncle who had been shot in cold blood. Although still gripping tightly to the smoking pistol, she would always consider Halag to be the innocent victim of an American intruder. As the onlookers began to disperse, and to Annaliese's dismay, she was finally able to distinguish the master of the weapon who had gunned down her uncle. In a hundred years she would have never suspected Dr. Carson. He had always been so kind, one of her favorite people, but in the blink of an eye, he had become a different person. She was shocked by the raging fury on his face. With his arm still extended, ready to fire again at even the twitch of a movement, one might have believed that his attack was personal.

Her despised uncle survived, but once the Third Reich discovered that he was paralyzed from the waist down and would spend the rest of his life in a wheelchair, they had no use for such a liability. When he heard that he was being transferred to Oranienburg (just north of Berlin) for more tests, he knew that his life was over - very aware that the asylum was home to brutal experiments done mostly on Jews and criminals, any and all that were viewed as flawed. These medical trials were all in the name of "good medicine." Good medicine and techniques that could save the lives of those in the higher order and faithful German soldiers who had fought for their country. For months, Halag lived there and was probed and ceaselessly used as lab experimentation. One day, in a moment of hopelessness as he was lying lifeless in his bed, an idea came to him that would prove to be his salvation.

Calling for the attendant, he demanded to speak to the head of the Gestapo.

"Tell him that I have information for the Fuhrer. Simply say the word *Enoch,* and he will know of what knowledge I speak."

As fully expected, he was visited by menacing leather coats who brutally interrogated him. He held nothing back, telling them much of what he knew about Benidette, such as the fact that he surveyed first hand her miraculous disappearance into thin air. After dangling that most enticing piece of information like a carrot, he refused to tell them any more. After much negotiation, they agreed to reinstate him as a member of the Third Reich, and make him the new Field Marshal, giving him all power, authority, and assets of the former. They agreed *only* if what he said was of interest to the Fuhrer.

When the arrangement was final, he instructed them to pull the hidden box from beneath the bed. At first, they resisted and became angry at what seemed to be a game, until he spilled the last detail about the secret compartment that held a frame - a frame that had the power to transport this girl to another time. He continued, telling them that shoe store "Schuh Coffee" was where he initially found her, and the shoebox bearing the same name held the frame that was secretly sent to her while staying at the Field Marshal's home. He went on to explain that the old shoemaker, Malachi, most certainly held the key to what they sought. When walking away with the container in hand, they heard something clanging inside. After several attempts at opening the puzzle-like box, they discovered several gold coins.

"What is this?"

He reluctantly informed them that those two pieces of gold were sold to the jeweler by this same woman, and the symbol that was deeply embossed was an emblem of the power. He wasn't sure how, but he knew that the coins were but a piece in the puzzle. Fully aware that his efforts would most likely go unnoticed, he reminded them, practically begged them, to make sure that they told the Fuhrer who he was, and not to forget about him.

Annaliese wasn't clear on the details after that point, but she did know that Halag wasn't released from Oranienburg until the war was over. He spent years there, simply because when the small army arrived at Schuh Coffee and proceeded to tear the store apart, nothing of interest was found.

Balancing the tray while quietly pushing the door open with her foot was no easy task for an old and tired woman. The room was dark, causing additional stress as she tried to maneuver through. When finally, she found the hospital table standing in the far corner, she was relieved. As always, she would open the venetian blinds just slightly to allow a gentle glow of light to fill the stuffy chamber. She stepped slowly and lightly as she returned back to the afternoon tea composition, and proceeded to create an artful medley of sorts, beginning with one cube of sugar, followed by a generous measure of cream. An experienced chemist in the art of umber brew, she streamed the well-steeped tea over the creamy concoction with exactly three stirs in a counterclockwise motion.

At first glance, this room would most certainly be construed as a sterile infirmary, as its only piece of furniture other than the table in the corner was a single hospital bed sitting against the wall opposite the window, with only a wheelchair as its companion. Like clockwork, each morning, afternoon, and evening Annaliese attended to the disheveled gentleman who lay day after day in the confines of this somewhat hidden room. The aged, practically primitive-looking man had very little hair, blotchy skin, and was extremely thin and frail. She held down the button that would prop the bed into a sitting position, and then rolled the small eating table directly in front of him. Placing the cup of tea and one blueberry scone within his reach, she broke off a tiny piece of his favorite pastry and placed it in his mouth. As she refused to make eye contact, he cleared his throat loudly to gain her attention.

She took a deep breath and prepared herself to divulge the impending information about the long-awaited visit.

"He came back, Father, just as you said he would."

Laboring to finish the bite of pastry, he spoke out with a raspy voice.

"What did he say?"

"He wanted to know if Benidette was here, *here in this house*! What does that mean? Why would he come here?"

The corners of the old man's mouth that seemed to be a permanent frown, slowly bent up into a twisted smile.

"It means that she survived."

"How do you know that? She wasn't with him, and he was hell-bent on finding her!"

Struggling to take a deep breath, the old man motioned for a sip of tea, and was incapable of answering her question for a time, until finally catching his breath.

"When last he came, my dear, he was seeking assurance that she was even still alive. Until that point, none of us knew if she had survived. Think, my daughter, of all that we have uncovered together! You know that there is only one origin of return, and it is not here. *Yes*, she has returned and *lives*. What should have killed her, though, was overridden by a greater power, the power I covet! She will be back, I know she will. Because she left so abruptly, abandoning a portion of her heart, she has no choice but to heed the voice of her calling. This declaration is like a *tolling bell* to her, like a mighty timepiece that is furiously calling her back to the young Field Marshal. He, along with the damned of that day, captured her heart. She will never rest until she knows what has become of them. I suspect that she is filled with great conflict and will come *here* looking for answers. When she does, you know what you must do. It's my last hope. Bring her to me."

Unable to speak another word, he turned his head and longingly fixed his eyes on the shrouded wall directly across from his bed. He knew that what lay beneath it held the solution to his paralyzing enigma.

Chapter 15

Brush with Surrender

*"How does one keep their mind occupied when it's
completely consumed by another?
Every fiber of my being ached for him, consumed to the
point that my soul cried out.
I was unsure if my inward distress was caused by the
calling of the Tempus Vector
or by a far deeper commitment of my heart."*
~Benidette Hammel~

It was difficult to remain lighthearted and engage in the festivities. There is nothing worse than a wet blanket to dampen everyone's mood, and I didn't want to be that person. Although the prompting of the Tempus Vector was prodding at my gut like a cow to the slaughter, I was determined to enjoy this time with my family. In the worst way, Dr. Dean ached to tell me what I wanted to hear - that all of this was a big mistake and I wouldn't need to return, but we both knew the truth.

He had earlier encouraged me with snippets of wisdom from my Aunt Adina.

"If she were here Beni, you know what she'd say! '*Pretend this is an adventure, smack dab in the middle of your favorite novel. Embrace the excitement and don't let fear dictate your life. Remember, fear is your greatest enemy! If you saw a dangerous foe approaching your house bent on destruction, would you invite him in? Of course not! You'd bolt the door and close tightly the windows, not allowing him to enter, ever!*'"

Obviously troubled, the doctor watched me from across the table with laser focused concern. As his intense stare met mine, I suddenly sensed a charge of warmth move through me, awakening a boldness that had been absent until that moment. His gift of healing obviously had even more dimensions than I realized. From the deeply-rooted passion of his own calling, he was somehow able, through a mere look, to remind me of who I was, and the incredible power that was at my disposal.

Just short of a miracle, my perspective was beautifully transformed, and was now one of blessedness rather than dread. With the eyes of my soul no longer focused on my dilemma, my heart overflowed with gratitude for this sweet time with my family. I was so thankful for each one of them, especially for my husband. I still couldn't believe that I was married to this magnificence of a man with green eyes, auburn hair, and a heart of gold. What did I ever do to deserve someone like him? Somehow my awakened resolve created an overwhelming joy, even in regard to my calling. The worry, fear, and pain, for now anyway, had been replaced with quiet confidence.

As it turned out, our first Thanksgiving was a mixed bag of perfection. Uncle Wil was the life of the party with his precisely-timed jokes and contagious laughter. Angelina glowed with satisfaction at her culinary delights. She was a wizard in the kitchen, everything flawlessly flavored and steaming hot. Then of course there was *us, the honeymooners*, still in la-la land. Our interlaced fingers dancing beneath the table, together with Carig's amorous Gaelic whispers, sent shivers up my spine. All of it played to the backdrop of college football cheers and chatter that was roaring from the big screen made for the best Thanksgiving I could ever remember. I didn't want any of it to end. If only for a moment, we were the most normal of families discussing tomorrow's Black Friday deals rather than the reality of what was on the horizon.

While helping Angelina and Mary wash up the dishes, I noticed Carig and the doctor talking in the back room. It was obvious by Dean's exaggerated gestures and Carig's irritated stance that they were having *the talk* ... confirming my imminent journey back to Friedlich. Until that moment, Carig believed it all to be a big misunderstanding, just like I did. There was no easy way of delivering the finality of it all, but the doctor was doing his best to cool the heated situation. In spite of his efforts, it wasn't sitting well. I understood Carig's frustration, but there was nothing that any of us could do to change it. His out-of-character temper tantrum was wearing on Dean, and in his no-nonsense doctor fashion, he quickly advised Carig to "calm the hell down."

"Listen here son, if you and Beni are ever going to survive this, you *both* have to start treating this like a job ... a secondary occupation, *not* the center of your lives. So far, you both have allowed *it* to become the focal point of everything."

In normal situations, advice from such a wise man would be heeded, but there was something very *abnormal* about my stiff-necked and jaw-clenching husband. Even the way Carig glanced down at Dean's hand as it squeezed his shoulder reminded me of a dog that was about to snap. Something very odd was going on with him. Even the doctor recognized it.

Mary had obviously been *filled-in* on the seriousness of their conversation, and when she saw Carig standing alone, she grabbed my dish towel and urged me to step in.

"Go check on him, Beni. I'll finish drying the dishes."

As I walked towards him, I could see that his mind wasn't here at our gathering, but in another world entirely. He was unresponsive to my presence as I wrapped my arms around him, and by his elevated breathing, I knew that it wasn't grief that held him captive, but anger.

"Are you ready to go, Beni?"

"Sure."

Like a rogue wave rising before a desperate ship, a wall had once again come between us, but this barrier was all too familiar. It reminded me of the one made of money and power that divided my father and me. My entire life was spent walking on eggshells around the *first* love of my life, and I had no intention of once again allowing such nonsense. My days and years spent in Bar Rousse had always been in a place of safety, but this attitude I was feeling from the heart I loved and trusted, bothered me more than anything else ever could, even the reality of returning to Friedlich.

The silence was deafening as we drove home. Why was he mad at me? This wasn't like him … *at all,* and I couldn't figure out what was driving this behavior. I understood his disappointment, I felt the same way, but we had talked through my unusual calling at the inn. We agreed, that whatever would come, we would get through it *together*. Were those just words said in a moment of passion?

Pulling up to the house and screeching to a halt, Carig stormed out of the car and headed straight to the tower, leaving me once again on my own. Even though I needed him to follow through on his promise, he left me. Normally I would have raced after him and given him a *what for,* but a small voice within me confirmed that something was possessing him.

Until the frigid wind began cutting through every layer of my garments, I stood waiting on the porch staring up at the platform toward the top of the lighthouse, hoping he would come back down, and we could work through whatever this was. As it turned out, my waiting was futile.

How does one keep their mind occupied when it's completely consumed by another? Every fiber of my being ached for him, consumed to the point that my soul cried out. I was unsure if my inward distress was caused by the calling of the Tempus Vector or by a far deeper commitment of my heart. Although I tried to stay awake, I fell into a deep sleep; the Lord calmed my spirit, knowing all too well that I needed the rest.

Minutes turned into hours as I woke to the blunt chopping sound coming from outside my window. The pale blue sheers were filled with the silhouette of Carig wildly chopping wood, *no, frantically* chopping as if his life depended on it. Although it was freezing, he had worked up a sweat, obviously trying to work out his frustrations. Time spent in the tower obviously didn't alleviate his frustrations. I was concerned about him, but at the same time, lingering in the back of my mind was the flashing reminder that I had to see Annaliese. It was imperative I visit her before returning to Friedlich. I didn't know why exactly, other than the shedding of light on my imminent journey. It was my hope that Carig would go with me to see her, but at this point, I didn't want to ask anything of him. He was so worked up, and I thought it best to walk away from his current state of madness.

By the time I got outside, he had ripped apart every last piece of wood and was resting on the stump, trying to catch his breath. I would have done anything to ease his pain, to let him know that no matter what, I was there for him.

"Good morning, mon amour!"

"Beni ... good morning, lass!"

"Are you okay?"

"I am now that I see you! Where ye off to?"

"Portland ... Annaliese."

"I don't think it's a good idea, I really don't. I'm not sure what happened to her, but it's not safe."

He undoubtedly knew by the expression on my face that I

was going, and *nothing* he could say would change my mind.

"Give me ten minutes to shower, lass. I'm goin with ye!"

"Alright, I'll wait for you in the car."

As he headed back to the house, I yelled out for him to wait. He turned around a bit flustered as he was in a hurry. I marched right up to him, held his face in my hands, and kissed him as if it were the last kiss I would ever give him.

"I'm all sweaty, Beni!"

"I know, but I don't care, I like it! I missed you last night!"

Carig didn't know exactly how to respond, as I spun around, and headed to the car, giving him one last glance that would hopefully light a fire.

Within ten minutes, both he and the fragrance that drove me crazy, sat down in the seat beside me. Unfortunately, *some* something also entered, lurking as a third passenger between me and my still-troubled husband. With the help of Doctor Dean, *I* had found peace in all of the chaos, but Carig was drowning before my very eyes.

The unchanging and dreary highway leading into Portland made it seem as though time stood still; the infinite road was without beginning and devoid of end. I was nervous at the notion of seeing Annaliese again, but Carig's apprehension escalated with each passing mile. I understood his uneasiness at the thought of once again entering the home of the "loose cannon," or as he put it, " the ol hag gone rogue." To him, going back made about as much sense as stomping on a rusty nail.

For some bizarre reason, Annaliese viewed Carig's presence as an act of war, setting her off like a time bomb of fury. Her unexpected and violent outbursts mingled with her even stranger appearance, sounded more like the devil himself blaring his trumpet of evil, rather than an old woman who had fled World War II Germany. Who wouldn't be completely unsettled by such a flashback? The rage and venom that spewed from her lips, like fire from hell, was not only disturbing but its poison was gnawing a wedge between my lifelong friend and me. As hard as he tried, he couldn't seem to move past the ugly scenario that consumed him.

It was difficult to stay positive and focus on the blessings. But as I glanced over at Carig, I knew without a doubt that he and I were favored, that God would only put such tasks upon strong shoulders, those that could bear the unthinkable. After all, in the entire world, no others at this particular moment in history were chosen for this task. Suddenly, a peace swept over me and I knew without a doubt that everything was going to be alright. Of course, normalcy would forever be cast from our vocabularies, replaced with unpredictable and adventurous bends and forks in the road ... perhaps even a few spoons.

Carig, my most beloved, had done pretty well until Dr. Dean dropped the bomb that got the best of him. I missed his spirit of lightheartedness ... it had all but vanished, leaving him completely preoccupied with a foreboding spirit that was waging war on his soul. Even more concerning was the queer darkness that shrouded his face. Until now, I chalked it up to a lack of decent rest, but it was obvious that his anguish went much deeper, stemming from overwhelming worry. At the moment, even though we were separated by only a few inches of console space, he seemed unaware that I was even in the car, let alone sitting right next to him. With his constantly-changing expressions, and the indistinct movement of his lips, it appeared that he was entangled in a troubling conversation, his thoughts raging like "The Running of the Bulls."

But with one squeeze of his hand, I reigned him back, instantly reminding him that I was there, and everything was going to be okay. For a moment it appeared that the spell was broken. With one deep breath, and a slight grin in my direction, he finally engaged in light conversation. Nonetheless, once the chattering ceased, he sadly returned to his encroaching thoughts. I was at a loss and struggling to keep a positive attitude was difficult.

Even though our thoughts were consumed by Annaliese, our perspectives remained parted, and in two different worlds. For me, it had been decades since I'd seen her. She would no longer be the sweet little thing with a crown of golden ringlets who donned lacy frocks of powder blue. She had turned old, strange, and unrecognizable. With the passing of years, her baby soft skin would now be withered and ashen, her hair coarse and gray, and her glistening blue eyes would now be dim. It wasn't her age that bothered me, but I couldn't fathom what events had caused her to go off the edge. Alrik, her wonderful father, adored her. I had no doubt of that. It couldn't have been because of him that she changed. I wondered if at some point in my young life, if I had unknowingly passed her on the street, would I have known? Would I have had any clue that I had just brushed shoulders with a daughter of the Third Reich? For some reason, the more I thought of her, the more uneasy and fearful I became. Maybe Carig's apprehension was contagious. Perhaps he knew something that I didn't. There was no way that I could completely understand what he had experienced, just as he could never fully understand what I had been through. Somehow, some way, we *had* to find a means of connecting with one another's intuitions ... find a way back to the solid ground where our roots were deeply planted.

My experiences thus far seemed more like a dream than reality. It was difficult to fathom that such things could actually occur. Who would have thought in a million years that I would have the great pleasure of meeting Malachi Coffee and Carson York? My time with them had been both wonderful and cutting rolled up together in a far-off piece of yesteryear. I found myself missing them terribly and feeling a deep sense of loss at never seeing them again. Then there was Alrik. Granting the fact that he held me captive by his compulsive obsession, I cared deeply for him and wondered what had become of the Field Marshal of Germany. I knew so little about this fleeting aristocrat who both plagued and consumed my journey. What event made his world turn in such a way that he left his homeland and moved west into enemy territory? And why, as an old man, did he seek me out? Was his objective only to give me a small wooden horse that would gather dust on my bedroom shelf? Or was it to kiss the hand of a little girl who would grow up into the woman to whom he would offer the world? There were so many unanswered questions. As a matter of fact, the "whys" were making my head spin and my stomach queasy.

Resting my head against the chilled window brought relief to my discomfort. The scenery of trees, snow-banked edges, and fluttering sky whisking by was the cure to my ailment. As I followed the profusion of colors swirling into gray, I was lulled into an unexpected slumber which led me back to the grand stairway of Alrik's estate. Alone, I followed the familiar ballroom music. The strains were not those of German waltzes, but instead big band sounds of the Catwalk Ball. From far across the room, I was taken aback by a stunning red velvet gown joined to a handsome black uniform, both with blurred faces atop the garments. Intrusive vivid hues spun wildly through the room, dancing to the upbeat tunes. With glitter and pomp, they tried to steal away my attention, while explosions of fireworks became my barriers as I fought to move forward through the chaos.

I was uninterested in the clamor of guests but drawn only by the two who moved in a sensuous manner as if they were making love rather than dancing amidst a room full of people. Struggling to distinguish who they were was like peering through a foggy glass. All that I could decipher was their shifting movements, with hands slowly caressing one another. I became frustrated, squeezing my eyes shut over and over again, trying to gain focus.

But then the vaporous veil was lifted, and I could see the couple clearly. The woman stared straight at me, not in a friendly way, but as if I were a drifter, secretly looking into her world. She on the other hand was no stranger, but my Aunt Adina, neither smiling nor frowning, only staring at me with a blank expression. Slowly, her dance partner, turned his gaze in my direction. To my astonishment, it was Alrik! With one glance, he abandoned his partner, and began charging in my direction. I was afraid and turned to run away. Once again, I broke through the closely-packed crowd, but this time, I felt cold fingers trace over my back, trying to grab hold. It wasn't Alrik, but something evil that was sure to entrap me. All at once, with the alarming thunder of gunfire echoing through my mind, I was jolted awake.

Still in a sleepy fog, not unlike the heavy winter air, I turned my face towards Carig. His expression was one of raw pain. Lack of sleep over the past week had plagued my poor husband with dark circles and a short fuse. Because of me, he was hurting, but through it all, he was more concerned about my well-being than his own.

"Are you alright, lass?"

"Yeah, it was just a bad dream. A really weird dream actually!"

"About Alrik?"

I didn't know what to say. How did he know that I was dreaming about Alrik? During the chase, I must have cried out the unthinkable.

"Yes, but it was a nightmare. He was with Adina. And then someone or something was trying to catch me, but it wasn't Alrik, I think *he* was trying to save me."

The dream spurred my memory of the lit poster. One of many that lined the path leading up to the entrance of the Catwalk Ball. When I asked Carig if he recalled the picture, he admitted that he didn't pay too much attention to very many things that night.

"Na, I was only lookin' for *one* thing that night, and wasn't a picture!"

"At the time, I only recognized Adina in the photograph. She was with a man whom I'd never seen or could remember anyway. But now, I'm positive of who it was! It was a picture of Adina and Alrik, Alrik Richter. They were standing in the middle of the dance floor, embracing one another. Everyone else was dancing and celebrating like it was New Year's Eve ... everyone, except for them. They were completely consumed with one another, just like in my dream."

Having sorted out the images that lined the path, I realized that there was, in fact, another man in Adina's life. Not just any man, but Alrik Richter. Now, more than ever, he became an even more significant factor in my life. My interactions with Alrik were by no means a coincidence, or even a journey that would end up posted on my wall, never to be thought of again. Somehow, he and Adina had found one another after, or maybe during, the war. I wasn't sure. But most importantly, and to my surprise, they were not just friends ... they were lovers.

With my somewhat confused and delirious account of things, I could feel an uncomfortable fuming heat radiating from Carig's direction.

"You must be kiddin' me, Beni! The two women I care for most in the world have *both* had a bloody love affair with the same bastard? Will I never escape him?"

"You go too far, Carig! That is absolutely not true! I did not have an affair with him!"

"All I know, lass, is that you almost married him! I have been so haunted by those blasted pictures of the two of you that I can barely think straight!"

"What are you talking about? Are we back here again? I thought we'd moved past this! You forget that I was only trying to survive!"

More than once in our lives thus far, Carig had accused *me* of being bullheaded, but it was he who would win the prize today.

His narrow-minded stubbornness was infuriating! I could have repeated the same story a hundred different ways, but he wouldn't hear it, and was determined to be mad. As I watched the way he glared out at the road with fiery vengeance in his eyes, I feared that he might never recover.

"Carig … Carig, look at me! Don't allow the enemy of doubt to tear us apart. I only see you, it's always been you! *Never* has there been anyone else for me! Don't you know that?"

Unexpectedly, he made a careless, sharp turn off the highway and slammed on the brakes, nearly running right into the side of a snowbank.

"What are you doing?"

He sat there, leaning his head on the steering wheel, grabbing it so hard that it looked as though the bones beneath his white knuckles would jut out of his skin at any moment. His breathing was escalated, obviously the result of emotions and frustrations colliding. I had never seen him in such a state of anguish and was determined to save him from this agony.

Slowly unclasping one finger at a time, I gently held his hands in mine. He closed his eyes and began to breathe easier and sit back as I kissed each tip of his fingers. Although this was not the time or the place, I was desperate for a solution. He had somehow ended up in the middle of a dry and weary state, ravaged by unquenchable flames.

This time, it would be me who would rescue him, deliver him safely from the harrowing "what ifs" that taunted him. Just as he never gave up on me, I would now redeem my most cherished husband and friend. My eyes filled with tears as I looked into the face of grief. He didn't deserve any of this. I wondered if I were to ask him at this very moment if he wanted to walk away, what path he would choose? All of this was too much to ask of anyone. The truth of it all was that there was nothing *I* could do, so I bowed my head, approached the altar of God and began to silently pray.

As my eyes opened, I began combing my fingers through his hair, and his far-off trance was abruptly broken, released from the darkness. My pleading on his behalf had broken the spell. Facing one another, not uttering a word, I was thankful for the power that was greater than I.

"Thank you, Beni!"

"For what?"

"For believing in me, for praying for me."

To be honest, I wished that I could have been by myself and just cried for an hour. But instead the tears were caught in my throat.

"I, I can't even begin to tell you how sorry I am for everything. You deserve much better than me. I'm sorry, I'm sorry!"

As the shake of his head told me that *I* was his deepest dream come true, he reached over and firmly held my face and kissed me with a desperate passion that was beyond being fueled by normal enthusiasm, but more by a rage-like intensity that had been bottled up until now. He was a strong man, who had a gift for making those around him feel safe ... and I rested in his cover of protection. At the same time, he had a heart that was gentle and kind, unused to being broken, and all of this had hurt him deeply. It was clear that nothing more could be said. Peace would not come by word, but only by laying claim to one another in a place where only *we* could go. We may have been sitting in a jeep in the middle of the snow, but it turned into a beautiful sanctuary where we held one another and wept tears that would heal the hurt. In despair, we held one another.

"I don't want ye to go back. I ... I can't stand it! Beni, tell me right now that you love me, and that you will always love me, no matter what!"

"I do! I love you today, I love you yesterday, I love you tomorrow ... nothing will ever change that! Just like last time, whatever it takes, whatever I have to do, *I'll come back to you!*"

He and I knew without a doubt that the road ahead would be difficult, and that the moments and experiences that we did have together must serve as powerful reminders of an unbreakable foundation on which our union would stand, no matter the storm.

Impulsively, Carig pulled me onto his lap and held me tightly. I was convinced that I could stay there looking into his eyes forever and I would be completely satisfied.

"Let me give you something right here and now that, no matter what comes, you can forever think back on as my undivided devotion to you. Close your eyes! Come, get lost with me in this secret place where only you and I can go."

With those words, Carig closed his eyes, and did as I had told him. The stress that he had endured as an unbearable yoke, disappeared with each button that I loosed. It was the deepest desire of my heart to satisfy him completely, to give him everything, asking for nothing in return while creating a benchmark of devotion that belonged to only us. Through this communion of intense passion, I quietly whispered lyrics that intensified the endeavors of my body on his.

"There are two ways of seeing: with the body, and with the soul. The body's sight can sometimes forget, but the soul remembers forever."

I lost track of how long we stayed on that snow-filled detour, but I soon began to recognize the man that I remembered.

"Do you know what I wish, lass?"

"Tell me!"

"This is how it should be Beni ... you and me here like this, makin' love every five minutes if we want. I just wish that *this* right here and now would never end!"

I slightly shifted and then giggled just a little.

"Really? You don't think it might get a little uncomfortable?"

"Naw! Not a chance! It would be heaven!"

"Carig, we're gonna be okay. We can get through anything if we do it together, even those times that seem so dark."

"I know, Beni. Let's go, lass, and get this over with. I don't wanna waste any more of our time together worrying about this old hag!"

With only a few miles left until we reached the gates of the Richter Estate, we were once again on our way.

I couldn't even imagine what Annaliese would do when she saw me. Hopefully, she wouldn't keel over from a heart attack. The whole idea was crazy. For me it had only been a few days, but for that sweet blonde haired, blue eyed little girl, I was a far-off memory. How would I explain the surprise of my appearance, completely unchanged after three quarters of a century? Before taking a step out of the car, I took a quick peek inside my backpack to make sure I still had the velvet bag that contained Caprice's pearl choker and the ruby ring. It was my hope that the two treasures would open the door to a civil reunion

Chapter 16

The Blood Caste

"Do you have any idea the chain of events you set off?
The moment you arrived a fuse was lit, and the moment you left
everything blew up,
left in shambles. Do you even know what happened after you left?
Do you even really care?"
~Annaliese Richter~

Aside from the smaller-scaled duplication of Alrik's greenhouse, the dwelling didn't remind me of him at all. The only thing that slightly resembled the family legacy was the extravagant "R" encased within a gold ring that embellished the front gate. Snow still covered the entire driveway leading up to the house, which made it necessary to park on the main road and walk the same path that Carig took just a few nights ago. It was obvious by the virgin condition that no one had gone in or recently come out. There wasn't even a trace that Carig had ever been there.

With great difficulty, we slowly trudged through the white powder until climbing the stairs that led to the front door. Carig wore a disgusted expression of *"I can't believe I'm bloody here again!"* as he willed himself to knock. At first no one answered, but then from behind the door we heard a quiet voice inquire as to who was there. Both Carig and I looked at one another, half hoping that one of us would have the gumption to leave.

"Annaliese, it's Carig Hammel. I'm here with Beni!"

"You came back? One, two, now three times! You're out! I already told you ... Beni's dead!"

I placed my mouth close to the door, so she could hear my voice.

"Annaliese, it's me, Beni. I know this may be difficult to believe, but I'm really here and I've come to see you. I have some things to give you ... that used to belong to your mother."

From the other side of the door we heard the lock disengage, and then the knob began to turn. Slowly, it opened, inch by inch, revealing her face. I was shocked by what I saw, not even her eyes resembled those of the little girl I remembered. *Hers* were deplorable. I'm not sure what I expected, but she no longer reminded me of her father, but of Halag. Her hair was pulled back in a tight bun, and her skin was dry and weathered. At first, she didn't say a word, but only stared at me intently, panting from her slackened mouth.

"Hello, Annaliese!"

Even after I spoke her name, she remained silent. Then, as if she was appraising a horse, she began inspecting me from head to toe. I now understood why Carig was so reluctant to come here again. She was beyond creepy, putting my senses on edge. I couldn't believe it was the same person. When she began to speak, I discovered that she was both insane and delusional.

"I don't believe you! There's a slight resemblance to Benidette ... and ... to my mother. What if you're not actually here, but only a figment of my imagination?"

"Annaliese, it's me! How about you let us come in, and we can talk?"

"No! Not until you prove to me who you are!"

I knelt down and began unzipping the front pocket of my backpack. I wholeheartedly believed that revealing the jeweled evidence of the past would quell her doubts, but she didn't want any part of it. Quickly switching gears from psychotic to irrational, she began loudly raving about the Benidette of her childhood, characterizing me as one of her dolls rather than an adult woman.

"There's nothing you have in that bag that could make me believe that you are *my* Benidette - shimmering brown hair and eyes of blue glass. How did you get here? I tucked you safely away in my secret room beneath the stairs, you should have stayed there! Now you think that you can just come here after all this time and prove that you are her? Perhaps it's true what they say, and you are a spy, traipsing around through time ... but pulling some trinket out of your satchel will never convince me. Blood is thicker than water, and scars are evidence of truth."

I wasn't sure what she was fishing for, but I did know that her thought process was deranged and twisted ... even rehearsed. Somehow it was all a game. I would have to enter into her madness in order to find out why I was prompted to go there. With each tainted word, I felt myself being pulled into her world, like a monarch caught in a sticky web.

"If you are who you say you are, tell me, by what power, what authority, could you infiltrate our lives so long ago and return unchanged here and now? I say it's impossible, and there is no reason I should believe you! Tell me who you are really, and what you want!"

I could feel Carig watching me closely, wondering how I would answer that question and hoping that I wouldn't say anything about my calling or the frame.

"I know that it's hard to believe, but there are some things none of us will ever understand. The evidence of your own eyes cannot be dismissed, Annaliese."

"That's not good enough. Now go away!"

Think, Beni! What is it that she wants from you? "Blood is thicker than water, and scars are evidence of truth".

"Wait, stop! I can prove it to you!"

As I stepped into her world, I threw off my jacket and scarf, and then began to pull off my sweater.

"Beni, what are ye doing?"

Standing there in the freezing cold, with my entire upper body exposed, I lifted my chin to show her the bruises on my neck, and then turned around and revealed my bandaged gunshot wound.

"For me, Annaliese, it's only been a few days. Does this, any of this, shed light on your doubts?"

She was surprised at my shocking display of candor and took a step back in amazement.

As I began putting my clothes back on, she left the door open and went and sat down by the fire.

Carig was slightly amused at my highly unexpected display, and even though none of this was very funny, we both got a slight laugh from it.

"I can't believe you did that, but well done, lass. That's one I'm never gonna forget! We'll be tellin' that one to our grandchildren!"

Cautiously stepping inside, we were met by the unexpected hospitality of Annaliese pouring each of us a cup of tea; another personality switch, I thought. Carig was leery of her out of character friendliness and kept pushing for me to say what needed to be said, so we could *get the hell out*.

"Beni, none of this feels right. She's madder than a March

hare!"

Of course, Carig was right. Her attempt at good cheer was as unbalanced as a three-legged stool.

"Sit ... sit ... have some tea!"

Most everything that filled the room was slightly familiar. It appeared that when they came to America, they brought with them bits and pieces of their old life.

"So, what do you want?"

Pulling the velvet bag from my backpack, I reached over, placing it in her hand.

"What is this?"

"Just a few things that belonged to your mother."

When she pulled them from the bag, I once again expected a reaction or an epiphany. But instead, she brashly placed the ring on her finger, and unevenly clasped the pearls around her neck.

"Did you steal these from my father?"

"No, of course not. I was wearing them when I came back."

"Who gave them to you?"

Going round and round in circles, I was already frustrated with her, and hadn't even begun to have any kind of real conversation regarding the real reason I was there.

"Listen, Annaliese. I just wanted to tell you that I'm sorry for leaving you. If I did anything to hurt you or your father, I'm so sorry!"

"You are sorry?"

"Yes!"

"Do you have any idea the chain of events you set off? The moment you arrived a fuse was lit, and the moment you left everything blew up, left in shambles. Do you even know what happened after you left? Do you even really care?"

Annaliese was clearly angry with me, and by the sound of it, my visit into their world of long ago had ruined their lives. Although I wasn't expecting her to recall the events so vividly, especially since she was very young at the time I left, she revealed every unpleasant detail of the moments prior to and after my leaving.

Like many tragic events that our minds try to suppress, she remembered this one at a snail's pace. Panicked voices from both her father and Dr. Carson imploring Halag to cease with the madness and to put the gun down, rang through her mind. Her father holding up his hands, trying to calm the heated situation with his cousin, which was beyond repair. The next thing she knew, Dr. Carson was aiming an outstretched pistol, cocked and ready, at her Uncle Halag. He begged and pleaded for him to lay down his arms, and then began a countdown. "Three!" On the count of three, if he didn't lay down his pistol, he would shoot.

"One, two … he never made it to three!"

Before Dr. Carson could finish the countdown, Halag took the shot. Gasps of disbelief resonated from the gathering crowd as the Field Marshal's bride fell. Almost simultaneously, a second shot rang out bringing down the shooter. With outstretched arm, unwavering like a god-like sculpture, Carson gripped the smoking gun.

Annaliese paused. She was clearly overwhelmed with emotion as she relived each detail of the event.

In the midst of the chaos, fighting to get through the hordes of terrified guests, Alrik paused at the sight of the horrific and gaping hole in the center of his cousin's back. When he regained his senses and looked back in my direction, I was missing. Only Annaliese remained, standing alone and frightened with the toes of her white patent leather shoes on the edge of my still fresh and blood-filled imprint.

Her haunted eyes stared right through me as, in a series of flashbacks, she lived the entire saga for the second time. Carig and I hung on every word she said, waiting in anticipation for what happened next.

"One second you were sinking in the mud, and the next, the ground had consumed you … you were gone from my sight. All that remained was your concave plot. Inch by inch, the waterlogged earth spilled into the hole. Curiously, all that was left behind was the shoe box from my playroom."

She went on to say that the grief-stricken Field Marshal fell to his knees, pleading with his sweet baby girl (who should never have been party to such things) to tell him what had happened, and who it was that took Beni away. Her explanation was both brilliant and accurate, but Alrik dismissed it as nonsense. She likened it to the white bunny that disappeared like magic from inside the magician's hat. She would never forget the look of disappointment on his face and how he sprang up and walked away from her. She felt invisible and alone as she watched him rally every last soldier to search everywhere until Beni was found.

During the weeks and months following that dreadful day, Alrik spiraled into a depressive pit and was consumed by his loss. Perhaps that was the beginning of the end for Annaliese Richter, when she realized that his obsession for a mere stranger far outweighed the love he felt for his own daughter, not to mention his disregard for his cousin who had been shot down like a dog by a visiting American who dared to take down a member of the German state.

Carson stood, still posed and ready to take down the enemy. After monitoring Halag for even the slightest movement, Carson dropped the pistol, and ran over to where my body had once been. As Annaliese babbled on about his reaction to my disappearance - of him falling to his knees and silently weeping - I once again became devastated over the ordeal that never seemed to end. She spoke in complete ignorance, unaware that he was my uncle, trying to defend me.

"To this day, I wondered why he was so emotional over someone he hardly knew. That was the last time I saw Dr. Carson - he never came in our house again. Some time later I heard that he had died. Poison I think it was."

"Poison? Dr. Carson was poisoned?"

"I was so young, I think that's what I remember hearing!"

I couldn't even begin to think about the fact that I told Carson not to get on a plane, and he wasn't killed on a plane. Even though I half-stopped listening to her after that bomb of information, she continued her recollection of long ago.

"I had never seen my father so panicked, not ever! He was yelling in every direction. 'What has happened here, where is she?' He ordered every guard that surrounded our house to begin searching the area, reminding them to be careful because you were hurt. 'Don't you dare come back without her!' It upset my father that Dr. Carson didn't join the search. The doctor kept telling him that you were gone and to stop the search, but he never did. Apparently, Dr. Carson knew something that my father didn't. More than anything, the doctor was angry ... *so* angry at Halag. When he walked past Halag's body, he was so filled with fury that he kicked him as hard as he could in the ribs, and then spit with contempt on his lifeless body.

"For the next nine months, my father used all of his resources to scour the countryside, never wanting to admit that you were gone forever. One day, out of the blue, we left Germany. Even though I was sad to leave, I hoped that it would be the end to his insane search, but little did I know that coming here was just a continuation."

Her recap was enlightening and also brimming with hostility. Even so, it helped me to understand some of what happened after I left. I wondered if I were to go back if I'd be able to do things differently. Maybe I'd never encounter Alrik and Annaliese and their lives wouldn't have been filled with such grief. But was I really the cause of all of this? Ivan clearly explained to me that Halag was the evil that should have been destroyed, not me.

Other than what I had already done, I couldn't see a reason why Carig and I needed to stay any longer. What she said about Alrik's lifelong obsession made me uncomfortable, but obviously made Carig uneasy.

"Well, Annaliese, it was nice seeing you again, but I think we'll get going."

All of a sudden, she seemed anxious that I stay, and became strangely cordial.

"Why don't you have some more tea! You haven't even noticed the photos of me in the hallway. They're from my younger days. Go take a look!"

Stacked one above the other were framed photos of Annaliese growing up. So many of them revealed the little girl that I remembered. While I examined each one, Carig spotted something that appealed to him sitting in the corner of the room. It was an extraordinary miniature-sized carousel, that was clearly hand carved by an experienced artisan, and one of the finest pieces of woodwork he had ever seen. He was impressed by each intricately carved detail. As he spun it around, he noted its precise balance. The horses glided perfectly up and down, like an authentic carousel. As it turned, he noticed aloud that one the horses was missing, leaving a hole in the outer part of the device. The poles were still in place, but the horse was gone.

As she continued rambling in Carig's general direction, she oddly stood in front of a small mirror by the fireplace and began fluffing her hair and pinching her cheeks as if she were preparing to attend an event. Once again, Carig had a front row seat to observe her truly bizarre behavior.

"It disappeared into thin air one day. I had a real one just like it when I was child. It was grand in stature, lighting up so brightly that it could be seen for miles. This *was* my most treasured possession until one day, probably twenty years ago, I came home to find one of my horses missing. Not just any horse, but my favorite one with the pink and gold saddle. Her name was Lily. She was just like the horse that my father gave Beni. She may not have told you this, I mean, why would she, but side by side, they rode out to Crystal Lake and stayed there the entire night."

With a devious grin, she turned and sneered at him.

"Oh dear, I've said too much! But speaking of Lily, she was Beni's favorite carousel horse as well. We rode it together, the best of friends we were! Did I mention how she absolutely adored my father?"

Carig could feel his blood begin to boil, once again reminded of this man who had now become a nightmare even though he had been dead for seventeen years.

Trying to ignore Annaliese's annoying chatter, curiosity turned his attention to a display that he noticed in the corner of the room that first appeared to be a unique piece of artwork. Upon closer examination, and like everything in this room, it instantly transformed into a strange sight. Exhibited in an orderly fashion, hung dozens of old wooden printer's trays. Within each tiny cubby sat identical amber-colored bottles ... hundreds of them. Carig was drawn to the unique shelving because his grandmother had used this same type of shelves, that had once been drawers which held alphabet pieces for printing presses, to hold her most valued thimble collection. The assortment of auburn bottles was slightly illuminated by the glow from a small refrigerator that sat beneath. Carig was perplexed by her obvious obsession, and when he reached up to touch one, she screeched out a violent warning. Upon her unexpected shriek, he knocked into the refrigerator, setting off the rattling sound of even more bottles.

"I wouldn't touch that if I were you!"

Carig pulled back his hand and began to walk away, trying to ignore the fact that she was standing so close behind him that he could feel her hot, foul-smelling breath on his neck.

"Venom! They were once filled with a venom that I created, but now they are just markers."

"Markers?

"Yes! Like tombstones, each one has its own story to tell. So small, yet so powerful."

Carig had no intention of engaging in any further conversation with Annaliese. Her insanity obviously had no bounds. If what she said was true, she was a murderer, using the cowardly method of poison as her weapon. She had pompously, and with no remorse, killed hundreds with her fatal toxin and kept the bottles as souvenirs.

Being alone once again with Annaliese was pure torture. Even though Carig wanted to get me and go, he wanted to make sure I had finished up what I had come here to accomplish, so that we would never again have to step foot into this madhouse. In retrospect, I shouldn't have listened to Annaliese, engaging in her long corridor of black and white memories - a pathway leading to a deadly trap.

Initially, I was captivated by her pictures. It seemed that horses were her life. Every single photo was either of her alone or on her horse. There were no friends or boyfriends or wedding pictures, and most strangely, none of her father. If I were judging by the wall display, it would appear that she spent most of her life as a loner, and it was sad. With every step I traveled down the hallway, darkness swept around me like an inescapable fog. I wanted to turn around and go back, but there were things to be revealed within this dark place, I could feel it. When finally, I arrived at the last of the framed images, and saw the eyes of Halag Sauer dressed in Hitler's best glaring at me, I could almost feel his hands around my throat.

All at once, I was distracted by the humming sound of someone mumbling from a partially-opened door at the end of the corridor.

A sudden and invaluable discernment rose up within me, instructing me to move forward in absolute confidence, leaving my shipwrecked faith at the door. I was entering into a place that was the origin of the darkness that I had felt was inching down the hallway.

The room was dimly lit, and from the doorway all I could

hear was breathing and mumbling. Someone was there, lying in a bed, trying to say something, and whatever it was, he hardly had enough breath for a whisper. As I drew closer, the stench of death and excessive elixirs seeped from his every pore, making it difficult for me to breathe without gagging. In the dimness I couldn't tell if he was awake or asleep; either way, he was suffering and barely holding onto life.

"Closer!"

Trying not to appear repulsed, I stepped closer just as he asked. His eyes were closed, yet he continued mumbling phrases that made no sense at all. He was obviously delirious. As I began to back away, his rantings became more elevated.

"Come closer!"

"Let me go get Annaliese - she can help you!"

"No!"

Again, he started mumbling words, when startlingly his eyes opened, and I jumped back. I knew those eyes, and even though he was as old as dirt, his twisted smile was even more disturbing than before. I wasn't sure if it was his putrid odor or the lack of fresh air, but I was suddenly revisited by increasingly severe stomach pain and nausea that intensified with every word he spoke. My pain became a mournful dirge to his lyrics of insults and accusations.

"I've been waiting for you, Benidette. You are nothing but a pawn in my game ... that's all you've ever been. I know that you are feeling inadequate. You are ill-equipped and have failed. Do you know why you have failed so greatly? In all the years I searched for the frame, the one who bore it before you did their job well, making it impossible for me to find them. But you, you made it so easy, and now that I've found you, I will take the frame, unless you wish to bring it to me."

He continued holding up a clenched fist toward me as if he wanted to give me something.

"Come closer, Benidette, I have something for you."

Although I was curious, I was reluctant to move too close, or for that matter, take anything from him. I realized as I laid eyes on this grotesque and shriveled up man, that his dark soul and inner ugliness had manifested itself perfectly into the monster before me. He continued holding out his gnarled hand, until I placed mine beneath it. With the drop of one single item into my palm, he silently spoke a thousand words. Somehow, he had gained possession of a gold coin. Not just any gold, however, but a coin that bore the knot of David, one that only the Carrier of the Tempus Vector should have. He was letting me know that he knew everything about me and my calling, all the way down to the distinctive gold piece.

The room began to spin and the pain within me seemed to grow in intensity. Maybe it was his evil presence bewitching me, but with each word he spoke I grew more ill and found it difficult to stand. I was dumbfounded to hear about how he had searched for the Tempus Vector, but it wasn't until I had arrived in Friedlich that he figured out that I was the Carrier. All of these years since then, he had followed me, waiting in the shadows of my life. And now he stood as my accuser. He told me that with the frame, and power of the nine, he would recreate his past and devise an entirely different future.

I was the Carrier of the Tempus Vector, but I soon discovered that he too was a carrier of a design; a plan that was established years before the fall of the Third Reich. This specific set of plans, backed by unheard-of amounts of gold, would not fail like the previous three. This one was created with no holes, no flaws. In addition to great wealth, all it required was the Tempus Vector, the power of God, to plant seeds in times past that would grow and twist together as one, creating the Fourth and final Reich of mankind that would rule the world with an unstoppable power. He somehow knew that with the Tempus Vector, there were nine other powerful tribes, one in particular that could restore him, heal him.

I was remembering the nightmare, the rise of the four pillars. Seeing and hearing his insanity was the reason I was meant to come here. No matter what, I had to go back and destroy him.

"Listen, old man, I will never give you the frame, and I refuse to stand here any longer and listen to you spewing lies. With my *life,* I will protect this sacred calling. It will never be tainted by you."

He only laughed louder at my declaration.

"It will happen. It's the perfection of God combined with a society of great minds. Look for yourself!"

With an eager jerk of his chin, he motioned for me to look beneath the shroud on the wall. I was hesitant, but curious at the same time. Pinching the sooty fabric between my fingers I began to lift the cover away. The blanket of dust that lay atop, dormant until now, infiltrated the already stuffy room, further aggravating my unusual and suddenly blurred vision and throbbing head. Trying to focus through the pain, I could see that the large parchment was in reality a blueprint filled with 9 evenly placed circles surrounding a much larger sphere with lines reaching in all directions. The labels and symbols were in German and too small for me to make out. The image of a solid black eagle with outstretched wings emblazoned the center band. Within its wingtips, four of the feathers extended out further than the others, not unlike the pillars that rose up from the ground in my dream. Clenched in the bird's talons was a gold swastika with arrowed tips facing north, south, east, and west. Struggling to raise my arms, I snapped a quick picture of the shrouded mystery with my phone. I wasn't exactly sure what this was, but it had the look and organization of a caste system, showing bloodlines from all parts of the globe systematically meeting at one crowning threshold. This was a lineage of powerful individuals that would help bring about a rule that was thought to be defeated long ago.

In a most disturbing and breathy murmur, the old man declared a warning that shook my world.

"You need to run, Beni. As we speak, there are those on their way to your house who will find the frame and deliver it to me. You see, my dear, you have lost and don't even know it yet!"

The room began to spin as I heard him laughing under his foul breath. I could feel my heart racing, and the twisting of the knife in my soul.

Carig had been entertained for far too long by Annaliese's insanity, and was standing at the front door waiting for me. With all my strength, I cried out for him. At that point, I didn't care about me, but the frame. As I rose up to my knees, I screamed even louder, and he heard me.

"Beni, where are you?"

"In here - help me!"

I was in such excruciating pain, crying out in agony, that I could hardly speak.

"What is it Beni, what's wrong?"

"The frame! I can't breathe, Carig, my stomach! I can't stand the pain. What's happening to me?"

Carig stood up and grabbed hold of the old man who was repeating the same two words, with a terrifying smirk on his face

"Auf Wiedersehen, Benidette ... Auf Wiedersehen!"

"What have you done? What have you done to her?"

The grotesque man grinned and laughed quietly with an eerie sound.

"Carig, stop, stop, listen."

I pulled his ear to my mouth and began whispering. What I had to say, I didn't want Halag to hear.

"Call Dr. Dean and Ivan. Tell them ... tell them to go right now ... up to the third story and take the frame and hide it. Tell them to be careful. Evil is coming to take it. They have to guard it with their lives. Do it now! GO! I'll be okay."

Annaliese walked in, unsympathetically glaring down at me as Carig ran out of the room nearly knocking her over. Neither she nor the old man seemed surprised at my condition. This pain was something more than the call of the Tempus Vector. This was taking me to the edge of where life and death meet, and I could feel myself fading. After a few minutes, Carig ran back in the room and swept me up in his arms.

"What did you do, what did you give her? Did you poison her?"

At first Annaliese said nothing, but like all psychopaths who long for fame, she could no longer remain silent.

"You'd better hurry, we wouldn't want Beni to go the same way as Dr. Carson."

Carig raced back through the snow, this time carrying me. Once we got to the car, he laid me down in the back seat.

"I'm takin' ye to the hospital. I think ye've been poisoned!"

"No, call Dr. Dean, he'll know what to do."

"There's not time, Beni. He's a good two hours away!"

"Just do it. Call him!"

In a panic, Carig once again called the good doctor. I could hear echoes of confusion surrounding my poor husband.

"Whatya mean a few minutes? This is at least a two-hour drive. What, do ye have a helicopter? Alright then, yeah I'm pullin' over now!"

"He's comin, Beni. Said he'll be here in a few minutes. I don't really know how that's possible, but he said to wait right here."

Even though Carig didn't yet understand how it was feasible, he was about to witness Ray Dean, Doctor and Overseer of the Tribe of Moses, achieve the impossible and once again save the life of the Carrier of the Tempus Vector by means of his incredible gift.

"There he is! Bloody hell! Impossible!"

Like the warm wind that had one time encircled and healed my throat, he again opened his black bag, this time preparing a vial of an antidote that pulled me from the shadows.

It was funny waking up with my head on Dr. Dean's lap. I had slept most of the way home.

"Is it safe?"

"Of course! Everything's okay, kiddo."

By the time we got home, I was thankfully able to get up and walk to the front door. It may have been completely inappropriate, but as we pondered on the unbelievable events of the day, and the fact that our difficulties weren't letting up at all, there was only one thing we could do ... laugh.

Waiting for us in the house, were Ivan and his brothers, who had all banded together upon his request. They were quite the motley crew, each with a pipe in one hand and a gigging spear in the other. Although they were a bit scary looking and smelled like fish, I was thankful for Ivan's wisdom of bringing in reinforcements.

Ivan walked up and gave me a hug and told me that he was glad that I was alright. He then turned to Carig and shook his hand.

"We good?"

"Yeah! Thanks for bein' here!"

Even though the poison had been taken care of, the persistent pain still remained, and Ivan could see it.

"Beni, I really do hate to say it again, but it's not gonna go away until you go back. I know that you've both had a long day, but time is of the essence. We need to talk about your journey back."

I knew that he was right, but I just didn't feel ready. Although now that I had been in contact with Halag, I couldn't put it off for too much longer.

"I'll leave tomorrow, but right now I'm gonna go take a bath."

As I walked up the stairs, I could hear the three of them talking. They all decided that until I left, it would be good if they stayed and kept both the frame and me safe.

Carig called for pizza to feed the group, and in the meantime, Ivan started jotting down what he knew about this journey that I was about to take. I was glad he knew. I was filled with questions.

Carig came in and sat with me while I soaked.

"I wish I could go for you. I'd have no problem killin' the old bastard!"

I just laughed.

"I wish you and I could go together, and I could watch you 'kill the old bastard!'"

"I just remembered somethin', Beni. I don't know if it means anything, but when I was alone with Annaliese today, I spotted her small carousel sittin' there, all covered in cobwebs. She said it had been hers as a child. One day about twenty years ago, one of the horses went missin. I just thought …"

"That's the horse he gave me. It has to be! You're bloody brilliant! I'll dry off, you go get the horse."

"How about I dry you off first, my beautiful 'goddess divine'?"

"Why, Mr. Darcy, you can dry me off anytime you'd like!"

We both smiled happily. It felt good, if even for just a few moments, to be playful and silly.

"Alright then, I'll be right back."

Chapter 17

Liebesbrief

"In his mind the agreement with Malachi was simple. No one would be paying attention to the comings and goings of a cobbler, where Alrik's every move was being monitored."
~Benidette Hammel~

Like every other trinket that finds itself abandoned on the highest shelf beneath a sea of dust, so was the fate of the white horse. Now that I thought about it, the silly thing never stood up on its own, and now I knew why. It was created to be a galloping carousel horse, impaled by a rod of bronze.

Carig pulled a knife from his pocket and began scraping a thick layer of white paint from the saddle. When he did, a pallet of pink and gold revealed itself.

"We were right, Beni. Here's the hole on the back and the belly was obviously puttied."

He began scraping the fill from the holes. The horse was solid other than an oddly placed wooden rod that ran horizontally through the body. Through the straw-shaped hole we could see a piece of paper strategically wrapped around. It had been in there for so long and partially covered with glue and paint, but finally with the help of tweezers, we were able to pull the note away from the inside spool.

Unfortunately, it was vague, and revealed very little information. On the first line in bold letters, it said WAR HORSE, and right beneath it, also in bold letters, it read TIGER LILY, but a red "X" crossed out the word TIGER.

We were both perplexed, it made absolutely no sense whatsoever! So, like anything that I've found difficult to understand, I read it over and over again, fast then slow, one letter at a time, even backwards, but I was still confused.

"For him to go to all that trouble, it means something, but what?"

"What did he say when he gave it to you?"

"He said that her name was Lily and that she was a great war horse that would always protect me."

"War Horse ... Tiger Lily, War Horse ... Tiger Lily. Wait, Lily was the name of the horse, and she was a war horse, but *War Horse* is a book, and Tiger Lily is a character in *Peter Pan.*"

I sat there thinking it through back and forth in my mind.

"Wait, I just remembered something. When Alrik told me the horse's name was Lily, I said 'like Tiger Lily in *Peter Pan?*' He's talking about books - two books - *Peter Pan* and *War Horse.* We have to find them!"

We both got up and began running for the library. For those few moments we were carefree like when we were kids. This scavenger hunt was so much fun. It was the kind of adventure that we grew up on. We ran all the way to the library, and he stayed right behind me, brushing me with his fingers, and promising that when he caught me he'd never let me go.

Every inch of Adina's library was filled with the best reads. However, they were not really in any kind of order, so finding the books would be no easy task. He began at one end, I took the other, and we searched, and we searched. After finishing the fourth row on the left, I took a step back and skimmed across the next section of books. But out of the corner of my eye, on the very top shelf, I noticed something oddly familiar. Sandwiched between *War Horse* and *Peter Pan* was a scarlet glass box exactly like the one that held Alrik's Purgatory Papers and the ruby ring! The contents of that box had been waiting for me for twenty years. I was curious as to whether or not Adina knew that he had left it for me.

The elegant leaden glass case, like the horse, was covered in a dense layer of dust. As I slowly opened the lid in anticipation of what I would discover, I couldn't believe my eyes! Sitting on top of a thick stack of papers, were my butterfly brooch and aquamarine necklace. I was thrilled and relieved! I had grieved over the fact that I would never see them again. It seemed unthinkable that I had worn them only a week ago, yet they had been in Alrik's possession since the 1940's. It was too unfathomable to even ponder.

The heavy sheets of parchment appeared to be a letter, handwritten by Alrik. Carig and I made ourselves comfortable as I read it out loud.

My Dearest Beni,
I am now an old man, old enough to be your

great grandfather. I have spent my entire life loving you, watching you from afar, trying to keep you close. I'm unsure of how to begin to tell you everything. These days, hours, minutes without you have ticked by slowly. Only in my thoughts of yesterday do I find you, like a vision, walking down the staircase to meet me. I read your warning to Malachi. I tried to rescue him, yet he wouldn't be saved. He sacrificed his escape for the good of another. Through an agreement that he and I made, safe passage was arranged for his sister and two brothers. They escaped under the protection and endorsement of my ranking. It was not until they arrived safely in America that Annaliese and I also fled. It is this arrangement made between myself and Malachi that I wish to tell you about. It began as a payment of freedom, but in reality, was a treasure-filled Pandora's box, or should I say crate, that ultimately led me back to you.

Alrik's commitment to save a people he didn't even know, on my behalf, was moving. All of these years, Adina blamed herself for not warning and saving Malachi, but in reality, it was he who saved her. As far as I could tell, it appeared that she was never aware that Malachi's people, Estee, Lavi, and Ira had survived.

Our curiosities had been sparked by this agreement, this payment of freedom that Alrik spoke of. As I continued reading, Alrik compared his journey to that of a maze. One swift and unexpected turn after another would lead to places and relationships that would change everything.

The letter turned out to be more of a journal chronicling important details. In his mind the agreement with Malachi was simple. No one would be paying attention to the comings and goings of a cobbler, where Alrik's every move was being monitored.

As the Field Marshal of Hitler's regime, he along with many other high-ranking Germans, had been given bars of gold that would forever tie them to the furtherment of Hitler. With it, these leaders committed to use the wealth as insurance policies in case the Third Reich failed. It was earmarked to give aid to fleeing war criminals in their escape, and in setting up new lives for them. In addition, this mass funding would support the "Werewolf" resistance which was code for their guerilla warfare against the allies until the Fourth Reich would rise.

Alrik knew that fleeing with a suitcase filled with 500-gram gold bars would be impossible. So, once Malachi was assured that Alrik would not use the gold for any purpose other than supporting his daughter and himself, together the men worked on devising another method to transport it.

Malachi was fully aware of the risks involved, and created a most brilliant camouflage, a perfect facade that no one would suspect. Day after day he melted down the bars of gold and transformed them into cobbler tools that were then covered with heavy layers of flat black paint. Once they were completed, he stored them within the compartments of a traveling trunk, adding in personal elements, books, clothes and such. He then crated it up and shipped it to America. Our understanding was that he would acquire the crate from his sister upon his arrival in New York.

It was then that the intricacy began. Alrik and Annaliese did in fact flee Germany, and he became hated and even hunted by those he once called friends, but never regretted leaving. When he arrived in New York, he inquired for many days as to the whereabouts of Estee Coffee. He discovered that she lived in a small brownstone apartment in Brooklyn. When he arrived at her door, she informed him that the crate was not there, but had instead been shipped to an address in Long Beach, California. She handed him a piece of paper with the name and address of the person that he should contact. She apologized profusely for the misunderstanding, but surprisingly, rather than being angry or upset by the news, he was intoxicated. He knew that the woman who exited his life almost as quickly as she entered, had come from California, and he viewed it as a sign. On the small piece of paper she handed him, there was both an address *and* a name. Adina York.

Immediately he traveled to Long Beach and discovered that the Adina York who once lived there had moved to a place called Bar Rousse, Maine. The crate had remained unclaimed for weeks until just recently being shipped to this woman's new location. He was greatly disappointed. Not only because of the crate but because his intuition about finding me was wrong.

I cannot express my grief at not finding you

there. I was so sure that this was somehow your way of reconnecting with me. My once exhilarated heart was again oppressed.

The small town feel of Bar Rousse appealed to me. The people there, however, were a bit put off by my German accent. I wasn't aware until arriving in the United States, the hate I would encounter for being a German, but I didn't blame them.

Finally, I discovered the address where the crate had been delivered. I was surprised to find an old broken-down estate that was in shambles. From inside I heard roaring music playing on the gramophone. I knocked several times, but no one came. From the lighthouse on the other side of the property, a man with a Scottish accent approached me with a hammer in hand and nails in his mouth. I pulled out the piece of paper and explained that I was seeking a Miss Adina York and wondered if she lived here. "Aye," he said to me, and then asked what I wanted with her. I explained that she had possibly received a crate that should have been sent to me.

While I waited for her to come out, I was taken aback by the view of the ocean from this property. It was clear to me why she chose it.

I couldn't even fathom what he must have thought when he first laid eyes on Adina. After all, it was she who was originally spotted walking down the streets of Friedlich.

I was lost in the peacefulness of that place, when she came up behind me and spoke. At that moment, I couldn't move nor could I speak.

"Kinda takes your breath away doesn't it?"

When I turned around, there standing in front of me was a likeness of you dressed in paint-covered overalls and a scarf pulling her hair back. Without even thinking, I called her your name. She apologized and told me that I had made a mistake, she had never heard of anyone named Beni. Then she

asked for a last name. When I told her Crawford, she
became agitated and asked who I was and I what I
was doing there.

I know what you must be thinking. That I was
taken by her beauty, just as I was yours. She was
stunning. There was no doubt about that! But Beni,
even though you believed differently, I was in love
with you, not your look. After merely a few moments,
I knew that she was most definitely not you.

Alrik didn't divulge *all* of what ended up happening with he
and Adina, but apparently, they became inseparable after their first
encounter. Adina, in all her glamour, at the side of a man who
relished the finer things in life, must have been a sight to behold.
From what I could gather, over the next few years their relationship
grew, and it filled the gaps of pain that they had both experienced.

Alrik and Annaliese moved to a large farm property in the
next town over so that he could both be close to Adina and also live
out his dream. He even admitted to falling deeply in love with her
with every intention of marrying her. He never claimed the gold
tools, nor did he tell Adina what they really were. It would have
opened up a part of his life that was better left a secret.

The amazing events that led to their meeting explained the
Catwalk picture that had been posted big as life. The more he spoke
of her, the more joyful his words became, but then without warning,
everything in his mood turned dark.

Everything did indeed return full circle back
to you. Since arriving that day and seeing Adina for
the first time, my life had never been happier. She
had spoken briefly about her husband but kept that
part of her heart very private. It seemed she had her
secrets, and I had mine. A platform of secrets will
eventually collapse, and so it did.

He spoke of an event that occurred shortly after the war
ended. What should have been the happiest of times was sabotaged
by a man who showed up at Adina's door one day. A man in a
wheelchair.

Chapter 18

Dead Man in a Wheelchair

"Alrik cursed the day that this man trespassed into their lives."
~Benidette Hammel~

*He introduced himself as Lars Wexler,
survivor of the Holocaust and patriot of the Allied
Forces. He told her that he had come to shed some
light. He wasted no time informing her of who I was,
or rather who I had been. He then revealed that her
husband, known as Dr. Carson, had worked for me
while serving an undercover mission in Germany. He
named me as the murderer of her husband, claiming
that I poisoned him and then covered the evidence of
his body in a staged plane crash. That was a lie. Dr.
Carson was like a brother, and when I heard of his
death I was deeply saddened.*

Alrik cursed the day that this man trespassed into their lives.
At the same time, he wished he would have been honest with Adina
from the beginning. This unfortunate evildoer was none other than
his cousin, Halag Sauer. It was true, he had survived the war, at the
expense of many, and then slithered his way back into his cousin's
life. The last words that were spoken by Adina to Alrik were words
of warning: *"Never make an attempt to see Benidette!"* He wasn't
sure why Adina would mention me. He had forgotten the day they
met, when he said my name and how she recognized it from the
diary. In fact, she not only knew that the next Carrier would be
related to her but that I had journeyed to his time and place, and he
had fallen in love with me.

Sauer was so clever, so deceitful, that he fooled even the
pages of history. Once he was discovered to still be alive on the night
of the incident, he was rushed to a hospital for Germans only.
Because of Alrik's fury, rather than sending him to a convalescent
hospital to recuperate, he had him transferred to a facility near
Dachau where Jews were sent for experimentation. Halag knew this
place well and begged not to be taken there. Experiments in spinal

cord repair were conducted to no avail. It was the intention of the Third Reich to master the technique of repairing spinal cords in order to aid battle-torn soldiers. Halag was the perfect candidate. He, along with others, also experienced massive experimentation with various drugs and untried techniques.

His days were lost, but his nights were fruitful as he spent the twilight hours speculating Beni's disappearance, the mysterious wooden box, and the lies of the shoemaker. He gathered enough evidence to prove that Beni was the key to the Enoch theory, and somehow Malachi was the key to her whereabouts. In order to save his skin, he demanded that the chief physician of the facility call for the council to the Fuehrer. At first, they refused, but then he threatened them, claiming that he held vital information that he had been collecting for Hitler himself. Just as Halag expected, a group of men dressed in long coats and black hats wasted no time in showing up at his door. He only agreed to talk if they could assure him quick release and the Field Marshal status. Although their word could not be trusted, they assured Halag that if his information did in fact, turn out to be useful, they would meet his demands.

Only hours later, Malachi's shop was ransacked along with the sleepy town of Friedlich. Nothing of any value was found in his store. Because of the bogus information he had given, Halag was forced to stay at the facility as punishment, but because he was of German descent, he was promoted to Head Facilitator. Even though he had personally endured the brutal experiments, he approved and condoned their continuation on the incoming Jews.

When the war was over, he was included on the list of the most notorious war criminals of Hitler's regime. To save himself at the last minute before the facility was raided by the allies, he took on the identity of a Jew, a Jew named Lars Wexler. He used his wheelchair as evidence that he was a patient and framed the real Lars as Halag Sauer. Like many others, out of mercy and pity over his circumstances, he was graciously given asylum in the United States. Because of the convincing portfolio of documents that would convict the real Lars Wexler, who was also in a wheelchair, of being the actual Halag Sauer, this poor man was hung in his place on October 16, 1946. When Sauer arrived in the United States, he continued his charade and moved to a small community outside of Portland.

I tell you this, Beni, as a warning. Halag knows all about you. It's true, I did search for you, but it was he who was completely obsessed - not with love, but power. He has waited for you all of these years. I know very little about the might of the frame ... but I know it's great and would be horrific in the hands of someone like him. I wish he had died that day! He <u>should</u> have died that day!

It required skillful pleading for many days in order for Adina to allow for me to see you for but a few minutes at the train station. You were just a little girl, and I knew that she would never permit me to tell you all of what I knew. You were far too young anyway. I said very little to you that day as we stood on the platform together, hoping that talk of Lily and War Horse would remain with you, and then I placed the white horse in your hand for safekeeping. Listen well, my dear, this stallion, a symbol of faithfulness, offers a piece of my heart, a restoration for the broken."

"Hmm? That's odd."
"What do ye mean?"
"Nothing. Just a mistake I guess."

Upon returning home, I wrote this letter. There really was so much to say, if only you could be here with me now. My life has been a series of unyielding burdens, but you must know, surrendering your necklace and pendant is like losing you all over again. It will be the hardest thing I've ever done. One more thing, please forgive me for ever making you feel afraid. There was no excuse for my actions. I had lost you once, I just didn't want to lose you a second time.

Of course, I knew what he was recalling. There was a time that I believed I would forever be a prisoner, both in his home and of that time period. However, his reference to losing me for a second time, left me perplexed.

I have treasured these pieces that once touched your skin - they have somehow made me feel closer to you. When the opportunity presents itself, I will hide the scarlet box between the classics, which would only make sense to you and no one else.

By now, I have probably been dead for many years, but just know that not a day has passed that you were not in my thoughts. I will always love you. I've made my peace with God, so that I will see you again.

Ich werde fur immer Dein sein,
Alrik

Carig and I just sat there in disbelief that any of this could be real. I felt bad for Alrik, while Carig just shook his head in complete irritation. After hearing the whole story, it seemed that Halag was at the center of Alrik's life-long difficulties, and for some strange reason no one was ever able to stop him. I appreciated him returning my pendant and necklace, but in all honesty, the mystery of the white horse was disappointing. He went to an awful lot of trouble to bring that horse to me, to keep all these years, just to return jewelry. It almost seemed like an anticlimactic ending to what should have been a great adventure.

Carig remained very quiet, and I could tell that he was bothered, so I snuggled up on his lap and wrapped my arms around him.

"You know, if you were an animal, you'd be a great big, muscular, beautiful, sleek, strong, muscular ..."

He smiled at me.

"You already said that."

"Well, I mean, just feel these muscles on you. They're worth mentioning at least twice."

"Aww, Beni! I don't want you to go."

"I won't be long, I promise."

"I think I've heard those words before."

"I know, I know! But this time I know more of what to expect. I mean, as far as the place and all. It'll be fine. Speaking of knowing what to expect, Dr. Dean suggested that I talk with Ivan. That he would be able to prepare me, and answer questions."

"Wait, before ye go, I dunno about you, but I'm still in

honeymoon mode. Why don't ye go back to talkin' about me bein' a war horse."

"Okay, okay, you be the War Horse, I'll be Tiger Lily!"

Chapter 19

My Old Friend, Friedlich

"With the sounds of footsteps coming up the stairs, Carig swiftly laced the backpack straps around my arms, set the frame in my hand, and pushed me out the door. As I turned around and glimpsed back, I saw two of the Taggart brothers, Audi and Gabe."
~Benidette Hammel~

By the time we returned, the pizza was gone, and the brothers were asleep. Dr. Dean and Ivan were thoroughly engaged in a deep conversation that ceased the moment we entered the room.

"Hey, there they are! We saved some pizza for you before the vultures could get to it. It's over there, on the counter."

Carig dove in, but I wasn't hungry. Although I didn't say much about it, the pain and uneasiness were raging within me, but even so, Dr. Dean insisted that I eat.

"Listen here, kiddo, you've been through more trauma in the last week than most people go through their entire lives. I'm already concerned about you taking a journey this soon. You have to eat! We were just sitting here talking, and there are a few things we need to discuss before you go."

He repeated several times how returning to the same place and time period was highly unusual, but then after saying it one final time, he suggested that Ivan take over.

"I'm not gonna candy-coat this, Beni. I realize that you've been through a lot, but I also know that the Tempus Vector is not just a thing. It's the power of God in you. Nothing's impossible, nothing's undoable if He's there. I know that you already know what's at stake here. Dean filled me in on what happened with you guys in the old hag's den. But here's what I know, and what you need to keep in mind!"

His wealth of information and knowledge put everything in perspective and commanded a call to arms. Even though Ivan was slightly quirky, his natural zeal and intensity reminded me of King Arthur and we, his knights, sat around Adina's round table. It almost felt that this room had been witness in the past to such notable conversations. The air was so intense that when Ivan bellowed out that *failure was not an option*, I couldn't help but salute him and answer with a bold "Yes, Sir!" At which point everyone broke out in laughter. It was obvious that he didn't appreciate my sarcasm. The bit of silliness was a welcome distraction that eased the tension, for a moment anyway. However, his all-inclusive descriptions concerning the delicate infrastructure of history and the frightening black cloud that now loomed above us, instantly subdued the mood.

This problem that we now faced began many years, rather decades, before Hitler's reign and unfortunately didn't end there. It was simply groundwork that would support the dark pillars of my nightmare that would explode with an unstoppable force. At this point only, Ivan truly understood the impact of my dream, and with great detail, began revealing its mystery.

"All of it together is quite remarkable! Imagine a line of perfectly placed dominoes, strategically positioned to tumble in flawless order."

I could tell that both the doctor and Carig grew weary of his lofty words that still gave no explanation, and Dean could stay silent no longer.

"Good God, man! Just tell us what *we need* to know and stop talking in riddles!"

"Okay, sorry! So, I think it's fair to say that the whole world has heard about the Third Reich. Why, you may ask? Simply because it was the most destructive of the three regimes. The corrupt Nazi movement was at the helm of a faction that was responsible for the most heinous crimes ever committed against humanity. What most people don't think about is that there were, in fact, three Reichs. There's tons of information if you wanna read about it, but since we don't have much time, I'll explain it in a nutshell. Keep in mind though, that each empire covertly built upon the next with one key element in common, *world domination.*

"The goal of the First Reich was to be like a *new* Roman Empire, ruling like the Caesars. If you recall, there was a time when Rome nearly *did* control the world. Each Caesar believed himself to be God and demanded that all citizens greet one another by acknowledging 'Caesar is Lord!' Those who refused, namely Christians, were either burned, crucified, or fed to the lions. Rome desired with a fury, control of all lands and all people, disregarding any who would stand against them ... world domination, right?

"The Second Reich set the stage for authoritarian power and the unification of Germany, bringing states together to create the German Empire ... only one ruler over many. A leader unleashed, ruling without consent. That kind of thing. They hailed allegiance to their emperors who, as history reveals, failed, but still authored, a platform of an absolute power to come.

"Well, then there was the Third Reich we all know about. Instead of 'Caesar is Lord,' the people greeted one another with a great big 'Heil Hitler!' - only if they wanted to live.

"All of this to say that the Fourth Reich is coming. The number four is highly notable in this instance and must not be disregarded. One, two, and three are all imperfect as numbers go, but four shows stability. It's a solid number that represents a foundation not easily broken. So, Beni, the moment you mentioned four dark pillars rising up with unstoppable force, with Halag standing at the helm of it all, I knew that stopping him before he began was your charge. I understand that it seems ludicrous that a shriveled up old man such as Sauer could do anything in such a feeble state. But your calling and this frame is more powerful than anyone realizes. If he gets his hands on the Tempus Vector, he will not only have the ability to go back and change pieces of history, ensuring the rise of the Fourth Reich but he'll also have unlimited connection to the powers of the other nine of the Lost Tribes. You do realize that means instant access to what I know, and the healing powers of Dr. Dean. It just can't happen, it can't happen!"

We were all bothered by his Armageddon-like revelation but could tell by his profound insight and wisdom that his gift of interpretation had been cast loose. Dr. Dean had shared only a bit about the remarkable intelligence and good judgment of Ivan's father that resulted in many safe returns for Adina. But until this very moment, none of us were truly confident in the son. Whether we liked what he said or not, his boldness was obviously inspired by God, marking this day as one that we would talk about for many years to come.

Together, we bore witness to Ivan paralleling his father's unimaginable abilities. Done ... finished! There would be no arguing about the matter, no ranting and raving like a tableful of politicians who believed they could change the world by merely talking about it. This would require action. Each one of us already knew what needed to be done. Ivan and the doctor had accomplished all they could thus far, and I was thankful for their unshakable commitment.

If I were to be honest, I didn't want to hear anymore doom and gloom, but Ivan had not yet finished revealing his laundry list of instructions.

"Now, Beni, going back to the same time and place, as you've already been told, is very uncommon. To be perfectly honest, it's kind of uncharted waters. When you return, you will have gobs of new stuff to write about for sure. I mean, who knows, maybe your photo will be sealed in gold. You will have earned it for sure."

He once again began babbling, and Carig and Dean gave him *the look*.

"Anyway, I'm gonna tell you what I do know. How I know these things is not important, you'll just have to trust me. You will not arrive where you left, but days or weeks before you did the last time. You will be a stranger to them. That really is a good thing, it will put you at an advantage. You've already been there and know what to expect, but they won't know anything about you. Also, this may sound weird, but I had the tiniest clip of a dream, and I'm not positive what it means except to say, you're somehow gonna land in a shadowy place, hidden from sight. You will see their faces, faces of many. They will see you, but they *won't* see you. That's really all I know about that. Regarding the length of this journey, I'm not exactly sure. It could be hours or days ... I guess my suggestion is to just be prepared for anything."

I knew that he was doing the best he could to prepare for me what was coming. Perhaps there were some black and white absolutes when it came to journeying with the Tempus Vector, but so far I found myself helplessly floundering in a muddled sea of gray.

"What does that mean, Ivan? They will see me, but they won't see me?"

"I'm really sorry, but I'm not exactly sure. That's it really!"

Immediately Carig sat straight up in his chair and asked about those waiting, namely himself.

"Will this be like the timin' of a regular journey?"

"I'd like to say yes, but quite honestly, *nothing,* absolutely nothing about this journey will be regular or normal. I don't know for sure, but we need to prepare ourselves for a bit of a long haul."

We could all tell how difficult this was for Carig to swallow, but they reminded him that they would be there with him, and together they would get through this.

"One more thing, Beni. I know that you've been told to journey wearing things that are of the era so that you'll blend in. But this trip you're gonna need to be able to move and move quickly. Fit in, but … you know what I mean."

Comfortable clothes didn't bother me a bit. I relished the idea of running shoes and leggings, but I knew that wasn't what he was talking about. My clothing and what I would wear seemed so insignificant in comparison to the profound impact that this journey could have on the world, but even so, I knew that every detail mattered and must be considered as important.

Carig grabbed my hand and nervously began stroking each finger. Along with the others, he was both overwhelmed and troubled. It was all that any of us could do to sit back and take a few deep breaths as we realized that the most problematic issue at hand had not yet been discussed. The risky and dreaded task of killing Halag Sauer sat like a bleeding elephant in the center of the table. How would I even begin to do such a thing? I'd never killed anything in my life. Me, of all people, who would go out of her way to preserve the life of a bug, was not simply the Carrier of the Tempus Vector, but had now become the weapon of choice.

Ivan could tell how burdened I was, and earnestly tried to make the solution to the problem short and sweet. Basically, an opportunity would present itself, and when it did, I would be given the strength and abilities to do what needed to be done. Not a one of us felt any kind of relief at his statement, but there was nothing left to do except move forward.

In an attempt to change the subject, Dr. Dean gave me one last warning that was accompanied by a serious gaze and a stern finger pointed right at me.

"Like Ivan said, you will arrive in the shadows ... you stay in the shadows! Keep that frame with you! When it's done, you get the hell outta there, you hear me? Most importantly, have faith in the plan that is set before you, even if you can't see the outcome. And remember, you won't be alone."

I knew that I wouldn't be alone, but that was only *part* of what was bothering me. Aside from not being able to fathom the idea of ending someone's life, I was concerned about how this would affect my first journey and the people I had met there. I had more questions and uncertainties about this trip. Would this cause the first one to be null and void? I now understood Malachi's and Carson's fates. They were meant to die, and according to my dream and Ivan's interpretation of it, there was nothing I could do to change their horrible dooms. Would that mean I would never meet them? Would someone else point Adina to Schuh Coffee, and would she ever find out that someone named Beni would be her successor? If not, would she still want to be such a big part of my life? What about everything with Alrik? How would he know to help Malachi's people escape? One question simply led to another, but Ivan reminded me of one thing.

"Beni, stop! You returning does not negate what was done the first time. You still went back! You did what you did, and that won't change. Let's just put it this way, this trip won't modify the first one, but will pave the way for the next. It's like any journey really. When you used to visit Adina, leave, and then come back, it didn't erase the journey before, it only added to it. Now, I understand that this is a bit different, but still similar. Because this journey takes place prior to your first, they won't know you, and it's probably best not to interact with them if you can help it. I wonder, I mean, perhaps, unbeknownst to you, they *did* remember you, but you didn't realize it.

"As haphazard as this all seems, remember, nothing happens by chance. If the events that occurred as a result of your journey are meant to be, they will be. I don't mean to sound harsh, but please don't make this about you! You went the first time with one task to fulfill. Along the way you touched each of these lives, and you care about them, I get it. But this was and is your task. A very, very important task. Keep focused on that, and everything else will fall into place as it should. You are not in charge of saving the world … well, you kinda are in charge a little bit. But as you will soon find out, if something is meant to be, this journey won't change it."

We were all tired and anxious, ready to get this done and over with. Ivan and Dr. Dean had done most of the talking while Carig had hardly spoken a word the entire time and seemed uncharacteristically annoyed.

"Are you alright, Carig?"

"Beni, I don't like any of this, but there's nothin' I can do to change it. Are we done here? If you gentlemen don't mind, I'd like to spend some time with my wife. It appears that no one really knows how this is gonna end, or when she'll be back. Is there no way that I can go with her? Or *instead* of her? Let it be me who kills him."

Ivan and Dr. Dean seemed curious about Carig's inquisition, as if they knew something that we didn't. Ivan just sat there rubbing his palms together, not saying a word, but Dr. Dean replied by telling him that he too wished that Carig could go instead of me. Everyone was so glum, and I for one, had had enough of the misery. I couldn't stand the thought of them being sad or afraid.

"I'd like to say something."

I stood up, intensely moved by the care and concern of the three men who sat before me. It was all I could do to choke back the tears as I explained to them just how much they meant to me.

"Thank you all … for everything! I really have no words to tell you how precious you are to me. I am not afraid because I have each of you supporting me, and I know that everything is going to be alright.

"Carig, if it weren't for you, I wouldn't be here at all. Even before I found out about the Tempus Vector, and this whole calling on my life, I was in love with you. It was because of you that I stayed. You believed in me before I believed in myself. It may sound silly, but you are my rock, and I am blessed because of you.

"And, Dr. Dean, what can I say? I would be dead by now if not for you. I don't quite understand how this all works and how you know when I need you, but I'm thankful that you do … thank you for being there."

As I made my way to Ivan, I couldn't help but smile and chuckle, on the inside of course.

"Ivan, if you would have told me that a day would come when you would be giving me wisdom and direction for my life, I would have never believed it. Somehow, I feel as though I've known you forever … you are a dear friend. And your brothers, how in the world did they get suckered into helping with all of this? They're here risking their lives, and I'm not even sure that I remember their names."

He reminded me that he was, of course, the youngest. Eddie was the oldest, followed by Audi, Zander, Billy, Elmer, Gabriel, and Quinn. He then did a slight recap of how his brothers never really cared very much for him, but then he readily admitted that he was difficult in every way. He went on to tell how he and his brothers finally overcame their years of adversity and came together.

"When pop died, we all showed up at Mr. Peevey's law office for the reading of his will. Like an idiot, so full of pride, I sat at the head of the table as if the will would be all about me. Feeding my already-inflated opinion of myself, Mr. Peevey did begin with me. He read a short message from my father. 'Dear Ivan'... he said. 'I have spent your whole life preparing you for the calling that is now yours. You know what to do.' Mr. Peevey then excused me from the table and informed me that the remainder of the discussion at hand did not include me. At that very moment, I once again became the baby brother. That humbling moment was my father's final lesson to me. My brothers discovered that they too had a calling ... to come alongside me. They each received a metal armory box. What each box held is still a mystery to me, but whatever it was, each contained a specific tool and instructions, or should I say expectations, of the roles they would play. All I know is that some of them received weapons, and other devices. Whatever my father revealed to them changed their lives as well as mine. Anyhow, that's kind of it. My brothers have become my partners, my confidants. I don't know what I would do without them."

Dr. Dean proudly looked at each one of us. Knowing that everything that needed to be said, had been said, he announced that we were in fact done. He agreed to take the first watch of the night. Until my task was complete, they would need to stay on high alert and take seriously Halag's threats to steal the frame. All I needed to do was pack a bag, and then Carig and I would spend our first night together as a married couple in the house that now belonged to us.

A bag? I no longer had possession of Malachi's suitcase. As I searched through the suitcases stored in Adina's closet, nothing seemed right. I was pretty sure that a red rolling suitcase would stand out in the1940's. I had no idea what I would use until Carig had a brilliant idea.

"Beni, what about this?"

With a big smile, he held up my backpack. That was it! Perfect idea! My oversized vintage leather backpack that fit me like a glove would become my new traveling companion. Not only would it fit everything that I needed but the zipper pocket on the inside wall would be the ideal hiding place for the Tempus Vector. I jumped up in Carig's arms and gave him a big kiss.

"You are bloody brilliant!"

"It suits ye far more than that ol suitcase, lass. I'll tell ye one thing, Beni, don't ye be gone like ye were last time. Do what the doctor said. Get it done, then get the hell out. Tell me ye will."

"Aye, lad, I'll be back quicker than you can say 'Yer bum's oot the windae!'"

Carig laughed out loud.

"Where in the world did ye hear that, ye funny girl?"

"Your grandfather, Killen, always said it."

"I remember, but it was usually when my Grandmother was spittin' and spewin' venom at him for smokin' and drinkin' too much. Kind of a 'you're speakin' gibberish, woman.' It's funny you remembered that."

"I have an idea. I'll finish my packing and figure out what I'll wear tomorrow, and well, we can spend the rest of the night um, playing cards."

Carig gaped at me like I had lost my mind.

"Yer bum's oot the windae, lass, if you think we'll be playin' a game o' cards."

"Well alright then, let me finish packing and I'll be right back."

I packed my bag with just the minimum I would need, just as Adina had instructed, except I did throw in gloves and a hat, since it was always so cold in Friedlich. As I continued packing, I realized that not only had I lost Malachi's suitcase but my leather journal, the pencil case, and Adina's measuring tape as well. At first, I slightly panicked, wondering if my journey would be a failure without those missing items. But then it occurred to me - the measuring tape and the little notepad that Adina would always take with her were just reminders to herself of who she really was, not a requirement of her success. I sat there wondering what I could bring with me that would always be a reminder of who I was and would represent a passion of my life. At that moment, I knew. I knew without a doubt what I would place in my backpack prior to every journey. In addition to my personal belongings and two gold coins, my original copy of *The Count of Monte Cristo* would travel with me.

Finally, finished, and ready to focus on something far more pleasant than my assassination journey, I went searching for Carig. First, I checked Adina's room, but he wasn't there. I next went down to my bedroom. As I walked in, there was only one thing that I could say as I saw my husband lying in my full-sized bed, under a blanket of pink and purple wildflowers, the bedspread of my childhood.

"Only you, my love, could look so incredibly handsome and manly lying under girly covers!"

"I think we may need a bigger bed, lass."

"Well, this will do for tonight!"

"Aye."

As it turned out, my childhood bed was the perfect size. We held one another and fell asleep in the wee hours of the morning but were abruptly awakened by the sound of Dr. Dean's voice.

"Carig! Beni! Wake up!"

"What? What's goin' on, Doc?"

"Beni's gotta go ... now!"

"Why? What's happening?"

I heard a frantic note in Dr. Dean's voice. He hastily explained as Carig and I rolled out of bed.

"Eddie's been sittin' on the tower all night, scoping out the area. About thirty minutes ago he noticed headlights comin' in this direction. The vehicle stopped about a quarter mile up the road and was just waiting. Then four more black jeeps pulled up beside 'um. Now they're comin' this way. You gotta go, Beni. Now!"

From downstairs, I could hear the Taggart brothers rallying together for a battle. I wasn't afraid for myself but for all of these who I was leaving behind. Carig kept listening to the ruckus going on with the boys and seemed antsy to go down and help.

I threw on the clothes that I had laid out to wear. I know it was totally opposite of what Adina would have chosen, but black stretchy pants, a black turtleneck sweater, and high-laced hiking boots would have to do. Lastly, I threw on a black leather jacket, Carig grabbed my backpack, and together we ran up to the third story room. There was no time for goodbyes as we heard the upsurge of chaotic yelling and a commotion that became louder and more violent.

"Hurry, Beni!"

With the sounds of footsteps coming up the stairs, Carig swiftly laced the backpack straps around my arms, set the frame in my hand, and pushed me out the door. As I turned around and glimpsed back, I saw two of the Taggart brothers, Audi and Gabe. They were frantically running into the room, yelling for Carig to get downstairs. He, along with the two boys took one last look at me as I passed through the door.

"I love you, Beni!"

"We're with ya too, Beni!"

I felt paralyzed. How could I move forward knowing that Carig, Dr. Dean, and Ivan and his brothers were in danger? I had no idea how violent this crew of thieves might be, and I would never forgive myself if anything happened to the people I cared about. I couldn't go back though, they were all counting on me. I had to move forward. Walking back into Friedlich and completing this task was the only way to help them.

I had stepped into an all-encompassing ebon-filled silence. The atmosphere was void of light and sound, and the air so heavy that I found it difficult to breathe. Unlike before, I couldn't hear the Bar Rousse waves breaking on the shore, nor feel a breeze. So dark, that I couldn't even see my hand in front of my face. Yet, as I moved forward, all the while wondering if I might suddenly fall from the side of nothingness into an unknown abyss, my leather boot tapped on the wooden bridge, my creaking entry into Friedlich. I wasn't sure how I would possibly find my way through a pathway absent of light, but I had learned very early on in my journeys that nothing seemed to hinge on what I knew or understood, I just had to do it.

Time was of the essence. Dr. Dean's voice kept running like a loop in my mind, "Have faith, Beni!" Faith! I had to have faith in every step that was before me. Faith that there was a bridge, faith that I would find the door, and faith that I would have the insight and wisdom to complete this calling successfully. As I thought of my group of warriors back home who were putting their lives on the line for me, I began to run. I kept my eyes peeled for even one inkling of light, but still saw none.

Stride after stride and hearing only my own breath for what

seemed like miles, I slowed as the sound of the wooden bridge below my feet turned into the crunch of gravel, hopefully signaling the near entrance into the city. Unlike the previous journey, I wasn't led by a sliver of light that would guide me, it remained dark. With my arms outstretched before me, walking at a steady pace, I collided with the door, leaving me stunned. Once I made sure that I was alright and gathered my wits, I pushed it open. Even passing over the threshold, it was as strangely quiet as it was dark.

By the familiar smell and dampness of this age-old city, I could tell that I had arrived in Friedlich. Before taking another step, I placed the Tempus Vector into the zipper pocket of my backpack where my laptop would normally go. As I continued walking forward, I could hear the low murmur of voices stirring. I stopped and remained still. I stared straight ahead, trying to make out the distorted sounds circulating in my direction.

Chapter 20

Blood Warrior

*"Listen, Colonel Klink, or whatever your name is, I find it rather
curious that if you are so certain of that ridiculous story that you
just told me,
why did you go to all the trouble of coming here?"*
~Ivan Taggart~

It was a stand-off. Ivan and his brothers, Carig, and Dr. Dean
stood at the entrance of the property, waiting for the caravan of black
jeeps that were rapidly approaching. The resounding racket of snow
chains slapping the spinning tires could be heard for miles. If it was
their intent to be stealthy, they had failed miserably. Eddie remained
in the tower watching them through his scope, with rifle set and
pointed in their direction. Just as their father had instructed, each
Taggart boy was armed and ready for the foretold evil that would
come their way. They would do whatever was necessary to both
protect Ivan, and more importantly, assure the safety of Beni and the
Tempus Vector.

Even though the brothers were generally laid back and spent
most of their time fishing, gigging, digging, and playing music
together, they knew the seriousness of this mission, and had
transformed into soldiers. Along with Ivan, they were more than
prepared for this very moment.

Their organization as a group was impressive. In addition to
knowing one another inside and out, they were clear as crystal as to
their role as a unit. Using earpieces that were connected through
two-way radios, they remained in constant contact. Eddie kept the
others posted on every movement of the incoming vehicles and
watched the surrounding area to make certain that no one was
covertly heading to the house on foot. He did most of the talking
while the others listened for updates. Audi and Gabe were the most
skilled marksmen, who each stood in the wings of the ranks. Their
extremely accurate ability to hit any target, even at longer than usual
ranges, was impressive. Generally speaking, the Taggart brothers
were known to be silly pranksters who played their banjos, guitars,

and fiddles till the wee hours of the morning, definitely more fun than serious, but to see them now standing as soldiers-at-arms was extraordinary.

Even with a definite threat coming their way, Ivan seemed to be preoccupied with his own thoughts, which was a common occurrence. One by one, each of his brothers spoke out.

"What now, Ivan?"

As the cars continued to approach, getting too close for comfort, their voices became more panic-filled. Eddie kept telling them to wait and stay calm, but Zander and Billy, the two with the hottest tempers of them all, became more upset and their tones elevated.

"Ivan, what do we do man?"

"He can't hear ya, brother. He's gone to that weird place in his head!"

"Come on, Ivan, they're getting closer. I've got a perfect shot!"

"Now's not the time to zone, Ivy!"

"All I know is, ya little bastard, if I see one inkling of a threat from those blackjacks comin', I'll shoot!"

To their relief, Eddie spoke up.

"Hold up, fellas. The herd of gas guzzlers just gridlocked a quarter mile down. They're not movin'!"

Finally, after the constant bantering between the brothers, and the prolonged silence of the one voice they were waiting for, Ivan spoke up.

"I'm walking out to them. Only Carig is coming with me!"

Zander had no patience for Ivan's far-fetched ideas and was usually the first to blow up at him. They all knew that however chaotic his ideas were, there was always wisdom in his chaos.

"What in the hell are you thinking, Ivy! He's not even armed, and that's who yer taking? You've gotta be kidding me!"

Ivan was focused, almost as if he could see something that the others couldn't.

"It'll be fine, you guys. I know you have our backs. Carig's armed with something you can't see. He's ready."

His brothers rolled their eyes at one another and shook their head.

"There he goes again, spouting a bunch of ballyhoo that none of us can make any sense of!"

"Zip it, Zander! You and me both know that we can trust what he's sayin', even though it sounds bogus!"

Audi and Gabe were hankering to hear the go sign to make target practice out of those shiny black jeeps.

"I say we take 'em all out, I am so ready!"

"I was born ready! Let me at 'um!"

Ivan once again reminded them to hold up.

Carig didn't flinch at Ivan's request to go. He wasn't afraid, but to the contrary, was filled with a roaring anger that had immediately sparked within the depths of his mind. All he could see was Beni's face, and hear her calling out to him repeatedly for help. With each cry, her voice became louder and more desperate. She needed his help, and he was so far away from her. All of it together burned like fire into his heart, and then shot like a bolt of lightning down his arms, causing a red heat to explode in the palms of his hands. He had experienced a slight version of this before, but never this intense.

As Carig and Ivan approached the jeeps that had paused for seemingly no reason, he asked Ivan what it was that they were doing. Carig was finding it difficult to stay focused on their conversation, fighting the urge to see red and not only go off on Ivan but whatever was waiting for them. Aside from the feeling that he would jump out of his skin at any moment, the palms of his hands were hot and itchy as if they had been attacked by fire ants. With every step they took, it became more excruciating.

"What in the hell are we doin,' Ivan?"

Fed up with the grumbling attitude of the bad-tempered Scot, Ivan stopped in his tracks and folded his arms in protest. When Carig realized that he was walking alone, he became even more irritated and raced back, nearly knocking over the *wee of a man* who was at least a foot shorter than himself.

Although a bit intimidated, Ivan stood his ground and spoke bold words that Carig never expected to hear.

"Control it, Carig! If you don't control *it,* it will control you!"

"What in the hell are ya talkin' about? What is it ya know? What's wrong with me?"

"That's all I'm gonna say right now. Stay focused, man! I

have one opportunity to talk to these people, but it has to be now. I need you, all of you, to be with me."

Ivan stuck his finger in Carig's chest.

"The fire is not your enemy!"

Carig was impressed with Ivan's courage as he walked up to the passenger-side window of the first car and knocked with great boldness. After a few seconds, and with the humming sound of the descending tinted glass, they were met by a grim-faced man and his three hapless traveling companions. Ivan's gift of destroying the prideful with clever distractions would begin with the bald-headed driver, whose attempt at alarming the young and witty Tribe of Yosef with his evil fixation, would fail before it even began.

"Wow! Look at you! Ya know, not too long ago, my brothers and I were fishing off the coast of the Ambon Island, and came across a coffinfish that looked just like you! Huh? Remarkable resemblance! Is that natural, or do you shave it? Anyway, what you've come here for is gone. When it returns, you will find, *my hairless friend*, that your entire purpose for living will be non-existent. So why don't you all turn around and go back to whatever hole you crawled out of."

Fuming at Ivan's blatant disrespect of his higher power, he discharged words of retaliation, all woven within a hardened German timbre.

"I'm not sure who you think you are, or what power you imagine you have here. You are nothing! Let's not pretend that I am unaware of the 'who' we are speaking about. We have watched her for many years, waiting for this very moment. Even now, she is being led down a slippery slope. Sadly, she will never return and neither will the frame. She will fail! The enormous power and wisdom from the Lost Tribe of Solomon that rules all the others will be ours … not today, but 75 years ago. So, my dear friend, it will be *you* left wondering what happened to your world. A great authority is soon to rise, and there is nothing that you can do to stop it."

Carig was furious at what he had said about Beni not returning. To him, those were "fightin'" words. But Ivan remained calm, and reassuringly looked back at his friend.

"I've got this, buddy! Don't believe everything you hear!"

"Listen, Colonel Klink, or whatever your name is, I find it rather curious that if you're so certain of that ridiculous story that you just told me, then why did ya go to all the trouble of coming here? You brought, what, 25 men with you? You and your plot-to-be are nothin' but afraid and threatened. I know very well, as do you, that she will succeed. Sauer is afraid! He sent you knowing that the moment she leaves this house, you'd all be done for and out of a job. You're the one who's too late! But no worries, Herr Dummkopf, I hear they're hiring a dishwasher down at Burger Barrel. I say you and your boys get the hell outta here, and don't ever think about comin' back. I'll see ya on the other side."

Not giving him a chance to rebuke him, Ivan and Carig turned and began to walk away when they heard a pistol cock from inside the car. Both of them immediately stopped, and Ivan said one last thing.

"I'd put that away if I were you. You shoot me, they shoot you. It's as simple as that. You've got two minutes to leave or they start firing. This conversation is over. I'm done wasting my time on you!"

From behind, they could hear the jeeps turn around one by one and leave.

Carig was curious about both sides of the conversation, which one was true, and which was not? The fearless and nervy voice of Ivan that Carig despised as a teenager, had become music to his ears.

"So, how did ye know what he was saying wasn't true?"

"I didn't. All I knew was they'd come to take the frame. If they were certain that Beni wasn't gonna be successful, they wouldn't have come in the first place. They were just hoping she was still here. I suppose we'll be seeing them again. They won't be far away, and they'll be keepin' tabs on Beni's return."

"Beni's return?"

"Yeah, they'll be watchin'. This is the thing, Hammel, they're only interested in the power. They don't care where it comes from or what they have to do to get it. For some insane reason, they think they're smarter than God, or that they *are* God. They're fools who see themselves as wise, and that's why *they* will fail, not us. I have faith in Beni and in the power of the Tempus Vector."

Ivan was so busy talking that he didn't notice Carig was no longer by his side. When he turned back to find him, he could see that he had dropped into the snow on his hands and knees. Not only was he breathing heavily but he appeared to be in great pain.

"You alright, kid?"

Carig stayed silent, except for his escalated breathing.

"Can you talk?"

"Somethin's wrong with me! It's burnin' like fire, startin' in my hands and moving up my arms into my chest. I felt it earlier, but it's just gettin' worse. It's freezing out here, still I'm burnin' up inside."

From a distance, Dr. Dean assessed the situation with curiosity. After realizing that something was terribly wrong, he quickly hurried towards them.

"What happened, Ivan?"

"I dunno, Doc! One minute Carig was walkin' by my side, and the next he was on the ground breathin' all hard and stuff. All he said was that he was burnin' up from his hands to his chest."

Ivan was taken aback by Dr. Dean's panicked expression. Rarely was Dean caught off guard over anything, and he was clearly alarmed over Carig's condition. Although still hunched over and most uncomfortable, Carig despised the scrutiny. Slightly embarrassed over the whole ordeal, he stood up and lashed out at the two.

"What the hell ye lookin' at? Doc? What's with all the fussin? Did I sprout wings or somethin'? You're lookin' at me like I'm about to take off and fly!"

"I don't know yet. Let's get him in the house!"

Carig stayed down another few minutes, and then together they helped him up. He was delirious, finding it difficult to walk upright. As they reached the house, the brothers were all waiting and wanting to know what was going on. Dr. Dean assured them all that he would be fine and not to worry.

While Dean helped Carig inside, Ivan's brothers congratulated their little brother for his bold courage in dealing with the psycho Nazis. Audi and Gabe were a little disappointed they didn't get to shoot anything and were more than happy to stand guard outside just in case they showed up again. The two waited in anticipation of spotting bright lights and shiny black jeeps plowing down the road.

Dean stumbled alongside the towering Scot, shouldering his weight until finally making it to the closest chair. More than just worry about a random and mysterious health issue that was affecting this normally able-bodied young man, was the doctor's lingering curiosity about the root cause of it all. The "something" that had been lying dormant in the recesses of Dean's mind, was now rearing its head. Something was happening inside of Carig that had nothing to do with medicine or science.

Carig was many things, but this sudden frenzied irritation was completely out of character. Even when they were all outside facing the enemy, Carig was antsy, keeping his eye on the third story balcony, half-present in both places. They knew something was up with him, but they didn't realize that his unyielding goal was to reach the door where Beni would return. The more Dean prompted him to sit, the angrier he became. Seeing him struggle was like watching an animal battle to free itself from a cage. His mind and heart were determined to climb the stairs, but his body wasn't willing. He was depleted of all strength, and strangely helpless. He was at the doctor's mercy, imploring him for help up to the third story room. Everyone looked at one another, perplexed by his unexplainable delirium.

"Good Lord, man, I don't think you can make it! Let's stop for just one minute and figure out what's going on here before you collapse!"

"Please, Doc, please! Just help me up there, then you can … whatever, whatever you want! I don't know what's wrong with me, except I'm gonna come right out of my skin if I don't get up there. I need to be near her. Somethin's wrong, I feel it!"

Dean was moved by his desperate request, and together they slowly scaled the stairs one step at a time. When finally, they reached the third story, Carig collapsed into his grandfather's chair, obviously disappointed that Beni was nowhere to be seen. It was clear that he had been stricken with a troublesome burden, one that the others didn't quite understand. Not yet anyway.

"Alright son, let's see what's going on with you."

"Na, Doc. Just let me close my eyes for a few minutes, please!"

Although concerned, Dr. Dean could tell that he was utterly exhausted, and left Carig alone. He hoped that sleep would cure what ailed him.

Ivan and his brothers were impatiently waiting for the doctor at the bottom of the stairs. Altogether, the still charged up anti-Nazi watchdogs bombarded him with questions and concerns about Carig. Their loud and obnoxious voices, while slightly annoying, were a normal occurrence in their world of fish stench and an overabundance of testosterone. Raised without a mother, or anything that half resembled *sugar and spice and everything nice,* they scarcely knew how to act within the four walls of a lady's house. Ivan, however, was much more insightful than the others, and in the thick of the mayhem, he and Dr. Dean spoke to one another through focused glances. They both felt deep down inside that this was not an illness that plagued Carig, but a transformation. There was only one true way of telling for sure if they were actually witnessing the rise of one they had heard whispers of many times but had never actually met. Their exchanged inquisitive glances practically screamed out "could it be him?" Together, they wondered if this young man with scarlet-stained hands, who had fainted into a death-like sleep, in fact be the Blood Warrior?

As Ivan and Dr. Dean sat eating lunch at the kitchen table, they heard a cry coming from the third story room at the first stroke of noon. Before their sandwiches had dropped onto the plates, they had already begun running up the stairs. Over and again they heard the excited bellowing of Carig calling out Beni's name; they hoped and prayed that she had returned. When they walked in, they found him pressed against the balcony door, looking out the window as if he could see her. Strangely, he was still asleep, senseless, and sweating profusely, all the while screaming out her name. Carefully, Ivan shook him and tried to wake him up.

Turning around and starting to come out of his trance, Carig was utterly out of breath, as if he had just run a marathon. Not only was his breathing elevated and he was dripping with sweat, but his eyes were dark and bloodshot. As he fell to his knees, Dr. Dean knelt down beside him and looked deep into his eyes. After a few moments, Carig snapped out of his lethargic trance and noticed that he was still wearing all of his cold gear - jacket, hat, gloves, and boots. In a state of confusion, he asked Dr. Dean where he was, and why he was dressed for the snow

"You alright, son? You're burnin' up! Why don't we get all this stuff off and cool you down, then maybe everything will make more sense?"

In curious expectation of catching sight of the one symbol that would validate their suspicions, they carefully watched as Carig removed each piece of winter gear. When at last he slipped the Duluths from his hands, and turned his palms upward, Carig gasped in horror. Whatever this painful and intense physical phenomenon was that made him question his sanity, it had actually transfigured his once blood-stained palms to a normal flesh-colored shade.

"What is this? How'd this happen?"

He was rattled to see the *something* that had always been part of who he was, suddenly gone. Ivan and the doctor however, seemed unmoved and pleasantly surprised at the sight … almost as if they expected it, which unnerved Carig even further.

"What is it that you know and aren't tellin' me? This can't be real! I was born with birthmarks. This is impossible!"

Ivan fixed his eyes on Carig, and then his palms as if he were going to say something, but instead turned around and faced the window.

"What? For the first time in your life you've got nothin' to say?"

When Carig continued interrupting Ivan's deep train of thought, probing him for answers, Dr. Dean pulled him back and told him to stop.

"Let him alone, son. He's only trying to help you!"

After what seemed to be an eternity of waiting, Ivan boldly declared that the time had come when silence would be broken and secrets that had been buried for years would now be unearthed to reveal a higher purpose.

There was nothing that could have prepared Carig for what he was about to hear, and since Ivan wasn't one to beat around the bush, sugar coat, or spare feelings, he turned around and blurted out the incomprehensible.

"Killen wasn't your grandfather."

Chapter 21

Secret Things

"Those from the Tribe of David, while mere mortals, remain united
by a tie of blood."
~Ivan Taggart~

"What in the hell are ye talkin' about? How dare ye say such a thing! Of course, he was my grandfather!"

"Don't get me wrong, you *are* related to him, and he loved you as his own, but he and Mari never had any children. He was your great uncle, brother to your real grandfather and uncle to your father. It all worked, and no one questioned it cause you were a spittin' image of Killen with your red hair and the blood-red birthmarks on your hands."

"My Gran didn't have red birthmarks like I do! Ye don't know what yer talking about!"

"That's where you're wrong! He was born with marks exactly like yours. Shortly after he and Mari moved to Bar Rousse, the same radical change happened to him."

"Even if what you say is true, what does it mean?"

"You, my friend, are the Blood Warrior! Dean and I have suspected it but weren't sure until you took your gloves off."

Ivan went on to explain that the red stains Carig bore at birth were the symbol of his charge from the Lost Tribe of David. Like David, Carig was a righteous man after God's heart, but who also had the gift of war, and would rise up and spill the blood of his enemies. While ultimately a seeker of peace and righteousness, this ancient calling would entrust to Carig the rights to take a life and to carry out divine vengeance. Although at this moment Carig felt that the life he had always known was both falling apart and reassembling all at once, he believed the profound testimony from this quirky lad from the Tribe of Yosef.

Before he even knew what was happening, Carig knelt down and allowed Ivan to bless and commission him for this new calling of his life.

"Those from the Tribe of David, while mere mortals, remain united by a tie of blood. This divine authority to take vengeance, enacting the final *Evening of Score or Justice,* is now given to you. You will now fulfill a most crucial posture in the continuing ascendency of the Tempus Vector, a privilege left in the hands of fortitude, willing to shed blood for the sake of Divine Justice. These hands branded from birth with patterns of splattered blood, will be given authority to strike vengeance against murderers or those who have come against the helpless and innocent, making what's wrong, right. However, with this herald of wrath comes great responsibility."

Once Carig rose to his feet, he felt better physically, but was distraught over learning about his Gran, and couldn't understand why he never told him the truth.

"Don't be mad at Killen. As far as he was concerned, you were, and will always be, his grandson. As for your calling, it wasn't his to tell, but one that could only be revealed by fire. I think you know what I'm talkin' about, right? This weird *thing* you've been going through for some time didn't just begin and end today. That unbearable heat was stamping you from the inside out.

"What you must remember, is that the entire time you were growing up, you *were* being trained for this calling but just didn't know it. Killen did his job well! Think about it. There were far more similarities between the two of you than your red mops. From the moment you came here after your folks died, you weren't preoccupied with childish things. You always had a desire to know everything he knew ... how many kids ever want that? By working closely with Killen, you became strong - all of the building, carrying timber, and wood chopping. It all played a part of who you are today. When Killen would take you hunting, you learned how to use every weapon - guns, knives, hatchets, bows until you mastered them all. To be perfectly honest, your respectable qualities, and the fact that you were so good at everything, always annoyed me to no end. I would have never admitted it then, but if truth be told, I wanted to be you. I believe it was you who reminded me *several times* that I stopped growing in the sixth grade, and all six-foot-whatever of you grew a new muscle every time I saw you. The final dagger of it all was when your future was revealed to me, and it included Beni!"

Carig couldn't help but feel bad about Ivan's plight, but even so, it was funny to hear him talk about himself that way as his personality and confidence were always bigger than life. He may have always been small in stature, but his sharp and quick-witted nature created an enchanting sex appeal that the girls could never resist.

"It's really okay, I'm over it. I'm not the person I used to be, Carig. Somehow when my father died, a switch turned on inside of me. Suddenly the spotlight that once shone on me, or so I thought, was redirected to something far greater than myself. The Tribe of Yosef is an intricate tool that will ensure the success of The Tempus Vector. As a whole, we're like a body. Apart we each play a vital role, but together we're like a well-oiled machine ... I mean, who knows? Maybe I'm the brain, but what good is a brain all alone? You, my friend, are the strong arm, and I for one am excited you're here."

"How will I know, I mean where ... what do I take with me? How will I know *anything*?"

"Well superman, I'll tell you exactly how you'll know. It's pretty simple. I've already told you about the burn and the blood, but there's more ... there's more."

Once again, Ivan became lost in his vast thoughts, continually discerning things that no one else could see. While in the middle of the conversation with Carig, he was surprisingly overcome by a more substantial empty stare and sudden stillness. More and more, his mind was becoming an uncontrollable chain reaction of non-stop brainstorms and containing them was like trying to capture the ocean in a mason jar.

Ivan's remarkable vision regarding Carig surprised even himself. Not only was he wide awake when it occurred but it was the first time that his foreknowledge included himself. Although he acted as if he were quite confident and unmoved by his skillset of notions and things to come, he was experiencing new and ever-clear perceptions that caught him off guard.

"What is it ye see, Ivan?"

"I saw myself standing right down there on the shore. Suddenly, a fog settled over the coastline, and I saw the shadow of a man breaking through the mist. As he came closer to me, I saw that it was Killen, but he was young, like you are now. In one hand he held a knife, and in the other, a bow. Strapped on his back was a quiver filled with arrows and tucked beneath his belt was a pistol. He walked onto the shore with blood dripping from his hands, and an expression of one who had victoriously conquered his enemy."

To Carig, this story of Killen was oddly inspiring, but he wasn't quite sure what it meant. He waited with bated breath for Ivan's interpretation.

Without warning, Ivan grabbed Carig by the shoulders and pulled him over to the window.

"You see those three large boulders down there on the shore?"

"Aye!"

"Okay, and then about twenty paces to the right are two smaller rocks that are covered in snow right now. Do you know the two I mean?"

"I do! But what's this …?"

"When you are called to go, your hands will burn and turn blood red. You will then enter between those two formations. The instant your shoes hit the water, you will be gone from here and be present there. That is also where you will exit and return home. Just as Beni is given wisdom when she needs it, and I receive visions, and the doc has the power and ability to heal, you will be equipped with whatever weapon is deemed necessary for your task at hand."

It then occurred to Carig that he made up the fourth tribe but wondered about the other six. When he asked about it, they immediately shut him down and told him that there are secret things that belong only to God, not to man.

Chapter 22

The Merchant of Venice

"Portia? He called me Portia.
I was smack dab in the middle of The Merchant of Venice!"
~Benidette Hammel~

Suddenly from out of nowhere, a bright spotlight hit me, leaving me blinded. I quickly shielded my eyes with my cupped hands, hoping that the uncomfortable light would cease and I would be able to see where I was. I began to hear faint whispers coming from every direction, but couldn't make out what they were saying, until they stopped and I heard only one voice calling out.

"Es ist fast Morgen!"

"ES IST FAST MORGEN!"

"ES IST FAST MORGEN!"

To my immediate left, I heard a voice loudly whispering that same German phrase over and over again. Each repeated word became louder and more irate. *Where was I? Did I even want to know where I'd landed?* Then, beneath my hands which were covering my face, I could feel something sitting over my eyes. As I carefully began examining it, I discovered that there was a mask on the top half of my face. My first impulse was to rip it off, but then I remembered what Ivan told me, that when I arrived I would be hidden.

As the beam of light lessened, I began to make out silhouettes of dimly lit faces. Not just a few, but rows upon rows of faces began to appear. Within the glistening of tiaras and feathers, I could see a theater full of people, an audience whose eyes were on me, or rather on the stage. I had somehow landed in the middle of a theater production, and according to the irate gestures and continual calling from the short, stocky man who was both yelling instructions at me from the wings of the stage, while also nervously twisting himself up in the stage curtain ... I was up.

It was time for me to say my line, and I couldn't even make out what he was saying. It was something about morning. I could feel the alarming stares from the other actors who were holding their poses, as well as their breath, in anticipation of my character finally saying her lines. I was utterly exposed before hundreds of people yet hidden behind the mask.

Nervously biting my bottom lip, I was quickly becoming a spectacle. This was my worst nightmare come to life. The only thing that could make it any worse was if my clothes had disappeared and I was standing there naked. As I cautiously looked down, praying that I wouldn't see my bare body lit up for all to see, I was instead pleasantly surprised by a gold gothic, most likely 16th century-styled gown. Guessing by the other costumes that surrounded me, the production had to be something from the Shakespearean era, but I wasn't sure which one. Without any further hesitation, I blurted out my lines as if I knew what I was doing.

"Es ist fast Morgen!"

Still, they glared at me intently. Continuing sheer panic consumed their faces. It was apparent that the four words I had just spoken were only the beginning of my character's address. The silence grew more profound as all eyes were on me. Not only did I not speak German, very well anyway but I had no idea what play this was. I was *completely* lost. In a mental flash, I remembered a friend of mine who was a theater major, and one of the most talented actresses that I had ever seen. She admitted to forgetting lines more than once, but those in the audience never knew. She would just laugh and say, "Half the time the audience has no idea what comes next. If you completely spaz out and forget your lines, just talk about something you know well, and say it with confidence and passion!"

Oh my gosh! What did I know … in German? I had no choice but to fall back on the basic phrases learned in Mr. Roth's German class. I closed my eyes and took a deep breath, repeating the one line from the play that I did know. But right before I opened my mouth, the actor standing next to me said one more line in an attempt to prompt me into action.

"Portia, ist es noch Morgen?"

Portia? He called me Portia. I was smack dab in the middle of *The Merchant of Venice!* How I wished I would have remembered even a few lines. I never liked this play very much, but I knew why the Third Reich did. This Shakespearean play was thought to be anti-Semitic, and because of that, one of the few productions that Hitler would allow during his reign.

"It's almost morning!"

Next, with great confidence and in a deeply dramatic call, I shouted out to the crowd as if I was making the most profound speech of my life.

"I have lost my bag … How are you? … I am tired," and then ended with a great big "Thank you."

The audience first looked at me in a confused manner but was unexpectedly cued by an outburst of laughter from an individual who was sitting up in the theater box. His jubilant stream of amusement at my complete and utter train wreck of a performance made everyone, including the actors standing beside me, break out in laughter. Before I knew it, all of the other actors joined hands, including mine, all standing in a line at the front of the stage, preparing for a curtain call. The man holding my hand was chattering angrily at me.

"Was zum Teufel war das? Nehmen sie ihre maske ab! Zieh es aus! Zieh es aus!"

I didn't know what he was saying, but he was fuming mad. He grabbed at my face, insisting I take off my mask, so the audience could see who I was, but I slapped his hand away. As we all bowed, everyone removed their masks and hats as the crowd stood to their feet, clapping and cheering. I was met by curious gazes from the other cast members, all wondering who I might be.

"Bist du die Zweitbesetzung fur Darla?"

Zweitbesetzung? He was asking me something about Darla. Perhaps that was the real Portia, the one who they expected to be standing beside them. Since I wasn't sure what he was asking or how to reply, I simply shrugged my shoulders and tried to turn a deaf ear. When the curtain went down for the last time, I was pushed with others back towards the dressing rooms. As I lunged forward to take my first step, something bulky that sat beneath my large hooped skirt became tangled between my feet and caused me to stumble. I went down hard, landing on all fours. I fixed my eyes on the ground in front of me, deciding not to move an inch until the busy group of people barreling past me had finally scattered. I had no desire to talk to any of them, but I mistakenly blurted out words of frustration when I hit the ground.

"Gosh darn it! What the heck was that?"

I was angry. Angry that I was dropped right in the middle of such a challenging situation, angry that I had made such a fool of myself, and now, angry as I cringed at the reality that I had just spoken out, in English no less, alerting a few passers-by that the stranger in their midst who came out of nowhere, was American.

Just as I was about to stand up, two pairs of shiny black shoes parked themselves directly in front of me. I didn't dare look up but prayed they would go away and leave me alone.

"Gehort das zu dir?"

I had no idea what he was saying, and yet I knew the familiar voice. In my wildest dreams, I never thought that I would see him again. But now, this strange reality left me paralyzed.

If I were guessing, and to my great dismay, the second pair of shoes was Halag, who thus far remained silent. Apparently, my backpack had been sitting safely by my side the entire time, and now hung from his glove-covered hand. Apparently, when I had begun to walk, the straps of my bag became entangled around my feet, causing me to trip. I didn't answer, nor did I even look at him.

Slowly, I stood up, checked to be sure my mask was still in place, grabbed hold of my satchel, said a quiet thank you, and then began to walk around them. Alrik firmly grabbed my arm and began sternly mumbling something in my ear. I had obviously offended him by my lack of respect at his presence. His rant was pouring out of his mouth so fast that I had no idea what he was saying or how to answer him. To make things even worse, my heart sank as I watched the stocky stagehand, the one who had called out lines to me, motion for Halag. The two of them began chatting, and by the looks of Halag's continuous glance in my direction, they were talking about me.

I could feel the intensity of their conversation from where I stood. By the time they were done, Halag's expression spoke a thousand words. I had been found out. Slowly, he sauntered back over and said only three words to Alrik, just loud enough for me to hear.

"Sie ist Amerikanerin!"

Alrik adjusted his neck as if his tie was too tight, and then gazed at me inquisitively. I expected a response of anger, but instead his disposition changed to one of intrigue. He said nothing about my being American, didn't ask my name or anything about me for that matter. I fully expected to be arrested, or at the very least, guarded. Instead, he invited me to the cast party and then allowed me to walk away.

"Champagne and hor d'oeuvres will be served at 10:00 sharp in the reception hall. I will count the moments until you arrive."

I jumped at the opportunity of freedom and continued my exit, but I could feel him appraising me.

My first thought was to get out of there as fast as I could, yet I knew that my being there was no accident. I was there because of Halag. As I turned the corner that led down the hallway lined with dressing room doors, I heard Alrik's voice. I didn't turn around until I realized that he was addressing me.

"I enjoyed your performance immensely. I don't generally appreciate the works of Shakespeare. I find them boring. But your rendition was quite unexpected and amusing. You single-handedly managed to dismantle Herr Vogel's near-perfect performance, which is not easily done. By the time you had completed your unconventional version, his character of Gratiano had become rattled to the point of tears. I have neither laughed so hard, nor felt that kind of amusement for many years. Thank you."

Still I said nothing, but only bowed my head and started down the hallway. But once again, he called out to me.

"Fraulein, this gathering is not a masquerade. I look forward to seeing the face that brought comedy to a most mundane drama."

I just couldn't help but like him. To me, he seemed like an old friend. He may have been addressing me in a superior "ivory tower" tone, but I knew his heart and I knew that he was not like the other Nazis who filled this great hall. I gave him a slight grin and walked away.

The golden taffeta costume that was as delicate as a bulldozer, annihilated everything that stood around me. The hallway was hardly wide enough to accommodate the two of us.

When I opened the first door I came to, it was filled with women who were not actresses, but appeared to be exclusive company for the single gentlemen, or for those who opted to leave their wives at home. If looks could kill, I would have been dead on the spot. As a group, they demanded that I get out and pointed to another room down the hall.

The next door was closed. After lightly knocking with no reply, I walked in. The room was small, and half of the area was filled with a rack of bulky costumes that appeared to belong to the infamous Portia. I was thankful to have found a place where I could be alone for a few minutes. Hanging on the outside of the rack was a shimmering white dress that was probably meant for the after-party, and on a second hanger, my traveling clothes. Glancing back and forth between the two, I wondered whether I should blend in with the others and dress in the white glimmering frock, or just put my clothes back on. Here I was again, in the middle of a dilemma.

As I stood there staring at my outfit neatly hanging on the rack, I was oddly encouraged. For the life of me, I was at a loss to remember the final moments of the entry to this journey that carried me onto a stage. It was as if I fell asleep in the darkness, and when I woke, I had been unknowingly prepared for my task. It was completely and utterly remarkable. If I didn't view all of this as a well-orchestrated plan, I was just a fool and didn't deserve to be the Carrier of the Tempus Vector.

With my clothes staring me straight in the face, my choice of evening attire became obvious. There was absolutely no way that I would leave my bag or the Tempus Vector behind. There was a purpose why it had been strategically placed beneath my feet. Never again would I allow myself to be parted from the frame. My next problem was getting out of the dress that was practically tied onto me. I would need help. I stuck my head out the door, and noticed a woman standing by the room of painted floozies. As they strolled out of their dressing room, she one by one, showered them with a cheap and horrific-smelling perfume that permeated the hallway. Once they had gone, I called her over and asked her to help me as I tugged on the laces of the dress.

"Bitte hilfe!"

"Ja, ich komme!"

What a process it was to remove the layers of this getup. While stripping off one piece at a time in complete silence, she asked me what my name was. Normally answering such a question would be a no-brainer, but here I was again, trying to figure out what I would tell these strangers about my identity. My last attempt definitely backfired, and I had no intention of giving a name or story that belonged to someone else. At the same time, I couldn't tell them my real name, because according to Ivan, they would encounter Beni later. There was only one name that came to mind. The beloved of Edmond Dantes.

"Mein name ist Mercedes."

"Ich bin Klara."

Klara was young and most likely the assistant to the costume mistress. Thankfully, she was shy and didn't ask any more questions. Once the dress was off, she offered to stay and help me change. She grabbed hold of the shimmering long-sleeved gown and began to unzip the back.

"No, Klara, this!"

Obviously disappointed at my all-black clothing and boots, she found it difficult to comprehend why I would choose the unfeminine garb over the bedazzled beauty. During the course of helping me change my outfit, Klara couldn't help but notice my dark bruising that stood out like a sore thumb. Her reaction was interesting. Most people would have been appalled at the black and blue handprints, but she walked over to a cupboard and pulled out a large makeup box, removing a small jar and sea sponge. Pushing my chin up and slightly back, she began dabbing a coat of flesh-colored concealer all over my throat, and then blended it onto my face and chest. Over the next hour, she transformed my grungy appearance, ponytail and all, to that of a starlet, hoping that I would change my mind and wear the dress. She knew that those who pledged their allegiance and the excellence of their craft to the Fuhrer should dress like royalty. To her dismay, I opted for my Zorro getup ... black pants, sweater, leather jacket, and matching boots, which was unacceptable.

Before I walked out, I grabbed my backpack, and in her final attempt to glamorize me, she dabbed gardenia perfume onto my wrists. I was thankful that she didn't attempt to spray me with *Evening in Tijuana* that was still lingering in the halls.

As I walked toward the party room, I immediately became the talk of the stagehands who were now cleaning the theater. The whispered rumor that there was an American in their midst was true. I'm not sure what they were saying, but their undivided attention made me feel uncomfortable.

During my long walk down the aisle, the non-stop stares resurrected insecurities. I put my head down, stuck my hands in my jacket pocket, and made a beeline to the door that would lead to the gathering room. Curiously, I felt something in my pocket that I didn't recognize. Along with a folded piece of paper, I pulled out a sealed bag that contained a small brown vial. Before leaving the auditorium, I sat down in the back row and began reading the handwritten note.

You are drop-dead gorgeous.
One trace of your beauty
could kill a thousand. ~ C

Although this note was in Carig's handwriting, it was vague, and sounded nothing like him. His romantic talk didn't generally sound like the lovesick rants of a teenager. I read it several times over and laughed a little at the "drop-dead gorgeous" part. I knew one thing for sure, this note had a higher purpose than an enduring compliment. It was an indirect message that he tucked into my pocket as he pushed me out the door.

He was trying to tell me something important, something that would help me. Within that one brief sentence, he mentioned death twice. The intention was not about me or my beauty but death by one trace, or possibly one drop, is what he meant. The contents of the vial were toxic and what Carig considered to be a method more suitable to carry out the deed I came here for … at least that was my interpretation. We hadn't spoken that much about the night at Annaliese's house, as our lives since then had been non-stop crazy. But what he did say after my near-death experience, was how Annaliese had become a servant of death, using a poisonous black magic as her weapon. All that I could figure was that amidst the madness at the Richter Estate that night, he had secretly grabbed a bottle from her shelf.

It was an incredibly sweet gesture, and made me miss him even more. Ever since we were children, he would always try to find a solution for my predicaments. The whole idea bothered him from the get-go, and he thought it crazy that I was saddled with such burdens. This obviously was not the time or place to be daydreaming about my husband, but I couldn't help it. He had a way of making everything better, and one thought of him set my heart racing. I found myself worried about him and the others back home, but my concern roused a boldness within me.

The haunting rendition of Beethoven's 5th Symphony entranced my body and soul   as I entered the fantastically beautiful reception. The concerto was performed by a tall man dressed in tails who passionately stroked the keys of the exquisite ebony grand as if he were caressing a beautiful woman. Like everything else that pertained to Alrik's existence, the illustrious party room in the midst of the Augustus Playhouse adorned with boundless ornaments of jeweled gold, was home to Germany's elite theater buffs. Each season they would assemble together in their finest frocks and feathers, top hats and tuxedos to enjoy the talents of the world-renowned Ziegler Players Theater Company.

The exquisitely decorated room, flowing with a sea of scarlet flooring, was elegantly furnished with dozens of glass top tables set atop bases of gilded tree trunks, spiraling branches, and hand-sculpted flowers. Encircling each table, sat velvet chairs that, like the carpeting, was a dramatic martial red. Lifelike cherubim fluttered amongst the painted heavens of the room which were sectioned and adorned with brilliant trimmings of gold. In the midst of it all, hung a gold chandelier, embellished with ruby and crystal inlays.

A banquet table ran the entire length of the hall, abounding with silver trays filled with meats, cheeses, caviars, and breads. Champagne was flowing from a fountain in the middle of the lavish display, crowned with a massive peacock ice sculpture. Maids clothed in black uniforms with ruffled white aprons pushed dessert carts from one table to the next, delighting taste buds with cakes, strudels, confections, and brulees.

As I joined the rich and spoiled assemblage, I scoped out the room, watching for Alrik and Halag. I still couldn't believe that I was actually pursuing the man of my nightmare. Until recent truths had been revealed, my goal was to completely forget about our encounter, but it wasn't meant to be. Nonetheless, here I was, in a room that was filled to the gills with theatergoers and, of course, an abundance of reeking party girls. It was obvious after walking through the leering hordes, that I was anything but inconspicuous and probably should have worn the dress. I didn't care though. All I cared about was finding Halag and returning home.

After searching for them to no avail, I noticed a space set apart in the far corner of the room, a private sitting alcove hidden behind an opaque room divider. Rising from the recesses was a cloud of smoke, and the sound of clinking glasses and giggling girls. Outside of the makeshift brothel, stood two armed guards who were protecting the group which had gathered on the other side of the fabric curtain. When I approached the two, they moved shoulder-to-shoulder as one, refusing to let me pass. They didn't ask me what I wanted, and quite honestly, I didn't know what I could possibly say that would allow entry. But then it came to me. His name alone was the key.

"Alrik Richter."

Yes. Those were the magic words, the secret password that would grant me passage into the presence of the elite of Hitler. For all I knew, Hitler himself could have been sitting at the table.

The small room was full. Every chair was double-occupied with a gentleman cradling a paid companion. Included in the already-intoxicated bunch were Alrik and Halag. As I walked in, the guard announced to the Field Marshal that I was asking for him.

"Sir, sie hat nach dir gefragt."

I'm not sure which of them was more shaken when they laid eyes on me, but in unison they abruptly stood up, causing their escorts to tumble to the floor. My presence had single-handedly ruined the festivities of the group, and Alrik and Halag appeared as though they were in the presence of a ghost. I glared daggers at Halag, then down at his half-filled glass, and then back up to his face. At the same time, I slipped my hand into my pocket and clenched the vial, while glancing down at the side-arm of the guard who stood right beside me. Neither option was feasible at that moment. I couldn't just walk over and pour poison into Halag's glass. That method would require a more opportune moment. As for grabbing hold of the gun and shooting him, well, I wasn't confident that I could pull the trigger, and I wouldn't be able to get to the frame before they would shoot me. Alrik's and Halag's reactions to my appearance was interesting, nothing like the time before. I could tell that my uncanny resemblance to Caprice sobered them right up, leaving them addled. In my previous journey, they somehow knew me - burning adoration from Alrik, and a deep loathing from Halag, but not this time.

Halag was disturbingly quiet. I hadn't heard even two words from him, but I could see Alrik pondering what he should do with me. Everyone in the room stood at attention, awaiting instructions from the Field Marshal. I wasn't about to wait around and be captured and imprisoned like last time. Before he could order his men to contain me, I had to flee. Stealthily, I began creeping backwards and exited the room before they had a chance to stop me. And then I ran, like a bat out of hell.

Without warning, and from out of nowhere, I could hear the sound of boots stomping from behind. Alrik wasted no time or manpower searching for me.

Thankfully, the wall-to-wall throng concealed my movements through the crowd. Amidst the dresses and suits, I squatted down and crept towards the side door of the banquet room. I didn't know exactly where it would lead, but at that point I just wanted to get away. The main entrance would be guarded to the hilt, so I knew through the side would be the smartest route of escape.

The exit led to the side alleyway of the theater. When I plowed through the door, standing there in a fog of cigarette smoke were the off-duty kitchen help, guzzling remnants of champagne that they had apparently pilfered. Judging by their wide eyes and deathly still postures, I had startled them just as much as they had startled me. Neither of us were looking to encounter a visit from the Field Marshal's guards, so they gestured to the left and told me to hurry and get away from them. The route they suggested led to complete darkness, but the other side was filled with rumbles of motorcycles revving by. I chose the darkness. Blindly trudging through potholes filled with water, I was met with the smothering stench of trash cans overflowing with rotten garbage that had been sitting there for God-knows-how-long. Halfway through, I couldn't stand the smell any longer and held my breath until reaching the other side. I quickly discovered upon exiting the long stretch of brick walls and ground slick with muck, that I had entered the part of town where decent men would never go.

If I hadn't known better, I would have thought that this particular part of town was the alter ego of Friedlich. The Twilight Zone version of that beautiful little town ... like walking onto the set of a real-life slasher movie. Since I didn't see another living, breathing soul, it stood to reason that I was the star of this horror movie. Perhaps people bustled about here during the day, but night was eerie, shutters were sealed tight, and I had a bad feeling about being here.

Meeting me head on stood a two-story ramshackled building. At first, I believed it to be a boat store. But as I focused more closely on the three small crafts standing side by side in the window display, I found that they were in reality, a trio of cheaply-made caskets of pine. Above the door hung a sign "Leichenhalle," the town's morgue. By the depressed feel of the section of town, this storeroom would serve as the only viable option for the poor and lowly to take their deceased. The most disturbing part, however, was the life-sized mannequins placed within each box. They were far too realistic and unnecessary ... it was a very strange sight.

The buildings adjacent to this *House of Wax* had darkened and broken windows. Ironically, one had been a men's haberdashery and the other a women's boutique, both abandoned. As I had no intention of knocking on either door for help, I briskly continued down the street that was now glistening from the light rain that had just begun. Perfect! Not only was the night windy and cold but wet as well.

As I hurried along, I was startled when struck by a blowing sheet of a poster-size announcement that was tumbling down the street. These public notices had been whisked from billboards and buildings, and now because of the rain, were glued to the ground, except for the one that was stuck to my leg. I peeled it off and held it up. Even though it was dark, I recognized the bright yellow poster from somewhere. I had seen it before but didn't have the time or light to examine it more closely. It would have to wait until later.

As I folded the paper and stuck it in my jacket pocket, I was all at once met by the soft glow of light, diffused with smoke-colored shadows that rose from the shoddy door of the town tavern. Of course, it was open! One could always count on the local beer joint to forever lure in and serve weak men who were trying to drink away their problems. I came to the conclusion that this section of Friedlich seemed to be good for two things, getting liquored up, and dying. Even though it was the only thing open as far as I could see, the saloon would not be my refuge.

I stopped in my tracks, scared away by the smutty and dangerous characters who waited like drooling hyenas to rob, kill, and destroy. Unfortunately, they spotted me the moment I stepped foot in their neighborhood. Quickly crossing to the other side of the street, passing right in front of the funeral parlor, I decided to go in the opposite direction. As luck would have it though, I was surprisingly met by a swarm of motorcycle lights speeding toward me. It appeared that I had two choices here - being captured by Alrik's men or risking the consequences of facing the worst of the worst. My fear, mixed with the bouncing lights of the motorcycles, played tricks on my eyes, making it seem as though the female mannequin in the middle box was winking at me. Most definitely the *Twilight Zone!*

My only escape was to disappear through a narrow opening between two buildings and hide from them all. Being snatched up once again by Alrik would ultimately lead to Halag, but I couldn't stand the thought of being held captive again. I'd rather stay in the shadows, moving in and out of their lives at such a breakneck speed that they wouldn't see me coming ... or going.

I breathed a sigh of relief as I saw the headlights pass, but then I noticed the group of troublemakers from the bar coming in my direction. By their rude and barbaric catcalling, I knew the intentions of their pursuit. Running through my head was the idea that I could grab the frame and be gone, but then it occurred to me, no matter what, it would be far better to be captured by Alrik than this immoral group that stalked me like a pack of dogs. I recalled Adina telling me about the dangers of her beloved German town. By day she would find something new and beautiful about it, but when night came, Carson warned her to never be out and about. Even he knew the dangers of this place. She knew that if he didn't return home before dark, it meant that he wasn't coming home.

According to what I had seen earlier, Alrik had sent out the troops. There were at least eight motorcycles that carried both a driver and a passenger on the prowl. As the shouts behind me grew louder, I began to panic. They were catching up and I couldn't run any faster. Hopefully, close by there would be an inn or boarding house where I could get off the street for the night or find somebody that would help me. I would have given anything if the end of this alley revealed the street where Malachi's shop was located. He would help me. He would let me in.

I would have to make a run for it and have faith that a way forward would be shown to me. Quicker than a New York minute, I bolted straight through to the other side, fiercely colliding head on with a wool-covered form that stopped me in my tracks, rendering me stunned. As I sat dazed and shaken, at first I didn't know what I had hit, but soon realized that I didn't run into a *thing*, but a person.

Feeling hands grab onto me, I instinctively began fighting to escape. But then I heard his voice.

"Fraulein, stop. I'm not going to hurt you!"

"Alrik, why are you following me? What do you want?"

"Why did you run? And you think you know me well enough to address me by my first name?"

"There was no reason for me to stay, and you did introduce yourself as Alrik Richter, right?"

Like clockwork, the thugs behind me emerged from the alley. When they saw their worst nightmare waiting in formation, they scurried like scared mice. Once Alrik realized what I had been running from, he wrapped his arms around me and tried to comfort me.

"I am not here to hurt you. Are you alright, fraulein? I feared for your safety, that is why I came after you."

"Thank you, Herr Richter!"

"You may call me Alrik."

He was so serious and had given me a hard time about calling him by his first name, so to break the tension, I decided to be a bit aloof.

"I don't know, I'll think about it."

He chuckled at my remark.

"You make me laugh, fraulein, and that is no easy task. Tell me, where exactly were you headed?"

If he only knew the truth! That I was on a mission to kill his horrible cousin who, if left to his own devices, would be perilous, destroying endless lives while breathing life into a movement that must never be allowed to rise again.

"An inn or boarding house for the night. Do you know of one?"

"A boarding house?"

I could tell he was filled with questions about why I was there. I hoped that before I would have to come up with too many answers, my job would be done and I would be gone.

"Of course, there are taverns, but the hour is late, and they are closed for the night."

"Well, Field Marshal Richter, I'm sure that they would open for you!"

"Yes, they would. However, it is not my intention to upset

the innkeeper at your request. It would, however, be a great honor to invite an American actress to stay at my home. I do believe that it is your only option."

His invitation seemed so normal, and he was right, I had no choice. Besides, returning to the Richter Estate was the only way that I could get close to Halag.

Alrik opened the passenger-side back door of the black sedan. For the second time in my life, I would enter this car and journey to the house of the Field Marshal of Germany. But this time, so I thought anyway, was of my own accord. Without wasting a moment, he climbed in the other side and slid over next to me. Directly in front of me sat Halag, and the same driver that I remembered from my last encounter sat next to him.

"So, fraulein, may I inquire as to your name? I am assuming it is not Portia."

Ugh! My name.

"I'm called … my name, I mean, is Mercedes."

"That's beautiful! I've never met a Mercedes before. Do you by chance know Edmond Dantes?"

"Only in my dreams, buddy."

Once again, my unexpected humor made him laugh out loud.

"You are quite funny. It is rare to find such humor and beauty wrapped up in one person."

"Thank you, sir, you are very kind."

"Alrik. Please call me Alrik. And by the way, the gentleman sitting in front of you is my cousin. He and I are the only members of our family who truly appreciate theater arts."

Halag turned around in his seat, held out his hand to shake mine, and introduced himself.

"Very nice to meet you, fraulein. Like he said, I am his cousin, Hermann Sauer."

Startled by his introduction, I pulled my hand back and gasped.

"Hermann? Did you say Hermann?"

He was obviously perplexed by my question, and slightly upset by my abrupt response.

"Yes, why?"

"I … no reason, sorry!"

I must have been losing my mind. I was at a loss. Was it his middle name? Not once had I ever heard that name, or more importantly, heard him refer to himself that way. Not only that, Halag, or Hermann, whatever his name was, was rather kind. Most curiously, something about him definitely wasn't the same.

By the humming sound of the tires I could tell that we were passing over the wood bridge, *the one that wasn't long for this world*, and nearing the Richter Estate. After the rather weird encounter with Halag, the car was brimming with an awkward silence. The dense fog outside the window made me feel as though we were in the clouds.

Although mesmerized by the billowing mist outside my window, I could feel Alrik's eyes fixed on me; the azure windows into his soul, spilled over with boldness. Even as I turned towards him, practically face to face, his gaze never left mine.

Turning down the long driveway, I half expected to see the house staff waiting outside. Thankfully, Alrik didn't insist that they *hop to* in their bed clothes, to attend to the unplanned guest. The moment the car slid to a stop, Hermann sprang from the front seat to help me out. Alrik was at my side in a flash and dismissed him with an unflinching stare that spoke volumes. Clearly irritated with Alrik, Hermann aka Halag, or whoever he was, stormed into the house, while Alrik walked me up the stairs and showed me to the same room where I had previously stayed.

"Your room, along with a hot bath, is being prepared. When you're settled in, meet me downstairs in the library, and we'll have a brandy and get to know one another."

As much as I didn't want to go downstairs and formulate another bogus story, I had to do it. I had to create as many opportunities to be with Halag as possible, until my task was complete. Although resolved as to what had to be done, I had a bad feeling. Something was weighing heavily on my mind that I couldn't quite put my finger on.

The moment I submerged myself into the steamy bath water, it hit me. I knew what it was that was bothering me. This whole mysterious charade that was going on between Alrik and Halag was just weird. I knew Halag Sauer. I had unfortunately experienced him up close and personal, and that man who turned around and introduced himself in the car was, in fact, him. Perhaps he had multiple personalities and the "good" Halag decided to come out to play. Even Alrik called him Hermann. *The name, the man, the everything* about Hermann was a mystery to me. Never once during my first journey had I heard even whispers of this name. I had to remember, no matter how nice he seemed now, that Halag was evil and had to be destroyed. I began thinking about what Ivan said. *They had not met me yet, so they might act a little differently, and this encounter is what created the love-and-hate-filled people that I meet later.* I think down deep inside I was afraid that I would somehow end up liking the person Halag once was, which would make my job all the more difficult.

I wasn't about to wear the nightgown and robe that were set out for me. After throwing on the same pants, white t-shirt and jacket, I went downstairs in search of the library. Everyone was asleep, and the downstairs was lit only by the light coming from the room that I had not yet seen. As I approached the door, I could hear Alrik and Halag talking. All I could make out was how the resemblance was uncanny, remarkable actually. They weren't talking to one another though, they were venting to a third person. As I quietly listened at the door, I could tell that they were talking about me. Their earlier calm, cool, and collected demeanors had escalated to keyed-up tones. Apparently, the news they had to share couldn't wait. They hadn't even taken the time to change out of their evening clothes.

Their enthusiastic zeal made it difficult to make out their foreign tongue, but through it all, I continued to hear my name, the fact that I was an American, and of course, "Caprice." Trying to gather all the information I could, I leaned in closer and then quietly cursed myself as the door let out a telltale squeak, alerting them to my presence. As if a spotlight was shining in my direction, my presence had suddenly been made known.

In unison, Alrik and Halag turned, and watchfully focused on their unexpected house guest. They were like a set of unmatched bookends; one made of perfectly chiseled marble and the other of tarnished copper flawed with dings and dents.

Even though *their* eyes were focused on me, *I* stood in awe of the magnificent extent of the Richter library. Obviously, I had been completely engrossed in the complications that were taking place on my previous journey and missed out on this magical place that overflowed with classics of every genre. The fireplace alone was so massive in height and width that it could have housed a roomful of furniture. Following the vast expanse of leather-bound wonders around the room, I was reminded of how everything in this house had been taken to the extreme, and they definitely spared no expense when filling three of the four walls from floor to ceiling with endless shelves of books. I had never seen such a library in a house. I wondered, as I scoped out the array of literature, if Alrik would adhere to Hitler's ruling to burn anything and everything that wasn't written by a German author.

There were not too many things that could distract me from such a heaven as this, that is until I noticed *him*. There was someone else in the room, a third man sitting on the couch who had joined the affair. He was facing Alrik and Halag, but his back was to me. His light hair was slicked back, and from what I could see, he was wearing a black and gold smoking jacket.

Alrik walked over to the door, took my hand, and forwardly kissed it.

"You smell lovely! Come, there is someone that I would like for you to meet."

Hand in hand, we walked over to where Halag was standing with a welcoming grin on his face that kind of freaked me out. The man who was sitting on the couch had almost finished a crystal carafe of hard liquor; I could smell him from where I stood. As I came closer, he set his glass down on the table, slowly stood up, and turned around. As our eyes met, the room began spinning out of control, my heart beat double-time, and I broke out in a cold sweat. I was in the middle of a nightmare that I didn't see coming.

In that split second, we were both overcome with emotion. His dramatic gasp was most likely due to my uncanny resemblance to Caprice. He hadn't believed what the others had told him until he saw for himself. At first, he seemed overjoyed as if he had seen an old friend, but then was suddenly withdrawn and poured himself another drink. *My* fight for breath, on the other hand, was one of disgust and dread.

There were two of them! Their people called it *eineiige zwillinge* ... twins. This had to be the Halag Sauer that I knew and despised, the one I came here for. I stared deeply into his eyes, searching for that lecherous, depraved leer that would reveal the heart of the animal I sought - one I failed to see in his identical twin brother, Hermann. To my dismay, I failed to see it in him either, and as far as his physical qualities, something about him was off. This Halag Sauer was a head taller, had a vibrant smile, and was breathtakingly handsome. He and Alrik standing together were all but perfect, like two gods. And then there was Hermann, who more resembled my attacking foe with crooked teeth and a greasy appearance, but his heart didn't seem to be dark. I had no idea what was going on. I was confused by it all.

Visions of Halag lying on his deathbed began to haunt me. Though he teetered with one foot in the here and now, and the other planted firmly in the depths of hell, he was amazingly confident of his ultimate victory and that my attempt in stopping the rise of the Fourth Reich would fail. I was suddenly afraid. That Halag, the one who tried to kill me, was a crafty and brilliant enemy who would not go down easily. It was almost as if he knew I was coming for him, and created a facade of confusion with these two, one that would cloud my judgment and encumber my mission. However brilliant he believed himself to be, and no matter how sly, my calling was led by God - The God who had no equal. He was with me and would give me wisdom to conquer this enemy of mine. All I needed to do was stay calm and move forward with my eyes wide open.

As I sat down on the soft green velvet armchair, I found myself instantly surrounded by the curious three. While Alrik and Halag wanted to know all about me and were attentive to my every move, Hermann sat at a distance with a sketch pad in hand and began to draw. When I inquired as to what he was doing, and before he had the chance to reply, Halag mocked his artistic abilities and referred to them as hen scratchings and childish finger paintings. Alrik immediately rebuked Halag's nasty remarks and began to brag on Hermann's impressive abilities as an artist. Through the insults, Hermann remained unmoved. It was obvious that when he opened his pad of paper, he entered into a world all his own, with eyes that effortlessly shifted from parchment to subject. It was obvious to me that Alrik had probably often served as a buffer between the Sauer brothers.

"You're just jealous of your brother, cousin! My dear Mercedes, Hermann is an extraordinary artist. When he's done, you will see what I mean. He was never formally taught, as his gift is God-given. My father commissioned him many times to paint members of our family. Every painting that I have of my late wife was done by him. He is remarkable!"

The more Alrik bragged about Hermann, the drunker and more obnoxious Halag became. Alrik had no idea that I knew the paintings he spoke of, those of Caprice that hung in the hidden hall, and I agreed, they were magnificent. When Hermann finished the sketch, he placed the pad of paper in my hand. Alrik was right, his talents were amazing. No more than half an hour had passed, and he had magically transformed a blank sheet of paper into a masterpiece. I stood up and walked closer to the fire so that I could see the drawing more clearly. He had captured me perfectly. Actually, I was far more attractive on paper. Alrik joined me at the fire, and stood behind, examining every line of the picture.

"Lovely, you are lovely! May I keep this, cousin?"

Hermann became oddly upset at his request.

"No! Not yet anyway. It needs a few finishing touches."

With his burst of frustration, he stuck the pencil behind his ear, said a perturbed *gute nacht*, and then raced out the door. In spite of his rather dramatic exit, he stopped right outside the door so that he could eavesdrop on our conversation. Absent from the room but not gone, he erupted in cursing from the hallway after dropping his stack of papers. While the attention was no longer on me, I felt it the perfect opportunity to return to my room.

"I think I'll go to bed too."

Alrik seemed disappointed, but then told me to sleep well and he would see me in the morning. Halag on the other hand, hypnotized by the flames, said nothing. My lack of discernment about these two left me confused and distraught. I had come here for one reason only, which was to find Halag Sauer and kill him. But now I didn't even know who was who. As a matter of fact, I half contemplated the idea of a third brother hidden away somewhere, due to his insane behavior? But it was doubtful.

As I headed out the door, Halag loudly began an inquisition from where he sat. When I stopped and turned around, he energetically arose from his drunken stupor and shuffled over to where I stood. Instead of Alrik objecting, he watched curiously.

"How is it that you have come to be here? Are you an

American spy?"

Terrific! Here we go again with the American spy theory. Trying not to appear nervous, and refusing to let him intimidate me, I took one step forward and stood toe to toe with my accuser.

"I have a very good reason to be here!"

I wish I knew what my very good reason was. As much as I hated to admit it, he had every reason to distrust me.

I thankfully remembered the folded piece of paper in my pocket, the yellow vintage poster that curiously latched onto me only hours before. I carefully peeled apart each section trying not to tear the water-logged edges. Even though streams of ink had slightly distorted the picture, after one quick glance I recalled where I had once upon a time seen this image. It sat within a black matted frame in the corner of Adina's sewing room. Because everything in her world was always neat and tidy, it struck me as odd that this one particular piece of her collection was covered in dust, like an abandoned and hated symbol that she refused to discard. It was identical to the one I now held in my hand, only more faded and timeworn. In all reality, it was a contradiction of sorts. Seemingly cheery and inviting at first glance, with its stein of beer and silhouette of a Ferris wheel, but then unfortunately branded by the twisted trident mark of the devil. I never understood why she kept such a dejected piece of history, but she would often remind me that the day we forget, is the day that history repeats itself.

"What is it, fraulein? You look troubled."

"No, I mean yes. It's just that when I was a little girl, my aunt had an old copy of this at her house. I just didn't know what it was until now."

"What are you talking about?"

Open mouth, insert foot! What had I done?

"What I meant to say was that this resembles something I've seen before."

Halag was alerted by my baffling statement, and drunkenly stumbled over to where I stood.

"How is it, fraulein, that you remember this poster as a child, long before it was created?"

For what seemed like an eternity, he peered into my eyes, obviously trying to intimidate me. He was clearly suspicious of me, but the longer he stared, the softer his disposition became, almost as if his mind was drifting into a memory from another time.

I was completely caught off guard when he suddenly spoke up and asked me a question. Not just any question, but unfortunately one that would test my mathematical skills, which was never my strong suit. My lack of mathematical genius mixed with nervousness, left me dumbfounded.

"Tell me … in what year were you born?"

At first, I couldn't even remember what year I was *in,* let alone what year it was 26 years ago. He was smart! What better way to test my true intentions than to ask me the simplest of all questions. But then I began subtracting years from 1940 in my head, only wishing that I could use my fingers. His continued observation of my every reaction was more than I could stand. I hemmed and hawed, and told him that it was very rude to ask a lady her age. Nervously, I looked down at the ground trying to further avoid his question, when I was distracted by a small but significant item that was lying on the floor. To my dismay, the amber-colored bottle filled with poison had fallen from my pocket when I had abruptly removed the poster. It was an ideal distraction from the age thing, but I wasn't sure which one was worse. Together, we rushed to grab it, but Halag got to it before I could.

"What is this?"

I calmly held out my hand.

"It's mine ... that's what it is. Please give it back!"

At first, I was going to tell him that it was a tonic that I needed for my health, but I feared he would make me drink it. My catty attitude towards him was risky to be sure, and at first it seemed that he was going to keep it, but then he reluctantly placed it in my hand. Not wanting to discuss it further, I held up the paper, trying to reroute his attention.

"This is why I'm here. I had intended to go to the Oktoberfest in Munich, but it's so far away. I've been traveling for weeks on my own and heard about this … this Festival des Sieges. It seemed like a perfect alternative."

"So, fraulein, you are not with the theater group?"

I began spinning a most absurd tale about how I was passing by the theater when a member of the crew frantically burst through the side door and began calling for Darla, who apparently was their missing Portia. It would have been hazardous and meant complete ruin for the production if he returned empty-handed. After pleading his case and sizing me up for the costumes, I agreed to help him. Before I knew it, I was dressed and standing on the stage, unprepared, surrounded by a sea of spectators who were waiting for the finale. It certainly didn't help that the "beefy and rather rude Herr Bossy Boots" was screaming at me from the wings. Once I realized that he was bound to be disappointed in my performance, I improvised.

"And that, gentlemen, is my story. My travels landed me here, and so far, it's been quite an adventure. The festival, well, it's on my bucket list. I mean ... I adore Ferris wheels."

I was nervous and kept rambling on about nothing. I just needed to stop talking before I completely unraveled my tale into the pile of hogwash that it really was. I was relieved when Alrik finally spoke up.

"Fraulein, the Festival des Sieges is an age-old tradition celebrating the finest beer and food in Germany, *in that order*. You are in luck! The Munich festival was canceled anyway, it would have been futile for you to go there. The Fuhrer has prompted communities of our homeland to carry on this tradition as long as Germany is honored in all of it. The first keg was tapped at noon today, and the celebration, which would usually last for two weeks, will conclude on Sunday. I hope you will stay at least until then. Tomorrow is the highlight of it all. How lucky you are to be here on such an occasion! People from Friedlich and surrounding areas will demonstrate their allegiance by wearing traditional German dress. There will be music and dancing, drinking and eating. If you'd like, miss, I will have an appropriate outfit delivered to your room first thing in the morning."

During Alrik's enthusiastic commentary about the Friedlich festival (that turned out to be a smaller version of the world-renowned Oktoberfest), I was preoccupied by the hateful expression on Halag's face that was intently focused on me. His barbed gaze spoke volumes; he didn't trust me. It was as if he could see right through my story. Perhaps even now he knew that I was the Carrier of the Tempus Vector and he was simply waiting for the first opportunity to take it from me. *This* was the Halag I remembered, with eyes that manifested the darkness of his heart. Be that as it may, it was Hermann who physically matched the person of my nightmares, not Halag. One Halag was enough for ten lifetimes, but *two* made me feel as though I was somehow being punished, and then there was the probability that instead of killing one, I would have to kill them both! Just the thought of it made me sick to my stomach.

The more his eyes burned through me, the angrier I became, and instead of making me cower, it struck me as a challenge. Even though his twisted approach was meant to bulldoze me into a state of fear, I had no intention of giving him the satisfaction. Along with my exaggerated zeal and excitement over attending the festival, I retaliated with a brazen death stare at Halag, until his face began twitching, causing him to finally turn away.

"I look forward to it, Field Marshal Richter! Goodnight, I will see you in the morning."

Alrik kissed my hand as Halag poured himself another drink and belched in my direction. I should have just walked away, but I wasn't in the mood to let such a foul-mouthed moron have the last word.

"Oh, Halag, I didn't know you were still here. I'm sure I won't see you tomorrow, you don't seem like the *let's have fun at the festival type*, so this is probably good-bye!"

Before he could say one more word, I walked out the door. By the sound of it, I had infuriated him and Alrik had to stop him from coming after me. I really knew better than to egg him on, but I couldn't help grinning from ear to ear as I made my way up the stairs.

The house was dark and quiet. Somehow though, I no longer felt like a stranger here. When I reached the top of the stairs, I stopped dead in my tracks as I noticed a shadow in the darkness. I nearly had a heart attack until I realized that it was only Hermann, waiting for me.

"For you, fraulein!"

With an outstretched arm, he handed me a gray portfolio that was bound with cotton twine.

"Don't open it now!"

"Why? Is this the drawing of me? I can't wait to see it. Alrik said that you are an incredible artist."

"It's much more than a picture … it's a story with a concealed beginning, and an unfinished ending."

I felt as though I had been put on notice with his brain-twisting riddle. Stricken by a swell of uneasiness, I turned around and began to walk away, but then I heard him call out my name.

"I'm sorry!"

"Why are you sorry?"

"Halag. He's cursed you know!"

I wasn't sure what he meant, but before I had a chance to ask, he quickly walked away and faded back into the shadows.

I was curious about Hermann's mysterious footnote about Halag being cursed, and whatever was in this portfolio. I had no doubt from the moment that Halag stormed into Malachi's shop that something was wrong with him, but to say he was cursed was an odd choice of words. If I were to be completely honest, the Hermann that I had believed to be sweet and artistic was becoming rather creepy. At least I knew where I stood with Halag. He was just mean, and slightly predictable. But Hermann was the smart one who seemed comfortable standing in the background. I was even more curious now as to what the portfolio held, and what it had to do with me. After checking every crevice and corner of the room, making sure that I was alone, I sat down on the bed and slowly untied the string.

I could tell at once that there was more than just one piece of parchment. The one on top was the picture he had just drawn of me. Alrik was absolutely correct in his assessment of Hermann's skill as an artist, it was brilliant. The next drawing was a much older and weathered piece of paper that was the initial sketch-turned-painting of Caprice, matching the main portrait of her that hung in the secret hall. It was an amazing likeness. We could have been the same person, just in different eras of time. Until the third drawing was revealed, I surmised that the story he spoke of was simply that I resembled the deceased wife of the Field Marshal. But as my eyes followed the turn to the next page, I was alarmed at what I saw. It was a messy, obviously hastily drawn image of the Tempus Vector frame, propped against my backpack, but that wasn't all … something was written on the backside that rendered me paralyzed.

Fingers that burn to etch the light of you.
Like mementos of blank parchment,
My sanity bides the day that I can trace your smile.
My mind is rendered numb … do you search for me as I

do for you?
The despondent slant of my quill recalls the contour of
your lips, as does my tainted heart.
My affliction is comforted only by my compositions.
It is in the tangled depths of furrowed parchment that I
find you.
 Frail and crumbling, only fickle peace stirs my bones.
My soul screams out, but only empty echoes return,
 Ensnared by an imitation that gnaws at my bones like a
dog.
Out of nowhere this deceiver came ... guided by a
carcass of embossed timber.

Terror consumed me on all sides, as the weird *Edgar Allan Poe-sounding* stanzas jumped off the page and taunted me. This was the story he spoke of, *my story,* or possibly how mine paralleled his. He was obviously filled with hatred, and tortured by my likeness of Caprice, but most disturbing was how he somehow gathered that the frame was responsible for me being here. He recognized that there was much more to me than what I had revealed to my hosts. In his warped way he was making a statement of power, a proclamation that he was one step ahead of me.

My blood was surging through my veins causing my heart to pound, still, I moved at a snail's pace to the table that held my satchel. *Breathe, Beni, breathe!* If the frame was gone, if he had taken it, I would know that the prophecy that Halag had declared on his deathbed was true. I had lost, even before I had arrived. But if it was still there, I would know that this was just a sick game. He was making a point that he could get to me. I held my breath as I unbuckled the outer strap of my bag ... it was difficult not to imagine the worst scenario, that I would reach in and the frame would be gone, and all would be lost. As I slid my hand into the side pocket, I collapsed with relief as I touched the edge of the frame. My overwhelming thankfulness was promptly replaced by an avenging wisdom, one that trumped my fear and refreshed my objective.

It was late, and I was exhausted. I couldn't remember the last time I had slept, so I, along with my leather traveling companion, slid between the cool sheets. I had no intention of letting the creepy clone of Halag get his paws on my bag again. Wound tighter than a top, I found it difficult to relax and fall asleep. It was a few hours after I had finally dozed off that I was awakened by a loud disturbance from outside.

Chapter 23

Festival des Sieges

"My sword of venom would change their course of being and resurrect those who had suffered at Halag's hand. Before I would leave this place, I would bend history."
~Benidette Hammel~

Booming thunder and fierce flashes of light tore through my room with the intensity of a war zone. I couldn't tell if the outside darkness was from the ebony-colored clouds, or if it was still night. Whatever the time, this was a violent storm that would surely prevent the Festival des Sieges.

Amidst the drumfire of the tempest, came a knock at the door. I yelled out for my guest to come in, but then there was a second knock. Wrapping myself in a comforter, I walked over and opened the door. Standing there, was Alrik.

"I came to make sure that you were alright, fraulein."

"I'm fine, thank you."

In the duskily-lit hallway, he just stood there, staring at me, saying nothing. As the seconds ticked by, the moment became more and more awkward.

"So, what time is it? Would you like to come in?"

"It's just slightly after 3:00. I hope I didn't wake you."

I told him that the storm woke me before he got there. He glanced around the room and shrugged his shoulders and crossed his arms as if he were cold.

"It's freezing in here. Let me light a fire for you."

Once the fire was lit, he insisted on calling for a tray of tea. I refused the idea of waking anyone up in the middle of the night to serve me. But I was starving, and I told him that if he would show me the kitchen, I would whip up an omelette. He was pleased with my offer, grabbed my hand, and like two kids who were trying to sneak out without making noise, we stumbled down the hallway and laughed all the way down the stairs and into the kitchen. I only knew Alrik to be intense and serious and hadn't seen this side of him in my last journey. I wondered what had happened to him this month prior that would rob him of his joy and create a man who teetered on the edge of a possessive delusion.

I could feel his eyes watch my every move as I cracked the eggs and crumbled the cheese over the bubbling concoction. I suggested that we return to the warm fires of my room with our early morning snack. This was my chance to be alone with him and "accidentally" gather information about Halag. Staying down in the kitchen was out of the question. In addition to being cold and drafty, it was also far too accessible with its dozens of storage closets and entrances on every side. It wasn't private from curious spectators, two in particular that I didn't trust. Halag was mean and condescending, and Hermann was slimy and sneaky, and together they created one perfectly horrible person. Even now I could feel eyes on me, like bait in a fishbowl. I wasn't afraid though, but rather filled with a boldness that I had never known until now. Little did they know that their intrusive investigation was double-edged. I too would watch and wait, only under the guise of the Tempus Vector. My sword of venom would change their course of being and resurrect those who had suffered at Halag's hand. Before I would leave this place, I would bend history.

I was suddenly distracted by dancing shadows that filled every dark crevice of the kitchen with visions of the enemy lurking. Realizing my preoccupation, Alrik tried to once again reel me into his world.

"Fraulein, fraulein! I have the wine, shall we go? Are you well?"

He placed the bottle and two glasses on the tray aside the two omelettes and followed me up the stairs. At this point, it was obvious that I felt more comfortable with him than he was with me. I had to stop and check myself. I knew his heart. It was lonely and desperate. I had grown fond of this man, but to me he was more like the brother that I never had. There was only one man who would forever be the love of my life. My time with Alrik needed to remain friendly, not romantic. I had no intention of playing with his heart and wanted to prevent any false assumptions.

I spread out the blanket on the floor, right in front of the crackling fire and then tossed several throw pillows on top, I sat down and patted the blanket.

"Here, give me the tray and sit down. We're gonna have an indoor picnic … that's what we do back home when the weather's bad outside. It's fun, sit!"

He stared down at me as if his aristocratic bum had never touched the floor before. As he slowly sat down and lounged back on a pillow, he smiled and soon discovered that he liked the floor. I handed him the cheese and mushroom omelette and was pleased by his response as he took the first bite. In all of the privileges and entitlements of his birthright, he had never experienced an omelette until now, and was savoring every morsel. For the next several hours, we talked.

I told him as little about myself as I possibly could. With each question he would ask about my life, I would turn the conversation back to him and his twin cousins. He told me that I was the only woman he had ever met who was more interested in him than in themselves. Although my motives were selfish, my probing questions and attention to his life sparked an unquenchable infatuation. Before my very eyes, he was conforming into the Alrik I remembered, the Alrik who loved Beni. He seemed to enjoy having someone to talk to about anything and everything and kept saying over and again how perfect it felt to be with me. His conversations quickly turned into flirtatious pillow talk that I tried to extinguish.

Through it all, I discovered that Halag was strong, always competing with Alrik even as children. They seemed to be more rivals than family, and their biggest competition while growing up was for the attentions of Caprice. But Hermann, on the other hand, was always sickly. At a young age, he contracted scarlet fever and almost died. He constantly struggled to keep up with the boys, but instead of striving to be like them, he began drawing, painting, and spending every waking moment with Caprice who had faithfully stayed by his side through his entire illness. She cared deeply for both Halag and Hermann, but her heart belonged to Alrik. After their marriage, Halag turned bitter towards the two, and Hermann escaped into his art. He became overly obsessed with capturing Caprice on canvas. His fixation explained the shrine of portraits that totaled more than all of the other family members' put together.

Of the two brothers, Alrik's father preferred Halag, and referred to Hermann as the "fatal flaw." Alrik, on the other hand, was more partial to Hermann. It was obvious that the two of them were close, which caused an additional contention between Alrik and his father. His tyrant of a father always thought him weak because he had compassionate inclinations.

At one point in our conversation, Alrik sadly admitted overhearing his father say that Halag was more suited to be his son.

As we lay there talking face to face, I could feel the weight of my travels combined with lack of sleep finally catch up with me. With a full stomach and the warmth of the fire, I found it impossible to keep my eyes open for another second. As I dozed off, I could feel Alrik's fingers gently comb through my hair, and before I knew it, I drifted off into deep slumber.

I could have slept forever but was alerted by the scrunching sound of leather boots parked directly in front of me, blocking the now smoldering fire. Impatiently, they began clicking together in perfect rhythm, until my heavy eyes opened. I was so warm and comfortable that I forgot where I was and what I was doing there. Alrik had covered me with a blanket and had fallen asleep next to me with his face buried in my hair.

I'm not sure how long this pair of boots had been standing there, staring down at the two of us, but the mere fact that he had come into my room uninvited, upset me. I bolted upright and yelled at the intruder to get out.

When Alrik heard my panicked voice, he stood up in one swift movement and faced Halag. Not holding back, they battled back and forth in staunch German tongue. I wasn't sure what the main issue was except that I was a mysterious stranger, and Halag was concerned with Alrik's total abandonment of his senses in letting a complete stranger invade their lives. It wasn't until Alrik threatened to have him dragged away like a dog that his cousin raised his hands in surrender and backed down.

Halag was fearful, I could see it in his eyes. He knew that the threat was not empty, and that with the snap of his fingers, the Field Marshal of Germany had the power to do it. He glared at me with hateful daggers and then stormed out of the room.

Still breathing heavily, Alrik turned around and reached his hand down to help me up off of the floor. As I raised to my feet, he gently wrapped his arms around me.

"I'm sorry for that, he doesn't understand."

"Understand what?"

"How I could so quickly surrender my heart to another. He and Hermann were fully committed to my late wife, Caprice, and feel that no other could take her place."

"Alrik, you don't even know me."

"There are some things that I just know to be true. I knew the first time I laid eyes on Caprice that she would someday be mine … I felt the same way when I saw you standing on that stage. You are unlike any woman I have ever met, choosing to serve rather than be served. I can't remember a more pleasant evening in my entire life. I enjoy *your* world, far more than my own, fraulein. Not only did you prepare a most satisfying omelette but we ate it on the floor, covered in blankets and pillows. It was far more agreeable than being at the finest banquet table in the presence of kings and queens."

As I chuckled at his overly enthusiastic response to a nonsensical practice that Adina and I had regularly enjoyed my entire life, I realized something. My prior journey that was yet to come, included the excessive spread of pallets and pillows beneath the old oak at Kristall Himmel, and was no accident, but a well thought out re-creation of last night. I felt horrible. He was exuberantly happy and so hopeful. Unfortunately, the more he talked, the more affectionate he became.

"Fraulein Mercedes, I must be frank with you. I could hardly stand to close my eyes for fear morning would come. It was all too perfect. So perfect that I thought perhaps it was a dream, and I would wake, and you would be gone. But you are still here. I promised myself that if this was indeed real, I would tell you, I mean ask you, to stay and never leave."

This probably would have been the time to tell him that I was unavailable, but I had learned from my last journey that it was best to say nothing about anyone or anything. It would only cause more questions and a tighter grip.

"Alrik, Halag is right. I can't allow you to give your heart to me. I can't stay and will be leaving after the festival today. I have to go home. It would be unfair to promise you anything, but I will always consider you my friend."

His hurt-filled eyes spoke volumes, a friend was *not* what he was looking for.

"Perhaps fraulein, before the day is done I might convince you otherwise."

Before I could reply, there was a knock at the door. It was

my old friend Gerda from my last visit. She excitedly walked into the room carrying a large box.

"Dein kleid fraulein!"

"Ah, it is your dirndl."

Alrik could tell by my confusion that I had no idea what she was talking about.

"The dress … the costume for the festival. It is traditional attire that everyone will wear. I will go now and let Gerda help you get ready. We will all leave for the Festival des Sieges together in one hour. You will be my special guest."

After giving my personal handmaiden some last-minute instructions, he left the room.

Immediately, Gerda began nervously buzzing around, pulling off my clothes and talking nonstop. By the looks of her showy garb, she too would be attending the event, and was trying to hurry me along. Not only giddy with excitement over the festival, but she was thrilled that the stormy weather had cleared into a beautiful sunny day. Piece by piece, she helped me put on the ruffled apron dress. I knew immediately by the way the bodice fit, that this style was surely invented by a man. It was far too tight, and lifted everything up, making certain assets appear bigger than they really were. The rest of it, however, was lovely, made of black velvet that was covered in red and yellow embroidered flowers. She attempted to put my hair in two braids and pin them into spirals on each side of my head, but I refused the "Princess Leia" do, and told her to take it down. When I stood up and viewed myself in the mirror, I was appalled and felt completely ridiculous. I resembled a floozy barmaid in a pirate movie.

Like a nervous nellie, Gerda kept prompting me to move my *arsch* and get downstairs. Most likely Alrik had warned her not to be late, but I refused to go without taking my packed satchel with me. Before placing my jacket on top, I pulled out the vial of poison and slipped it into my apron pocket. This event, with its hordes of drunken people, would be the perfect platform to finish what I had come here for. Even though I looked utterly ridiculous, I knew that my ensemble wouldn't compare to the trio of straight-laced Germans waiting for me at the bottom of the stairs all dressed in lederhosen. *That* would be a sight to behold.

To my dismay, they were not dressed in short leather

britches and suspenders, but in crisply pressed uniforms that reeked of German rule.

Even though I was slightly embarrassed to be the only one dressed up, I said nothing. Halag and Hermann whispered back and forth, silently mocking my snug attire, but I refused to give them the satisfaction of becoming ill-humored.

"Well, check out the three of you! You're about as much fun as a root canal."

With furrowed eyebrows full of contention, they glanced at one another quizzically, making me wonder if they even knew what I was talking about. Maybe root canals were a slight wrinkle in my timeline? So, I continued in another way to express my disappointment in their lack of spirit for the occasion.

"You did say we were going to a beerfest, right? Or are we going to a funeral? I'm afraid that not a one of you will fit in … they may not even allow you to come in at all. As for me, I am ready for *F - U - N!* Okay, gentlemen, let's go!"

Alrik was amused by my ribbing, but Halag and Hermann were not entertained one little bit.

I scooted past the uniforms and scurried out the front door, leaving the trio behind. Unexpectedly, I was met outside by a caravan of vehicles filled with armed guards who would be joining us at the festival. I crawled, *as lady-like as possible considering my garb,* into the backseat of the lead car. Within a few minutes, they walked out together and quietly got in. Alrik slid next to me saying nothing, intensely studying my every contour. As the cars began to move, I stared out the window remaining indifferent to his attention and trying to focus on the beautiful countryside.

I had it in my mind that the festival would take place in the center of Friedlich, but to accommodate the sheer masses of people that would travel from all around, it was held on a large plot of land that bordered Steinway, the next city over that was home to one of the busiest train stations in Germany with tracks stretching in all directions. Because it rained all night, I had visions of a *Mudfest* rather than an *Octoberfest.* Either way, I was anxious to get there … this car ride was becoming unbearable! Alrik's mad infatuation had begun and would continue on into the next journey; he had become smitten with me overnight. It was inevitable that he would fall head over heels for the ghost of Caprice who he believed had come to him, just as she had foretold. With each passing moment, his fine breeding went right out the window as his fervor hijacked his self-control. Each bump in the road gave him the excuse to move closer, making it notably difficult to ignore his breath on my skin and his eyes wandering to places they didn't belong.

"See anything you like, Field Marshal?"

"Forgive me, fraulein, but you are beautiful. As hard as I try, I can't seem to look away."

Seeing the zeal in his eyes was actually painful. This, all of this, would eventually end with heartbreak for him. I cared deeply for him as well, but just not in the same way.

Within a few moments after turning onto the main street, I was surprised to see that we had arrived in the middle of a bustling interchange. People were moving in all directions. Some had suitcases in hand and were heading toward the train station, frantic to catch the last one of the morning. Most, however, were excitedly walking towards the festival. I'm not exactly sure what I envisioned this celebration to be, but I didn't expect the awe-inspiring display that lay before me. Colorful tents, elaborately decorated booths, merry music, and of course, the fantastic Ferris wheel covered in twinkling lights filled the normally vacant lot. If not for the notorious German flags that were strung from one end to the other, it would have been completely magical.

The commoners were required to park in a distant lot and walk, but our cars pulled right up to the front, and one by one the doors to the vehicles swung open. Everyone seemed to watch as the staunchly pressed uniforms and token bar maid stepped out of the sleek black sedans. Like clockwork, faces in the crowd that were just a moment ago filled with joy, quickly turned somber at the arrival of the suits. Quite honestly, I didn't blame them a bit. They were only trying to escape their fearful reality and drown their sorrows in barley pop.

I was glad to see that everyone there was dressed in their traditional bests. Although this event was familiar to the trio, Alrik, Halag, and Hermann immediately hampered everyone's fun with their intimidating Nazi egos, pushing their way past the people like proud peacocks. I on the other hand, would have no problem mixing in with the normal everyday folk.

The air was filled with delicious and unique flavors of

freshly baked bread and pastries, spicy sausages, and fragrant sauerkraut. I even sensed the black licorice spice of anise that was delicate in comparison to the malted perfume that overpowered the atmosphere. Perhaps it was the pools and barrels of beer that were everywhere, but the air was so thick and heavy with malt alcohol that even normal breathing made me tipsy. It was so odd watching children fill their steins right alongside their parents; it was a family affair to be sure. Apparently underage drinking was not a thing, and no one cared if little Hans was lying drunk as a skunk in the dirt. For all who attended, it was unacceptable to allow one's glass to become empty, and there was no excuse, for that matter, as every few feet you practically tripped over another spigot attached to a different brew.

Alrik held my hand tightly with no intention of letting go. For a short time, Halag and Hermann walked closely behind us, and then left for the main tent where they could eat, drink, and dance until they passed out. Alrik's ideas were quite different than theirs … romantic, always romantic. It was his goal to win my heart before the day was done.

We arrived at a booth labeled Lebkuchen, which was the source of the powerful anise fragrance that I had noticed earlier. Hundreds of heart-shaped gingerbread cookies frosted with romantic phrases had been strung on ribbons and tied into necklaces. When a gentleman wanted to announce publicly his feelings for the one he loved, he would purchase one of the aromatic and appetizing strands and place it around her neck. The sweet and spicy secret ingredient was said to warm any heart into complete submission.

As Alrik placed the delicious necklace around my neck, he bent down and kissed me on each cheek. When he did, all of the people standing around applauded and yelled out to me "Kuss ihn!" They were urging me to kiss him back, but I had no desire to. I didn't belong to him.

Once again, the words of Malachi ran through my mind, recommending that the Carrier of the Tempus Vector never marry. Maybe this was why. This was not the first time that I had been faced with a decision that would require me to surrender the moment and go down a path not of my own choosing, and I feared it would not be my last. The longer I hesitated, the more awkward the situation became, and with every passing second the crowd seemed to grow and chant even louder. I didn't want to kiss him, but I didn't want to embarrass him either. All eyes were suddenly focused on me, waiting in anticipation for my next move. Then they began chanting in unison.

"Kuss ihn! Kuss ihn!"

I took a deep breath, wrapped my arms around his neck, and kissed him good and hard, and he kissed me back. We thrilled the people with our display, and they cheered just as though we'd won a race. I pulled away from his arms and took a step back, but he remained stationary with his eyes still closed, not realizing that I had stopped. He opened his eyes and gaped at me, apparently entranced, and whispered three small words.

"Kiss me again!"

I couldn't help but give a slight grin at his seemingly enchanted affection. To break the spell, I grabbed his hand and pulled him away from the licorice-scented voodoo hut that was causing him to act so strangely.

"Come on, Valentino. Take me on the Ferris wheel ... I think we need some fresh air!"

The more I was around this German casanova, the more I realized how touchy-feely he was, far more than myself. We couldn't even stand in line without him holding my hand or fondling the apron strings of my dress.

There were so many people in attendance, all from various walks of life, making every car of the Ferris wheel, a story. Elderly couples, jubilant children, and impassioned lovers spun round and round feeling as though they could fly, if even just for a few moments. I would have been happy just to stand there and people-watch for hours, when all at once my attention was drawn to one particular couple. At their first turnabout, they were embracing and kissing, making it difficult to see their faces. Although dressed for the occasion, he in lederhosen and the silliest green hat, and she in a tasteful cream and white apron dress with a matching scarf tied around her head, they were somehow different than all the others. On the next revolution, I was struck by their contagious joy and laughter. It was obvious that they adored one another.

The third time they came around, I could clearly see that the couple was none other than my aunt and uncle! His face was buried in the nape of her neck, but she unexpectedly glanced up, and we connected. To me, it was a most familiar and comforting gaze. I smiled from ear to ear at the sight of my Aunt Adina and Uncle Carson sitting there together. She, on the other hand, was most obviously astounded to see a mirrored image of herself staring back at her. My presence instantly put her on high alert. Shifting and twisting in their seats, I could tell that she and Carson were both hanging over the sides, struggling to get a better look. I was stricken with a horrible feeling in my soul, warning me that this encounter couldn't, or rather shouldn't, happen.

As much as I wanted to see them one last time, nothing good would come from me meeting Adina and Carson. As a matter of fact, it would be disastrous. For their sake, I had to prevent Alrik from seeing them, alert Carson to Alrik's presence, all the while not letting either of them know my motives. My uncle had kept his marriage and private life completely hidden from those within the circle of his alter existence of secret agent. It was his way of protecting Adina, and I had every intention of helping keep her safe and hidden. But I needed to act fast. The Ferris wheel was being unloaded efficiently, and the two of them would soon be at ground level. I had to do something drastic. If I didn't, the second they stepped off, everything would all fall apart.

"Alrik, umm. Let's go. I don't really want to go on this ride. I'm uhh, super hungry. Let's go eat … with Halag and Hermann. They're probably waiting for us!"

I grabbed his hand and pulled, but he didn't budge. He only stood there, slightly laughing at my panicked state.

"We're here, and almost at the front of the line … it will be fun."

To make matters worse, our place in line would parallel their disembarking. In just a few moments, we would all be standing face to face.

"Are you alright, Mercedes?"

Still, he was smiling and finding humor in my totally stressed state.

"What are you laughing at?"

"The way you talk. I've never known someone to be so hungry that they were 'super hungry.' You make me laugh!"

"I'm so glad I amuse you!"

"No … not amused. Rather, you fill me with overwhelming

joy!"

I didn't even hear what he was saying. All I knew was that Adina and Carson were sitting there, now trying to make head or tails of the two of us. The reasons for their shocked expressions were two-fold. First, my uncanny resemblance to Adina, but even worse was, secondly, the look on Carson's face as he realized that the two worlds that he had kept hidden from one another would now collide. I could tell that he wanted to hide as he pulled his hat down over his face, but before I could divert his attention, Alrik saw him too and called out to his friend, Dr. Carson.

To prevent the inevitable, I grabbed hold of Alrik's shoulder and turned him towards me, and away from Adina and Carson.

"Alrik, there's something I need to tell you, it's ..."

It was all unraveling so quickly! I didn't know what to say or what to do.

"What is it, fraulein? What's wrong? Come, there is someone I would like for you meet!"

I couldn't believe what I was about to do. Grabbing the lapels of his jacket, I pulled his lips to mine and spontaneously kissed him. In order to divert his attentions, I placed my hands on either side of his face and drew him into my world. For the greater good, I surrendered a part of me that was not meant for him, yet he gladly indulged. I had no intention of yielding until the two of them had a chance to get away. Even after every car had been emptied and the line of people waiting to ride grew longer, no one dared to disturb the Field Marshal who was curiously making out with a girl in line. When I opened my eyes to take a peek, I saw that my aunt and uncle had disappeared, and *all* was clear. I on the other hand was in the midst of a feverish love session that would need to be interrupted delicately.

Alrik was happily lost in the moment, and temporarily forgot where he was until I pulled my head back and told him that we were holding up the line. Once he refocused, I noticed a flame of torment in his eyes. He appeared confused over my sudden change of heart, almost as if he knew that I was deliberately deceiving him.

"Fraulein ... there's so much that I don't know about you. I don't know your last name, where you're from, how you got here, or even why. But what I do know is that I'm completely smitten. This may sound strange, but I'm in love with you! Stay here! ...

always ... with me. Don't leave!"

All at once I was overwhelmed with agonizing regret over what I had done. My grief was so paralyzing that I could barely utter a word. I had not only kissed a man who wasn't my husband, but my aggressive behavior would send Alrik on an obsessive journey to search for me after I was gone. It was all starting to make sense to me now. He didn't accidentally stumble upon Adina walking down the streets of Friedlich, he was on the hunt for me, and caught a glimpse of her. No wonder he had behaved so oddly and was so obsessive during our first meeting a month from now. And no wonder he approached me as if he knew me. He had lost me once and had no intention of losing me again, even if it meant making me his prisoner. For a reason unknown to me, my journeys had deeply intertwined with Alrik Richter. There had to be a higher purpose that I could not yet see. In the midst of it all, I found myself caring deeply for this man, and it broke my heart that I would cause him such anguish.

As I stared deeply into his eyes, my throat burned with welled up tears that broke into streams of misery, flowing down my cheeks.

"I'm so sorry! I'm so terribly sorry! Please forgive me, I shouldn't have done that. Alrik, I can't stay here ... I have to go!"

I couldn't bear to look at him for one more second, it hurt too much. Now was the time to seize the day and finish what I had come here for. I turned around and ran, breaking through the crowds of curious spectators who had gathered around. I heard Alrik yelling out my name, but his voice only fueled my desire to run even faster. His frantic call was quickly replaced by the sounds of horns, tambourines, and the shouts of vendors hard-selling their goods. This was the moment I had dreaded, the moment when I would actually take a life. I wondered if Adina had ever done such a thing, or if this daunting commission had been reserved just for me ... I hated this place, and never wanted to return.

Finally, I came upon a large red and black tent that was most likely the central meeting place for the entire event. Because everyone inside was fully engaged in a drunken party, no one seemed to notice when I practically flew through the door. Every inch of the enormous space was moving wildly in all directions. On the makeshift stage that was the center point of the room, second only to the ever-flowing barrels of beer being guzzled like water, was a motley group of musicians performing traditional Bavarian tunes. Upbeat melodies flowing from horns, violins, and accordions filled every corner, promoting joyful dancing and singing to the country's most cherished tunes of patriotism. Rows of wooden picnic tables lined the tent walls, all filled with platters of sausages and kraut. Like pigs surrounding feeding troughs, hungry patrons gorged themselves to the tune of their own music of the clanking cheers of ceramic steins. Although it was cold and windy outside, the atmosphere within the four walls of canvas was musty and humid. All of it together, made my stomach turn.

It was pure craziness, and I knew it would be impossible to find Halag without a better view, so in the midst of it all, I stood atop a barrel and began scanning the entire room. Without warning, from behind someone grabbed my skirt and pulled me backwards. Before hitting the ground, I felt them reach down to catch me. To my surprise, it was none other than the one I had been searching for, Halag Sauer. He was in his normal state of intoxication, hardly able to hold himself upright, let alone hold on to me. With slurred words and eyes half open, he began speaking what seemed to be complete nonsense.

"Dance with me, Caprice! I've been so lonely without you!"

I shook my head and breathed a heavy sigh. *Good grief!* All I knew is that Caprice must have been one hell of a woman to make three men feel so desperate without her. He held me tightly in his arms and swirled me onto the dance floor where dozens of other couples were moving to a waltz that was totally unfamiliar to me. Halag however, just held me and buried his face in the curve of my neck, barely moving as if it were a slow dance. He kept saying the same thing over and over again.

"Lass mich dich einfach Caprice halten!"

And then he began to cry like a child. He went on about how sorry he was for what he had done. Part of what he mumbled was in English and part in German. If I understood correctly, this story of Halag and Caprice went much deeper than a rival crush from afar.

Caprice adored Halag, but the brotherly affection she felt for him didn't compare to the undying love that she had for Alrik. Their marriage was a complete secret, hidden from Alrik's father and Halag and Hermann as well. Although the brothers realized what the future held for her and the Field Marshal of Germany, they never lost hope that someday she would give her heart to one of them instead.

From what I could tell by his destructive lifestyle, Halag took the news much harder than his brother. When he learned of their marriage, he disappeared from the Richter estate, vowing never to return. One night, months later, he stumbled upon the small cottage where the newlyweds had hidden themselves. He knew that he should run away and leave them in peace, but instead, he began watching from the shadows, all the while growing more desperate and more obsessed. His fixation could only be numbed by the constant infusion of hard spirits.

He waited patiently for the day when she might be left alone, one of the few times when Alrik would go into town without her. When that day came, he knocked on the door in desperation. Being the gentle and caring spirit that she was, Caprice felt great pity at the sight of his brokenness, and invited him in. During the events that followed, Halag referred to himself as a monster who deserved to spend all of eternity in the pit of hell.

In order to protect Halag, Caprice never said a word about what took place. Several weeks later she discovered that she was pregnant, and nine months later she died during childbirth. Whether Annaliese was his child or not, only he and Caprice knew what had happened. All of these years since, torture had become Halag's closest companion, accompanying him wherever he would go. As he continued on with one of the saddest accounts I had ever heard, he said that this life of anguish was his punishment for murdering an angel. Now I understood the cryptic caution that Hermann had uttered. Cursed indeed was this man who stood before me.

Without warning, Halag's body went limp and he collapsed in my arms, causing both of us to fall to the floor. At first, I just thought that he finally passed out from his drunken state. But then, his body began convulsing and his mouth foaming. I tried to calm him, but as his condition worsened, I screamed out for help.

"Halag! You're alright, you're going to be okay!"

What was I saying? This man had to die, and here he was, dying before my very eyes, but his demise was not my fault. What was wrong with me? I couldn't stand to just watch him die, no matter what.

"Someone help me! Please!"

The crowd began to spread out and watch as I held this man in my arms, screaming for someone to help. And then, unexpectedly, appearing right in front of me was Hermann, glowering down at me holding Halag. Although his very own brother was dying before his eyes, he didn't seem distressed or upset, but unusually calm.

"What are you doing just standing there? You've got to help him!"

He knelt down and lightly placed his hand atop Halag's mouth.

"He's not breathing, he's dead! I found this vial sitting next to his drink." He held the small amber bottle between his thumb and forefinger.

"This belonged to you ... did it not? You! American! You have killed the cousin of the Field Marshal!"

I loudly proclaimed my innocence and told everyone standing around that I didn't kill him, but hatred-filled stares had already passed a judgment of condemnation. He then yanked me up off the floor and plunged his pistol into my ribs.

"You are under arrest, fraulein, for the murder of Hermann Sauer. You will be executed for this great crime!"

I was completely thrown for a loop. What was he talking about? He was Hermann! Conveniently, he had a strand of rope in his pocket that he threw at one of the eyewitnesses, ordering them to tie my wrists together. As he hissed threats in my ear to stay quiet and remain still, the stench of his breath and sound of his voice brought to mind the horrible recollection of coarse hands wrapped tightly around my neck. Until that very moment, I had failed to see the obvious. This bastard who now wore his brother's leather coat, was the Halag Sauer that I remembered. But it wasn't Halag at all. It was Hermann! To my dismay, I quickly realized that the wrong brother had fallen at the hand of his twin. The entire scene was bizarre, as Hermann had already *in his mind* become Halag Sauer, the Assistant to the Field Marshal.

"Someone go and find the Field Marshal and tell him what has happened. I will take this criminal and lock her up!"

He led me out through the back of the tent, grasping the rope with one hand and his stabbing pistol in the other.

They hustled me past all the booths and tents, and across a

large grassy field that stood between the festival and the train station. We weren't headed for the car, but to a place where Alrik wouldn't think to look. Hermann had strategically created his own agenda that was now leading to a train that would take us God knows where. This encounter was both a curse and a blessing. I had become the hostage of a madman, but at the same time, being close to him would create the perfect opportunity to kill him. At my first opportunity, I would kill him with *his* very own pistol.

I was suddenly overcome by a feeling that I couldn't explain. Even though I was being kidnapped by a man I knew to be completely insane, and I was running from safety into harm's way, I wouldn't attempt to escape. The Tempus Vector had once again sent me here for the sole purpose of being with this monster at this exact moment.

Chapter 24

The Burden of Power

"That's my Gran's bag. He'd always bring it when we went huntin' or campin'.
What does it have to do with anythin'?"
~Carig Hammel~

Carig refused to leave the third story room. He was a man of his word and would stand watch and wait for Beni to walk through the door. Although Dean and Ivan made several attempts at luring him away, he wouldn't budge from Killen's chair. Their concern for him was not only his mad focus on the door but his constant preoccupation with his hands. He watched them like a clock, as if at any moment they would chime red. The two understood Carig's uneasiness. They both remembered that daunting fear of failure, the anxiety of becoming *the one* that single-handedly erred and destroyed both the Carrier and the Tempus Vector. For Carig, doing his job well was not just about personal accomplishment, but about Beni and keeping her safe.

Whether he was ready or not, the time for Carig's wake-up call had come. Like the others before him, he was strong in every way and had always been able to muscle through the toughest of situations. This new season of his life would be different. He needed to die to himself and acknowledge and rely on the fierce origin of this power that had been given to him. Until he did so, he would be unable to effectively move forward. This privileged wisdom and guidance would be unmasked by Ivan who had been suffering physically for Carig's cause.

The time was short as the throbbing pain that filled Ivan's head and his tormented spirit signaled that the instant was rapidly approaching for Carig to go. Along with the nagging pain, cries of anguish rushed through his mind. He was tormented by Beni's cry for help, while sensing the pain of a steel barreled gun poking into her rib cage. She was in trouble, and unless Carig could get himself together, he would be no help to her whatsoever.

Ivan was desperate to capture the attention of the stubborn Scot and knelt down before him, which caught Carig completely off guard. In a loud, bold voice Ivan sternly insisted that he come with him …"now!"

Carig was initially irritated, wanting nothing more than to deck 'im a good one. But as he studied Ivan's eyes, they revealed a clamorous dilemma, one that stirred Carig's blood and shifted his attitude. With a sharpened mindset, he followed closely behind Ivan as they walked down the stairs, out the front door, then straight into the woodshop on the ground floor of the lighthouse. Even as the door closed behind them, Carig felt a pang of intense urgency and heat rising within him, while Ivan on the other hand, remained unemotional, staring out the window, once again lost within a vision.

All at once Ivan's silence broke as he turned and pointed at the wall beyond a pile of firewood.

"What's that?"

At first Carig thought he was ridiculous to point at everything and nothing, as every inch of the room was overflowing with unfinished carvings, projects, and tools. He had no idea what Ivan was referring to.

"What are ye lookin' at?"

Ivan didn't say another word, but focused unwaveringly, and began gesturing at one particular item.

His interest was not in the leather apron that hung from an

old rusty knob, but the haversack made of animal skin that was all but invisible beneath it. At his inquiry about this most unique satchel, he was brought back to reality from his far-off trance.

"That's my Gran's bag. He'd always bring it when we went huntin' or campin'. What does it have to do with anythin'?"

As if a divine bolt of lightning had struck, Ivan could now see clearly the revelation that was given him from the heavens. All at once, he knew what had been hindering both Carig's peace of mind, and his lack of preparation for what lay ahead. It wasn't a pep talk or encouragement that Carig needed, that would be like giving a soldier a butter knife. His call to arms, his war cry, simply lacked instruction. With one glance at the deerskin bag with a top flap distinctly engraved with the knot of Solomon, they both knew that his apprenticeship was over. He had now become the master hunter, filled with boldness and unafraid of the size or scale of beast or battle. The haversack was like a book, not only filled with memorable lessons but also abounding with every weapon and device that he would need to fulfill his call as the Blood Warrior.

As Carig lifted the worn bag from the wall, he skimmed his hands across the three tassels made of rabbit's feet, now dingy, and held only by tarnished chains of silver. These "lucky charms" always appeased Killen's superstitions, preventing *in his mind,* any misfortune.

It was powerfully obvious to them both that this was the one item that Carig was meant to take with him. Like the one time that Beni joined them on their annual turkey hunt and referred to Killen as the Scot with the bottomless Mary Poppins' bag, then teased him all the way home that his smelly bag held a magic far too deep to comprehend.

Studying the fur pack sparked a thousand memories for Carig of his time with his Gran. Killen *had* prepared him for this journey in more ways than he would ever know. Carig had never really thought about how incredible the Scottish haversack was, nor could he fathom its ingenious capabilities. No matter the situation or whatever the moment called for, his grandfather was wondrously able to retrieve the ideal tool or weapon from his bag.

Strapping the pack onto his back and fastening the chest strap, with a sigh of relief Carig dropped his head backwards and exhaled as if he could finally breathe.

"Thank you, Gran. I now know what you once knew. All of it together was far too profound to explain."

Ivan witnessed a boldness in Carig that he had not yet seen and could tell that the torment was over. The Tribe of David, the power of the Blood Warrior, had fallen upon him; it was both finished, but it had also just begun.

Carig feared nothing as he turned his palms towards his face, and his eyes flamed with fire at the reflection. In humble reverence, he lifted his hands before God, and then towards his face, as both he and Ivan witnessed a scarlet glow. His journey had begun.

Before he walked out the door and down to the water, he turned around and reassured Ivan that he would not only return with Beni but also with the soul of the tyrant.

Chapter 25

Two O'Clock to Berlin

"My convictions for the advancement of a new world,
are perfect and sharp like points of the bent cross."
~Hermann Sauer~

His grip was powerful, and tightened with each step, along with his escalating fury. His putrid hiss whispered threats in my ear to stay quiet or he would kill me like a dog in the street. How had I missed all the signs? Unquestionably, this was *the* Halag, a premeditated and atrocious result of stolen identity. Beneath the long leather coat that dragged along the ground, were the emblems and stripes that belonged to his brother. The more I thought about it, the more perplexed I became. On my journey a month from now, there was no talk of a twin, no talk of Hermann even from Alrik, only this imposter. Little did he know that I had put up with him long enough. A hate such as I had never experienced rose within me, fueling my mission. If it was the last thing I would ever do, I would rid the world of this man.

"How could you do it? How could you kill your own brother?"

"It was your poison that killed him, not mine ... he deserved to die! He murdered her! Then like a coward, became a drunk. His vision for the future was muddled through a dark veil of loss, and he became nonessential. *My* convictions for the advancement of a new world, are perfect and sharp like points of the bent cross. The rise of the Third Reich is only the beginning, and *you* will help me to succeed. The flag of the ultimate solution will soon wrap the globe."

"You're crazy!! What makes you think that I have the ability to help you? I have no power to do such a thing, and even if I did, I would rather die than be a part of your madness!"

"The choice to live or die is yours, fraulein, but please, don't insult my intelligence with your lies. YOU ... HERE ... NOW ... are *my* destiny. I am your purpose for being here!"

You are damn right about that, you prideful son of a bitch!

"Although surrounded by idiots, greatness has always been my destiny. Alrik's Achilles' heel is his pathetically tender heart. It blinds his vision and weakens his power. If not for his birthright, he too would be expendable. His romantic inclinations will be his downfall. I'm shocked that he was so blind ... so ignorant of *your* red flags. He believed you had come for him, but I knew there was much more to the American woman who showed up out of nowhere - alone. Well, not completely alone are we? You are accompanied by a rare traveling companion, one to which you are closely connected. It is this harbinger that interests me ... and the Fuhrer."

His knowledge of the frame left me speechless, and he found great pleasure in my fear-filled expression.

"You see, my people are far superior to your people."

His arrogance was infuriating. Images of Indiana Jones putting his whip aside and shooting the turbaned warrior dressed in black strongly crossed my mind. His ego inflated like a hot air balloon, but amidst the prideful chatter, I discovered the origin of his knowledge about the frame.

Hermann went on to say that Alrik and Halag were the only family members summoned to attend a secret underground meeting in the heart of Berlin. Because they were both in seclusion after the death of Caprice, they could scarcely function and refused to hear anything about it. That was the day he discovered the power of position. Clothed in his brother's uniform with all its stripes and medals, he became Halag, and nobody could tell the difference. When he walked into the room, he was respected and welcomed by what he called, the god of this age. Hitler himself sat at the head of a massive table, surrounded by his most trusted comrades, and suddenly Hermann was one of them. There were no windows, and only one way in and one way out. He wasn't sure as to why they had been called until the lights switched off and the room was filled with darkness. With one click, a beam of light began projecting mind-altering images onto the concrete walls. The strategies of the most twisted thinkers of the age were instantly on display.

Not only had the stage been set for a most brilliant plan but within the complex photos was an ill-fitted photograph of an old man in a coat and hat, holding onto a small wooden device. They didn't know who it was, but I did. It was Malachi. The Fuhrer referred to the frame as a harbinger that would herald Mother Germany to absolute success, and then challenged each of them to find *it* and the Carrier. Hermann was possessed in both body and soul by this evil cult, I could see it in his eyes. His eerie and demented description of Hitler resembling an angel set aglow by the light of the projector was disturbing to say the least. More upsetting was how much they all knew about this power that was not meant for them. At the conclusion of the meeting, Hitler executed the Nazi salute while holding between his fingers a unique gold coin that was stamped with a knot.

"Find the gold, and you'll find the frame!"

Then, as an incentive, he offered up a place of honor, right by his side as a reward to the one who would find it.

"Is that where we're going ... Berlin?"

"Yes. I have seen myself sitting at the right hand of the Fuhrer. His request for the frame and the Carrier is the only reason I didn't take the frame from your bag. You understand its magic. If you behave yourself, perhaps I will allow you to live and serve me."

There were so many things that came to my mind that I could say to him, but I restrained myself and stayed close to him, waiting for the moment that I would end this.

As we stepped onto the platform, he stumbled over the hem of his coat, and yelled at me as if it were my fault.

"I have nothing to do with the fact that you're the short brother, you son of a bitch!"

With hate in his eyes, he glowered at me, as if on the verge of a violent meltdown.

The man at the ticket window saw us coming and was clearly frightened by Hermann's presence. He had obviously dealt with him before. I couldn't fully comprehend the exchange between the two, but I did recognize the continual name-dropping of the Field Marshal that the poor man took seriously. Whatever Hermann said, it worked, as the ticket attendant and his assistant boarded the train that was about to leave and began furiously blowing a whistle, demanding that every last person exit the three-car train. We stood there and watched as each man, woman, and child hurriedly disembarked, making sure not to make eye contact with Hermann. They were obviously afraid of him and would do anything to protect themselves from trouble.

When the train was completely empty, Hermann and I stepped into the back door of the now vacant caboose that was just beginning to move. I stared out at the people who stood on the platform, and they stared back with expressions of compassion and empathy over my situation. It was ironic, their eyes were filled with pity for me, but because I knew their imminent future, I found myself grieving for them. I wanted nothing more than to yell out, *get out of here as quickly as you can!*

As the train began to speed up, Hermann pulled me into the car and the door slammed in my face.

Chapter 26

This Ought to be Interesting

"Here goes nothin'... Oh God in heaven, help me not to kill em!"
~Carig Hammel~

Just as Ivan had told him in his dream, he pointed the toes of his shoes into the sea that was still thick with ice. The second the leather and salty water touched, he was carried as with angels to a faraway destination that would lead him into the presence of the Carrier of the Tempus Vector, his bride whom he would gladly surrender his life to defend. Like a dream, he flew through the heights of the heavens, surrounded by a beauty that was far beyond anything he had ever seen. From above, he heard a choir of a thousand singing from the holy of holies, its beauty echoed amongst the clouds. Instantaneously in unison, the angels arrived at the forefront of his journey, and released him like from the talons of a bird onto a rough pebbled landscape that was surrounded by railroad tracks pointing in all directions.

As he heard the whistle of a departing train, his focused sharpened, and he scoured the area for Beni. If only he would have arrived seconds earlier, this could have ended here and now. But as it stood, the train was moving away from him at a charging pace, and as the caboose door slammed shut, he saw Beni's face.

It was not his intention to waste even a second, nevertheless, he needed a moment to gather his wits. His power may have been given by a divine source, but he was only human, and fully comprehending the reality of traveling to another place and time was difficult to fathom. In a windstorm of dust and smoke, the train was gone. He instantly panicked, hoping that he didn't miss his only opportunity, and wouldn't be too late to help her.

Carig needed a vehicle, some form of transportation that would move fast, but was small enough to follow along the tracks. Without wasting a moment, he combed the area, and couldn't help noticing the mass of travelers who were up in arms about something - the "something" having to do with the train that just left.

From out of nowhere, a car screeched up to the platform, causing Carig to dive out of the way. A man dressed in a black uniform, who seemed oblivious to the near accident, jumped out of the vehicle and made a mad dash up the stairs onto the train platform. Without missing a beat, he made a bee-line up to the attendant who was distracted and clearly upset by his futile attempts to calm the crowd. When they saw the Field Marshal approaching, the people opened a pathway, and quieted to a hush. After a short discussion, the man in black placed his hand upon the attendant's shoulder as if to say he was sorry, and that he would fix this disaster. When he turned around and walked back to the car, standing there waiting for him was Carig, who unbeknownst to Alrik, was the American Scot who had studied him and was familiar with both his past and his future.

Even though Carig hoped to avoid contact with the man who tried to steal Beni's heart, there they stood face to face. His hopes of dealing exclusively with Halag, "one down and done and then get the hell out," suddenly turned into a soap opera. To make things even worse, he could tell by Alrik's stressed behavior, that Beni had fallen back into the vile grip of his demented cousin, and it infuriated Carig. In spite of his outrage, he had to stay cool and use this situation to his advantage. He would heed the words of Ivan and put aside his feelings and mental images of the Wikipedia wedding photo, and focus on his mission. Carig knew that he could use Alrik's extensive knowledge of the countryside, and easily ride his coattails of power to get where he needed to go.

Here goes nothin'... Oh God in heaven, help me not to kill em!

"Is there somethin' I can help with, sir?"

"Who are you?"

"Just a traveler, who like all these other fine folks, watched the train haul off carryin' all our valuable belongin's. The item that belonged to me, was priceless, and I'll be damned if I'm goin' home without it."

Alrik was suspiciously curious about Carig. He could feel the urgency of this red-haired foreigner who was passionate and a bit on edge about recovering his personal property.

Carig was both conflicted and honor-bound in regard to *his* adversary. Their like-minded "objective" that had just sped away on the 2:00 to Berlin, was an unhinged kind of connection between the two. Carig knew from the ongoing chatter of the crowd, that the final destination was Berlin, but had no idea how long the journey would take, and most importantly, where they could go to head off the steel beast. The sooner he would gain entry into Alrik's dilemma, the quicker he would find Beni.

"By the looks of it, sir, there's somethin' on that train you want as well. Maybe we could help each other. Do ye know where it'll be stoppin next?"

Alrik continued to stare curiously at Carig, clearly disturbed at the ignorance of this stranger who acted oblivious to his high rank and status.

"A Scottish man who speaks English here in Germany? That's odd, don't you think?"

"Aye, it's strange for sure. We can talk about it later over a pint, but don't ye think we oughta get goin'?"

Alrik exhaled loudly, knowing that his window of opportunity was short. Like Carig, he too was more anxious to intercept that train than he was to examine this stranger.

"Fine. As I left the festival in such a hurry, without any of my men, I find that I am currently in short supply of manpower. I would appreciate your help in this matter."

Both men anxiously slid into the backseat of the limo. While Alrik yelled instructions to the chauffeur, telling him to drive as fast as he could to the town of Gustel, Carig was only concerned with exactly how long it would take to get there. The awkward silence between the two was too much for the Field Marshal who was curious about this out of place stranger. Carig on the other hand, wanted no part of senseless talk and was in no mood to chat. Rather than be buddy-buddy with this pretty boy German, he had to fight not to punch his lights out.

"So, how long till we get there?"

"Normally, Gustel is about an hour and a half drive. But in order to arrive before the train, we must fly."

At the reminder, Alrik once again yelled out for the driver to go faster.

"Beeile dich, geh schneller!"

"I am Alrik Richter … and your name?"

"Carig."

"I once traveled to Scotland."

"Did ye now? I haven't been there myself since I was a child.

My parents were killed, and I was sent to America to live with my grandparents."

"So, you're American?"

"Yeah."

"What is it again you left on that train?"

"It's uhhhh ... precious, a uhh, a valuable diamond, one that can never be replaced. What about you? What's so important on that train that made you leave all yer men behind?"

Alrik didn't answer, but only stared out the window. He was obviously distracted. After a few moments of silence, he answered the question.

"The only family I have left are my two cousins, and one of them was murdered today ... poisoned. I just can't believe she would have done it!"

"Who? Who ye talkin' about?"

"A girl. She was like a cool breeze that drifted into a stuffy room, bringing life and joy to everything she touched."

Carig knew exactly who he was speaking of. He felt the exact way about Beni in his own life. The day she came back, the moment he heard her voice, she brought to life what was once dead. Carig couldn't help but notice that Alrik had climbed down off of his high horse as Field Marshal and had simply become a normal guy who was sharing his heart.

"It seems like an entire lifetime since my wife died. She ... my wife ... told me on her deathbed that someday someone would come, but I never thought it was possible. Until yesterday, until the moment she walked into my life, I'd been so alone, and then suddenly, her ... and now she's gone. So, what's on that train? Her! Halag took her. He told the train conductor that I had given instructions to empty the train so that he could take this criminal who killed a soldier of the German army to Berlin to face charges. But then another witness said that Hermann collapsed in her arms and she had no idea what had happened. She sat there on the floor holding him in despair, calling out for help. If she had murdered him, she would have run, not stayed and called out for help. As far as I am concerned, she's innocent. But Halag, he cannot be trusted. I have to get to her before he does something ... something terrible."

When finally, they had reached the station in Gustel, they watched in great disappointment as the train blew straight through the train depot. That's what both men had feared. Hermann had used the power and authority of the Field Marshal to strike fear into the engineer, warning him not to think about stopping until they reached Berlin. Unfortunately, that would result in another six hours. At the quick pace that they were moving, they would soon run out of fuel. There was no way in hell that Carig was willing to wait it out and risk losing sight of the train. It wasn't in his nature, and he'd already wasted enough time.

"I'll tell you what. Get me close enough to that train, and I'll jump on. I'll get it to stop, I promise ye!"

"You would do that to help me?"

"Na, not for you. Like I said, I'm not leavin' here till I get what's mine, and I won't be playin' this game of cat and mouse any longer. Tell your driver to step on it and pull up as close as he can right alongside the train. Closer! Come on man! It might seem like yer gonna hit it, but ye won't! Now … go, go, go!"

As they pulled up next to the train, Carig opened the door, hanging onto the car, and reached toward the back rail of the caboose. The train began steaming away as he was still straining to grab on to the massive caboose.

"Come on! Ye gotta move faster, ye son of a bitch!"

The driver didn't like Carig's demanding tone, but after Alrik gave him a nod of affirmation, he pressed the accelerator to the floor as if his life depended on it, and apparently feeling as though this might be the final act of his life. Alrik was quite impressed as he watched Carig launch himself off the car like a catapult and onto the back rails of the caboose. Barely holding on by the tips of his fingers, and with his shoes dragging along on the tracks, he was finally able to pull himself up.

Chapter 27

The Battle for Power

"I knew what Hermann referred to. The secret hall filled with Caprice images. In his torn heart and twisted mind, he believed that his paintings would somehow resurrect her from the dead."
~Benidette Hammel~

The outside of the train was sleek and shiny, like a silver rocket that would blast through the countryside with ease, a product of cutting-edge technology. The inside was clean and modern ... state of the art decor, covered in black and red leather, bound in cold steel. There was no inkling of charm or romance. It was as far from the inspired design of the Orient Express as *I was* from home.

Hermann forced me into a seat that sat directly across from him. It was sterile and uncomfortable, not unlike his bizarre and unflinching gaze that didn't waver for even a second. He was a loose cannon. I knew this because I had already been a victim of his uncontrollable vile moods, and still had the bruises to prove it. One minute he was filled with a violent rage, and the next he responded like a somewhat normal person. His personality was like a roulette wheel, one never quite knew where the marble would land.

As I sat there face to face with this demon man, it occurred to me that there is nothing more disturbing than being the object of an emotionless stare. Even worse, he analyzed every curve of my face and body as if he were drawing a picture, except this time, he had no pad of paper ... no pencil. It was no longer hateful, but lustful, and that was far worse. He was completely offensive and made me want to escape and never come back to this horrid time and place.

I had missed all of the obvious signs from the moment I got there. Feeling completely ignorant as I leered once again at his corrupt face, I wondered why in the world I hadn't recognized it ... I didn't recognize *him*. He killed and maimed with no remorse. It was now so obvious to me. Strangling me was one thing, but taking the life of his own brother, his *twin* brother who was part of him, was another. Just being near him made me want to retch.

I was no expert on the matter, but Hermann was obviously

insane. One moment striking out at me, the next flirting, intermingled with surges of blank stares. He was oddly processing through memories of Caprice and the reality of me, trying to figure out which was real.

Unbeknown to him, in the midst of his preoccupation, I was watching for the perfect opportunity to grab his sidearm. If I could get close enough and take it from his holster, I could kill him and be done! I just wanted it to be done! The question was this ... could I stand the stench of his breath long enough to remain that close? *You have no choice, Beni!* I was growing weary of this journey and ready for it all to be over. I would do whatever was necessary, which meant that it was time to turn on the charm. As Carig would say, "Show me those eyes that would lure a lion from its prey, lass."

"Hermann, it's me, Caprice. I couldn't stand to be apart from you for even one more second. Our waiting has finally come to an end! You rescued me from Alrik and Halag, just like you said you would. They were never you, not even close. They mean nothing to me, it's you I love. Please, Hermann, take me away from all of this! I just want to be with *you!*"

He was intrigued. My plan to capture his attention and throw him off of his game seemed to be working. For the first time since I had met him, his demeanor became gentle instead of defensive, as he slyly slithered right up next to me, and peered deeply into my eyes.

That's right, you son of a bitch! Go right ahead, come closer! Your next step is straight into the pit of hell.

"Caprice! Is it really you? I wasn't sure, I thought you were gone forever. Alrik said that she wasn't you, but I knew you weren't dead, they had only hidden you from me. I knew I would find you. It was the paintings that brought you back to me, they kept the vision of you alive."

In his torn heart and twisted mind, he believed that his paintings would somehow resurrect her from the dead.

"Remember how we used to sit together for hours while my brother and cousin played and did all the things I wasn't able to do? They never included me, they didn't want me with them. But you were always kind, and became the inspiration for every sketch, every stroke of my brush. You alone healed my brokenness."

Semi-sane Hermann all of a sudden departed, leaving the

mental door wide open for his darker, irrational side to enter back in.

"Wait, wait, something here isn't right! My brother, he hurt you. She was pregnant, *you* were pregnant ... it was his fault, he lacked self-control and then you died. You were so beautiful lying there, like delicate china tucked within the pleated wall of satin. I leaned over and touched my lips to yours ... our first kiss. Life had abandoned you. I hate him, I'm not sorry he's dead. He's been dead for years, but just didn't know it."

As he ran his finger over the silhouette of my lips, I knew this was my opportunity to make my move. I put my face right up to his and ran my hand down his chest and around his waist. As our lips were only inches apart, I yanked the pistol from his holster. In one swift move, I cocked and buried the barrel into his side, all the while keeping my face next to him. To my surprise, his reaction was much different than I believed it would be.

"Do it, fraulein! You are simply one more image of Caprice that will forever leave my heart broken. Always choosing another over me. Do it! Do it now!"

I dug the pistol in even further with my finger on the trigger, ready to shoot. Little by little, I began to squeeze. But when it came down to it, I just couldn't pull the trigger. When he saw my weakness it infuriated him, and he firmly pushed me into the wall of the train, holding my hands tightly behind my back. I could hear him unzipping my backpack with his other hand. My struggle to break free resulted in his grip tightening. All he said over and over again was to be still or he would kill me right then and there. I frantically struggled as I heard him pull the frame from my backpack. I had to do whatever it would take to get it away from him!

At that point, I didn't care what happened to me. My duty, my calling would take priority over my safety. With all of my might, I lifted my feet and pushed against the wall, causing him to tumble over the seat and fall to the ground. We both watched as the frame slipped from his hands and flew through the air. I couldn't stop it as it hit the corner of a seat and fell to the ground in pieces.

Without hesitation, I flung myself onto the floor, clutching the frame. I was right, it was broken, and I immediately began crawling on all fours, searching for the missing handle. Devastated and completely panicked once again that I might be stranded here forever, I continued searching in every direction. Finally, I saw it, hidden deep beneath the very front seat of the car. With all of my might, I crawled forward. I could hear Hermann panting and stomping like a bull behind me … and then, there he was, standing right above me. I turned over and began kicking his hands away, and then with one swift kick, I booted his knee so hard that he screamed out in pain and fell to the floor. When he did, adrenaline propelled me along the floor towards the broken piece, until finally, I snatched hold of the splintered handle. I had to get away from him, or this wasn't going to end well. Standing up, I began running to the exit of the second car, quickly reaching for the door handle. In a rage, he ran right at me, fiercely shaking in anger, he began to wrap his fingers around my throat and pushed me against the door.

"You are now mine ... the frame is now mine … the power now belongs to me!"

As he hissed these words, and clung even tighter, I thrust the sharp dowel straight into his heart.

"I don't think so, you bastard!"

Instead of stopping him in his tracks like I hoped it would, it enraged him, even empowered him. I could tell by his ferocious expression that if I didn't get away from him right now, he would kill me. He had finally surrendered himself to pure unadulterated rage.

With all of my strength, I kicked him in the groin, which sent him to his knees, giving me a chance to escape his clutches. As I bolted towards the third car, I glanced down at the Tempus Vector. The one thing I was given to care for and protect, was now in a broken state, and it dawned on me that for that reason I may be stuck here forever. Regardless of my outcome, one thing was for damn sure, I would stop this mad man. His insane ideals about the rise of the Fourth Reich would stop here and now, no matter what it would take. When I suddenly noticed that he was once again up on his feet like an unstoppable cyborg, and powering after me, screaming insanely like a locomotive on the verge of running me down, screaming insanely, ready to kill and destroy.

I stumbled my way down to the exit of the railroad car and slid open the door. Even though the train was moving at full speed and the connectors were perilous and narrow, I jumped onto the next car. Along with the screaming gale blasts of wind, my eyes were immediately drawn to the grimly dark sky, one like I had never seen before. It was like blackened plums, lit up with veins of lightning that tore through the heavens as if a battle between good and evil had been waged.

Even though it was a creepy feeling not seeing another soul, I was relieved to make it to the other side. With each passing moment however, the scene of it all reminded me of a chiller; this place, this time was a pit of monstrosity. Why was it, that although I hated edge-of-your-seat suspense, I continued to find myself in the middle of it? And for whatever reason, Hermann, aka Halag, was forever in the starring role of my nightmare, resurrecting himself like Freddy Krueger. Although wounded, he was still right behind me, and I began to fear that I would never be able to stop him. I could hardly believe that I had just stabbed him in the heart and it didn't stop him but seemed to intensify his strength and resolve.

Passing through the final outside connection of the third car to the caboose, my options for escape narrowed. Unless I jumped off the train, this was it. I would face Hermann here and now, and either kill or be killed. This had to end ... *now.*

I stood in the middle of the aisle and watched as he ran toward me. The showdown had come. It was so strange to see a rod sticking out of his chest, seeping with blood, yet it didn't even phase him.

"You will never escape me! You and I are meant to be together, don't you see it? You are mine. Give me that frame, fraulein. Give it to me now!"

"No! I won't do it!"

"Have it your way."

Hermann pointed his pistol straight at my head, and I squeezed my eyes shut. At the sound of the cocked and ready weapon, all I could think to say was *forgive me,* and that I was sorry for not being about to complete my journey. At this point, I couldn't even fathom breaking the news to those who were waiting back home for me. They had done their part, but I had failed. Without waiting another moment, I grabbed onto the fractured device, hoping and praying that it would take me away from this place. If I didn't leave now, the frame would become his ... the choice was simple. I had to go back. But when I took hold, nothing happened. To my great dismay, the frame wasn't working right! The option for escape, with my task undone, had come and gone.

At least I knew that none of the powers of Germany would rise if they had possession of the Tempus Vector since it was in disrepair. I closed my eyes knowing that the pain of a bullet to the head would be but a second and then I would stand in the presence of the Lord. It was then that it happened. My eyes were squeezed shut when I heard the deafening blast as the gun fired.

I was relieved. It was over, and for that matter, completely painless. Too painless. I felt the warmth of the flow of blood covering me. With the sound of the shot, the brakes of the train began to screech to a halt. When I opened my eyes, Hermann was looking at me with a blank expression. In a panic, I patted all along my head, trying to find a wound, but there was none. Perhaps it was shock, but I couldn't comprehend what had just happened.

The gush of blood that had unknowingly spattered all over my face, was not my own, but Hermann's.

"Wait, what's happening?"

I didn't understand … we were both covered in blood. As he clung tightly to my arms, face to face, he began to collapse and then fell to the ground, taking me with him. As he fell, he uttered only four words.

"I love you, Caprice!"

I'm not sure how long I sat down on the floor holding him. I was half afraid to turn around and then I heard my name.

"Beni."

I knew that voice. It was the voice of home.

But it couldn't be! Surely, it was my imagination, or maybe I too was dead. The familiar inflection that spoke my name was utterly unbelievable ... impossible! Then, I heard it again.

"Beni, I'm here, right behind you!"

Still looking straight ahead, I took a deep breath. I was afraid to turn around and risk disappointment. There was no possibility that Carig could be here. Maybe I had gone mad, and it was really just voices in my head, but I felt him, it was real. *Please Lord, let it be him!*

I stood up, and slowly turned around, and then his eyes met mine. Not only was it Carig but his arm was still outstretched holding a pistol. I could hardly believe the evidence of my own eyes! I had finally lost my mind and was afraid to draw near to him. The impossible was standing before me. Maybe I *had* died, and Carig was the face I saw as I stepped into heaven.

Paralyzed where I stood, he lowered his arm and holstered his pistol. Without hesitation, he grabbed me up and embraced and kissed me joyfully.

"Thank God you're alright, Beni!"

Even feeling him, smelling his bewitching scent, I was afraid to believe, and peered at him as if he were a stranger.

"Beni! Lass ... it's me. Everything's alright."

"Carig, why? How is this possible? Why are you here? How?"

When I finally realized it was true, I was overwhelmed with joy, and collapsed into his embrace. I didn't know how this could be happening, but somehow it unbelievably was.

"Thank you, thank you, Carig! I thought I had failed."

"I'll always be here to help you, lass. He's a goner for sure - I'd say your task here is done."

"Wait, what just happened? How in the world are you here?"

"I'll explain it all when we get home, but now is the time to go."

Even though the train had stopped, the door got caught in the clutches of the bitter wind and slammed open. Still locked in one another's arms, we turned and saw Alrik emerge from the shadows where Hermann had fallen.

He was obviously in shock. First, over losing one cousin, and then another, and finally me ... so I thought anyway. I quickly discovered by his confused distress, that it was not about me or Hermann at all, but about Halag. He had earlier been advised by a trusted attendant that Hermann had perished by *my hand.* Although grieved by the news, Halag was by far his favorite of the two brothers, and he was relieved. He had even resolved in his mind that he would forgive Halag for pulling the crazed stunt of stealing me away. The consequences of such an act would be dire to be sure, confronting him with the command and rage that could only be delivered by the hand of the Field Marshall, but it would soon blow over and they would carry on as usual.

However, now grief consumed Alrik as he stared down at the pale and ill-favored cousin who always wanted to be the "admirable brother," and had underhandedly claimed an identity that could never be his, one that would last only a few hours. The thought that they were both gone, was more than he could bear.

"Unless you've killed Hermann twice, fraulein, it seems as though both of my cousins have departed from this world, because of you. What have you done? They were the only family I had left! I believed you to be the blessing I had been waiting for. Tell me it's not true that you would do such a thing?"

I stepped away from Carig and walked towards him. He was devastated, and I felt horrible. I too felt his unbearable grief.

"No, Alrik, I didn't kill Halag. Hermann did, and then he yelled out for everyone to hear that I had killed Hermann. He was completely confused and told me that his brother didn't deserve to live because of what he did to Caprice."

"What are you talking about? What did he do to Caprice?"

It didn't occur to me that Alrik didn't know about the secret encounter between the two, and there was no way I would break such disturbing news to him on top of everything else.

"He didn't say. I guess it was a secret between brothers, something that only they knew."

I had grown very fond of Alrik. Through our encounters, I had come to know his heart, and I could see that it was breaking in two. He had just lost his last remaining family members, and he could obviously tell by the way Carig had been holding me, that he had lost me too. But then I remembered Annaliese. Although he had not yet introduced me to his daughter, I knew about her, and I knew that the fight for her, and the desire to get out of this country, would be his motivation to carry on.

He suddenly changed gears from grief to rage and came after Carig.

"You! Who are you? What did you come here for? Was it for him or for her?"

Carig was armed and ready to take him down. In a way, he almost hoped that the German bastard would make a move, but I told him to let me handle it, and then I met him where he stood.

"Alrik, I have to go, but promise me that you will leave this place. Germany will lose this war. It won't end well for you or Annaliese. I can't explain, just promise me that you will leave!"

His eyes filled with sorrow, stared back at me.

"Does that mean I'll see you again, fraulein?"

"Yes! We will see each other again. Do whatever you have to do and leave Germany. I know how hard it is to lose your cousins, but they were poison. Live your life always for the greater good. Everything will be alright now. Stay close to your daughter and leave this place."

As I turned and walked back over to Carig, I agreed that it was time to go home. However, before I could say another word, he was swept away before my very eyes. Whatever power had delivered him here to help me, had abruptly taken him back. There I stood, just Alrik and me. I should have been following right behind Carig, but I felt nothing. No pain, no prompting, no nothing, and I didn't understand why. Both Halag and Hermann were dead, yet I was still here.

Although stunned by Carig's disappearance, when Alrik saw that I was still there, his desperation broke into hope.

Chapter 28

Severed

*"I have a gut-wrenching feeling that things are not as they seem ...
If I could only see into the world from whence you came, just for a
moment!"*
~Ivan Taggart~

Rushing up from the seashore towards the house, Carig hoped that I was already waiting for him, but remembered the concern in my eyes as he was whisked away while I stood there and watched. For some reason, it bothered him more than he could have imagined to leave me behind, especially with Alrik.

When he ran through the front door, there sat Dean, Ivan and his brothers. While Ivan was overjoyed at his return, and the perceivable success of the journey, Carig was preoccupied.

"You did it, Red! I can feel it! What's wrong? What happened? Where's Beni?"

Carig just stared at the group, and then hauled up the stairs to the third story room. They all rushed behind him, trying to see what was going on. When they arrived, I was not there. In unison, Dean and Ivan began asking the hard questions, demanding to know what had happened. Carig was so distraught that he tried to break through the two of them to once again run down to the shoreline and return to me, but together, they stopped him.

"Let me bloody go!"

"You can't go back! Not until you're called!"

"Where in the hell is she?'

Ivan, the voice of reason, tried to calm him down.

"Carig, Carig ... you gotta focus, man! Tell me what happened!"

"When I walked in, he had a gun to her head, but I shot him first. Then ..."

"Then what?"

"I was called back. She had the frame in her hand, and I thought she was right behind me. She was right behind me ... where the hell is she? ... Let me go ... get your bloody hands off me!"

When Ivan and the doctor could no longer contain him,

Carig lunged forward, landing face first on the floor. He was geared and ready to get up fighting, but then the door from the balcony blew open.

There I stood, on my own two feet, all in one piece. Somehow, even though the Tempus Vector had been broken, what was left of it, whisked me up and brought me safely home ... no new wounds or bruises. It may have seemed silly to most, but I was thrilled beyond words as I passed over the threshold, like a child taking its first step. This arrival home was a completely different experience than the first one. *So, this is how it feels!* I had done it. Not by myself of course, but I had completed what needed to be done, and I was back. This perfect feeling of accomplishment had to be the driving force that compelled Adina to continue on until the day she died.

Waiting for me, bigger than life, were my friends and allies who had been with me in spirit, fulfilling the promise that I would never be alone. Most curiously, however, was the sight of my unanticipated defender lying on the floor with his head resting on his clasped hands. I knelt down before him and placed my hands and my head on his. He was my home, and just as *he had* promised, he had kept me safe.

"Are ye prayin', lad?"

He neither said a word nor even moved a muscle at my playful question, but I didn't realize that he was silently weeping. Little did I know that when I failed to arrive back in a timely manner, he had spun out of control, faced once again with the possibility that I would not return. When he heard me come through the door, the downrush of everything that he'd been through nearly did him in.

"Carig, I'm here, right here. Thank you for saving me. I don't understand how or why but thank you!"

Slowly sitting up, he held me tightly.

"I would do anything for you, lass, but I'll be damned if I'll be leavin' before you next time."

We were not only surrounded by the doctor and Ivan, but all of the brothers had made their way upstairs as well, bringing with them several buckets of chicken, each with a liter of soda in hand. They were all glad to see us but disappointed all the same that they didn't get to use their weapons.

"Speaking of not leaving before me next time, you all wanna

tell me what happened while I was gone? How it became possible for Carig to travel to where I was?"

None of them seemed to know where to begin with the explanation, but of course it would ultimately be Ivan who would step up with the answers. He was in a funny mood, and for a moment, I saw glimpses of the old Ivan, the one I used to know.

"Beni, sweetheart, give me a big hug! Come on, bring it in!"

"I don't think so, buddy! What are you up to? Back away!"

With one cutting glance from Carig, he began again.

"Geez, calm down, Red. I was just trying to give Beni a friendly welcome home and say well done! From what I can see, you've snuffed out the flame of the Fourth Reich. Now, as far as your husband's transformation, the 'David Banner turned Hulk thing,' the doc and I have suspected it for some time now."

"David Banner turned Hulk thing? What in the world are you talking about, Ivan?"

"Well I mean, he's like me and the doc now, like superheroes, but better! You see Beni, the sudden onset of erratic symptoms was all brought on by his calling. As it turns out, he's takin' up the torch ... the legacy that once belonged to Killen. He, and he alone, was given the power of the Tribe of David to step into your near-death experience and pull the trigger, so you wouldn't have to. He's The Blood Warrior, Protector of the Carrier."

Neither Carig nor I ever knew until recently about Doctor Dean and Ivan. We knew that Adina and Killen were close, but not that he had stepped in on many occasions and saved her. There was a battle raging that could be fought and won using our God-given gifts and abilities. Because of the power of the Tempus Vector, and that the representatives of the Ten Lost Tribes were rising up at every turn, evil such as that of the Fourth Reich could be crushed before it began.

Carig and I were both relieved to find out what it was that had been plaguing him. I smiled from ear to ear and told him that I thought it was super sexy being married to someone named The Blood Warrior. Just like in the great novels of old, he kissed my hand, and declared his loyalty.

"Beni, today and always, I am at yer service."

As all good things eventually come to an end, so too would the joy of this triumph cease. Amidst the talking and celebration of a job well done, Ivan was suddenly distracted. Trembling, he walked over to where I had left the frame and gazed in fear at what he saw. He guardedly reached down to pick up the Tempus Vector, as if it might bite, and then fell to his knees while running his fingers around the edges. None of us knew what to say. It was obvious that something was very wrong. In an angry tone, he began scolding me as if I were a child.

"Beni … what happened to the frame? How did this break?"

I told him the whole story. With each sordid detail, he was filled with anguish. Even more so when I revealed that Halag Sauer had a twin named Hermann.

"WHERE IS THE HANDLE? The piece that broke off, where is it?"

"I told you, I stabbed Hermann in the chest with the broken rod. It never crossed my mind to pull it out and bring it back with me. I didn't know!"

The excitement over our return was all at once replaced with an unexpected outburst. Ivan was usually so cocky, so sure of everything, but I had never seen him so utterly and thoroughly distraught. I walked over and knelt down beside him.

"Ivan! What is it? What's wrong?"

He wouldn't look up but remained hunched over the frame.

"Ivan, talk to me!"

Everyone else in the room stood as still as statues, caught off-guard by the *something* that Ivan was privy to, but hesitant to say out loud.

"Beni … the Tempus Vector is crippled. Until it's made whole, you will never be able to fulfill your calling as the Carrier. But even worse, the piece that was left behind can be used to change the course of history."

"What are you saying?"

"Something catastrophic is happening here. The Tempus Vector in its current and broken state will take you to only one more destination … the location of its possible restoration. If it's not restored there, both you and the frame will forever be stranded. There will be nothing that any of us can do to get you back. This place is not only hidden from me but as you can see by the dark matting … no photo, no symbol marker, nothing … it's also hidden from you. It could take you anywhere, and you wouldn't know what to look for once you got there! This concealed journey comes with a monumental warning. The broken piece, and the one who carries it, will also have the ability to meet you there and challenge you for the power."

Carig rolled his eyes at Ivan's obvious overreaction to the situation.

"Calm down, man! This is a simple fix, I can make it like new. No one will ever be able to tell it was ever broken."

At this point, Ivan had zero patience for stupid suggestions.

"Carig, just stop. You don't know what you're talking about!"

"I don't know what *I'm* talkin' about? What in hell is your problem?"

Although Carig was just trying to help, Ivan was steaming mad. No. It went far deeper, he was riddled with fear.

"I'll tell you the problem. YOU CAN'T JUST FIX THIS FRAME AS IF IT WERE A FREAKING CHAIR IN YOUR BOTHY!"

Every last one of us was stunned by Ivan's rude and heated tone. Even his brothers who only moments before were gorging on chicken, quickly changed their focus. At this point, none of us quite understood the gravity of the situation. Not until Ivan peered out of his own little world and noted the confusion of ours, was he able to make any sense.

"I'm sorry, Red! All of you, I'm sorry! How could you know such things? This frame was cut from the cedarwood door of Solomon's Temple. *The* Solomon's Temple! The one that was destroyed by Nebuchadnezzar, hundreds of years before Christ. Like the sacred temple where God dwelt, so is the Tempus Vector. It's not just a piece of wood that can be reshaped in a woodshop. It can only be restored in one of two ways. Either by locating the broken handle or by cutting a new piece from the one door.

"This unexpected dilemma comes with both good news and bad news. The good news is that I can see the frame restored to perfection as clearly as I can see you all right now. What I can't see is how, or by whom, or for that matter, who will be left holding the frame in the end."

Ivan was still talking in riddles, and none of us could quite understand what he meant by "whom."

"Ivan, hold on a minute. We still have the Tempus Vector. Maybe not all of it, but most of it. How could someone else create a new one out of a fragment?"

"It doesn't matter who's got which part! Even the smallest piece of The Tempus Vector can be the foundation for a new frame. *We have* to find that piece or the door before they do! If we don't, well, let's just say that the consequence will make the threat of the Fourth Reich seem like a day at the circus."

"What enemy are you talking about, and how could they get ahold of it? Even if they did, how would they know what to do with an old wooden dowel that looks more like a piece of tinder than a magic wand?"

"Pardon me, miss, but let's review the facts! The man, Halag or Hermann, or whoever the hell he was ... did he by any chance have even the slightest knowledge or wisdom about the frame in your backpack? And to go one step further, when you left that place and returned here, *who* was in possession of that '*old wooden dowel?*'"

His questions were hypothetical, of course, asked only to make a bigger point.

"I'm not sure exactly how much he knew about me or The Tempus Vector, but he was definitely aware of the fact that the frame has great power ... and as far as I know, the slivered rod, well, it was left *buried* deep within the chambers of Hermann's black heart. In all honesty, I CAN'T IMAGINE THAT HE SURVIVED!"

"Beni, this is very important. Can you say with one-hundred percent certainty, that both brothers were dead when you left?"

The room was quiet, and all eyes were on me.

"Yes! I mean no. I mean I can't say for sure. Halag was poisoned by his own brother, and I stabbed Hermann and Carig shot him. He couldn't have survived that!"

"But you don't know for sure. Carig was called to leave right away, to come back here, but not you. Ya know, when it comes to the power and will of the Tempus Vector, there is a reason for everything, nothing happens by accident! There was a valid basis to your delay. Could it be that the job wasn't done? What happened in those minutes before you left? Think Beni!"

I lashed out at Ivan, insisting that he hold off on his accusations. I didn't know what he was getting at with his blame game. Only moments earlier, he had been all cheery and congratulatory, declaring that *we did it*! We stopped the rising of the Fourth Reich, which could only happen if Halag was killed, which meant that he had died. Ivan was going completely sideways on me. *Now maybe he didn't die?* Ugh! My head was spinning, I was beyond upset.

Ivan, still learning about his role in all of this, remembered that his father could control any situation by remaining calm. After mellowing his approach, bringing it down a few notches, he continued on.

"Beni … you're right. What was accomplished, what we stopped, was huge. I'm not saying that the man who was about to bring to life the next holocaust *wasn't* stopped, because he *was*, absolutely; prevented because of your efforts! It's just … it's now been revealed to me that … well, a nightmare of a different magnitude has awakened. This twin you speak of is just as evil as the first, and his existence changes everything. For some reason, I didn't see it before now! The entire rise of the Fourth Reich, although a real threat, was all smoke and mirrors, a brilliantly planned distraction that would ultimately lead to a far more disastrous pursuit than we first realized. They had no intention of sparking a movement into flame but resurrecting a fallen one."

You could have heard a pin drop in that room full of witnesses who couldn't believe their ears. I, along with the others, hoped that Ivan's overreaction stemmed from his slight tendency to see a glass half empty. He had no real proof of any other agenda, yet he was clearly convinced.

"What was it you didn't see, Ivan? Maybe you didn't *see* anything else because there's nothing else *to* see!"

"I didn't pay enough attention to your dream, to the details. Perhaps Halag and Hermann were so closely linked in mind, body, and soul that I only saw one headstone, but there were two all along, cleverly hidden behind the etched HS that symbolized either, or both. I see it … I see it now. One of them remained in the shadows, waiting and watching. Even though it appeared that only one brother knew about the power of the frame, I'm bettin' ten to one that both brothers were savvy to its divine abilities. They were waiting for you. Ultimately, they wanted the entire frame, but were aware that even a piece would do, the piece that was left behind."

Ivan's riddle twisting was so frustrating that I just wanted to shake him. But his brothers who knew him well and were wise to the ways of his calling, stretched out their arms, creating a refuge of protection for Ivan to sort out and piece together this frightening enigma. Like a bottle that was spinning round and round, Ivan's gaze swirled about the room until his eyes settled on me.

"Beni, tell me quickly what happened in the last few minutes that you were there! Every detail, don't leave anything out!"

I didn't want to think about it, not any of it, but before I even realized what was happening, I began spilling every detail as if I no longer had control over the words that fell from my lips. I could feel the uncomfortable invasion of Ivan peering straight through into my deepest memory, as if he didn't trust my ability to reveal truth.

"Even now, the whole things seems like a dream, like it didn't really happen, and in the middle of the unimaginable, Carig appeared from out of nowhere. Even when I heard his voice and saw his face, I hardly believed that he was there. And then he left as quickly as he appeared. But before he did, and without hesitation, the echo of his firearm resounded off the wall, and then Hermann fell to the floor. As he was falling, he looked at me, with eyes like mirrors. At first, I could see my reflection in the pools of blue, and then they turned dark, he was gone. Blood consumed him, no movement, no breathing, nothing. I didn't examine him, but he was clearly dead, I saw it in his eyes."

"What about the twin, how did he die? Were you certain he died?"

"Halag, I actually witnessed him die, first hand, in my arms, to be exact."

"See again Beni ... for the second time and tell me what you saw."

I sunk deeper into this powerful trance originating from the Tribe of Yosef. For those next few moments of having the undivided attention of every soul in the room, I took an emotional step back onto that train, trying to remember something that might help. But for some strange reason, what stood out to me, more than anything else was the grief in Alrik's eyes, and his lips uttering the same two phrases over and again, "Please don't go. Stay here with me!" It was a sharp dagger in my heart, and I couldn't stand myself for what I had done to him. Shame filled my soul, and I could hardly speak another word.

"Really, it was just me and Alrik at the end. He was just as astounded as I was. I know they had to die, and I'm not sorry for it. Halag and Hermann were equally deserving, but I felt ... I feel terrible for leaving Alrik so alone, completely abandoned by those he cared for. For the second time, I left him behind, and he didn't deserve it. He wasn't like the others. It was never power that he wanted, he just wanted me. And then all of a sudden, the broken but faithful frame, the Tempus Vector of whom I am the Carrier, brought me home."

As my mind and heart once again became present in the here and now, I hardly remembered what I had just said. But I could tell by the expression on Carig's face, and the awkward stares from the others, that I had just spilled a bitter truth that would have been better left unsaid.

With incessant blinking and some master rerouting, Ivan tried to change the subject.

"Let's think about this. The events of *this* journey occurred a month prior to your first encounter with them. Halag or Hermann, or whoever it was that first time around, was alive and well, huh? Beni ... one of the brothers survived!"

"What are you getting at? How do you know for sure?"

"I'm saying that this journey is not yet over. If only I could see what happened once you left. Be present in the room where their bodies lay, taking note of a heartbeat ... observe, like a fly on the wall, who it was that took possession of the broken piece. If only this blasted veil was lifted from my eyes so that I could see for just a moment the movements of the Field Marshal ... whether he's innocent or shrewd, I can't tell. I have a gut-wrenching feeling that things are not as they seem. If I could only see into the world from whence you came, just for a moment!"

There is nothing more bitter than being left behind. Alrik sat on a cold metal chair in the Friedlich Morgue with Halag on one side and Hermann on the other, still in shock that they were both gone. They may not have been the perfect kin by any means, but they were his family. Not only were they gone but the woman whom Caprice predicted would come to mend his broken heart had disappeared before his very eyes. For the first time in his life, Alrik was without the companionship of his cousins; the grief was more than he could bear. Heedlessly, he fell to his knees onto the tiled floor, entombed between the two bodies and wailing bitterly, not unlike the day he had lost Caprice. This time he was certain that the weeping would never end. Minutes turned into hours of complete agony ... a pain that could not be eased by words or sympathies filled with sorrowful glances. He cried out for death, he begged for it, but the angel of darkness favored only his closest relations. At his darkest moment, he was distracted by a single forsaken star twinkling in a black sky, rescuing him from a certain shroud of agony. In his final cry of anguish, he caught sight of fingers thumping from beneath the white sheet, revealing life.